The Mourning Dove

Book 1 of the Baramayan Chronicles

Deborah Millitello

Word Posse

Dedication

To my mom, Patricia Ann Laslie

Acknowledgments

I want to thank my writing group: Laurell K. Hamilton, Mark Sumner, Martha Kneib, Sharon Shinn, Lauretta Allen, and Tom Drennan, for all their help and insight. Thanks to my family for understanding my writing obsession. And Carl, you're still the love of my life.

From Word Posse

The Naturalist, Mark Sumner

Sleeping the Churchyard Sleep, Rett MacPherson

Pandora's Mirror, Marella Sands

The Water Girl, Deborah Millitello

Thor McGraw & the Ice Man, Tom Drennan

Restless Bones, Marella Sands

Do Virgins Taste Better? and Other Strange Tales, Deborah Millitello

Fortune's Daughter, Marella Sands

On Whetsday, Mark Sumner

The Angel Share books by Marella Sands

Volume 1: Through a Keyhole Darkly

Volume 2: What the Thunder Said

Visit us at www.wordposse.com

Like us on Facebook: facebook.com/WordPosse

Follow us on Twitter: @WordPosse

This book has been typeset in Fanwood. Titles and headers are in Darleston. Cover design Word Posse. Cover art by Danielle Shimchick.

ISBN-10: 978-1-944089-05-4

ISBN-13: 978-1-944089-05-5

I

Water dripped from Cordwin's dark hair and trickled down his forehead to his straight nose. He started to wipe it with his sleeve, then stopped. His red and gold guard uniform was as drenched as his hair. *A fine way to arrive at Tarolin Castle after a two-week absence*, he thought as he tried futilely to wring out the hem of his surcoat.

A shiny blue-green opal fly buzzed around his face and kept trying to land on his nose, but he swatted the annoying fly away. He shivered in the cool spring breeze that blew through Rindolar Woods, and he glared at his red-headed cousin Daikin, who at twenty was only a year older than Cordwin but heftier and half a head taller.

Daikin gave him a mock-innocent grin as they stood facing each other. "I didn't mean for you to fall in the creek, Cord. Honestly, I didn't."

"You sneak up behind me while I'm filling my water bottle and you shriek like a banded hawk, and you expect me to believe it was an accident?" Cordwin asked, eyes dark as storm clouds. He picked up his saddle bag from the creek, opened it, and poured out water and wet clothes on the grassy bank. "And all my extra clothes are drenched!"

Daikin's green eyes glinted as he spread his arms and shrugged. "Really, Cord, I'm sorry. Besides, it's a beautiful day. How could anyone be unhappy?"

Cordwin swatted at the opal fly. "I should have stayed on the main road with our escort instead of riding through Rindolar Woods, but no. You wanted to go through the woodland path and camp in the open air."

"And when was the last time we managed to get away on our own?" Daikin asked. "And it was only for one night. We haven't been camping for almost three years."

Cold and miserable, Cordwin stretched his aching back and winced. "Barg's breath, I'd forgotten how hard the ground is to sleep on. Animals stole our food, so we have nothing for breakfast. And these opal flies circle me as if I were a banquet laid out just for them." Frustrated, Cordwin swatted at the fly again. "Then I fall in an icy creek, and I'm drenched to the skin. Why do I let you talk me into things I *know* will be trouble? Now I'll probably be late for the council meeting with Clevil, and I'll have to change clothes before I attend."

Daikin laughed, his freckled nose wrinkling. "Your brother won't care if you're a little damp or smell like a wet horse."

"But *I* care! I won't drip all over the council chamber floor!" He squeezed water from his hair and finger-combed it from his forehead. "And I can imagine what the counselors will say if they see me like this!"

"Oh, Cord, you're a bit too vain," Daikin said, laughing.

"I'm not vain!" Cordwin said. He looked down at his soggy uniform, stained with mud, and sighed. "I just don't want to do anything that would embarrass Clev or make him ashamed of me. He's my brother as well ss the Lord of Vorlik"

"You couldn't do that, even if you tried," Daikin said, resting his hand on Cordwin's shoulder. "You know that. He loves you."

"It's just that...he was so ill." Cordwin halted and swallowed hard. He shivered, and his stomach tightened into a cold knot. He blinked back tears that blurred his vision. "I was so afraid...so afraid he might die of winter fever just like our parents did. So afraid he'd leave me alone. I wish," he paused a moment, "I wish the Wizard Casslin were here. I know Clev would be all right then." Cordwin touched the silver eagle amulet he wore, a gift from the Wizard.

Daikin stopped smiling and looked serious, something Cordwin seldom saw his cousin do. "Cord, the physician assured you that Clev was recovering before we left the castle. That's the only reason the counselors let you out of Tarolin. You're second in line to the throne after Clev's son, and the counselors are..." Daikin paused, "very conscious of that, especially since Bren is only a baby."

"And you're third in line, but they let you out of the castle all the time." Cordwin sighed. When Daikin had been sent on an inspection tour of southern and eastern Vorlik, Cordwin was delighted at the chance to go along. It was so rare that the counselors were willing to see Cordwin travel outside the castle, but everyone knew the tour would be completely free of risk. "Look," he said, "everyone knows I'll never be lord of Vorlik, and I'm glad I won't be. I never wanted to rule anything. All I've ever wanted is to be the best officer I can be and to make Clev proud of me."

"He is," Daikin said, giving Cordwin a genuine smile. "He couldn't be more proud of you. And he trusts you. That's why he sent *you* on this inspection tour, since he was too ill to go himself."

Cordwin shivered again. The early morning sunlight barely trickled through the thick leaf-covered branches overhead, not enough to warm him or dry his clothes. His feet and hands felt numb. The cold felt as if it had soaked all the way to his heart. "I'm so cold, Daik," he whispered, unable to stop shaking.

"Barg's breath!" Daikin felt Cordwin's forehead. "Cord, you need to get out of that wet uniform. I don't want to be responsible for you coming down with a fever. Your brother would never forgive me, and I'd never forgive myself."

"Neither would I," Cordwin said and gave his cousin a weak smile. He crossed his arms over his chest and rubbed his upper arms for warmth. He didn't feel any better. "But my other uniform is as drenched as this one is."

"I have a spare uniform," Daikin said. "A bit large for you but at least it's dry, and right now that's what's important."

Daikin turned to his cream-colored horse and untied his pack from the saddle. He pulled out a pair of black wool pants, a loose black cotton shirt, his spare red and gold surcoat of the Tarolin Guard, a pair of dark woolen socks, and linen underwear. "Sorry I don't have an extra pair of boots," he said as he handed the clothes to Cordwin, "but with dry socks your feet should be warmer."

Cordwin stripped off every last one of the wet, clinging clothes. The cool breeze raised goose bumps on his lightly tanned skin, and he shook with cold.

"A good thing there are no ladies passing by," Daikin said, leaning an arm on his saddle, resting his jaw on his fist, and grinning at Cordwin. "They might faint from excitement."

Cordwin shook his head and said through chattering teeth, "Don't you ever quit? You're always so...exuberant."

"I have to be," Daikin said with a grin, "because you're always so dour."

Once Cordwin was dressed, Daikin handed him a small towel, and Cordwin rubbed it through his dripping hair. Daikin was right; the clothes were a bit too big, but at least they were dry. They felt so good against his chilled skin, and the surcoat over everything added an extra layer of warmth.

Daikin slipped a blanket around Cordwin's shoulders. "Feeling better, I hope."

"Yes," Cord said, hugging the blanket close. "I can almost feel my toes and fingers now."

"Good. Now let's go home." Daikin mounted his horse. "We should be there in another hour even at an easy pace. And stay wrapped up in that blanket."

Cordwin gathered up his wet clothes and stuffed them in his pack with the other wet clothes. Mounting his horse, he and Daikin rode west side by side through the cool shadowy woods. Daikin began humming a tune, then sang a bawdy tavern song in his rich baritone voice.

"Stop that," Cordwin said, scowling.

Daikin grinned then began a more risqué song. Cordwin shook his head, resigned to enduring his cousin's vexing sense of humor. He pulled the blanket over his damp hair and clutched the blanket close to his throat.

Daikin kept singing songs, each one worse than the one before.

"Where do you hear such ribald songs?" Cordwin asked, blushing so much his face felt hot.

"In the barracks," Daikin said, a satisfied smirk on his freckled face. "You should spend more time there. You'd be amazed what you can learn from other soldiers."

"There are some things I don't want to learn," Cordwin said disapprovingly.

Daikin just laughed out loud.

The warm blanket chased the chill from Cordwin's body, and he began to enjoy the ride through the woods. The sun had crept up high enough, its golden light flickered off spring green leaves. The air was filled with the scent of damp earth, wild flowers, and the moldy odor of years of fallen leaves.

Cordwin suddenly remembered a time his father had taken Clevil and him riding on that very path through the woods and had pointed out the different kinds of trees and flowers growing there. *That was the white oak where we saw the banded hawk,* Cordwin thought. *And that was the weeping willow where the doe and her fawn were bedded down. And there was the cluster of wild violets where the baby rabbits had huddled motionless. And that was where Father stopped to pick a bouquet of wild Sweet Williams for Mother.* Had it only been ten years ago? Cordwin still remembered it as if it were yesterday. It had been the last time his father had taken Clevil and Cordwin with him before...before Cordwin's parents had died.

Tears came unbidden to his eyes. His grief wasn't as sharp as it used to be when he was younger, but sometimes, a memory would come to him, and his grief would catch him off guard with a sudden blow to his chest. His throat felt tight, and it hurt to breathe. *Why did the Wizard Casslin leave Vorlik just when he was needed,* Cordwin wondered bitterly, closing his eyes for a moment, *when the epidemic of winter fever killed so many? If he'd been here, my parents wouldn't have died. Daikin's parents would still be alive. Why did Casslin leave us?*

"Hey, Cord, look," Daikin said and pointed to a break in the trees ahead, "the Tironza Road. We're almost home."

Cordwin gave a grateful sigh. "I'll be glad to sleep in my own bed tonight."

The Tironza Road was the wide main north-south trade route from Tarolin Castle to Tironza, the largest city in Vorlik. The road passed south for several miles through the thick old trees of Rindolar Woods, then went across wide plains and gentle hills for more than ten miles until it reached the great city of Tironza. A rider with a good horse could make it easily from Tarolin Castle to Tironza in less than a day.

They had just turned north on the broad road toward Tarolin Castle when Cordwin's horse shied suddenly.

"Barg's breath! What's that?" Cordwin said.

A lathered brown and white horse shuffled riderless in the middle of the muddy road. Lying face down at the horse's feet was a man wearing the yellow and gold uniform of the Southern Guard at Tironza. An arrow protruded from the man's back. His dented metal helmet lay several hand spans away.

Cordwin and Daikin slid from their saddles and knelt beside the man.

Daikin felt the side of the man's neck. "He's alive, barely."

Cordwin touched the blood-soaked back of the surcoat. "Looks like he's lost a lot of blood."

"That arrow needs removed, but not here, not by us. He needs a physician—now. Who did this to him? And why?"

Cordwin cautiously lifted the man's head and turned him over on his side gently, careful not to move the arrow. Blood crusted the man's short brown hair and the left side of his lean face, and stained many slashes in his surcoat. "I think I recognize him. He's Corporal Trell of the Southern Guard."

The man groaned, his eyelids fluttered opened, and his greenish-brown eyes blinked several times, then widened. He clutched at Cordwin's arm. Breathing in gasps, the man said, "Sir Cordwin, Southern Guard...Tironza...attacked...must warn...Lord Clevil. I have...to report...what happened!" A choking sound rose in his throat, and his body twitched. He collapsed, unconscious.

Cordwin stared at Daikin, and they both whispered, "Invasion."

"We can't lay him over his saddle," Cordwin said. "And we have to reach the castle as fast as possible. I'll hold him in front of me. I'm lighter than you are. My horse can carry both of us. You lead his horse. "

"What about the arrow?" Daikin asked. "You can't hold him with the arrow protruding like that."

"Hold him still for a moment." Cordwin stared thoughtfully at the shaft for a moment. "I don't recognize the fletching pattern."

Daikin held the injured guard so the man's arms were pinned to his sides. Cordwin fetched his knife from his horse's saddle sheath and knelt behind the injured man.

"Ready?" Cordwin asked.

Daikin nodded.

I hope I can do this right, Cordwin thought. He measured one blade's width on the shaft from the man's back, then began cutting a notch above and below. "Now, keep him completely still."

Daikin nodded again.

Taking a deep breath, Cordwin rested his knife blade flat under the shaft between the notches and the man's back, then jerked the fletched end of the shaft down. The shaft snapped off, leaving only the blade's width. The guard groaned, stiffened, then went limp again and remained unconscious. Cordwin blew out his breath and stuck the broken shaft through his belt.

"Let's get him on his feet now," Cordwin said.

Daikin and Cordwin each put one of the guard's arms around their shoulders, pushed to their feet, and practically dragged the man to Cordwin's horse. Daikin bent slightly, grasped the guard around the waist, and lifted the man on his shoulder. Cordwin mounted his horse, backed his horse a few steps, then turned his mount so Daikin was on the right side.

Bending over cautiously, Cordwin held out his arms. Daikin stretched as much as he could until Cordwin grasped the guard under the arms and pulled him across Cordwin's lap, legs dangling to the right. Daikin sprinted to his horse and mounted, grabbed the reins of the guard's horse, then the cousins kicked their horses into a gallop straight north toward Tarolin Castle.

Lady Baramay, please, let us reach the castle in time to save this man's life, Cordwin thought. *He has to live. We have to know what happened to him.*

Half an hour later, the woods gave way to a flat grassy plain, and in the northeast corner of the crossroads of the Tironza Road and the east-west trade route sat Tarolin Castle. The red granite wall surrounding Tarolin Castle gleamed in the morning sunlight, while the white limestone walls and turrets of the three-story castle glowed as if the sun had burnished them with gold. Soldiers walked the battlements, and the pennants of the five Guards of Vorlik flapped in the light breeze above the gatehouse.

Daikin grasped the yellowed horn slung at his side and blew a series of three short notes and one long one, then repeated the signal. Soldiers patrolling the walls halted, and someone shouted, "It's Lieutenant Daikin and Sir Cordwin!"

"Bows at the ready!" another voice shouted. "Guards to the gate! Ready the portcullis!"

Soldiers on the balustrade slipped bows from their shoulders, nocked arrows, and knelt behind the crenellations.

Cordwin and Daikin rode through the castle gate, across the muddy courtyard, past a squad of soldiers with drawn swords, to the castle steps. The soldiers sprinted after them.

"Close the gate!" Daikin said as he leaped from his horse and ran to Cordwin's side. "We have to report to Lord Clevil!"

"Gently," Cordwin said as he eased the guard down to Daikin's shoulder. Cordwin dismounted and rubbed his cramping left arm and shoulder.

Two stable boys took the reins of the three horses.

"Take care of them," Cordwin told the boys.

"Yes, Sir Cordwin," one of the boys said.

Cordwin took one of the guard's arms across his shoulder; Daikin took the other. Together, they carried the guard up the steps to the foyer. Captain Bailoc met them, saluting Cordwin.

Staring with wide grey eyes at the bloody guard, Bailoc said, "What--"

Cordwin cut him off. "Tironza's been attacked!"

"Barg's breath!" Bailoc said. "Let me take him, Sir Cordwin. Lord Clevil's waiting for you in the Audience Hall."

Cordwin let Bailoc take the guard's arm, then raced ahead through the open castle doors to the wide entry hall. Shouting for guards to open the doors to the Audience Hall, he hurried across the granite floor of the great high-ceilinged room, lit by numerous candelabras. Guards standing like statues along the side walls grasped their swords, ready to spring into action. The assembled counselors parted as Cordwin sprinted toward the dais where Lord Clevil of Vorlik sat, wrapped in furs and as pale as his snow-blond hair.

Clevil stared at his younger brother, a scowl pulling his eyebrows almost together. "Cord, can you explain why—" he halted as Cordwin approached closer. His blue eyes grew wide. "What wrong? Did something happen? Is that why you didn't return last night? Where's Daikin?"

Cordwin hurriedly knelt and barely clapped his fist to his chest. "Vorlik has been attacked!"

Over the clamor of the council members, Clevil asked anxiously, "When? Where?"

Cordwin quickly climbed the dais and stood before Clevil. "Daikin and I found a messenger from the Southern Guard on the Tironza Road. He was injured severely and barely conscious but told us that Tironza was attacked."

At that moment, Daikin and Bailoc came through the Audience Hall entrance, half carrying the guard. Cordwin turned toward them.

The wounded man tried to stand on his own and salute, but gasped in pain as he raised his arm. Daikin and Bailoc had to hold him up.

"Corporal Trell...of the Southern Guard, my lord," the soldier said, his voice shaky and barely audible. "An army...entered...southern pass...hidden by a shadow...We didn't see them...until they attacked...the Southern Keep...three hours after midnight...killed many of the guard...burned our barracks...attacked Tironza...before dawn today. My lieutenant...sent me to warn you...but someone shot me. I hung on to my horse...as long as I could...but I passed out."

"Do you know who they are?" Clevil asked, leaning forward. "Where they're from?"

"We don't know...who they were...my lord."

Cordwin pulled out the broken arrow shaft. "And here's the arrow we took from his back. The fletching pattern isn't known to me. Does anyone else recognize it?"

Soldiers and counselors shook their heads.

"And no signal towers or fire beacons to warn us sooner!" Clevil said. "I knew we should have rebuilt them!"

"But my lord," said a white-bearded scribe named Wogen, "who would want to attack us? *Especially* from the south. We're on exceptionally good terms with Lord Merrik of Peltik. And we're on good terms with the rest of our neighbors—except Drambit, and we've kept the towers and beacons from the western border to the castle."

"We're being attacked now, scribe," Clevil said tightly, "and *not* from the west."

Wogen bowed his head. "Yes, my lord. I pray your pardon."

Clevil pulled the fur tighter around his broad shoulders, shivered, and pushed to his feet, swaying. Cordwin hurried to his side, slid an arm around his brother's waist, and steadied him as Clevil leaned heavily on Cordwin's shoulders. *Clev feels so frail still,* Cordwin thought, worry filling his heart. *The fever has sapped so much of his strength. It might take weeks or months before he's as hale as he used to be. Why did this have to happen now?*

"Can the Southern Guard delay the invaders until more forces arrive?" Clevil asked the guard.

Trell struggled to speak. "They're outnumbered...many dead...more will die...but while they live...they'll fight." Groaning, Trell passed out and sagged in Daikin's and Bailoc's arms.

"Take him to the physician!" Clevil ordered, leaning on Cordwin. Two guards from the side walls ran to take the guard from Daikin and Bailoc.

"I'll bet those worm-eating Drambini pigs are behind this," Bailoc muttered as he relinquished his hold on the guard.

"Captain Bailoc, sound the battle horn," Clevil said. "Send scouts south to Tironza. Wogen, prepare carrier pigeons for the Eastern, Northern, and Western Guards. Instruct the Northern Guard to be ready to send troops if we call. Tell the Eastern and Western Guards to double the soldiers at the border keeps, especially on the Drambini border, but assemble as large a force as can be spared to march to Tironza with all speed." He paused, then added, "And send for the priest of Baygor."

Captain Bailoc bowed and hurried from the hall. Moments later Cordwin heard the Battle Horn of Tarolin for the first time in his life, blowing clear and sharp throughout the castle.

Cordwin leaned back against the cool stone wall just inside the large antechamber of Clevil's rooms. He didn't dare speak while Clevil and his wife, Lady Ellisa, were arguing. They stood across the room, before the limestone and brick hearth, but Cordwin could hear them plainly. Clevil and Ellisa seldom argued, but when they did, Cordwin knew better than to get involved. And they were both already angry that he'd traveled without an escort. Cordwin didn't want to remind them how furious they were with *him*. He tried to be mouse-quiet and rabbit-still.

Ellisa paced back and forth from the crèche where her son Bren slept to the fireplace where Clevil struggled to put on his armor. Ellisa's green velvet dress flared every time she turned around. Her gold and pearl drop earrings swung like angry pendulums. She stopped in front of Clevil, trembling, her hands in tight fists at her side. "This is madness," she said in an angry whisper.

She clutched his arm while he tried to buckle on his steel breastplate. He ignored her, but had to lean on an oak table next to his velvet-covered chair to keep from falling.

"Clev, stop!" Ellisa said, pulling on the breastplate. "You can't do this! You're too ill! Today was the first day the physician let you leave your room!"

"I have to," Clevil said, sweat beading on his forehead.

"No, you don't!"

"Yes, I do!" He shook free from Ellisa's grasp and nearly collapsed to one knee.

Golden hairpins tumbled to the stone floor as Ellisa's walnut hair fell loosely to her waist. Gold flecks glinted in her brown eyes as Ellisa wheeled toward Cordwin and rested her tight fists on her hips. "Cord, can *you* make him listen to reason?"

Startled, Cordwin shrank back for a moment, then pushed away from the wall and walked hesitantly toward Clevil. His throat tightened, making his voice sound higher than normal. "Clev, how can you even *think* about going? You barely made it up the stairs with my help. How can you possibly bear your armor, mount a horse, and ride all the way to Tironza? You're not well enough."

"I'm well enough to protect my people." Clevil fumbled with the leather shoulder straps on the breastplate. "Ellisa, help me fasten this."

"No!"

"Ellisa!" Clevil stared at her, his mouth open, his eyes wide.

"I won't help you kill yourself! And I'm not going to be a widow and raise our son alone!" She stood glaring at him, her slender body rigid, her jaw clenched, and her arms folded across her chest.

Cordwin jerked back a step, shocked by her vehemence. He'd never seen her so livid. Clutching Clevil's shoulders, Cordwin said, "Clev, stop! You can't lead the army, and you know it! Please, let me lead the army in your place!"

"No!" Clevil started to turn away, but his legs almost gave way.

Cordwin gripped him tighter. "But why?"

Clevil tried to pull back and failed. At twenty-six, Clev was in his prime, but the fever had left him weakened. Worry danced in Cordwin's chest. Winter fever had killed his parents nine years earlier. He refused to risk losing Clev to the same illness because of Clev's pride.

"Why?" Cordwin repeated intensely. "Just tell me why!"

"You're just a boy," Clevil said but kept his eyes averted, "You may have studied and practiced, but you've never been in a real battle."

"Neither have you. So give me a chance!" Cordwin said, not caring if it sounded like he were begging. "I've trained since childhood to lead Vorlik's army and to serve you! It's what I was born to do — to keep Vorlik and her people safe! Let me do this in your place."

"But *I'm* responsible for my people!" Clevil said, straining against Cordwin's hold. "*I* have to protect them!"

"And what would *they* do if you died because you were too proud to admit you were ill?"

Clevil stiffened but before he could answer, Cordwin said softly, "Clev, please, you know you're not well enough for battle. In your heart you *know* it."

Clevil resisted a moment longer, but finally his shoulders sagged, his forehead glistening with sweat. "Damn, Cord," Clevil whispered, "you're right." He sank to the velvet chair, then took the breastplate off and let it slide to the floor. "I know you're right."

He looked up at Cordwin, breathing in short gasps. "I give you command of Vorlik's forces."

Ellisa touched her fingertips to her trembling lips, eyes shining with tears. "Thank you," she whispered and knelt to help Clevil unbuckle the rest of his armor.

Cordwin knelt and pressed his fist to his chest, his heart pounding with excitement and fear. "Clev, I swear on my life, I'll defend our people."

He started to stand when Clevil embraced him with a fierceness that astounded Corwin. "Just come back unharmed, Cord," Clevil said.

"I will." Cordwin's arms circled his brother's chest and returned the embrace. "I will, I promise."

Pulling back a little, Clevil stared deep into Cordwin's eyes. "I hope my son is like you when he grows up."

Cordwin's throat tightened so much, he couldn't speak, and his heart beat so hard, it felt as if it would break through his ribs. He had to blink his eyes several times to clear away the grateful tears that blurred his vision.

Clevil grasped Cordwin's forearm and nodded slightly. "May a friend guard your back."

It was a common luck-wish of Vorlikian soldiers, but it surprised Cordwin. This was the first time Clevil had ever treated him as a soldier, not just his younger brother. His head held high, Cordwin grasped his brother's arm and gave the traditional reply.

"May you not die alone." He rose and turned to go.

Ellisa blocked his way, stood on tiptoe, and flung her arms around him. "Be careful, Cord. Please, please, be careful. And don't you come back with so much as a scratch!" Her tears wet his cheek as she kissed it.

Too choked to speak, he nodded, pulled away from her, and hurried to his chamber.

Pellin, Cordwin's young page, stood at attention at the foot of Cordwin's bed when Cordwin entered his room down the hall from Clevil's rooms. It had been Cordwin's bedchamber since childhood and still held all his boyhood treasures. The room was small, cozy, comfortable, his safe haven. A fire blazed on the hearth, chasing the spring chill from the room.

Cordwin's chain mail coat, helmet, sword, and a surcoat of the Tarolin Guard were already laid out on his narrow bed. A clean set of black pants, shirt, and socks, and off white linen underwear lay across the leather and oak chair before the hearth. A worn pair of black boots sat on the floor beside the chair. And a spare set of clothes was tied into a tight bundle.

"Master," Pellin said as Cordwin took off his belt then stripped off the surcoat and shirt, "I know there is no time for a bath, but I thought you might want to wash up a bit, so I set out a basin of water for you." He pointed to the small trestle table next to the bed. Steam rose from a large ceramic bowl half filled with rose-scented water. A cotton towel and square cloth lay folded beside the bowl. "And there's a plate of food on your bed, just a bit of meat and bread and cheese."

Cordwin smiled to himself. Pellin was barely eleven years old and had been with Cordwin for less than a year, but already the boy was an efficient page.

"Thank you," Cordwin said as he sat on the side of the bed and began to pull off his damp boots. Pellin knelt and started to help, but Cordwin stopped him. "No, I can do this myself, but I want you to send word to the stables to saddle Moon Shadow for me. He's the only horse I want to ride into battle."

"Yes, master." Pellin bowed and started to leave the room, then turned back. "Am I going with you?" he asked eagerly.

Surprised by the boy's request, Cordwin gaped at Pellin for a few moments. "Go with me? You mean, go into battle with me?"

The boy nodded enthusiastically.

Cordwin just stared at him. How could he take someone so young into such danger? He shuddered. No, he wanted Pellin to be safe behind the castle walls, away from harm. "No," he said slowly, "not this time."

The boy looked hurt. "But I went on tour with you, even though you sent me back with the escort last night."

"But this is war, and I want you to stay here."

"But who will lay out your clothes and sharpen your sword? Who will bring you food and wine? Who will take care of you?"

I can take care of myself, Cordwin thought, but Pellin looked so disappointed, Cordwin didn't say it aloud. "I'll have to manage somehow," he said, smiling at the boy, "though not as well as you would. Just have a fire blazing when I get back." He looked at his bed longingly, wishing he could nestle in the soft bed under warm blankets, and sighed deeply.

The page nodded slowly and turned away, but Cordwin called him back.

"Pellin, these clothes I'm wearing belong to Lieutenant Daikin. While I'm gone, please take them to the laundress, and when they're clean, see that they're returned to his room."

The page bowed again and left.

Cordwin removed the boots and socks, then stripped off the pants and underwear. The heat from the blazing hearth felt good on his bare skin. Dipping the cloth in the hot water, he wrung out most of the water, then quickly wiped off his face, neck, and lean body, breathing in the delicate rose fragrance in the steam. He unfolded the cotton towel, almost the size of a bed sheet, wrapped it around himself, grabbed the plate of food, and hurried to his chair to huddle as close to the hearth as he could without scorching his skin.

His stomach growled, and he realized he hadn't eaten since noon the day before. The cold roast chicken and mild cheese tasted like a banquet to him, and the bread filled his empty stomach. For a moment he closed his eyes, sated, then sighed, knowing he couldn't stay by the fire. Drying off hurriedly, he dropped the towel on the stone floor, then began dressing.

By the time Pellin returned, Cordwin was fastening the surcoat over his chain mail coat. Pellin slid the leather sheath holding the sword onto Cordwin's belt, then helped him tie it around his waist. The chain mail coat was heavy on his shoulders, but Cordwin had spent many days wearing it to become accustomed to its weight.

Cordwin caressed the hilt of his sword. It was a gift from Clevil on Cordwin's eighteenth birthday. This would be the first time it was used for anything but sword practice. *Great Baygor,* he thought, *let me be worthy of Clev's faith in me.*

Pellin looked up at Cordwin, biting his lip, a disappointed frown on his young face. "Fight well, master, and...be safe. Baygor protect you."

Cordwin gave the boy's shoulder a light squeeze, nodded, and left his room. He strode through the torch lit corridor, trepidation flowing through his body, tingling in his fingers. He ran down the three flights of spiral steps, crossed the stone floor of the Audience Hall to a small door behind the throne, and entered the small council room.

Wrapped in furs, Clevil sat at the head of the narrow oak table, Ellisa sitting beside him and holding their son on her lap. Captain Bailoc, counselors, scribes, and the four lieutenants of the Tarolin Guard, including Daikin, were seated on either side of the table. At the end of the table sat Kella, the young priest of Baygor who served at the castle chapel. It was the first time the priest had been summoned to a council meeting. He was still wearing his gardening clothes; he took his self-imposed responsibility to care for the castle gardens as seriously as he took his duties as a priest. His grey eyes were wide, and he shifted in his seat nervously. Everyone glanced at Cordwin as he entered and sat down across from Daikin, then they all turned back to the discussion.

A yellowed map of Vorlik lay on the table, showing Tarolin Castle in the center, the main north-south and east-west roads, the wide swath of Rindolar Woods, most of the towns and villages, and the Circle Mountains surrounding Vorlik, as well as the lands bordering the mountains. A tiny marble figurine weighed down each corner of the map.

Bailoc tapped the southern area. "My lord, if we leave within the hour, the vanguard of our troops could reach the northern edge of Tironza in four hours; three if pressed. Supply wagons and the physicians' wains will travel as quickly as possible."

"Good," Clevil said. "We'll keep sending wagons with more supplies as soon as we can load them." He leaned close to the table. "Lieutenant Rayvil, you and the First Watch will attack from the plains here," he used a dagger to tap the map, "on the west side of Tironza. Lieutenant Loren, you and the Second Watch come in from the east beyond the barrow ground. Lieutenant Daikin, you and the Third Watch go straight through the northern gates of Tironza. Lieutenant Tude and the Fourth Watch will provide reinforcements until the Eastern and Western Guards arrive and also provide men to protect refugees and help the healers set up tents for the wounded."

Tude nodded, her dark braid falling over her right shoulder.

"Cordwin, you were in Tironza recently," Clevil said. "Is there anything else we should consider? Any weaknesses we should know about?"

"No, this is a good plan," Cordwin said, "unless the enemy has taken Tironza and is marching north right now."

Clevil leaned his elbow on the table and rested his temple in his palm. "If that happens, well, you know the land between here and there. Keep the same attack pattern: left, right and center. You'll also have to warn the villages and farmsteads between here and there."

Cordwin nodded.

"Wogen, have the carrier pigeons been dispatched to the Eastern, Western, and Northern Guards?" Clevil asked.

The scribe nodded. "Yes, I sent them myself just before coming to this council."

"Good. All three guards should have the messages within the hour. Are your troops ready?"

Bailoc nodded. "They stand in the courtyard, ready to ride as we speak."

"What about the defense of Tarolin Castle?" Counselor Shola asked.

"I've sent for the sheriff of Tarolin Town and any men he can bring with him," Clevil added, "and Captain Bailoc will stay here with three squads."

Shola's face became as grey as his hair. "But...but who will lead the army?"

"My brother Cordwin. I've named him captain."

Scribe Wogen looked as if he'd been drinking sour wine. "Is that wise, my lord? Since you are not recovered from your illness, Captain Bailoc is the senior officer. Besides," he raised a bristly brow as he stared at Cordwin, "your brother is but a youth and has no battle experience."

Clevil answered in a slow, quiet voice, emphasizing each word. "He will—after today."

The silence was as thick as honey in winter.

Wogen squirmed and cleared his throat. "Forgive me, my lord. My concern is Vorlik's safety."

A kindly smile crossed Clevil's face. "As is mine. Cordwin is well trained, and I trust him."

Wogen bowed his head.

"Questions?" Clevil's blue eyes glanced around the table.

"Are three squads and the sheriff's men enough to guard the castle?" Shola asked, plucking at his eyebrow.

"We can always summon the Northern Guard. Anything else?" Clevil glanced around the room. No one spoke. "You know the plan. Prepare to leave."

Everyone stood and saluted or bowed to Clevil. The four lieutenants and all the counselors left the room, but Cordwin lingered with Ellisa and Clevil. Cordwin gazed at his brother and sister in-law and their young son. The child wasn't quite a year old, but

Cordwin could see the boy had Clevil's blue eyes and Ellisa's walnut-colored hair. Cordwin touched Bren's cheek, so soft and warm, and smiled. *I would do anything for these three,* Cordwin thought. *I'd die to protect them.*

"Cord, it's time to go," Clevil said quietly. "Be careful and...come home soon."

"I will," Cordwin said, his voice cracking. He turned away and hurried to the Audience Hall where the lieutenants waited for him.

Followed by the lieutenants, Cordwin reached the doors to the courtyard, where the Tarolin Guard waited. Cordwin walked down the steps to the courtyard and mounted his favorite stallion Moon Shadow, as white as moonlight, the silver bridle flashing in the midmorning sunlight. He rode to the head of the army, the standard bearer at his side, and waited as the lieutenants joined him. Some of the men and women of the guard looked surprised to see Cordwin there, but he tried to ignore their doubtful looks even though apprehension pulsed through his own body.

Clevil, leaning on Captain Bailoc's arm, walked from the castle entrance, followed by Ellisa carrying Bren, the priest Kella, and all the counselors. Clevil surveyed the assembled troops, then gazed intensely at Cordwin and nodded.

Standing with arms spread wide, the priest said in a reverent tenor voice, "Great and merciful Baygor, preserver of life, grant your protection to these your servants and keep them safe in this dark time. Hand to heart." He placed his right hand over his chest.

"And heart to heaven." He raised his left hand to the sky.

"Hand to heart, and heart to heaven," the soldiers said prayerfully.

Cordwin drew his sword, raised it above his head, and said, "For Vorlik and Lord Clevil! May Baygor protect us!"

"For Vorlik and Lord Clevil! May Baygor protect us!" the soldiers echoed his words.

Sheathing his sword, Cordwin gazed at his family one last time. He wheeled his horse and urged it through the castle gates, leading more than two hundred horsemen and numerous wagons with physicians, healers, and supplies to Vorlik's first war in a hundred years.

2

Cordwin rode at the head of the army, Daikin on his right, the standard bearer on his left. The other three lieutenants rode behind Cordwin. The army traveled four horsemen abreast at a brisk walk on the Tironza Road south through Rindolar Woods. The healer's wagons brought up the rear. The sound of horses' hooves and the creak of wagon wheels echoed loudly through the woods, nearly blocking out the sounds of birds twittering and opal flies buzzing. The towering trees bent over the road, limbs and branches entwined so thickly they shut out most of the morning sunlight.

We have to keep a quick pace, Cordwin thought, glancing over his shoulder at the troops following him, *but not so fast that the horses will be exhausted before we reach Tironza.* Even so, it was late morning before the army reached the southern edge of the deep woods.

Sunlight almost blinded Cordwin as he rode from the shadow of the trees. He shaded his eyes and squinted as he rode ahead until his eyes adjusted to the bright light. To the east he saw fields greening with newly sprouted wheat and corn. To the west a herd of sheep and goats munched fresh green grass in a fenced pasture. Just beyond the pasture, pink and white petals from an apple orchard fluttered across the road with a cool northwestern breeze, surrounding Cordwin and the army with a delicate fragrance. He noticed a few puffy white clouds rising above the western mountains, but most of the sky was clear blue. *Except directly south,* he thought. There, he saw columns of black smoke smudging the sky.

My first battle, he thought, his stomach churning. *My first real battle.* But what if he failed? What if the enemy defeated him? And what if his failure brought death and destruction to the people of Vorlik? No! He couldn't fail Vorlik or Clev!

Moon Shadow seemed to sense Cordwin's anxiety and tossed his head back nervously several times. Cordwin stroked the horse's warm neck. "It's all right, Shadow. Everything will be all right," he said. *I hope,* he added to himself.

Soon he passed rows of grapevines, pale green tendrils and leaves seeking support on wooden trellises, and he knew he was close to the town of Yarrow, known for its wines. He had sampled cups of deep red and clear white wines when he'd passed through on the inspection tour. Daikin had sampled several pitchers full of each. Cordwin smiled to himself. Next to women, Daikin's favorite thing was good wine, and Yarrow wines were the best in the northern lands.

At midday, Cordwin and the army reached the town of Yarrow, comprised of a score of houses, an inn, a smithy and stable, a small chapel, and a general merchandise shop. Yarrow was the only town between the castle and Tironza. As Cordwin rode into the center of town, he saw a crowd of townspeople gathered in the market square, worry on their faces. Fretful children clung to their mothers' skirts and stared at the soldiers. Women smoothed their children's hair and hushed them soothingly. The rotund innkeeper, the village priest of Baygor, and the forge-blackened smith stood before the inn, arguing anxiously when Cordwin rode up to the crowd.

"Sir Cordwin, what's happening?" the innkeeper said, bowing, a troubled look on his round face. "First we hear a horse racing toward the castle before dawn. And when the sun comes up, we see smoke rising in the south. Then an hour or so ago three Tarolin soldiers come galloping through town like they're being chase by the Hound of Darkness and heading toward Tironza. Everyone's so frightened, me included. Please, tell us what's going on!"

Cordwin halted Moon Shadow and gazed at the anxious faces. These were some of the people he had to protect. Doubt crept into his heart, and suddenly, he felt inadequate. "Tironza has been attacked," he said. "We don't know by whom, but we're on our way to help the Southern Guard."

"Great Baygor!" the priest said, his eyes wide. "Are we in danger? What should we do?"

"I don't know if Yarrow is in danger," Cordwin said. "I don't know who has attacked Tironza. But whatever happens, we'll protect you with all our strength. People will likely be fleeing Tironza to Yarrow. We need to set up a safe area for them. This would be an excellent place. Lieutenant Tude," Cordwin called over his shoulder.

She rode up beside Cordwin and saluted. "Yes, captain."

"Leave half a dozen men here to help set up camp for the refugees."

"Yes, captain." Tude saluted again, wheeled, rode back to her troops, and began calling out names.

Cordwin turned back to the priest. "Help the soldiers with the preparations. The people will need shelter, food, and water, and some may be injured and need tending."

"My wife's a healer," the innkeeper said. "The injured can be brought in here. I'll send word to the surrounding farmsteads to come help." He paused, swallowed hard, then asked, "Do you think we'll have to fight?"

"Not if it's in my power, but . . ." Cordwin gazed south, "keep your swords close."

"We can build barricades around the town," the smith said. "And we'll fight with scythes and pitchforks, even stones if we have to."

"Hopefully, you won't." Cordwin whistled to Moon Shadow and started down the road again.

The sun had passed its zenith when Cordwin spotted the first refugees—mostly women, children in night clothes, and old men, straggling north on the road, carrying only small bundles. Gazing at their faces smudged with dirt and soot, eyes filled with fear and disbelief, Cordwin felt guilty, as if he were responsible for what had happened to them. In his head, he knew that was foolish, but he found it painful to look the refugees in the eye.

Farther down the road he passed several women dragging carts packed with children and supplies, and children leading younger children. He saw a large yellow dog pulling a small wagon holding an old woman, whose arm was burned severely. Farther south, Cordwin stopped by a wagon, overcrowded with children and old women, pulled off the road to let the troops pass. A horse-faced old man sat on the bench seat, holding the reins.

"It's bad down there," the old man called in a voice like rusty hinges. He pointed to the billowing column of smoke that darkened the southern sky. "You'd better ride fast, or there won't be anything left."

Cordwin nodded to Daikin, who blew a signal on his horn. The army shifted from a fast walk to a quick trot, passing lines of people, old and young, fleeing from the battle. Some were burned, some, bleeding, Some were on crutches; some had slings. All stared at the soldiers as they passed. Many looked dazed and dejected, as if they felt betrayed.

Cordwin averted his eyes to avoid the accusing stares. "Lady Baramay," he prayed, "please, let us be in time to stop the invaders!"

The sun was halfway between its zenith and the western mountain tops when the wind shifted. Blowing straight from the south, it carried the acrid odor of fire and a fine grey ash that made Cordwin cough. As he climbed a last rise before the descent to the plain of Tironza, Cordwin swallowed hard, fearing what he would see. Only two weeks ago he had ridden up this slight hill toward Vorlik's largest city. At the hill's crest, he halted and gazed across the flatland with its farmsteads and fields, and the great city of Tironza in the center.

The southern half of the city was in flames, great tongues of fire belching clouds of black smoke into the air. The northern edge of Tironza wasn't burning, but people streamed from the city up the road to the north. Faint shouts and screams, mingled with the sounds of metal on metal, wafted toward Cordwin.

Moments later, the three scouts, who'd been dispatched by Clevil, came racing from the city toward Cordwin and halted before him. One looked at Cordwin, surprised. "Sir Cordwin?"

Cordwin sat erect, trying to appear in command, even if he didn't quite feel adequate. "Captain Cordwin."

The guard saluted. "Guardsman Alswick, Captain. The enemies have taken the southern third of Tironza, maybe more. Much of it's burning."

"Do you know who the enemies are? Where they're from?"

"No, captain. They bear no standard; they wear no insignia on their armor or helmets."

"How many?" Cordwin asked.

"Perhaps two to three hundred inside Tironza," Alswick said, his brow furrowed. "Perhaps more. It's hard to guess how many are packed into the streets and alleys. I'd say there are at least another two hundred reinforcements just south of the city."

"Any sign of the Eastern and Western Guards?"

"No, sir."

"Well done, soldier."

Wheeling, Cordwin faced the lieutenants. "We stick to the plan," he said quietly. "Rayvil, take the west side, keeping behind the hills surrounding the plain for cover. Loren, do the same on the east. Daikin and I will go straight south into the city. Tude, come with me, and Baygor protect us all."

"Baygor protect us," the lieutenants echoed softly.

Cordwin turned Moon Shadow south and led the Third and Fourth Watches toward the city.

The massive oak North Gate in Tironza's stone wall was wide open and packed with citizens struggling to get out of the city. Half a dozen guards wearing the yellow and gold uniform of the Southern Guard tried to keep order and speed the people through the gate to the safety of the north road. The fleeing crowd was wedged in so tightly, Cordwin knew it was impossible for his troops to enter the gate without trampling some of the people.

"We can't ride into the city like this," Daikin shouted above the noise. "Should we leave our horses by the wall?"

Cordwin chewed his lower lip for a moment. "No. We don't want to give up our advantage. We have to find a way into the city."

One soldier of the Southern Guard sprinted from the gate to Cordwin's side and saluted. "Sir Cordwin, I'll see you get into the city." He ran back to the gate. "Clear the way!" he shouted. "Make way! Quickly! Make way for Sir Cordwin!"

People poured out of the gate at a run and fled to both sides of the road. Others still inside the city pressed as close as possible against the sides of buildings until there was just enough room for two guards to ride side by side down a broad avenue toward Market Green, the wide plaza in the center of the city. Cordwin, Daikin, and Tude led their troops past cheering people toward the sounds of fighting and crackling fire.

"Keep them safe," Cordwin said as he passed the Southern guardsman.

"Baygor protect you!" the guardsman called back as the riders entered Tironza.

Cordwin rode as fast as he could, past the terrified citizens and crowded alleys, past deserted houses and empty shops. Fear and excitement pounded in his chest nearly as loud as Moon Shadow's hooves pounded on the cobblestone street. Finally, he entered the wide plaza called Market Green.

On the southern side of the plaza the roof of The Temple of Baygor, a blue marble and gold leaf building, collapsed, sending up smoke, ash, and searing sparks. The crash of timbers and stone almost blotted out the screams from inside the building, but not quite. Soldiers of the Southern Guard, backed by farmers and tradesmen armed with staves and stones and clubs, formed a line of defense near the northern edge the plaza. Facing them were scores and scores of invaders, all armed with swords and spears and axes. More of the enemy fighters poured in from the southern streets adjoining the plaza.

Daikin sounded his horn as Cordwin led his troops to join the attack. The weary defenders glanced over their shoulders, their eyes widened, then they cheered the reinforcements.

"For Lord Clevil and Tironza!" Cordwin shouted, drawing his sword.

The Vorlikian soldiers echoed his words and plunged into the battle.

Injured men lay like broken dolls on the plaza, spilling crimson life on the smooth white stones. Cries of agony and despair rose above the clang of steel against steel. The air was thick with acrid smoke that made Cordwin's eyes water, and the metallic scent of blood filled his nose and rested on his tongue like a copper coin. He fought through the enemy ranks, barely thinking of anything except killing the foe in front of him at the moment. He had no time for self-doubt; he simply tried to stay alive. Soon his red and gold surcoat was stained darker red and was soaked with enemy's blood.

Still more foes poured in from the south, but Cordwin led the Vorlikian guards and the defenders until they had driven the enemies almost to the burning southern edge of the plaza. Just when Cordwin thought he'd trapped the invaders between his troops and the Temple fire, the enemies split their ranks. Half cut their way to streets running to the east. The other half smashed doors of houses on Market Green's west side, breaking through back exits to flee down narrow alleys.

"Daikin, take the Third Watch west!" Cordwin called. "Tude, you and the Fourth follow me!"

Cordwin rode east down a wide avenue, picking his way around bodies and fallen stones. Cobblestones became so slick with blood, Cordwin feared his horse might slip. Rubble made the street more treacherous. Thick grey smoke rolled between the buildings, stinging Cordwin's eyes so badly he could barely see where he was going. Sweat stuck his clothes to his skin and trickled down his face. His throat felt dry and raspy, and the heat and smoke felt like they scorched his lungs with every breath. He tried holding part of his surcoat over his mouth and nose, but he still coughed and choked. Moon Shadow trembled beneath him and shied back from the fumes. Cordwin had to drop the fabric from his face and use both his hands to control his mount and force Shadow onward.

Suddenly, the smoke began to dissipate, and Cordwin saw an opening ahead. He'd reached the eastern edge of the city. Enemy troops fled through the East Gate to the grassy plains beyond. Cordwin rode after them, gasping hard, his chest hurting from the smoke he'd breathed in, sweat-drenched hair plastered to his forehead. When he reached the open gates, he darted a glance outside. The foes had turned and arrayed crossbowman kneeling in a line, backed by archers, ready to attack the guardsmen when they emerged from the gate. Cordwin pulled back and called Tude to his side.

"We can only ride through the gate six at a time," he said, leaning close to her so he didn't have to shout, "and our enemies could pick us off easily. How can we reach them before they cut us down?"

Tude bit her lower lip for a moment, her eyes troubled. "We need a diversion. Otherwise everyone who rides through the gate will be dead in moments."

Suddenly, a horn sounded north and east of the gate, a Vorlikian horn, Lieutenant Loren's sharp staccato signal. A moment later, another Vorlikian horn rang out, then another, the sounds building on top of each other until Cordwin could feel the sound vibrating in his chest. Hooves pounded from the east, kicking up clouds of dust.

"The Second Watch has come and the Eastern Guard!" Cordwin shouted, hope rising in his heart. "Follow me!"

Cordwin galloped from the East Gate, leading the guardsmen. The enemies—faced with forces from east, north, and west—were in disarray by the sudden shift in advantage. One of them sounded retreat, and they all shouldered their weapons and fled southwest toward the pass through the Circle Mountains.

Evening shadows lengthened as Cordwin and the Vorlikian guards pursued the retreating fighters to the southern edge of the city, killing most of them. At the entrance to the Southern Pass, Cordwin saw large numbers of invaders escaping to Peltik, but near the Southern Gate of Tironza a remnant of their force fought the combined troops of the First and Third Watches and Western Guard. Cordwin led his own forces to attack the enemies from behind. Retreat cut off, the grim foes turned to confront the Vorlikian troops. For the first time, Cordwin was close enough to realize their faces wore barbaric tattoos. He had no time to wonder why.

"Surrender!" Cordwin shouted. "You are surrounded and outnumbered! You can't survive!"

For a moment the foes hesitated, then one of them, the captain, shouted back, "To us, surrender *is* death! We will fight to our last breath! No surrender!"

"No surrender!" the other fighters echoed and charged the guardsmen.

Cordwin slashed toward the center of the cluster of fighters as the sun hung barely above the western mountains. At last, he faced the enemy captain, a man with more scars on his body than hair on his head. Strange dark blue tattoos covered his face, and his arms bulged with knotted muscles that decades of training brought. Cordwin staggered as their swords clashed; he knew that by himself, he was no match for the man. Daikin appeared at Cordwin's right side, then Rayvil arrived at his left side. The scarred captain fought and parried their attacks with ferocious skill, but the three Vorlikian fighters were too formidable together. Cordwin blocked the captain's sword, and Daikin slid his sword past the captain's shield to his heart.

As the sun set, the last enemy was slain. A shout of victory filled the cooling air as the forces of Vorlik surrounded Cordwin.

Cordwin coughed harshly, his throat dry and aching, then he finger-combed his damp hair from his forehead. His surcoat was blood-soaked and sweat-stained, and his chain mail coat felt intolerably heavy. Exhausted but heart still pounding, he struggled to raise his sword, which gleamed crimson in the fading daylight. Chest heaving, skin glistening, he cried, "Praise Baygor!"

"Praise Baygor!" echoed the guardsmen.

Cordwin raised his arms for silence. "Send word of our victory to Lord Clevil. Take the wounded to the physicians. We'll bury our dead with honor, but the enemy dead," he paused for a moment, his jaw tight, "we'll burn them in disgrace."

More tired than he ever remembered being, Cordwin dismounted and picked his way slowly across the battlefield. His legs felt unsteady, and his lungs still ached from smoke. Even his sword felt almost too heavy to bear. Daikin walked beside him in the fading orange light.

"We need to close the southern pass until we know where this army came from," Cordwin said wearily as he leaned heavily on his sword hilt and coughed again. "We should seal all the passes. We'll leave thirty Tarolin guards to help rebuild and man the guardian keep on Peltik's border and another forty to reinforce the Southern Guard for now." He paused, looking at the growing heap of bodies, his eyes narrowed with rage. "Hound of Darkness, who were they? What did they want?"

Daikin scanned the battlefield, his red brows pulled together in an angry frown, his jaw tight. "I wish I knew!" he said. A cool wind blew his copper hair across his square-jawed face, as soot-covered and sweat-streaked as Cordwin's. One sleeve of his surcoat was torn away, although the chain mail sleeve was undamaged.

Cordwin nudged the body of an invader, turning it over, and chewed his lower lip. "There were too many to be just raiders, but look at them. Not one of them carried a device on their armor or shields. There was nothing unusual about any of these men, except the tattooed ones – and I've never even *heard* of their like before. Look at that tattoo in the middle of his forehead." Cordwin pointed his sword at the dead man's head. "A black circle with red eyes—the symbol of the Hound of Darkness. Only two kinds of people that we know of worship that creature – Sorcerers and Drambini – but I've never heard of Drambini tattooing themselves."

"We don't even know if Sorcerers still exist," Daikin said. "And if these raiders really *were* Sorcerers, why didn't they use magic in the battle?"

"I don't know. I'm just trying to make some sense of this." Cordwin shrugged as he scanned the battlefield. "If these raiders hadn't crossed the border from Peltik, I'd swear Drambit was behind this."

Daikin spat on the ground. "Who's to say it isn't?"

"But why did they attack now? And why here, in the South?"

Daikin shrugged his broad shoulders. "Who knows?"

"We'll send a messenger to Peltik. I can't believe Lord Merrik had anything to do with this. He's always been an ally of Vorlik."

"He wanted you for a son-in-law," Daikin said, giving Cordwin a weak smile.

Cordwin just shook his head. "Dispatch a messenger to him. Maybe he has some word of these...villains." The word felt like acid on his tongue.

Daikin turned to face him and gasped with alarm. "Barg's breath, Cord, you're wounded! We're going to the surgeons. Now!"

Cordwin glanced at his left arm. A deep slice ran from below the cap sleeve of his chain mail coat almost to his elbow. The wound oozed slowly, blood already crusted on his surcoat sleeve. He hadn't even felt it, but now burning pain shot up his arm. "I'm fine, but Ellisa's going to be furious. Give me some cloth. I'll bandage this myself."

Daikin bent down and tore a strip of relatively clean cloth from one of the enemy's shirts. "Let me help." Daikin wrapped the cloth around his cousin's arm and gave the bandage a jerk.

Cordwin cursed between gritted teeth and cradled his elbow. "You did that deliberately!"

"Who, me?" Daikin smiled wickedly. He put Cordwin's good arm around his shoulder. "Don't argue, Cord. Just come with me to the healer's tents. Or would you rather I throw you over my shoulder and carry you there?"

Cordwin was too tired to protest. He just nodded.

Daikin glanced around the battlefield, then shouted, "Tude, take charge of mine and Captain Cordwin's horses."

Tude waved her acknowledgement and headed for the pair of wandering mounts.

Daikin led Cordwin to a cart carrying the wounded to the healer's tents. Cordwin sank down on the back edge of the cart, too fatigued to crawl farther inside. Daikin walked beside the cart as it headed north.

The physicians and healers had set up their tents between the North Gate and the hills north of the city. Daikin helped Cordwin out of the cart and led him to the red tent of chief surgeon Tothim.

"Here's an obstinate patient," Daikin said as Cordwin collapsed to a small stool, coughing until his chest hurt. "Don't be gentle with him. He'd rather bleed to death than face a little needle!"

White-haired Tothim raised a bushy eyebrow as he scowled at Cordwin. "You're supposed to set an example for your men, Captain Cordwin. Surely, you're not afraid of a tiny needle."

Cordwin swallowed hard but said nothing. He had never won a battle with Tothim.

Cordwin winced and breathed in sharply as Daikin helped Cordwin remove his surcoat and chain mail coat, then Daikin took the mail and surcoat and left the healers tent. Tothim cut away the blood-soaked black shirt sleeve and examined Cordwin's arm, then washed the wound with oil and wine. While a healer applied a heated poultice of woundweal to the area, Tothim held his precious thin steel needle in a candle flame, threaded gut for stitching, then dipped needle and gut in a basin of wine.

Although woundweal numbed the arm, Cordwin still felt the needle going through his flesh. His stomach churned uneasily, and he felt like he might vomit. He clamped his jaws shut and closed his eyes, trying to calm his stomach.

"You can open your eyes now," Tothim said. "I'm finished."

Cordwin opened his eyes and stared at his arm. The wound was closed, black stitches in a line more than a hand span long down his arm. Tothim applied honey to the incision to keep down the infection, and wrapped a bandage securely about Cordwin's arm and put it in a sling.

"Drink this," Tothim said, frowning as he handed Cordwin a cup of hot red liquid. "I'd tell you to rest, but I already know you won't do anything I tell you to, so I won't bother. This will help you. But only for a while. If you don't rest sometime tonight, you'll pay for it later."

Cordwin inhaled the swirling steam rising above the cup, a wholesome fragrance mingling the scent of mint, apples, linden blossoms, and ginger root with something earthy, subtle, yet pervasive. Simply breathing in the aroma relieved some of his weariness and eased the aching tightness in his chest from all the smoke he'd inhaled. "Roborant?" he asked.

Tothim nodded. "And peppermint and coltsfoot for that cough. The infusion will ease the coughing and give you strength for now, but only for a while. Before the night is over, you *must* rest. And eat something."

"I will." Cordwin blew on the cup until the infusion was cool enough to drink. Warmth flowed through his body, soothing his aching muscles. His exhaustion melted away; his legs felt strong enough to support him again. Gradually, he could breathe without gasping.

Daikin returned just as Cordwin left Tothim's tent to search for Moon Shadow. Cordwin found his white stallion with other horses guarded by several of Lieutenant Tude's men. Tude directed some guards to help the physicians and healers care for the wounded, and others to help organize the refugees who couldn't go farther from the city. Not only was Tude a good soldier, she was an excellent leader. Noticing Cordwin, she saluted, then went back to her duties.

Twilight and a bright full moon cast deep shadows on the city as Cordwin and Daikin walked through the North Gate, down the now deserted wide avenue to the Market Green, to survey the destruction. Fire still blazed in places. Rebuilding would take many months. Cordwin had always loved the elegant city with homes of fine woods and polished marble, granite, and limestone quarried from the Circle Mountains nearby. Tironza's Market Green drew caravans from every country to trade for goods found only in Tironza, such as the flawless diamonds mined in the nearby foothills. Even the poorer quarter in the city had been clean, well-built, and decorated with colorful murals of mountains and rivers.

A squad of soldiers, commanded by Lieutenant Rayvil, and all of the surviving uninjured townsmen formed a bucket brigade to save as much of Tironza as possible. The houses surrounding the plaza were charred but no longer burning. The soldiers and citizens moved down streets to the south, dousing smoldering beams, doors, and furniture.

"Lieutenant Rayvil," Cordwin called, "how bad is it?"

Rayvil saluted, then wiped his eyes with his sleeve, streaking dirt across his dark brow. "The entire southern section of the city has been destroyed. Many buildings collapsed and will have to be rebuilt. But the worst," he paused and gazed at the south end of the plaza, "the worst is there—the Temple of Baygor."

Rayvil led Cordwin and Daikin past dozens of people trying to clear the plaza to the ruins of the temple. Cordwin stared, appalled, as soldiers of the Southern Guard carried the blackened bodies of priests from the gutted temple and laid them out reverently on the stone pavement. Cordwin felt sick to his stomach, and tears leaked from his eyes as he walked slowly toward the rows of dead.

One of the Southern Guard stood gazing down at the bodies, tears in his pale blue eyes. He looked up when Cordwin approached. "Most of the priests fought beside us to give two of their number enough time to evacuate children from the temple orphanage," the guard said. "They got the children out, but the invaders cut off the escape of all the other priests and forced them back into the building." He swallowed hard. "It was already burning. We tried to reach them. We tried so hard. But there were too many enemies between us and them. The ceiling beams collapsed and...merciful Baygor," he whispered, "I'll never forget their screams. Never."

Cordwin trembled and felt sick to his stomach. He clamped his jaws shut to keep from vomiting, forcing down the acid in his throat.

A pair of injured priests, the only survivors of the temple, trudged slowly toward Cordwin and bowed awkwardly. Their red robes were singed and torn. One had a broken arm. The other priest's hair was burned to the scalp on one side, and his face was blistered and bleeding.

Cordwin turned to Rayvil and said, "Bury the priests beside our fallen soldiers." He faced the priests and rested his right hand gently on the burned priest's shoulder. "They gave their lives to save others, and they are worthy of the highest honor and our gratitude."

Amazement filled the priests' faces, and they knelt before Cordwin. "Thank you," said the severely burned one, his voice quivering.

"I should kneel to you," Cordwin said earnestly and held out his right hand.

The burned priest took Cordwin's hand hesitantly and stood up, then helped his fellow priest stand.

Cordwin glanced at Rayvil. "See that these brave men are taken to the healers and their injuries are cared for—and make certain that they are treated with the dignity and deference they deserve. They are true heroes."

Rayvil nodded and called for a cart to transport the priests.

Slowly, Cordwin turned and stood gaping sadly at the ruined Temple of Baygor. The blue marble walls were blackened, and the gold-covered dome that had shone like the sun for miles had collapse into the sanctuary. "We need to hire carpenters and masons to restore the Southern Barracks and destroyed buildings in the city," he told Daikin softly. "Especially the temple. And we need to clear the streets of debris. Have Rayvil and Tude organize crews to help." He gazed at the ruins. His skin felt cold, and everything around him seemed flat, as if it were a painting, almost unreal. "So many deaths, so much destruction. Why? For what? It's all so...senseless!"

"War usually is," Daikin said quietly as he gazed at the destruction. "Right now, you need to rest." He held up a hand when Cordwin started to protest. "We know what to do. Just let us do it. Go rest in your tent." He held up his hand again when Cordwin started to speak again. "I had it set up while Tothim was sewing up your arm. It's just behind the main healer's tent. I'll come for you when it's time for the burial."

"All right," Cordwin said, nodding slowly. The roborant infusion still flowed though him, but he felt exhausted, almost numbed by the amount of death he had seen.

Daikin motioned to a black-haired woman wearing the colors of the Tarolin Guard. "Escort Captain Cordwin to his tent and stand guard."

She saluted and placed herself to Cordwin's left, her hand on her sword hilt. Beside her, Cordwin trudged back to the North Gate and out to the healers tents. Just behind them was a small red tent with the standard of Vorlik. Before it was planted a white banner with the color of one the four border Guards in each corner and the red and gold banner of the Tarolin Guard in the center. A man wearing the uniform of the Tarolin Guard stood statue-still beside the standard, hand on his sword. He clapped his fist across his chest in salute as Cordwin approached. His escort took her place on the opposite side of the tent opening and saluted Cordwin.

He shuffled to the tent, ducked through opening, and spotted a small cot near the east wall. Too worn out to undress, he sank down on the cot and pulled a thick blanket over his shoulders and chest. Lying down on his right side, careful not to move his injured left arm too much, Cordwin immediately fell asleep.

Someone shook him gently and called his name. Curled up on his side, he pulled the blanket tighter around him and tried to sink back into the warm dark comfort of sleep.

"Cord," a voice said. "Wake up."

He opened his eyes and saw Daikin kneeling beside him, a lantern on a makeshift table of planks and crates the only light in the closed tent. Cordwin pushed up on one elbow and knew instantly that the roborant had worn off. Every muscle ached; his wound throbbed.

"Here," Daikin said and handed Cordwin a cup of hot roborant tea. "Tothim thought you might need this."

Cordwin winced as he sat up and took the cup in his right hand. "Thank you." He blew across the steaming liquid and took a quick sip, but the tea wasn't too hot to drink.

"It's time to attend the burial," Daikin said, standing up. "But you might want to wash up and change clothes." He pointed to the table. A pitcher and bowl sat beside the lantern, with a small cloth, a towel, and a pile of folded clothes on the other side of the bowl. His mail coat hung on a stand to the right of the table. "And I brought you a meat and potato pasty. Tothim insisted you eat something, too."

Cordwin inhaled the strong earthy fragrance of the medicine, took another sip, and felt its warmth flow through his chest, arms, and legs, soothing his raw throat and lungs, renewing his strength. "I *really* needed this," he said, arching his back and stretching.

"Drink up," Daikin said, smiling. "Everyone is waiting for you. Let me help you off with your boots."

Cordwin finished the medicine as quickly as he could and bit into the pasty then nearly stuffed the entire thing in his mouth, while Daikin carefully removed Cordwin's boots and socks.

Daikin laughed. "Slow down or you'll choke to death."

"But I'm starved!" Cordwin said, his mouth full. "I just didn't know it until now. This tastes better than a banquet! You wouldn't have more of them, would you?"

Daikin grinned and handed him another pasty. Cordwin devoured it almost as quickly as the first one.

Slowly, Cordwin stood, grimacing as bruises he didn't know he had began to smart. He tried to strip off his bloody clothes, but couldn't do it one-handed. Daikin had to undo the sling before Cordwin could take off the shirt. Daikin untied the shirt and helped Cordwin slip out of it.

Blood had soaked all the way through to Cordwin's linens and stuck them to his skin. He winced as he pulled off the pants and underclothes. Walking stiffly to the table, he poured water from the pitcher into the bowl. He dipped the cloth in the water, surprised it was so warm, then squeezed out the cloth as much as he could one-handed, and wiped off his face, chest and left arm. Daikin had to wash off the right arm.

"Would you like for me to have one of the women come wash your back?" Daikin asked, his green eyes twinkling.

"I can take care of the rest myself," Cordwin said, taking the cloth back and frowning at his cousin. "When will you ever stop?"

"When I'm in my grave," Daikin said, grinning.

Cordwin rolled his eyes, quickly washed the rest of his aching body, then Daikin helped him on with his clean clothes, but left off the mail coat. Cordwin didn't think he could bear the weight at the moment. In the northwest corner of the tent was a small depression — a hastily dug latrine. Cordwin relieved himself, Daikin replaced the sling, then they walked out of the tent together.

The full moon was still in the eastern sky, perhaps two hours from midnight as Cordwin and Daikin and the two soldiers guarding the tent walked to the barrow ground. Generations of Tironzans had been buried in the wide treeless field northeast of the city. Marble mausoleums and limestone tombs stood beside great stone-covered barrows from ages ago. And gathered at the far eastern edge of the barrow ground were the soldiers of Vorlik.

A newly raised mound, surrounded by spears, stood beside a second, smaller mound, circled by white stones. The two surviving priests of Baygor stood at the head of the smaller mound, singing a hymn of mourning. Vorlikian guards stood silently, heads bowed in the bright moonlight. A few held blazing torches.

Cordwin and Daikin walked to the head of the soldiers' mound and waited reverently while the priests sang. When they'd finished, the one with facial burns knelt and brushed his fingertips across the mound.

"Sleep peacefully, dear brothers and sisters." The priest's voice cracked, and tears trickled down his raw face. "May Baygor wipe away the grief of this life and give you rest from your labor. And may we meet again in Barg's kingdom."

The other priest laid a hand on the burned priest's shoulder and wept, too. Finally, the burned priest stood, trembling but no longer weeping.

Daikin leaned closed to Cordwin and whispered, "You need to speak now."

Cordwin gazed at the large mound, lit by moonlight, and his mouth and throat felt dry. His chest was so tight, it hurt to breathe. Several times he tried to speak, but no sound would come. Swallowing hard, he tried again.

"Let us honor our dead in our hearts. They died that others might live, and I can give them no greater praise. May they find rest and peace in Barg's kingdom."

His voice cracked; his vision wavered like ripples on water. He cleared his throat, took a deep breath, and continued. "It is said that the dead will live forever as long as one person remembers them. Let the list be read."

Daikin unrolled a scroll while a guard bearing a torch stepped up beside him. "Derwin of Tironza."

A man wearing the yellow and gold of the Southern Guard stepped forward. "I stand for his memory."

"Kel of Tarolin."

One of the Tarolin guards stepped forward. "I stand for his memory."

And so Daikin read the list, with one of the soldiers stepping forward to vow remembrance of the dead, until all thirty-seven guardsmen had been named. Cordwin listened to the list of names and wept. Never again would he spar with Swordmaster Cyril. Or raise a mug with Kel. Or learn from Horsemaster Tulley to gentle a horse with quiet words. So many friends gone. So many faces he'd never see again. All lay in the soft earth, senselessly killed. Cordwin wiped his tears away with his sleeve.

Then Daikin took out a second list and began reading names. "Eulin, high priest of Baygor."

For a moment, there was silence, and the priests looked stunned.

Cordwin stepped forward and said, "I stand for his memory."

"Lynneah, priestess of Baygor."

"I stand for her memory," said Lieutenant Rayvil.

The priests sank to their knees and wept again while the rest of their fellow priests were named. The burned priest looked up at Cordwin, clasped his hands together, and bowed his head until his forehead touched his hands. Cordwin returned the bow to the priest.

Gazing past the priests, Cordwin saw the pyre of enemy bodies, set far apart from the barrows. The bodies were piled with branches and timbers scavenged from ruined buildings. His eyes narrowed, and he clenched his jaw. His hand tightened into fists as he strode toward the heap of dead. He stood glaring at them, rage and cold deliberation warring in his chest. Rage won out.

"You'll find no rest beneath our fields!" he said, his face hot despite the cool air. "Let fire burn you to ashes! Let the wind blow the ashes to the sea! Let the sea hide them in its depths! And may the Hound of Darkness *never* let your souls know peace!"

Taking a torch from a soldier, Cordwin hurled it at the pyre. Others threw more torches. Soon crackling flames rose to the sky like a pillar of fire, coloring the night saffron and crimson. The nauseating stink of burning flesh permeated the air.

At least Vorlik's safe now, he thought with a sigh of relief as his arm began to throb again.

Suddenly, a sentry shouted, "Sir Cordwin, the sky! Look at the sky!"

Daikin pointed north frantically. "Cordwin, look! Look at the sky!"

Thick blue-white clouds had started rolling in from the northwest, portending a coming storm. But straight north the clouds were tinged red by the reflection of flames. Only something large burning would cause such a pronounced reflection.

Fear shivered down Cordwin's back as he stared north, toward Tarolin, toward home, toward..."Clev!"

3

Cordwin raced to Moon Shadow, so scared he felt sick to his stomach. Daikin ran close behind.

"Leave forty men to guard the wounded!" Cordwin said as he pulled the sling off his arm and grimaced as pain shot up to his shoulder. "Have all able-bodied guards mount and follow me as quickly as possible! Daikin, you're in charge!"

"Captain...cousin...Cord!" Daikin grabbed the silver bridle as Cordwin almost leaped into his saddle. "You can't go alone! Wait for the army to assemble!"

"There's no time!" Cordwin tried futilely to wrench the bridle from Daikin's grasp.

"You *can't* go alone!" Daikin said. "At least, wait for me! Let me come with you!"

"No! You lead the army! I have to go to Clev!"

Daikin held on to the reins, his eyes hard and determined. "You're not leaving without a guard! If our worst fears are true, *you* may be the lord of Vorlik now!"

"No!" Cordwin cried, terrified by Daikin's words. "Don't say that! Clev's alive!"

"Maybe!" Daikin shouted as he hung onto the reins, though Moon Shadow dragged him several yards. "And maybe not! Either way, I'm coming with you, whether you like it or not!"

"Then you'll have to catch up with me!" Cordwin clapped his legs against Moon Shadow's sides. The white stallion leaped forward, jerking the reins from Daikin's hands. Daikin shouted orders and ran toward his horse, but Cordwin didn't wait. He wove north through the hurrying mass of troops to the Tironza Road, toward Tarolin Castle and Clevil. He heard Daikin's voice calling him, but Cordwin didn't slow down. He heard shouting, running feet, and horses neighing and knew a large part of the Guards were preparing to follow him, but he didn't dare take time to look back. It would take him nearly four hours before he could reach the castle.

Cordwin's arm throbbed, the air stung his face as his horse galloped through the chilling night, but nothing else mattered to him except reaching the castle. He cursed himself angrily, and he was frightened, more frightened than he'd ever been in his life. "A ruse! Hound of Darkness, it was a ruse! Clev, I'm coming! Please, Lady Baramay, let me be in time!"

He rode past darkened farmsteads and numerous small camps of refugees. Some of the refugees jumped to their feet, startled by the pounding hooves in the middle of the night. The closer Cordwin came to Tarolin, the redder the clouds grew and the more frightened Cordwin became. Moon Shadow galloped so fast, the moon was barely past midnight when Cordwin reached the town of Yarrow.

Cordwin saw tables and wagons used for barricades had been pulled to the side of the road as he galloped into Yarrow. Sliding from the saddle, Cordwin pounded on the inn's door until the innkeeper unbolted the latch and opened the door. "I need a horse right now!" Cordwin said.

"Sir Cordwin?" The innkeeper's eyes were barely open. He scratched his sparse hair, then blinked a few times and shook himself. "What's wrong? A messenger said you'd won the battle."

"We did!" Cordwin said, breathing hard and fast. "Where are the Tarolin guards left here?"

The innkeeper rubbed his eyes. "They helped the refugees set up camp north of town, then went back to the castle when the messenger rode through with the news several hours ago. We thought everything was all right so we all went to bed." He gazed at Cordwin with a worried look. "Everything *is* all right. Isn't it?"

"No!" Cordwin said desperately. He grabbed the innkeeper's arm and pointed to the clouds in the north. "Tarolin's burning! I need a fresh horse, and I need my horse stabled for the night!"

The innkeeper's eyes snapped wide open as he gazed at the red clouds above Rindolar Woods. "Baygor protect us!"

"I need a horse, now! Have more ready for the soldiers following me!"

"Y-yes, sir."

The innkeeper led Cordwin quickly to the stables and ordered a sleepy stable boy to saddle a horse for Cordwin and tend to Moon Shadow. The white stallion was lathered and breathing harshly. Cordwin unbuckled the saddle, slid it off, and handed it to the stable boy.

"I'll be back for you soon, Shadow, I promise," Cordwin said, throwing a blanket over the stallion's sweat-drenched coat and sliding the silver bridle from the horse's head.

The stable boy saddled a black mare. Just as Cordwin mounted the fresh horse, Daikin and half a dozen guards halted in front of the stable.

"Change mounts and follow me quickly!" Cordwin shouted to Daikin, then spurred his horse toward the castle, clinging close to the horse's neck. *I can't wait for them,* he thought. *I can't lose my family!*

"Cordwin!" Daikin called after him, but Cordwin didn't stop. Faintly, he heard the innkeeper shout, "But we don't have that many horses!"

Cordwin passed the refugee camp, with barely a glance at the sleeping people. He focused on the flickering red clouds above the towering trees of Rindolar Woods. The glow became brighter and more intense the closer he came.

Entering the great woods was like entering a cave. No light penetrated the thick boughs overhead. "Lady Baramay, guide this beast and me through the darkness," he prayed as he laid his cheek against the horse's neck.

It felt like hours before he spotted light ahead, but it wasn't soft, white moonlight. The red glare of fire flashed at the end of the dark woods. As he left the huge trees, his heart sank.

The iron portcullis was up, and the massive castle gate was wide open and burning. The bodies of several guards lay on the ground inside the gateway. Fire blazed high above the walls, sending ash and smoke into the night sky.

Cordwin's horse shied from the flames and balked at entering the gateway, no matter how hard Cordwin tried to force the frightened beast. Abandoning the attempt, Cordwin leapt from the horse and ran through the burning gateway to the courtyard.

"No!" he cried softly, stunned as he surveyed the courtyard. He'd seen a great deal of death in Tironza, but the sight of carnage and destruction in the castle, his home, brought him to a standstill, horrified, unable to move. *Oh, no, please, not here, not my home!*

The last standing timbers of the Guard's barracks collapsed with a hollow crash, sending up sparks high above the castle walls. Smoke stung his eyes. All the stables were only smoldering ruins. The air was filled with the sickening stink of burned flesh. Two of the stable boys, only a few years younger than Cordwin, lay before the remains of the stable doors. The boys' bodies were blackened, skin peeled back from raw flesh. There was no life in their eyes.

Guards lay scattered across the wide courtyard, bodies hacked and limbs severed, amid numerous bodies of unknown men. A handful of guards lay sprawled on the steps to the castle. And before the open doors lay the body of Captain Bailoc, a sword still in his hand, his severed head lying in a bloody pool. Beside him lay Scribe Wogen, his chest split open, his sword lying in his blood on the stone portico. Around Bailoc and Wogen lay more bodies of invaders.

Tears streamed down Cordwin's face. He clapped his hand over his mouth, trying to still his stomach, but everywhere he looked, he saw pale bodies of people he'd known all his life, people lying in dark purple pools of blood. His stomach lurched, and he vomited on the steps. His hands felt clammy, and his body felt so cold, he couldn't stop shivering. One thought pushed him onward: Clevil, Ellisa, and Bren — his family.

The castle was silent, so still. There was always noise in the castle, the sound of people moving, talking, but not now. Cordwin ran through the entrance hall, dashing over dead bodies, and slipped on blood-slick floors. He fell on his injured arm and cried out as some of the stitches broke open. Pushing to his feet, he ran for the wide stairs. "Clev!" he screamed. "Ellisa!"

No one answered, only the echo of his own desperation.

He raced up the spiral stairs, passing more dead guards and several servants, and shouted his brother's name. At the top of the stairs lay the body of Kella, the priest of Baygor, a quarterstaff still in his hand. Three invaders lay crumpled around him. Cordwin didn't stop. He couldn't. He ran down the corridor shouting his brother's name, fear pounding in his head and ears like thunder.

Finally, near the door to his brother's rooms, he found Clevil, lying in a puddle of blood, surrounded by a dozen dead guards and a score of dead raiders. Clevil's blond hair was matted with blood from a head wound. Blood crusted rents in his shirt and trousers. His face was paler than when winter fever had gripped him.

"Clev, be alive! Please, be alive!" Cordwin fell to his knees and lifted his brother in his arms. Clevil's forehead was cold. Cordwin felt his brother's chest, but there was no breath. Touching the side of Clevil's throat, Cordwin felt no pulse, no throbbing of life. "No," he whispered, "please, please, no!"

Tears cut gullies down Cordwin's face. He pressed his brother's cold body to his chest and sobbed, rocking back and forth. "Clev! Clev! Don't leave me! Please! Don't leave me! Don't leave me!" He gazed up at the ceiling, tears stinging his face. "Merciful Baygor, bring him back!" he begged. "Give him breath again! Let him live! Don't take him from me, please, please, please!"

He laid his cheek against Clevil's blood-streaked hair, and wept until he felt almost numb, wept until he knew in his heart that Clevil would never open his eyes, never laugh, never give Cordwin a secret smile again, wept until he admitted to himself that Clevil was dead. And Cordwin wanted to die, too.

Glancing into Clevil's room, he gasped as he saw Ellisa lying on the floor. Placing his brother's body on the floor, Cordwin half-crawled over three dead men to where she lay. Dried blood left a dark trail from the corner of her mouth to her long, matted hair. Wine-colored streaks, like spokes of a wheel or threads of a spider web, radiated across her white gown from a dagger in her breast.

"No," he whispered, fresh tears blurring his sight. "Oh, gods, no, not her, too."

With the same gentleness Ellisa had always shown him, Cordwin lifted her in his arms and caressed her pale, lifeless face. His tears wet her soft but cold cheek as he kissed it. Ellisa had soothed his fears and sung away his nightmares. She'd kissed his bruises and bandaged his scrapes. She had been like a second mother to him when his own mother had died, and he loved her even more than the mother he remembered dimly. Blinking his eyes, he tried to stop his tears, but they kept burning down his cheeks.

"Lady Baramay, why? Why her? Why did you let her die? You've taken everything from me! Everything!" He buried his face in her tangled hair. "I should've been here," he said, sobbing. "I should've been here to protect you."

He heard a groan, and his eyes caught a slight movement. His nephew's nurse lay on her belly beside the child's crèche, a dagger in her back. She pulled herself an inch or two across the floor with her thick, stubby fingers through a smear of blood, then went limp.

Laying Ellisa down tenderly, Cordwin crept to the nurse's side and cradled her in his arms as if she were a small, frightened child. "Can you hear me? Please, tell me what happened!"

Her green eyes, flecked with dull gold, flickered open and took a moment to focus on his face. "Cordwin?" she whispered.

"Yes," he said softly, "yes, I'm here."

The nurse dug her fingers into his arm and clutched his sleeve convulsively. Tears washed down her cheeks. "They killed her. They killed my lady."

"Who?" Cordwin asked desperately. "Who were they? Where did they come from?"

She tried to speak, gasping painfully. "A shadow...like a cloud of darkness...fr-from the north...the n-north. They t-took Bren, my baby."

"Bren's alive?" A tiny ember of hope flickered in Cordwin's heart. "Are you sure? Who were they? Where did they take him? Tell me!!"

The nurse didn't answer. Her last breath bubbled from her mouth in a stream of red froth.

"No!!!" The empty castle echoed with his anguish. He placed the nurse back on the floor and crawled back to his brother. Cordwin sat back on his heels and wept. He'd never felt so alone, so lost, so desolate. The ones he loved most were gone; only Daikin remained alive. There was only a faint hope that Bren might still live.

Cordwin felt dizzy and cold, so cold, but something warm ran down his arm. It took all his will to turn his head and look at his arm. Blood ran down from the reopened wound, soaking into his shirt sleeve, but the blood seemed almost gray, as if most of the color had been leached from it. Everything looked flat, like a painting, the colors faded. The sound of the fires crackling and timbers falling was dim and muffled, as if he were under water. He felt as if he were trying to move through a vat of honey, as if he had no strength left. His whole body was tingly numb, and he cried until there were no tears left.

Daikin and the other guards found him beside Clevil, dazed and shivering.

"Cord," Daikin said, kneeling beside him, "Cord, there's nothing you can do now."

Slowly, Cordwin looked up at his cousin, his eyes hot and aching almost as much as his heart. "Why?" he asked softly, his throat so raw he could hardly speak. "Why did this happen?"

"Baygor only knows," Daikin said, resting a hand on Cordwin's shoulder. "Cord, come away from here."

"I should have been here," Cordwin said, rocking back and forth as he stared at Clevil's body. "I should have been here to protect them."

"You would have died, too."

"You don't know that," Cordwin whispered. He wrapped his arms across his chest, shivering he was so cold.

"Yes, I do!" Daikin said, grasping Cordwin's shoulders and shaking him. "And so do you!"

"No," Cordwin said, shaking his head slowly. He barely had the strength to move his head.

"Yes, you do, Cord." Daikin knelt and put his arms around Cordwin. "You know it's true."

Cordwin leaned his head against Daikin's shoulder, his heart so filled with grief, he couldn't speak.

"Cord, you couldn't have prevented this," Daikin said gently. "You know it in your heart."

Cordwin buried his face against Daikin's shoulder and cried.

"Barg's breath!" Daikin said, his hand resting on Cordwin's forehead. "Cord, you're burning up!"

Slowly, Cordwin looked up at Daikin for a moment, his vision edged with black, yellow and black spots swimming before his eyes. He tried to speak, but collapsed, unconscious.

Cordwin opened his eyes to see familiar wooden beams in the stone ceiling of his own room. Late morning sun gilded the floor as a warm breeze blew across his face from the narrow bedside window. His mouth was dry, and his lips felt cracked. He pushed back the sheet and grey woolen blanket, and the odor of old sweat rose from his body. His left arm was in a sling, but he didn't remember how he hurt it. The air on his bare skin made him shiver, and he realized he was wearing only linen underwear. He pulled the blanket back over himself and tucked it around his chin for warmth. His eyes burned; he rubbed them with his right hand.

When his vision cleared, he saw Daikin sitting in the chair beside the hearth. Daikin's clothes were as rumpled as if he'd slept in them. A stubbly red beard covered his cheeks and chin. His green eyes were bloodshot and dark-circled, as if he'd stood watch for days without rest.

"Daik, you look awful," Cordwin said and winced as his left arm ached.

"Not as bad as you do," Daikin shot back, his green eyes twinkling, although he sounded worn out.

"I must look like something even a rat wouldn't touch."

"Worse."

"Thanks."

"It's good to see you awake," Daikin said, lines cutting across his forehead. "I was beginning to think you'd never wake up." He suddenly looked grave. "You had a fever.

You were delirious. Tothim...Tothim wasn't sure if you'd . . ." he paused and cleared his throat. "But the fever broke yesterday, and Tothim says you're going to be all right." Almost whispering, he added, "Thank Baygor."

"What day is this?" Cordwin tried to sit up. His head spun, and his stomach lurched threateningly. He sank back against his pillow and groaned.

"Serves you right." Daikin gave him a smug grin as he walked over and sat on Cordwin's bed. "You lie right there."

Cordwin glared at his cousin. "You're enjoying this, aren't you? What day did you say this is?"

Daikin hesitated before answering. "The fifth day since the battle."

"Battle?" Cordwin's throat constricted. He felt as if a lead weight had just dropped on his chest. He remembered everything – the messenger, the battle at Tironza, and finding Clev and Ellisa. "Oh, gods," he whispered, "it wasn't just a terrible dream."

Daikin looked away. "No."

Cordwin moaned, and his eyes blurred with tears. He wished he'd never awakened from safe, dark sleep.

"Cord, I'm sorry." Daikin squeezed his cousin's shoulder. "While you were unconscious, we searched the invaders before we burned them but found no clue to who they were or where they were from, just as in Tironza. *These* raiders each had a small velvet bag, filled with a strange powder, stuck in their pockets. We searched everywhere for the raiders who took Bren, even just inside the border of Drambit." Daikin looked grim and muttered, "We found no trace of him or his abductors. The only thing we found was the body of a murdered peasant seven miles north."

"North?" Cordwin levered himself up carefully on his right elbow, hardly daring to hope. "The nurse said something about the north! Send a messenger immediately to Formia's Council of Tribes. Their trackers might find a trail."

"I already contacted the Council in your name, and they dispatched trackers at once. They found tracks of a few wagons, numerous horses, but no trace of an army or any indication that a large group of riders had crossed their land. And if Formian trackers can't find a trail, no one can. They did say that a few of the farmsteads near the mountains reported a great darkness covering the foot of the mountains for days."

"Did Lord Merrik send word yet?"

"Yes. He sent his hopes for your quick recovery and said a thick fog covered the base of the Circle Mountains for days, much like the Formian Council reported. No one saw the invaders come or go. The only explanation I can think of is too bizarre, too unbelievable."

"What?" Cordwin asked.

"Sorcerers."

"That's insane," Cordwin said. "No one has seen or heard from the Sorcerers for generations."

"That doesn't mean they don't exist still, hidden somewhere. Suppose all the dark tales and legends we heard growing up were true. Suppose they were involved. That's the only thing that could hide such large forces. And if it were Sorcerers, we mightnever learn who the raiders were."

Desperate, Cordwin tried to rise, and was surprised at how weak he felt. "Daikin, we have to. We have to! Bren's the only family I have left, except for you. He's Clev's only son, Ellisa's son, and heir to the throne. I have to find him, rescue him, for their sake. I can't fail them again. Please, you have to help me."

Daikin forced Cordwin's shoulders back to the pillow. Cordwin felt too weak to resist.

"You can't do anything about it right now. You need rest." Daikin gazed at Cordwin, then slowly continued. "Today at sunset, we'll mourn Clevil and Ellisa. If you're strong enough, you should be present."

A sob escaped Cordwin's lips. The memory of Clev and Ellisa, murdered, lying on the bloody floor, was like a blow to his chest. He could hardly breathe through his grief.

"*You* are the ruler of Vorlik now," Daikin said. "Your people need you now more than ever. They need to know they can count on your strength and leadership. And as ruler of Vorlik, it's your duty to lead the ritual at the funeral." Squeezing Cordwin's shoulder again, Daikin whispered, "I know, Cord. I loved them, too."

Cordwin stared at the ceiling and blinked back tears. He felt as empty and alone as he'd felt at his parents' death. Clevil and Ellisa had held him then, cried with him. This time, only Daikin was here to comfort Cordwin. Practical, laughing Daikin. *But he needs comfort, too,* Cordwin thought, *just as much as I do.* He reached up and rested his hand on his cousin's shoulder. "Thank you," he said. "Thank you for being my strength."

They were both silent for a long time.

Finally, Cordwin spoke. "You're right about attending the mourning. You're always right. Send Pellin to me." He looked up sharply, suddenly feeling sick. "Is...is Pellin alive?"

Daikin nodded.

Cordwin closed his eyes for a moment and said a silent prayer of thanks. "I don't think I could bear one more death."

"He survived the attack by hiding in your trunk. He...he thinks he's a coward, not worthy to serve you, so be gentle with him, Cord."

"I will."

Daikin bowed and started to leave when Cordwin said, "Wait. Moon Shadow—did you bring him back to the castle?"

"Yes, although the stables haven't been rebuilt completely, but he's well cared for."

Cordwin smiled weakly. "Thank you. For everything."

Daikin nodded, then left Cordwin alone.

Cordwin stared at the ceiling. How could *he* rule Vorlik? He knew he didn't have Clev's wisdom or skill, and he didn't know how to be the kind of leader his people needed. "Lady Baramay," he prayed, "please, tell me what to do."

Pellin entered and bowed, his auburn hair falling over his pallid face. "You sent for me, Lord Cordwin?"

Cordwin's heart stopped for a moment. He'd never been called lord before. It sounded so wrong. Clev was lord of Vorlik. *But Clev is dead. Whether I wanted it or not, the lordship of Vorlik is mine. I have to make decisions for the good of the people, my people, including this boy standing before me now.* Taking a slow breath, Cordwin sat up and tried to keep his voice soft and steady to reassure his page. "I need you to lay out clothes for..." Cordwin halted and cleared his throat, "for my brother's funeral."

"Yes, my lord." Pellin's red-rimmed green eyes sparkled with relief.

Cordwin smiled, noticing for the first time that Pellin had started to change from child to youth. "I'm so very glad to see you're alive."

The spark in Pellin's eyes vanished, and he hung his head. "I should've died like the others."

"No!" Cordwin said, distraught. "Don't say that!"

"I ran away!" Pellin cried as he turned away. "I hid like a coward. I should've died!"

"Pellin, come here!" Cordwin pointed to his bedside.

The boy spun around and hurried to stand rigidly before Cordwin.

"Could you have killed the invaders?" Cordwin asked gently.

Pellin's lips quivered. "N-no, my lord, there were too many of them."

"There was nothing you could've done to save Lord Clevil and Lady Ellisa?"

"No, but—"

Cordwin held up his hand to silence the boy. "Then the only thing to do was what you did: survive. Survive and report everything you know. Something you heard or saw may be vitally important. You may be the only one who can help us find Bren."

Pellin looked up, his eyes wide with surprise. "Do you really believe I can help?"

Cordwin nodded. "Yes, Pellin, I'm certain." He paused. "All right?"

Pellin gave him a tentative smile, full of hope.

"Now, see that my mourning clothes are ready. And later, after I've rested, bring me something to eat. My stomach is telling me that I haven't eaten for days."

Pellin blinked several times, then bowed deeply. "Yes, my lord." He turned and left.

Cordwin stared after the boy for a while, then closed his eyes and fell asleep quickly, still exhausted.

He woke to a room that was dim and chilly. Pellin knelt by the hearth, adding a log to a newly laid fire. On the chair before the hearth lay a black shirt and pants, and a black tabard embroidered with silver stars — black and silver, the colors of mourning.

Cordwin groaned as he stretched. He felt stiff and sore, and his arm throbbed and itched slightly.

Pellin looked up instantly and smiled. "My lord, there is a cup of roborant tea on the table beside you. Physician Tothim thought you might need it. He came in to check on you while you were sleeping. And there's a bowl of meat broth and some bread for sopping on the table, too."

Cordwin sat up slowly, feeling only slightly dizzy, and brushed his oily hair with his fingers. "What I wouldn't give for a hot bath," he said quietly.

"My lord." Pellin pushed the chair away from the hearth, revealing a large wooden tub filled with steaming water. A towel and cloth lay across a wooden stool beside the tub, and a cake of cedar wood soap sat on the cloth. "There's more hot water for rinsing," Pellin said as he hung a small kettle on the hearth hook.

Cordwin smiled and cautiously swung his legs over the edge of the bed. "How did you manage all of this without waking me?"

Pellin just smiled and added small branches of wood to the fire.

The roborant tea had cooled enough Cordwin could drink it. He hadn't realized how thirsty he was until he took his first sip, then he drank it straight down. Within moments he felt strength pulsing through his whole body. The throbbing in his arm subsided. Bruises stopped aching. Even the itching on his left arm lessened.

His stomach growled. Tearing off a piece of brown seed bread, he dipped it in the broth and popped it in his mouth. The broth was rich and seasoned with onion, sage, pepper and rosemary. The bread's crust was chewy, but the inside was soft.

"What time is it?" Cordwin asked between bites.

"Perhaps an hour before sunset."

Cordwin halted, a bite of bread halfway to his mouth, when he remembered what would happen at sunset. *It's almost time,* he thought. He gazed up at Pellin. "Time to dress for the ritual."

Pellin nodded slowly. "Yes, my lord."

Suddenly, Cordwin's appetite was gone. He started to set the bowl and bread back on the table, but Pellin stopped him.

"Please, my lord, you must eat," the boy said, kneeling in front of Cordwin with wide frightened eyes. "Physician Tothim said you have to eat something. You have to get well. You have to. We need you. We all need you."

Cordwin sighed deeply, his shoulders drooping, and nodded. Pellin looked relieved, stood, and turned back to the hearth to add more wood to the blaze. Cordwin stared at the broth for a few moments, then sipped it. It seemed bland now. The bread was dry and tasteless. He ate it anyway. *Pellin's right,* Cordwin thought. *I have to care for the people of Vorlik and continue to search for Bren, and the only way to do both is to get well.*

When the bowl was empty and the bread gone, Cordwin set the bowl on the table. Slowly, he started to stand, but his legs felt too wobbly. He sank back down on the bed.

"Let me help, my lord," Pellin said. He sat down beside Cordwin, put Cordwin's arm across his own shoulders, then said, "Now try to stand."

With Pellin's help, Cordwin struggled to his feet. The boy was surprisingly strong for his size. He helped Cordwin reach the chair, which Cordwin grasped. Untying the drawstring on his underwear, Cordwin let them fall to the wooden floor and carefully stepped into the tub of water. With Pellin's help, Cordwin eased himself down into the tub.

The water was warm but not too hot, and felt delicious. Using the cloth and cedar wood soap, Cordwin worked up a lather. The spicy wood fragrance filled the room. Cordwin closed his eyes and breathed in the scent of the soap, his favorite scent. It reminded him of his father, who had always smelled of cedar wood, too. Scrubbing the stink of old sweat from his skin, gently where bruises were turning purple-green and on his left arm, he began to feel more awake, more alive. He rubbed the soap in his hair and washed it thoroughly, careful to avoid getting soap in his eyes. Pellin swung the hearth hook out from the fire and tested the water temperature.

"Are you ready to rinse, my lord?" he asked.

"Yes," Cordwin said reluctantly. He closed his eyes, bent his head forward, and waited. Warm water cascaded over his head, down his shoulders, back, and chest, rinsing all the soap and dirt away, and surrounding him with a warm cloud of steam. It felt good to be clean again. The last real bath he'd had was over a week ago at the Eastern Guard barracks. Sitting in the warm water, the cedar scent enveloping him while the warm fire crackled on the hearth, Cordwin sighed, content to stay where he was forever, stay and relax and forget.

A knock on his door snapped Cordwin out of his pleasant reverie. "Come."

Daikin entered, wearing a clean red and gold uniform. His face was shaved, and his copper hair was combed back. "Not ready yet?" he asked with a grin, then glanced at Pellin and added, "My lord."

"No," Cordwin said with a sigh, "not yet."

Daikin dropped to one knee beside the tub. "It's almost time, Cord," he said very softly.

"I know." Cordwin ran his fingers through his wet hair. "I know. Help me up. I don't think I can stand by myself."

Daikin and Pellin each wrapped an arm around Cordwin, and together they lifted him to his feet. Pellin wrapped a towel around Cordwin, then Daikin helped him to the edge of the bed. Sinking down on the bed, Cordwin shivered and pulled the towel tighter.

"My lord," Pellin said, a worried frown on his lean face, "are you able to walk to the barrow ground?"

Cordwin looked up at him. "I am," he said wearily. "I have to be."

"Maybe I can help," Daikin said. He went back to the door, stepped into the hallway, and came back with a carved staff. "I found this in Lord Clevil's room. Do you remember it?"

Cordwin gazed at the dark wood, carved with twining vines and crowned with a dove. "Yes, I remember," he said slowly as he let his fingertips brush across the smooth dark wood. It felt oddly warm and comforting when he grasped the staff. "The Wizard Casslin gave it to Father when I was very little, just before the Wizard left. I'd forgotten about the staff."

"You could use it with your right hand and let me support your left arm. If you falter, I'll be there to help."

Cordwin looked up and smiled gratefully at Daikin. "As always."

"And now that you're up and around, we can move your things to the lord's chambers."

"No!" Cordwin said adamantly. "I'll never go to those rooms again! I want the doors shut and locked." He shuddered. "I couldn't bear to see them again, much less sleep there."

"All right." Daikin rested his hand lightly on Cordwin's shoulder. "I understand. Now you need to get dressed."

Cordwin pulled the black shirt and pants on, and decided against putting his arm back in the sling. Pellin helped with the boots and the black and silver tabard. Standing in front of the wash table and steadying himself with one hand, Cordwin combed back his damp hair, then looked in the small polished mirror on the wall above the table. A pale young man with dark sorrowful eyes stared back at him, and he wondered how he could face the funeral. Glancing at the reflection of Pellin, Cordwin turned around, leaning on the table, and said, "Thank you, Pellin, you may leave us."

"Yes, my lord." The page bowed and left.

Daikin cleared his throat, then reached inside his tabard. He pulled out a golden chain with sunburst amulet.

"Your symbol, my lord," Daikin said, holding it out to Cordwin.

Cordwin nearly choked. "Daik, I-I can't," he said, his voice shaking. "I can't wear it. That belongs to Clev."

"Cord, it's yours now, and your people need to see you wearing it." Daikin knelt before Cordwin and looked straight up at him. "Take the symbol of Vorlik, Lord Cordwin, protector and ruler of our people." He paused, then said, "You have to, Cord."

Trembling, Cordwin took the chain and caressed the medallion. He remembered the first time he'd seen Clev wearing the medallion—at their parents' funeral. "Daik, I'm not capable of being Vorlik's lord."

Daikin stared straight at Cordwin. "A man who thinks he is, isn't."

Reluctantly, Cordwin slipped the chain over his head. It felt lead heavy and ice cold.

Daikin stood up, and Cordwin embraced him tightly. "I'll need your strength to face this," Cordwin said. "I'll never be the ruler Clev was. I don't have his knowledge and experience, so I'll have to depend on you help me, keep me from making too many mistakes."

Daikin pulled back to gaze at his cousin and rested his hand on Cordwin's shoulder. "There's strength and wisdom in you, Cord, more than you realize, just waiting for you to summon them. Just trust yourself. But I'll always be here. My sword is yours."

"Thank you." Cordwin brightened as a thought bloomed in his mind. He gave Daikin a crafty smile. "And just to make sure you're always here when I need you, I'm naming you chief guard of Tarolin Castle...Captain."

Daikin stared in disbelief. His jaw dropped open, and his hands hung at his sides. "No. You can't. You wouldn't do this to me," he sputtered. "I can't take Bailoc's place. Many others are more qualified and experienced than I am. And I'd be so...restricted."

Cordwin clasped his cousin's shoulder. "Look, I know I can trust you. You have the respect of all the soldiers. I need you beside me. Please, Daik, I need you."

Daikin's shoulders sagged. "All right. I'll stand at your side." He raised an eyebrow, and a slow smile lit his face. "Hmm...Captain Daikin...that has a nice sound, doesn't it? Might not be so bad. After all, women adore officers, and I just adore women. This promotion may have its benefits."

Cordwin shook his head and clapped his cousin on the back. "You never change!"

Daikin gave him a martyred look. "Can I help being so attractive to women? It's just a curse I have to bear."

"Maybe I should make you my fool instead of captain of my armies."

Daikin rested a hand on his cousin's shoulder. "I'm glad I can make you laugh."

"You're family," Cordwin said and embraced him. "You make the pain bearable."

"Time to join the procession."

"I know," Cordwin said softly. "I know."

Daikin handed Cordwin the staff, offered his right arm to support Cordwin's left one, and together they walked down the spiral stairs.

The main hall was filled with people wearing black-and-silver mourning clothes and holding torches. At the head of the procession were several of the older priests of Baygor from the temple west of the castle. Black cloth swags hung above the castle door. Dried flower wreaths dyed black and laced with silver cords hung on the closed doors to the Audience Hall. Sprigs of rosemary were scattered on the stone floor; the strong evergreen scent filled the air with each step. Rosemary for remembrance.

Daikin supported Cordwin as the new lord took his place just behind the priests. To the doleful beat of drums, they walked slowly down the granite steps and across the partially cleared courtyard in the orange-red light of sunset. The procession passed through the newly replaced gate and turned east to the burial grounds of the lords of Vorlik. Cordwin stumbled a few times, still unsteady and weak, but Daikin kept him from falling.

The barrow ground was deep in the castle's shadow. A great mound covered the soldiers who had died in the attack. A little distance away a stone-covered mound had been raised over Lord Clevil and Lady Ellisa, together in death as in life. Torches ringed the barrow ground, casting sunset shadows on the mourners' faces. Cordwin stood beside the grave, leaning on Daikin for support. One of the priests offered prayers for the dead, but Cordwin barely heard them. He felt numb. His vision blurred, and he blinked back tears. Everything seemed unreal, like a waking nightmare. Even the torchlight seemed dim and dull.

Daikin gave Cordwin's arm a light shake and whispered, "It's time for you to speak."

Cordwin glanced around. Everyone was gazing at him, waiting. He swallowed hard and cleared his throat.

"Let us honor our dead in our hearts," Cordwin said, his voice cracking as he spoke the funeral ritual. "May you find rest beneath this earth and happiness in Barg's kingdom. We, the living, lament your passing for we are lessened by your deaths."

He swallowed hard, cleared his throat, and forced himself to continue. "It is said that the dead will live forever as long as one person remembers them. Let the list be read."

Daikin placed Cordwin's left hand on Daikin's shoulder, unrolled a scroll, and began to read. "Lord Clevil of Vorlik."

Cordwin's chest tightened, but he said, "I stand for his memory."

"Lady Ellisa of Vorlik," Daikin said, then immediately said, "I stand for her memory."

Cordwin gazed over at him and nodded slightly. He could barely see through his tears.

Daikin read the next name. "Bailoc of Tironza."

"I stand for his memory," said Lieutenant Rayvil.

As Daikin spoke each name, a member of the Tironza Guard stepped forward to promise remembrance.

While Cordwin listened to the names, he sank to his knees, holding onto the staff, and caressed the stones covering Clevil's barrow. "Clev," Cordwin whispered, "Clev, I promise I'll find out who did this, and I swear on my life I'll find Bren and I'll bring him back home."

4

Lord Paxell of Drambit sat at a whitethorn wood desk and studied a book bound with black leather. He was twenty-five years old, but his cavernous eyes held knowledge beyond his years. His short cropped hair was jet black, as were his narrow eyebrows. His lightly tanned skin looked almost pale against his black shirt and pants. He was new moon shadow and winter midnight. His darkness was broken only by a silver snake on his black surcoat, a silver circlet, a silver amulet with a coiled snake embossed in the center, and silver and schorl ring on his hand. Black and silver. In most lands those werethe colors of mourning. In Drambit they were the colors of royalty.

The book he was studying was old beyond the memory of men. Its pages were yellow and brittle, and Paxell had to be very careful handling them. The book contained some of the knowledge of the Sorcerers, a race from tales told on moonless nights. Among people in other countries, it was whispered that the Sorcerers once lived in Drambit and that the lineage of the lords of Drambit included Sorcerers' blood. In Drambit it was known to be true.

Paxell had obtained the book nearly two years ago, not long after his marriage, from a now dead thief. The Drambini lord studied the book intently, sometimes day and night. He'd learned a few of the spells scrawled in blood-red ink in the ancient language of the Sorcerers. He frowned for a moment, then his eyes widened and he smiled slowly as the meaning of the words became clear: a spell to change another's form.

"Yes, it might be interesting to change a servant into a horse or a worm," he said with a quiet laugh as he gazed out the narrow window of the tower room. "I can almost see that old tutor of mine crawling on his belly. Revenge for all of those tedious lessons in the ancient languages. But," he looked back at the book and carefully ran his fingertips along the edge of the leather binding, "without his teaching, I'd never have been able to comprehend this book. I *am* grateful for that."

Advancing footsteps echoed on the stone steps of the spiral staircase beyond the wooden door to his study. Moments later, someone knocked on the door.

"Come," Paxell said, looking up from the book.

A man, wearing scale mail and helmet with no device, burst into the room, panting. Quickly, he dropped to one knee and inclined his head. "Lieutenant Barlin reporting, my lord. We have returned from Vorlik."

Paxell jumped to his feet, his eyes glittering with expectation. "Well, what news, lieutenant?"

The soldier stood at attention. "We've slain the lord of Vorlik and captured the heir to the throne, my lord."

"Captured him?" Paxell's voice became as soft as drifting snowflakes on a killing-cold night. "*Captured* him? You were ordered to *destroy* all the house of Vorlik."

The soldier trembled, and his face paled.

Slowly, Paxell sat back down and interlaced his fingers. "Tell me everything," he said deliberately.

The soldier swallowed tightly. "My lord, the army from the south drew most of the troops away from the castle, just as you said they would. The charms you gave us kept us invisible until we reached the castle. Your agent set fires inside the castle walls and opened the gate for us. But once we dismounted, our horses became visible so the Vorlikian knew we were there. And the charms didn't hide the sounds our feet made. But we killed most of the guards before they could strike back."

Just as I'd planned, Paxell thought. He nodded for the soldier to continue.

"Getting into the castle was hard," the soldier said. "The door was guarded by two men who were more able and canny than most of the others. Even a young priest with a staff killed several of my men, but we finally took him down. Lord Clevil was like a wild animal protecting his family. We'd been told he was deathly ill, but he killed six of my men before we cut him down. His wife was just as deadly. She killed three of my best men before we got her.

"Only five of us survived. On our return, we killed a peasant who saw us. We'd forgotten to use the charms you'd made. We avoided the Northern Guard and finally made it out of Vorlik. I thought we'd never get out of Formia. If not for your protective charms, their trackers would have found us."

"What about Clevil's brother?" Paxell asked anxiously.

The soldier swallowed tightly, then continued. "Clevil's brother wasn't at the castle when we attacked. Your agent said he led the forces sent south."

"Cordwin?" Anger churned in Paxell's stomach. "Cordwin...is still alive?"

The soldier said, "Y-yes, my lord."

"Hound of Darkness!" Paxell leaped to his feet and clenched his fists.

The soldier dropped to one knee, stark terror on his face.

Paxell turned away and stared out the narrow window that faced east toward the mountains that separated Drambit from Vorlik. *My agent swore to me that Bailoc would lead the army south and that Cordwin would be at the castle when my men attacked! I wanted him dead even more than Clevil!*

He took a deep breath and blew it out slowly, cooling his anger. *No, Cordwin's time will come. At least, I'll wait for the mercenary army to return from Vorlik before I do anything. And perhaps...perhaps the brat may be useful.* Paxell turned back to the soldier, who was pale and trembling. "You said you brought the heir with you?"

"Yes, my lord," the soldier said, his voice quivering. "I thought since Cordwin wasn't at the castle, we might need the baby for bargaining later."

"And only five of you survived?"

"Yes, my lord."

"Only you five know about the babe?"

"Yes, my lord." He paused, then added, "And Captain Callas."

"My agent in Vorlik, what happened to him?"

"He was killed in the battle."

Paxell swore to himself. He'd paid well for the information the agent had sent him, paid in Drambini emeralds. "The babe, where is he?"

"One of the kitchen wenches is nursing him. The only thing he's had for days was just enough wine mixed with water to keep him asleep and quiet."

"Very wise." Paxell smiled and nodded. "You've done well, lieutenant. Keep the child hidden until I decide what to do with him. I want the names of the other survivors. You'll all be rewarded. Get something to eat and take three days rest from duties."

"Thank you, my lord." The soldier named the other men quickly, his face showing relief. He bowed, then hurried down the stone steps.

Paxell stood staring at the open door. Perhaps, he could use the magic he'd just mastered to guarantee the five men's silence. Something innocuous such as hutch rabbits or chickens for the stewpot. He shuddered. No, that thought turned his stomach. But he had to insure the secret would be safe. No one but Callas could know he had the brat. His forces might have control of Vorlik at that moment, but he'd keep the boy for now, just in case.

Descending the stone steps from his tower study, he reached the office of Captain Callas, leader of Drambini's army and his chief military advisor.

Seated at a small table, Callas was just finishing a duty roster for the week. Wearing a black tabard with silver piping over his black shirt and pants, Callas looked up as Paxell entered. The raven-haired captain rose, clapped his fist to his chest, and inclined his head respectfully. "My lord."

"Has there been word from the southern army?"

"No." Callas' weathered face was dark with doubt. "And that disturbs me. It's been a week since the attack."

Paxell paced the floor, considering the implications. His fists clenching and unclenching, he stared out Callas' eastern window at the mountains toward Vorlik. Since before history was written down, the two countries had been at odds with each other.

Paxell wanted to rule Vorlik as much as some men were obsessed with women or craved wine. "I must know what's happening!" he said.

"The pass to Vorlik through the mountains has been closed," Callas said. "None of my spies have been able to get through."

"And our agent at the castle is dead," Paxell said with a frown. "I must know what's happening! Keep watch at the border for any of our informants." He braced his hands on the stone windowsill, gazing at his lands. Whitethorn tree thickets sprang up between small patches of crops. A few streams wandered through the rolling land, nourishing tyneberry briars and pastures. Drambit wasn't as harsh a land as Hargrim, but it wasn't as lush and fertile as Vorlik. Only Drambit's wealth of gems, particularly the prized emeralds, kept the Drambini treasury filled.

Paxell gazed over his shoulder at the tall, stocky captain. "We have another problem to deal with," he said.

Callas' eyes narrowed. "Yes, the child—and his captors. I hate to lose them. They are good soldiers, and we can't afford to lose any more. If only they'd followed their orders!" He sighed. "There's a boar hunt tomorrow. Boars are dangerous and unpredictable. Sometimes men die."

Paxell nodded, then turned back to stare at the mountains. Callas understood what had to be done without being told. Turning from the window, Paxell said, "I'll leave it to you. And declare a full day of mourning for each of them." He sighed. "I hate to lose good soldiers, too."

Callas bowed slightly. "It will be done, my lord. As for the child, I know a woman who could serve as his nurse and she's a cook in the castle as well, if you desire. She's cared for my own son for seven months since his mother died."

"As you will." Paxell strode through the door and down the corridor to double doors. Opening them, he entered the slate and granite great hall of Abasette Castle. Chairs of carved whitethorn lined the walls like bleached skeletons. Worn tapestries and enemies' shields were the only other decoration. Centered in the northern half of the hall, on a white marble dais, stood an ebony throne, the arms carved to resemble snakes. Three other doors opened into the hall: single doors on the east and west walls, guarded double doors on the south wall.

The east door to the kitchen opened as Danneah, Paxell's wife, entered the hall. For a moment Paxell's heartbeat quickened. He had loved her from the first time he saw her, and he was certain that she had loved him, too. But something had changed between them. She had grown distant and withdrawn, and he didn't know why, didn't know what he'd done to turn her away from him.

Now she reminded him of a faded sunflower. Barely twenty years old, Danneah's belly was swollen with their first child. Her blue eyes were as dull as the sky blasted by summer heat. Her face was thin and pale, as if the child were siphoning her life away. She halted when she saw Paxell coming toward her, then she averted her eyes and curtsied awkwardly. "My lord."

"My lady," Paxell said bitterly, "what has brought you from your room?"

She glanced up at him. "I was...asking the cook to prepare a tyneberry dessert for you."

"You were?" Paxell blinked in surprise. "For me?" He stepped closer and took her hand. He felt her stiffen. She gazed at him with cold blue eyes. He let go of her hand and took a step back. "You should take care of yourself. Our child will soon be born. I think you should return to your room—now."

"Yes, my lord." She curtsied again, then shuffled as quickly as she could toward her quarters. Occasionally, she halted, inhaling sharply.

Paxell's dark eyes followed her. *Why did I threaten her like that?* he thought, cursing himself as sadness filled his heart. *She's still so beautiful. So very beautiful. I hope she's carrying a son to rule after me. Maybe...maybe when she holds our child, she'll remember that she loved me.* He sighed deeply. *Now I want to see that spawn of Clevil.*

He strode through the eastern door to the steamy, fragrant kitchen. Cooks and serving girls bustled about. One seasoned stew. Others removed golden rounds of bread and two bubbling, dried-apple pies from an oven. On a spit turned a whole deer, basting fat popping as it dripped. The aroma made Paxell's mouth water.

A nine-year-old scullery boy with sunken cheeks walked into the kitchen, awkwardly carrying a bucket of dirty water. Not watching where he was going, he bumped into Paxell, sloshing some of the bucket's contents on the lord's clothes. The boy cringed, wide-eyed, his open mouth trembling as he stared up at Paxell's face. Before the boy could say a word, Paxell backhanded the boy, knocking him across the room. The bucket clattered to the floor, flooding the stones with grey-brown water, as the boy crashed against the stone wall and crumpled, unconscious.

From the far corner a woman cried out and sprang to her feet, nearly dropping the infant suckling at her breast. Quickly handing the child to another cook, the woman ran to the boy and cradled him in her arms. Staring up at Paxell, her eyes vacillated between terror and anger, but she said nothing.

Looking about the room, Paxell saw that the rest of the servants stood like marble statues. Only the infant's whimper broke the deadly silence.

"Clean up this mess," Paxell said, startling the others in the room.

Servants scattered, grabbing rags and mops to sop up the water. All carefully avoided meeting Paxell's eyes.

The lord strode toward the woman holding the crying infant. "Is that the child Lieutenant Barlin left?"

The woman clasped the child to her chest and stuttered, "YY-yes, m-m-my lord."

"Take it to Captain Callas."

The woman almost ran from the kitchen with the baby.

Paxell glanced around the room again. Work continued but with a tension that hadn't been there before. He turned and strode from the kitchen. His steps echoed as he crossed the great hall to the western corridor leading to his rooms. Halfway down the passage was Danneah's quarters. The door was closed at the moment, though he heard her pacing inside. He leaned against the door, lightly caressed the wood, and wished he were welcomed within.

He remembered his first glimpse of Danneah in Peltik. He'd attended the Midsummer Festival at Castle Lecida. He didn't know why Lord Merrick had invited him, although they were distantly related on Paxell's mother's side. Merrick trusted Drambit about as much as Clevil had. But Paxell had gone to Lecida and had lost his heart to Danneah.

She was a sunbeam come to earth, and he'd dared to love her against hope and reason. Lord Merrick had tried to secure a marriage between Danneah and Clevil's brother Cordwin, but she hadn't shown an interest in the Vorlikian lord's brother beyond numerous dances at the Festival. Still, jealousy raged in Paxell every time Cordwin touched her hand. When the Festival was over, Danneah had asked Paxell to stay for another week, and although Merrick wasn't pleased, he'd extended the invitation.

Paxell hadn't known he could be so happy as he was during that week. Walks in the garden, rides among the giant trees of Peltik, picnics in the courtyard, quiet moments on the castle walls watching the stars – Danneah had captured his heart with her laughter and gentleness. When he'd asked her to be his wife, she'd accepted with no hesitation.

His chest ached with the memory of their wedding. Her braided hair had circled her head like a golden crown, her pale blue dress enhancing her fair skin. A riviere of sapphires about her neck had sparkled as brightly as her eyes. Desire tightened his body as he remembered her silken skin and loving surrender to him. Was it only two years ago? Bitterness and mistrust had replaced her affection. When had he lost her love? Not long after he'd obtained the ancient book of the Sorcerers and began planning his campaign against Vorlik – that was when he'd started to notice a change in her. But that couldn't be the reason she'd turned from him. She didn't know about his plan; no one did except Callas.

Paxell caressed Danneah's door one last time. His heart ached for her, and he longed for the days before she'd grown afraid of him, before she'd come to hate him.

He turned from her door, continued to his own room at the end of the hall, and opened his door. The room was austere for a lord. Heavy black curtains hung from plain whitethorn rods on three sides of his large bed. An unadorned wooden chair sat before a blazing hearth. A cedar chest stood at the foot of the bed. To the right of the bed against the stone wall stood a whitethorn wash table with a brown pitcher and matching basin. A polished mirror hung above the wash table. The one luxury in the room was a sable rug beside the bed.

Paxell shut the door behind him, stripped off his boots and dripping clothes, and dropped them beside the hearth. Pouring water from the pitcher into the basin, he quickly washed the scrub water smell from his body with lemon-and-thyme scented soap, shivering from the cold. He opened the cedar chest at the foot of his large whitethorn bed, and took out a set of clean black clothes. He pulled on the clothes, then replaced the discarded wet boots with black boar skin ones, comfortable veterans of many hunts.

Removing his silver circlet, he ran fingers through his tousled black hair and stared into the mirror above the wash table. Reflected was the door that conjoined Danneah's chamber with his – a door that was locked against him. Beyond power, what he desired most was Danneah's love. Now – all she gave him was icy submission.

Why do I love her when she hates me so much? He leaned heavily on the table and hung his head. *Why can't I be like my father? He only kept a wife until he had a son.*

He gave a bitter laugh. *Half of Drambit might be my father's bastards. I could take any woman in the land, any woman at all...but she wouldn't be Dannee!*

5

A scream came from his wife's room. "Dannee!" Paxell ran to the joining door and jerked at the latch. "Dannee, are you hurt?" The latch wouldn't yield no matter how hard he pulled. "Dannee!"

Abandoning the locked door, he raced through the hallway to Danneah's door and shoved it open. "Dannee? Are you all right?"

The stout red-haired maid who had come with Danneah from Peltik was pulling a cotton gown over her mistress' head and down her swollen body. Suddenly, Danneah's face twisted in pain, her hand supporting her back. Breath came in short gasps followed by moaning sobs.

"It's her time, my lord," the maid said. "She's been having pains all day."

"Let me help," Paxell said as he ran to her side, put his arms around her, and started to lift her.

"No!" Danneah said, shivering as she tried to pull away.

"Dannee, please, don't fight me."

She struggled against him with surprising strength. "Don't touch me!" she said, cringing. "Don't touch me!"

Her words clawed at his heart. His arms dropped to his sides, and he stepped back as the maid edged closer. Danneah sobbed and slumped against her maid's thick arms.

The maid guided Danneah to the bed, eased her back against the pillows, and covered her with the linen sheet and golden furs. Turning to Paxell, the maid said softly, "My lord, please, send for the midwife. I'm afraid to leave my lady alone."

Nodding, Paxell sprinted to the great hall. "Summon the midwife to Lady Danneah's chamber!" he shouted to the door wards guarding the open doorway to the hall. "Now!"

The door wards saluted, and one of them hurried away. Paxell wheeled and fled back to his wife's side.

Danneah clenched her teeth, and her moans intensified. Paxell took her tiny hand, but she jerked away, glaring at him with blue eyes as cold as a winter day. Another contraction doubled Danneah's body. Paxell firmly enfolded her hand and lifted it gently to his lips. Once she'd smiled at him, had welcomed in his touch, had loved him, but no more. Had his ambition been the reason he'd lost her love? Was there anything he could do to win her back?

She stiffened and sucked in a sharp breath. She drove her nails into his hand, drawing blood, but Paxell ignored the pain.

The white-robed midwife arrived just then, her knotted, grey hair held tightly with wooden pins. Her leather bag of medicinal herbs was slung over her sagging shoulder, and a small, iron kettle was in her wrinkled hand. She set her implements on the end of the bed, then walked to the head of the bed. She felt Danneah's forehead, placed a hand over the pregnant woman's heart for a short time, touched the side of her throat for a few moments, then felt Danneah's abdomen for contractions.

Paxell saw the midwife frown. "What's wrong?"

The midwife looked at Paxell, then at his wife. "My lord, may I speak to you a moment?" She motioned toward the door.

Paxell gazed at Danneah, her eyes closed. Her forehead was beaded with sweat, and her breast rose and fell with short gasps of breath. He released Danneah's hand, turned, and followed the old woman until she stopped near the door. "Something *is* wrong, isn't it?" he said.

She didn't answer, just stared with a worried look at Danneah.

"Tell me!"

The midwife cleared her throat and shifted nervously. "She's not strong, and her hips are unusually narrow. Her heartbeat is too fast; her breathing, too shallow. This isn't good for her or the child."

Like an eagle clutching its prey, Paxell grabbed the midwife's arm. "Nothing must happen to her!" he said. "Nothing! If she or the child dies, so will you. Do you understand?"

The midwife's blotchy face was as pale as a winter sun veiled by grey clouds. "Y-yes, my lord, I-I understand."

Paxell released her arm and strode back to his wife's side.

"Light a fire," the midwife ordered the maid, who rushed to the stone fireplace and began laying kindling on hearth. The midwife kept checking Danneah's heartbeat and contractions while Paxell paced at the end of the bed.

When the fire was blazing, the midwife called the maid. "Go to the kitchen and get Marta. I'm going to need her help since both of my apprentices are away on deliveries. And both of you bring back a bucket of clean water."

The maid ran from the room.

The old woman turned to Paxell. "My lord, when the maid returns, you must leave. Expectant fathers aren't allowed to be present during births. They often tend to vomit. I won't have time to treat you when she needs all my attention."

"I won't leave her!" Paxell said. "I'm staying with her while our child is being born."

The midwife was silent, biting her thin bottom lip. At last, she spoke. "Very well, my lord, but you will do as *I* tell you. Here, *I* am mistress. Her life or her child's may depend on your obedience. Do you understand?"

"Yes," Paxell said, worry tightening his chest. "But, please, what can I do to help?"

The midwife massaged her forehead as she studied the pregnant woman. "For now, just what you're doing: hold her hand, talk to her, try to make her more comfortable.

When the maid returns, wipe Lady Danneah's face and wet her lips. Later, you can massage her back or belly. When the delivery time comes, you must help her bear down. But if you question my orders or become ill, I'll throw you out myself."

Paxell nodded. Midwives were the only authority that everyone, even lords, deferred to.

The midwife began searching her bag. "Let's see. Woundweal for pain, roborant for strength. Somewhere I have mint and wintergreen," she said as she ruffled through bundles, bottles, and boxes. "I wish I had fresh foxglove and valerian. I'll have to manage with dried ones. Where is that woman with the water?"

Danneah drew her knees up, rolled over on her side, and buried her face in a pillow to stifle her cries. Hurrying to the side of the bed, Paxell knelt and slid his arm under her neck and pressed her head to his chest, kissing her hair and whispering soothingly. Danneah clung to him, sobbing and clutching his shirt, her forehead clammy, her golden hair damp.

Paxell couldn't stand to see her hurting so much. His eyes blurred with unshed tears. "Can't you do something for her?" he pleaded with the midwife.

"Not until I have some boiling water!" she snapped, measuring out small quantities of the herbs. Under her breath, just loud enough that Paxell heard her, she added, "And I hope I have it soon." At that moment, she met Paxell's worried stare and seemed to age before his eyes. "My lord, just try to comfort her. If she'll take long, slow breaths and relax, she'll tolerate the pain better."

"All right," he said and turned back to his wife. "Don't cry, Dannee, don't cry." He stroked her pale cheek. "Do you remember the summer before we wed?" he whispered close to her ear. "The hunt we rode? I do, as if it were yesterday. Your horse cut mine off. I fell over its head into a briar rose. You laughed at me, all scratched and covered with dirt and leaves. You were so lively, so exciting, you captured my heart. When you accepted my proposal, I was the happiest man in the world. I loved you so much. I still love you, Dannee."

The midwife walked to Paxell's side. "She can't tighten up like that," she said and turned Danneah on her back. "Go see what's keeping that water."

Paxell started to rise, but his wife clutched his hand tighter.

"Don't leave me!" Danneah said, her eyes wide with fear.

The midwife placed her hand on Paxell's shoulder. "I'll go. You stay. Anything to reassure her. And remember, slow steady breaths."

Paxell nodded. The midwife started for the door only to be met by the maid and the cook who had taken the Vorlikian babe to Captain Callas. Each one carried a bucket of water.

"Here," the midwife said, handing her kettle to the cook. "Fill this with water and bring it to a boil." She paused, glanced at Paxell, then added, "And hurry."

The cook nodded, glanced fearfully at Paxell, then began filling the kettle with water from the bucket.

The midwife turned to the maid. "Bring the other bucket over here. I'll need clean cloths to wipe her face with cool water, a basin of warm water to bathe the child, and a blanket to wrap it in. And tell me when the water is boiling."

The cook hung the kettle on the hearth hook and swung it over the fire. The maid opened a wooden chest below the room's only window, took out carefully folded clothes and a soft woven black woolen blanket, and set them at the foot of the bed. The midwife removed a willow wand from her bag and finished measuring herbs for the infusion.

"Pull the table over to the head of the bed and pour cool water into the basin," the midwife told the maid.

The maid pushed the wash table next to the head of the bed, the legs making a screeching sound on the slate floor, then poured water into the basin.

"Now, give him a cloth." The midwife turned to Paxell. "Sponge her face with the water. If she's thirsty, dip the cloth in the water and let her suck on it, but not too much or she might vomit."

Pushing up his sleeves, Paxell dipped a cloth into the basin, wrung it slightly, then dabbed Danneah's forehead. She groaned, gritting her teeth with each pain, and gripped Paxell's hand. For a moment he glimpsed the maid open-mouthed and staring at him. When she met his eyes, she turned away quickly.

Paxell half-smiled to himself, a bitter smile. He didn't suppose anyone would believe he could care about someone, anyone.

"Water's boiling," the cook said.

"Watch her," the midwife said. "And check the strength of her contractions."

The cook crawled up on the foot of the bed and placed her hands on Danneah's abdomen while the midwife walked to the hearth. She swung the hearth hook from the fire, added a little wintergreen, valerian, and foxglove, stirred the boiling potion with the wand, then added woundweal, roborant, and mint. A wholesome fragrance wafted through the room.

Ladling the green-gold liquid into wooden cup, she brought it to Paxell. "Have her sip this," the midwife told him. "She must drink it all, slowly, a sip at a time, but remember: it's hot. It'll ease the pain and strengthen her. After she's taken all the tea, I want you to move some of those pillows, remove your boots, and slide in behind her. You'll have to help support her and rub her back to relax her and relieve the tension. You can also massage her belly if she asks you to. Do you know how?"

"Uh—yes," Paxell said. "At least, I think so."

The old woman felt Danneah's belly.

Paxell blew on the tea until it was cool enough to drink, then pressed the cup to his wife's colorless lips. "Drink some, Dannee. It'll ease the pain. Please, just a few sips."

Danneah sucked at the fragrant liquid. Paxell felt her relax gradually as the tea's warmth and strength flowed through her. When she'd finished drinking, Paxell pulled his boots off and scooted behind her. Closing her eyes, she slumped against his chest.

Paxell rested his cheek against her soft hair, his eyes slitted. Rhythmically, he massaged circles on each side of her belly, felt the muscles harden as the contractions increased. Something warm and sweet, deeper than desire, something he could only name love, ached in his chest. *She feels so good,* he thought. *I've needed her so much. I haven't touched her, held her close since...since she realized she was carrying our child. Even before that, she hated my touch. But maybe...when our child's born, when she holds him in her arms, maybe she'll love me again.*

The midwife felt Danneah's pulse and the strength of her contraction. Worry deepened in the old woman's eyes.

"Tell me," Paxell said

She leaned close to whisper. "She should be ready to deliver, but the child isn't coming. This may be a very long labor."

His eyes as dark as a well, his voice like ice, he whispered back, "Remember my promise, woman."

The midwife swallowed hard and searched her bag, muttering, "I'll give her something to speed labor."

The contractions continued into late afternoon, growing more intense. Danneah grew weaker despite the tea Paxell forced her to drink at the midwife's insistence. Soothing Danneah's aching back, Paxell tried to encourage his wife, speaking lovingly to her. Still, Danneah didn't seem to care. Her eyes were vacant. Her skin was clammy.

"Dannee, try!" Paxell said desperately as he rubbed her shoulders while her head hung limply against her chest. "Don't just give up. Please!"

Danneah suddenly bent almost double, screaming as hard labor took control of her body.

The midwife knelt on the foot of the bed and called for the maid. "Take the knife from my bag. Heat it in the fire until I tell you. When I ask for it, plunge the knife into the infusion in the kettle and bring it quickly." She turned to Paxell. "She has to bear down now, but she's so weak, you must help her. Bend her forward to push the child out. Talk to her, soothe her anyway you can, but she must bear down with the pains."

When Danneah screamed again, Paxell pressed her forward. Again and again cries clawed from her throat, each one wounding Paxell's heart.

"Let it be over!" he shouted. "Just let the pain stop!"

With a final drawn out scream, their child was born.

"You have a daughter, my lady, a healthy little girl," the midwife said as she tied the cord with a black thread. "Bring me the knife."

The potion hissed as the maid plunged the heated blade into it. Running, she gave the steaming knife to the old woman. Quickly, she cut the cord and handed the whimpering baby to the maid to be bathed. Pressing hard upon Danneah's belly, the midwife delivered the afterbirth and wrapped it in bloody cloths.

Paxell held his exhausted wife, kissing her sweat-drenched hair and neck, joyful tears falling down his face. "I love you!"

"Let me see her," Danneah said, her voice weak from exhaustion. "Let me see my baby."

The maid brought the baby to the bedside.

"She looks just like you, Dannee," Paxell said. "She's so beautiful."

Danneah touched the child's cheek. "She's so tiny, so vulnerable." She paused. "Miria. Her name is Miria." Suddenly, she became limp in Paxell's arms, her eyes closed, her breathing raspy.

"What's wrong? What's wrong?" Paxell demanded frantically.

The midwife compressed the woman's belly, cursing through gritted teeth. "Too much blood. She'll bleed to death if I can't stop it soon. Marta, help me!"

The cook knelt on the side of the bed and pushed with all her strength on Danneah's abdomen, but blood kept flowing from Danneah's body.

Paxell saw the maid, pale and wide-eyed, holding his daughter and backing away. Tears on the maid's cheeks, she fled the room, but Paxell didn't care. Nothing mattered except Dannee. Weeping, he held her tightly in his arms, his face contorted with fear. "Dannee, don't leave me! I love you so much! Don't leave me! Please, don't leave me!"

The cook scrambled from the bed and ran for the door.

Danneah opened her eyes and tilted her head back to see his face. She smiled at him oddly, without hate, but without love, also. "Thank Baygor," she whispered. "At last, I'll be free." She gazed up at him, her blue eyes filled with tears. "I know about Clevil's son," she said so softly, he barely heard her. "I know about the attack on Vorlik, and about that book, that evil book, you keep in your study. I know many things you thought secret." She paused as Paxell blanched at her words. "I chose to marry you instead of Cordwin because I loved you with all my heart. He was kind and quiet, and I cared for him. Father urged me to make such a favorable marriage alliance, but I refused because I loved you. I wish I'd listened to him."

Tears arced down her gaunt cheeks and pooled in dark stains on Paxell's shirt. "I watched you change. Desire filled your eyes and heart, but not for me. Power, revenge – those took first place in your heart, and that book fed those desires. Why couldn't you have been content to rule Drambit and to love me? Why?" She gasped for breath. "I loved you, more than life. But you killed my love, just as you killed Clevil, Ellisa, and all the other victims of your ambition. There was gentleness and goodness in you, but you killed those, too, with your hunger for power."

Breath came in wheezing gasps that rattled in her shrunken body. Eyes stared sapphire hard at Paxell. Lips once full and red were transparent blue and trembled as she spoke. "My poor little Miria. How I wish she'd died...before her first breath. You'll destroy her...just as you've destroyed me. Someday, Paxell...you'll pay for my death...and the coin...will be...your own blood." She slumped in his arms, her last breath bubbling from her throat.

"No-o-o!" Paxell held her to his chest, his tears falling on her colorless skin. "Dannee, you can't die! You can't die!"

The midwife quietly backed toward the door. As she stooped to retrieve her bag, Paxell glanced her way.

"Get out," he said in a quavering voice.

She froze, her hand almost touching the strap, and stared at him with saucer eyes.

"Get out!" he shouted hoarsely. "Leave us alone!"

Leaving the bag, the midwife ran out and slammed the door behind her.

"Dannee," Paxell whispered as he cradled her limp body in his arms and wept against her neck, "Dannee, why? Why did you leave me? Why?"

Later, he heard Captain Callas knock on the door and call, "My lord? My lord!"

Paxell ignored him and continued sobbing Danneah's name.

6

Briella ran her fingers through her short blond hair, then massaged her aching temples. Her blue eyes burned from lack of sleep, and her body felt leaden. Her great-grandfather, the Wizard Casslin, was seriously ill. She was afraid he was dying, and she wanted to be with him every waking moment, but she had promised she'd teach a class for Loremaster Gilfan, who had injured his back. She tried to hide her fear and forced herself to smile at the children sitting in a semicircle at her feet.

A gentle breeze rustled through the grove of giant callum trees surrounding the Teaching Glen. The air was just cool enough, Briella was glad she'd worn her long-sleeved blue dress. The children, eight- to twelve-year-old boys and girls, were as restless as leaves in a breeze, laughing, talking, jostling each other. Briella sighed. She was only twenty herself and remembered how hard it was for her to study when the air was scented with lavender and midmorning sunlight warmed her face. *How can they keep their minds on school when the sky is so blue and the day is so perfect for climbing trees and skipping stones in the pond?* she wondered.

Today they were more disorderly than usual. Two of the older boys elbowed each other. A brown-haired boy snatched a ribbon from a cornsilk-blonde girl; she leaped up and chased him. Two of the younger girls played clapping games. And none of the other children seemed interested in learning. They squirmed and fidgeted so much, Briella understood why Loremaster Gilfan had asked her to teach this class.

He doesn't have the stamina to deal with children anymore, Briella thought. *Sometimes, neither do I. And I know they aren't being deliberately uncooperative. They're just being children.*

Briella sat up straighter on the limestone bench and clapped her hands for attention. "Now here is the tale of the beginnings of all things."

"Again?" grumbled Addis, one of the older boys. "I've heard it hundreds of times."

"But the younger children haven't heard it before," Briella said. She paused, and her eyes brightened. "Maybe *you* could tell the story. I know you know it by heart."

His eyes widened. "I guess I could," he said hesitantly.

"And let's do something a bit different this time," Briella said. "While Addis tells the story, I'll make pictures for you."

The children looked at each other, then clapped their hands. "Yes, yes!" they cheered.

Addis stood up, looking uncertain, walked to stand beside Briella, and faced the other children. He cleared his throat and began.

"Before the world was made, before the sun was placed in the sky and the stars were scattered across the heavens, before a tree grew or a bird flew, before anything was created, the god Barg was alone on a throne of light for uncounted ages."

Briella drew a sigil in the air and spoke a word of command. Before her appeared an image of Barg on a glowing throne. The children stared at the picture with wide eyes, and they gasped gleefully.

"'There is nothing in the universe except me,' Barg said. 'I will make other beings so I will not be alone.'

"As Barg thought about how to create the new beings, a strange thing happened. Barg became two: the female Baramay and the male Baygor. These two made all that is."

Briella waved her hands. An image appeared of a tall, slender woman with pale skin. Her black hair was bound with a silvery circlet set with a glowing white gem. Dark eyes flashed from her delicate face. She wore a gown that shimmered like moonlight.

Beside her stood a taller man with skin as golden as his robe. His golden hair was bound with a golden circlet set with a shining yellow gem. His eyes were the color of a summer day.

"Both looked at the emptiness about them," Addis said.

"'I will make a world,' Baramay said.

"She cupped her hands and blew into them. A mist began to form and swirl into a tiny ball. It began to harden into a ball of earth. Into the dark void she rolled the sphere which grew larger and larger. As the ball turned, Baramay breathed upon it, and green plants and trees sprang from the ground. Baramay was so happy that she wept tears of gladness, which fell upon the sphere and become seas, lakes, and rivers. We call our world Baramayan, which means Breath of Baramay," said Addis as Briella created an image of the creation of their world.

"Again Baramay breathed on the world," Addis said. "Creatures both small and great appeared: some on the land, some in the water, and some in the air. Baramay was so pleased that she sang for joy. The birds in the sky heard the song and tried to mimic her. When you hear a bird singing in the distance, you are hearing an echo of the Song of Baramay."

"Oh-h-h!" the youngest children said in unison.

"Baygor watched as Baramay made the world. When he heard the song she sang, he clapped his hands with joy. Shining sparks sprang from his hands and scattered across the dark sky, which had been lit only by the brightness of Baramay and Baygor. The sparks became the stars, the Sparks of Baygor."

Briella created a night sky overhead with twinkling stars in familiar constellations: Barg's Throne, the Sickle, the Harvest Maiden, the Diadem, the Formian Bear, Tressa's Stallion, and many more.

"'The world and all you have made are wondrous,' Baygor said as he gazed at Baramayan. 'I will give a gift to all living things on your world.' He held one hand over his head. 'The plants will bear fruit and seeds to begin new life; the creatures will bear offspring. Thus will life continue."

"What's offspring?" asked one of the little girls, a puzzled look in her violet eyes.

Addis rolled his eyes and looked annoyed. "Children."

"Oh."

"Baramay shouted with gladness," Addis continued. "She danced around the spinning world until her circlet fell off. It kept spinning about the world, the shining white gem slowly turning from the world and back again. That's why we call the moon--"

"Baramay's Circlet!" shouted a lean lad of eight.

Briella smiled, glad that the children seemed really interested in the story.

Addis nodded. "When Baygor saw the moon lighting the darkness, he decided another light was needed for the plants and creatures. He took the golden circlet from his head and sent it spinning around the world opposite the silver circlet. Always facing the world, the yellow gem gleamed brightly, warming the world as the plants and trees stretched toward the sky. We call Baygor's Circlet..."

"I know! I know!" With the eagerness only the young possess, the lean young lad tugged at the sleeve of Briella's blue dress. "The sun! It's the sun!"

Briella gave him an approving smile. "That's right." She created an image of the sun and moon circling the world, then gave Addis a nod to continue.

"Now, after many ages Baramay and Baygor looked upon the world. The trees were tall and straight. The plants covered the earth with flowers and fruit, grasses and bushes. It was a lovely, peaceful world where birds sang and animals played in meadows, where fish swam in the waters and all things lived in harmony. But Baramay and Baygor still had no one else to talk with, to share with.

"A time came when Baramay started another creation. She took rock from the mountains and formed bones. She took water from the sea and soil from the land. She mixed

them together and formed flesh on the bones. Catching a warm breeze and a ray of sunlight, and mixing them with her breath, she breathed life into the body and created Siteon the First One."

An image appeared of a being whose skin was the color of ripe acorns, with hair and eyes as brown as oak leaves in autumn.

"Siteon wasn't male or female, but Baramay and Baygor gifted him with great knowledge and mighty power so that he knew the future and was able to create things from nothing. Siteon talked with Baramay and Baygor often and learned many secrets.

"For many ages Siteon walked the world alone except for the animals and the gods. More and more often, Siteon sat alone, gazing silently at the world. One day, Baygor noted sadness in Siteon's eyes that seemed to grow with time.

"'Siteon is lonely,' Baygor told his wife, 'even as we were lonely when we were Barg. As Barg became two, Siteon will become male and female. I shall give to them the gift of offspring so they may continue.'

"Baygor called to Siteon. When Siteon came to them, Baygor took one hand and Baramay took the other. They pulled Siteon's hands until two bodies, a man and a woman, came from the one."

Briella waved her hand and another image appeared before the children. Baygor held the hand of a dark-haired man with eyes the color of earth and golden skin like Baygor's. Baramay held the hand of a pale, golden-haired woman with eyes the color of the sky.

"'Yo

ur name is Kitch,' Baygor said to the man, 'and this is your life mate.'

"'Your name is Nira,' Baramay said to the woman, 'and this is your life mate.'

"They became the parents of all the Wizards. They lived in a special land called Vorlik. They learned the ways of magic and used it wisely, as did their children and their grandchildren. And everyone was happy in Baramayan."

Addis lowered his voice and gave the other children a somber look. "But one of their great-grandchildren didn't use the magic the way he was taught. Canzet sought dark secrets. He wanted the power to control people, to make others do what he wanted. He chose to become evil, and he led some of his companions to join him. Soon Canzet's deeds were discovered. He and his followers were told they had to leave. They went to live in a land where they used their evil magic, becoming the first Sorcerers."

The littlest children squealed in fear at the mention of the dreaded enemies. Even Addis shivered before he spoke again.

"The Sorcerers became strong and powerful until one day they decided to attack the Wizards. Instead of fighting the Sorcerers, the Wizards moved to this secret valley in the north. Canzet and his followers destroyed much of the land with misused magic until Baygor became angry. He sent a lightning bolt which killed Canzet. The other Sorcerers ran far away to a hidden place in the south."

Briella shivered herself, and she didn't make an image of the Sorcerers War and the death of Canzet. She didn't want to frighten the children more than they already were.

Addis cleared his throat again. "When Baygor had healed the land, Baramay made her last creation. She took dust from the earth and water from the sea, mixed them together, and formed a man and a woman. Breathing into their mouths, Baramay gave them life. They were Ekivan, the father of men, and Riom, the mother of men. Baygor gave to them the gift of offspring and the freedom of the world. But men were weaker and shorter-lived than Wizards and Sorcerers, and men were easily fooled. So Baygor told the Wizards to guide and teach mankind and to protect them from the Sorcerers.

"So in Baramayan there are three races: Wizards--"

"That's us!" said a pert golden-haired girl.

"Wizards," Addis repeated, scowling at the interruption, "Sorcerers, and men."

The children cheered as he finished the story. Whether because they liked the tale or were relieved it was over, Briella wasn't certain.

The clapping of hands drew her attention to the edge of the clearing. Amaly, Briella's childhood playmate and closest friend, stood grinning at her, gold-brown eyes sparkling mischievously.

"Can we go now?" asked the green-eyed girl hopefully, her copper-colored hair quivering with anxiousness.

"I think we should all thank Addis for telling us a wonderful story," Briella said.

"Thank you, Addis," the children said in unison.

"Now can we go?" the green-eyed girl asked again.

"Yes, class is over," Briella said, then sighed with relief.

The children squealed as they tried to outrun each other.

Amaly's yellow shift swished softly as she walked toward her friend. "Difficult day?"

"Not too bad. Addis was a great help. That boy will be a great teacher when he grows up." Briella smoothed back her straight, blond hair, then massaged her forehead, trying to relax the tight muscles that threatened a colossal headache. "But some days the children can't sit still for five minutes. Especially on a beautiful day like today."

"I know," Amaly said, nodding. The breeze blew a strand of her long brown hair into her mouth. She spit it out and pushed the strand back behind her left ear. "I taught them for two weeks when Loremaster Gilfan broke his leg last year. I'll never willingly do that again!"

"At least, I won't have to anymore." A frost seemed to settle around Briella's heart.

"I know." Lines marred Amaly's forehead, and a frown pulled at the corners of her mouth. "I'm going to miss you so much. Do you really have to go?"

"I'll miss you, too." Briella embraced her friend tightly as if trying to hold on to childhood happiness by holding Amaly. "But we all go out into the world, even you, someday. This is my time to serve mankind. Wizards made the mistake of hiding once, and the Sorcerers nearly destroyed the world. We can't do that again."

"But you don't have to go now, do you?"

Briella released Amaly and nodded. "You know I do. Vorlik needs me, now more than ever." She tried to sound confident, but she didn't feel that way.

"But it's so...dangerous," Amaly said softly. "So many of our people have been killed by Sorcerers or have just disappeared. And you shouldn't have to go to the lands of men for many years yet. Most Wizards don't leave the vale until they're at least twenty-five years old. Even Maren was twenty-three before he left."

Sighing, Briella touched Amaly's arm. "You know why I have to go. Glisande Shadowmaster's dream told him it was vital that I leave for Vorlik now. I have to go, just as you will one day go to serve and protect men, just as Maren did. Have you heard from him?"

Amaly frowned thoughtfully. "Let me think. He left two years ago, and I heard from him a year later but not since then. I don't know where he is right now. If that brother of mine doesn't come home or send word soon, I'll go looking for him myself! And when I find him, he'll wish I hadn't!"

Briella grinned, her blue eyes twinkling. "Oh, he'll be sorry, especially when you give him the scolding he deserves." She smiled wistfully. "When he does return, tell him I wish him happiness always. Tell him he's the brother I never had."

Amaly touched Briella's arm gently. "I'll tell him, but he doesn't think of you as a sister."

Briella winced. "I know," she said softly. She rested her hand over Amaly's. "I want him to be happy. He *deserves* to be happy. I wish I could love him the way he loves me. But when I looked in his eyes, I knew he wasn't my life mate, my one true love for all my life. I'm sorry. I wish it were different."

"I'm sorry, too, for both of you." Amaly slipped her arm around Briella's arm, and the two of them ambled from the Teaching Grove, leaving the cool shade of the massive callum trees, to the sunny path that led to the main part of the settlement. They passed Rose and Lily, identical twins, who were on their knees in soft black dirt and planting a new bed of healing herbs. Briella and Amaly waved when the sisters looked up and smiled at them; the twins waved back with dirt-covered hands. Several youths raced past them on the worn paths from the center of the settlement, most likely on errands for various Wizards. In the distance, Briella heard some screeching notes from Warrith the Harper's school as he tried to teach one of the ancient ballads to his apprentices, just as he'd taught Maren. Briella smiled at the thought, glanced at Amaly, and realized she was thinking the same thing. They smiled at each other, then grinned.

"I remember when Maren first tried to play a lute," Amaly said. "He was terrible! I told him he'd never be a minstrel."

Briella laughed. "And now he's wandering the lands of men, singing and playing everywhere. He's famous if the reports we hear are true."

"My brother, the famous minstrel – who could have imagined it?" Amaly laughed.

Briella's thoughts wandered to the day Maren left the vale. He'd told her he loved her and had asked her to wait for him. She'd tried to tell she loved him as a friend, but then he'd kissed her. Suddenly, she'd felt uneasy and tense, and he'd never made her feel like that before. He'd walked away from her then, leaving the Wizard's Vale. She'd felt upset and relieved at the same time.

"Briella!" a voice called. An apprentice to Briella's great-grandfather sprinted into the main plaza where the women stood. "Master Casslin is calling for you. Please, come home as soon as you can." He turned and disappeared as quickly as he'd arrived.

Amaly's golden eyes dimmed with worry. "He's very ill, isn't he?"

Briella nodded, her throat tight. When she tried to speak, her voice was barely a whisper. "And that makes leaving the vale even harder. He's the only family I have left, since the Sorcerers killed my grandparents and my father, and since Great-grandmother Ireena died eight years ago. I barely remember Father. And Mother died when I was born so I don't remember her at all." She paused for a moment. "But Casslin was always there for me. Always there." Her eyes filled with tears.

Amaly put her arm around Briella, and Briella leaned her head on her friend's shoulder for comfort.

"I was ready to leave the vale," Briella said, "excited and curious, until Grandfather became so ill. I know I have to go to Vorlik, I truly want to go, but now I'm afraid if I leave the vale, I'll never see him again."

Amaly leaned her cheek against Briella's hair. "And I'm afraid that if you leave," she said, her voice barely a whisper, "I'll never see you again. I'm afraid I'll lose you forever."

Briella heard a strange tone in Amaly's voice. "Are you all right?" She pulled back and looked into her friend's eyes. "Do you know something? Have you seen something?" Wizards didn't often have visions or prophetic dreams, but when they did, they were true warnings. Was this one of those rare times? "Tell me, please," Briella said.

Amaly took Briella's hand and squeezed it gently. "No, I...I haven't seen anything. I just have this uneasy feeling. I'll be fine, really." She looked straight at Briella. "We've known each other all our lives, done everything together since we were old enough to walk. You're my best friend, closer than a real sister. I just can't imagine you not being here."

"I know. Neither can I. I'm sorry. I really have to go to now."

"I know," Amaly said, her forehead lined with worry. "I know. Take care of yours elf. And please, promise me you'll come to see me before you leave."

"I will. I promise." After another hug, Briella turned and ran down the path toward her home.

Her heart filled with worry, she raced past wheat fields already ripening from green to gold, past several of the hot springs that kept the Wizard's Vale warm and snow-free even in winter, and past the silversmith's forge where Amaly had learned to fashion elegant items and jewelry. Her footsteps echoed as she ran across the small arched bridge over a clear rushing brook, and in the distance she heard the creaking of the great wooden water wheel at the grist mill and a pair of mourning doves cooing to each other. A cool wind scented with wild flowers caressed her face as she ran by meadows where flocks of sheep and goats grazed, by neighbors' houses grown from opals or rubies or diamonds, and tall stacks of drying hay.

How can I leave my home? she wondered. *How can I leave Grandfather and everyone and everything I've ever known and loved? I wanted to see the world so badly, but how can I leave right now?*

By the time she reached her house, sparkling like emeralds in the morning sunlight, she was flushed, out of breath, and troubled.

7

The Wizard Casslin was dying.

His eyes were closed when Briella quietly opened the door to his room. She stood at the door gazing at him as the morning sunlight drizzled through the open window across the room, and her stomach knotted in worry. He looked so thin, so fragile lying in the bed. His skin was ashen. His breathing was ragged, gurgling in his chest. Tears crept down her face, and she wiped them away on her sleeve. She'd given him every potion she knew, every medicine she could brew. Nothing had helped, not even callum bark tea. He was the greatest healer in the Wizard's Vale, but even he couldn't stop death.

Tiptoeing to the bed, Briella knelt beside her great-grandfather and gently held his hand. His fingers were gnarled and brown, and his hands were cold. Her face felt hot and chilled at the same time, and her cheeks were sore from the tears she'd wiped away. Her lips trembled, and her throat was so tight, it hurt to breathe. She lightly smoothed the thick, grizzled hair from his pale, clammy forehead, trying not to disturb him, but she failed.

He opened his clear green eyes and smiled weakly. "Ah, Briella, how did your class go today?"

"Very well," she said, trying to smile. "Addis was bored as usual, but that's only because he's so bright. He's like a sponge that soaks up everything. I had him tell the beginnings story to keep him interested, and I made pictures of the story while he spoke. He really needs to be given harder lessons. I know he'll be a great Loremaster someday." She paused thoughtfully. "All the children are so eager, so young, so . . ." Her voice trailed off as her facade of cheer dissolved. "Oh, Grandfather . . ." Tears started trickling down her cheeks again.

Casslin stroked her hair tenderly. "Don't cry, little dove."

"But I'm so afraid," she said, and she shivered down to her toes. "I don't want to lose you."

He lifted her chin until she gazed straight at him. "I've lived three hundred and fifty-seven years, and I'm not afraid of dying. I have so many memories, some bad, some good," he stroked her cheek, "mostly good, but I'm ready to go. Soon I'll be with your Grandma

Ireena and your grandparents and your mother and father, and we'll never be separated again. You don't begrudge me that happiness, do you?"

Briella's hands suddenly felt clammy. The thought that her grandfather would leave her sat on her heart like cold lead. "I don't begrudge you happiness, but do you have to take mine away? I need you to teach me, to guide me."

Gently touching her face, wiping away tears with his thumb, he shook his head and smiled wanly. "You've learned everything I can teach you about healing, shape-changing, enchantment, and so much more. You're the best healer I've ever taught...and my greatest joy. Now you must use what you have learned. Today you must leave for Vorlik."

"How can I leave you now? Like this?" she said, her heart in such anguish. "I know I promised to go to Vorlik, but that was before you became so ill. I can't leave you now. Who'll bring you callum bark tea? Who'll make warm broth the way you like it? Who'll hold your hand and sing to you at night? Who'll take care of you like I do? Please, Grandfather, let me stay with you a little longer!"

He stroked her cheek gently. "I have many friends to care for me. Amaly will watch over me as if I were her own grandfather. You know that." He paused. "The new lord's coronation is in three days. You must go to Vorlik and offer your service to him. He'll need your help and protection now more than ever. And be cautious. I'm certain the Sorcerers were behind Clevil's murder. Even in Vorlik, Wizards are not always safe."

Briella sat still, telling herself over and over how important going to Vorlik was. "Tell me again. What's he like? Lord Cordwin, I mean. Will I like him?"

"I haven't seen him in ten years." Casslin's eyes seemed to focus beyond her, and the corners of his mouth twitched, as if he tried to smile but couldn't find the strength. "He was only nine when I left Vorlik."

"Ten years ago?" Briella said softly. "That was when my parents were killed by the Sorcerers. That's when you came back to take care of me, wasn't it?"

Casslin nodded slowly. "Yes. Ten years ago. Children grow and change so much in ten years. I might not even recognize him now, but if he's anything like his father and older brother, he's a good man. He's a year younger than you. Actually, he reminds me of Maren in many ways. He played a flute quite well even as a boy. If he'd been born a Wizard, he could've been a minstrel. He was kind-hearted, occasionally impulsive, sometimes he was too serious, and he lacked self-confidence. But he'd give his life to protect his friends or his people."

Briella tried to imagine how Cordwin would look when they met. "Is he handsome?"

Casslin turned his head to look at her directly. "Handsome? I don't know. He was a comely child, but it's been many years since I last saw him. You'll have to judge for yourself." His smile and a twinkle in his eyes made her blush. "Tell him I send greetings and my deepest affection, then give him the gifts I've prepared. Tell him how much Clevil's death grieved me, how all the master Wizards searched for the murderers with all their powers but that we couldn't find any answers. And assure him I'll continue to search—" the old man stopped short and clutched at his chest. His breathing was like wind through knotholes, hollow and rough. "As long as I'm able. We all will."

"Don't talk, please." Briella kissed his forehead. "You need to rest."

Casslin shook his head. "There's so much I need to say," he whispered hoarsely. "I love you more than anything else in this life. In the eighteen years since you were born, you've filled my life with more joy than I thought possible. You are my heart's most precious treasure. Now, I'm sending you to Vorlik to protect its people. Love them, care for them." He coughed, struggling for breath. "Always remember, my little mourning dove, how very much I love you."

Leaning her head on the side of the bed, she wept again.

He stroked her tousled hair, then lifted her pale face and smiled at her, though his voice cracked and his eyes shimmered. "Briella, it's time. You have to go now or you won't arrive in time."

"I can't!" she said, her voice muffled by tears. "I just can't!"

"Yes, you can. You have to," he whispered, his own tears trickling down leathery cheeks. "Cordwin needs you more than I do. Vorlik needs you. So many lives depend on your protection, your skills. Besides, you gave me your word, and you've never broken a promise. Not ever."

"But that was before you became so ill! Please, just let me stay a little while, at least until you're better."

"I won't get better. You know that. By the time you reach Vorlik, I may have already entered Barg's kingdom." He stared into her eyes. "And you gave your word. You can't break your promise. Wizards don't. The last Wizard who did was Canzet."

Her shoulders sagged, and she nodded. Even if he'd have agreed to let her stay, she couldn't go back on her word. Like lying, that was something Wizards didn't do. "But...I won't see you again." She rested her cheek against his side.

Casslin rested his hand on her head. "We'll see each other again. I'll be waiting at the gates of Barg's kingdom for you."

She lifted her head and gazed at him through tears.

His half-smile carved lines in his cheeks and brow. "I'll always be with you. Be careful and wary, little dove. Watch out for our enemies. They are everywhere. Far-thell, and Baygor protect you."

Briella bent to kiss his forehead. "Far-thell, Grandfather. I love you!" She stood and ran from the room.

Briella shut her bedroom door and slumped against it. Her body shook with sobs; her head pounded. Her throat was as tight as her chest, and her heart felt torn in two. *How can I leave him when he needs me now more than ever?* she thought.

Slowly, she pushed herself erect. No, she'd promised her grandfather and the master Wizards that she would serve and protect Vorlik. She'd given her word, and she never broke a promise, no matter what. *Grandfather,* she thought, *I'll try to be worthy of your faith in me.*

She turned to her bed where she'd set her spell book, a small bag of treasured mementoes, and a drawstring purse containing a number of gems, since she didn't have coins from Vorlik. Beside them was a tightly packed bundle of clothes, a sack of medicines, and her silver-grey hooded cloak. She placed her clothes, mementoes, and spell book into a pack to tie to her back. After slipping all the other items into the cloak's inner pockets, she turned to her bedside table. A small, rosewood box rested there. Inside were a set of silver bracers made especially for Cordwin by her grandfather, and a silver and emerald ring, an heirloom of the house of Vorlik that Cordwin's father had given to Casslin. Now it would come back to Cordwin.

She slipped the box into a wide, deep pocket, tied the pack to her securely, then put her cloak around her shoulders, making sure that the clasp didn't snag her silver pendant, shaped like a dove. She gazed at her reflection in the oval silver mirror on the wall. She wondered what Cordwin would think of her and if she were dressed properly for a coronation. Her blue dress was clean but plain, and it made her eyes seem bluer. Her black slippers with ankle straps weren't made for rough journeys, but she wasn't going to walk long distances. Her face was pale, her eyes were red-rimmed from crying, but that wouldn't last. With a last glance about the room which had always been her retreat, her haven, she turned to the crystal windows and opened them. She spread her arms, spoke the spell, and became a gray dove, her favorite changeling form, winging through the air, rising with the winds.

In ever-widening circles she flew above the Wizard's Vale. She tried to imprint every detail in her mind, knowing she'd never see it again. She flew above her green crystal house where Grandfather slept and past the clear-gold house of Glisande Shadowmaster. She saw fields and meadows, the grist mill, the weavers' school where skeins of colorful yarn dried on racks in the sun. There below was the white marble cottage of Warrith the Harper, his music school, and the amphitheater where Wizards exhibited their musical and theatrical talents.

As Briella flew over the main plaza, she saw many of the Wizards stop, shade their eyes, and wave to her as she dipped lower for a moment, then flew on toward the callum trees in the Teaching Grove of Loremaster Gilfan. Scattered throughout the vale she saw the hot springs that kept the valley warmer in winter, although it was far north. There, southwest of the Teaching Grove was the red crystal cottage of Amaly and her brother Maren.

Briella spotted a slim figure in yellow in the middle of a multi-colored rose garden along the walk from the cottage. Amaly looked up at the dove-Briella in the sky, shielded her eyes from the sun with one of her hands, and waved with her other one. Descending,

Briella alighted just inside the white slat fence surrounding Amaly's cottage and changed to human form.

Amaly took off her work gloves and hurried from her garden to greet Briella. "I'm glad you came before you left." She looked somber as she scanned her friend's face. "Your eyes and cheeks are red."

Without thinking, Briella reached up to touch the corner of her right eye.

A gentle smile brightened Amaly's face, and her dark eyes glowed with understanding. "It's all right. If anyone has a right to cry, you do. Is Master Casslin any better?"

Briella shook her head. "He said he may die before I reach Vorlik."

Amaly took her friend's hand and gave it a light squeeze. "I promise I'll look after him for you. Everyone will."

"It's not the same thing," Briella whispered. "But I have to go. I know I do. I'll try to come home for a visit."

Amaly hugged her. "Make it soon."

"I will." Briella pulled away slowly and smiled. She started to turn away when her friend stopped her.

"Your dove pendant, the one I made for you, are you wearing it?" Amaly asked.

"Of course." Briella unhooked her cloak and pulled out the chain that held the silver dove. "It's my dearest treasure. I wear it next to my heart."

Amaly gazed at the pendant, then in a faraway voice said, "Never take it off, no matter what. Not when you sleep. Not even when you bathe."

Briella blinked. "Why?"

Amaly looked troubled. "I don't know why. All I know is you must *always* wear it. Please, promise me!"

"All right," Briella said. "I'll always wear it."

Nodding, Amaly gave her a hug and whispered, "Goodbye, dear friend, and be careful. Baygor protect you."

Tears threatened to spill down her face again as Briella changed back to dove form and launched toward the sky. *I'm going to miss her so much,* she thought sadly. *She's always been part of my life. I can't remember a time when we didn't spend at least part of each day together. And Grandfather – how can I go on without him? So many memories of things left behind now. Why can't life be simple? Why do things have to change?*

She turned southward, a cold and empty ache in her heart.

Deeply drifted snow of the encircling mountains yielded gradually to desolate tundra. The wind was icy, chilling her breath and tiring her wings. By nightfall she had traveled nearly four hundred miles. Exhausted, she found a solitary picket pine growing beneath a steep cliff, sheltered from the fierce wind. She nestled close to tree trunk, cast a small sphere of warmth about her, and fell asleep surrounded by fragrant pine needles.

She woke before the sun pinked the sky with dawn. Rising on the cold, clear air, she glided far above the mossy tundra teaming with herds of caribou, over dark forests of picket pine and red spruce, past roiling rivers and misty falls, above meadows green with spring. At sunset she landed in a tall spruce, her grey wings aching with their effort, her stomach empty. Drowsy, she huddled against the tree. *Four hundred miles yesterday, she thought, and nearly six hundred today. Tomorrow I'll reach Tarolin Castle.* As she fell asleep, she wondered what Lord Cordwin would think of her, and what she would think of him.

With the first blush of dawn, she rose above the tree tops, rested but so hungry, she thought she could eat a bushel of wheat or millet seeds. She crossed great stretches of wilderness, passed the forests and plains of Formia, and by midmorning she reached the northern edge of the Circle Mountains encompassing Vorlik. She flew above the northern pass, beyond the barracks of the Northern Guard. Following the main highway south, she saw towns, villages, herds of cattle and flocks of sheep, orchards, and green fields. As the sun reached midday, she heard the echoes of trumpets and sighted the limestone towers and red granite wall of Tarolin Castle. Her wings ached, and she felt faint. Her strength was nearly depleted from the changeling spell. But she sighed with relief. Her journey was almost complete.

8

Vorlik's gold and ruby crown weighed on Cordwin's head like grief weighed on his heart. The red velvet knee-length robe and matching trousers, embroidered with gold thread at the cuffs and hem, seemed tight and stiff. His sword belted at his side was unbearably heavy. His heart was numb, and he felt cold, yet the room felt so stiflingly hot, he could hardly breathe. He desperately wanted to be anywhere but sitting on the throne, Clev's throne.

Light streamed through the high windows above the gallery, opened to admit the warm spring air. The newly repaired Audience Hall was filled with spring flowers. The banners of the five Guards hung on the north wall. And lining the east and west walls an arm's length apart stood soldiers of the Tarolin Guard in red and gold uniforms. Everything was as it had been before the fire. *Except Clev isn't here,* Cordwin thought, his head and heart aching. *Clev and Ellisa will never be here again.*

Heralds' trumpets sounded as the senior priest from the Temple of Baygor said, "Long live Lord Cordwin!"

The words made Cordwin cringe.

Officials, merchants, and peasants, crowded into the hall and waiting to present their gifts and good wishes to the new lord of Vorlik, echoed the priest. "Long live Lord Cordwin!"

One of the younger scribes stood before the throne and announced each visitor, who bowed before the new lord. For Cordwin, the faces blurred together, the names echoed at the edge of his consciousness, and the gifts and good wishes were meaningless. He felt as if a horse had kicked him in the center of his chest, and his eyes burned with tears he blinked back. He fingered his eagle amulet above the gold medallion of Vorlik, just wanting the ceremony to be over. *I don't believe this,* he thought. *I don't want to believe it. Please, let me wake up from this nightmare.*

The eagle amulet suddenly began to tingle and vibrate between his fingers, and made a low sound like bees humming. The silvery metal glowed slightly red, as if caught in the last light of day. Cordwin stared at the amulet, startled; he'd never seen or felt anything from it before. *This is Wizard crafted,* he thought, *but what does the red glow mean?*

"Minister Haller of Peltik," the scribe announced, drawing Cordwin's attention back to the ceremony.

A tall, lean man with brown hair, graying at the temples, stepped forward and bowed to Cordwin. "Greetings, Lord Cordwin. Baramay's blessings to you. Lord Merrick sends his good wishes and sincere regrets that he could not attend your coronation himself."

Cordwin leaned forward anxiously. "He's not ill, I hope."

Haller shook his head slowly. "No, my lord, but Lord Merrick and all Peltik are in mourning."

"Mourning?" Cordwin said, worried. "Who has died?"

The minister looked pained, then said, "Lady Danneah."

Cordwin inhaled sharply. "When? How did she die?"

"In childbirth nearly a week ago."

Cordwin winced, remembering how kind she had been to him. They had known each other since they were children, and he and Danneah had vowed to be friends forever. How they had laughed together at the way her father and his brother had plotted their marriage. Now, she was dead — she and Clevil and Ellisa. He covered his eyes with his hand. *Too much death,* he thought, his head throbbing.

Finally, he looked back at the minister. "Please tell Lord Merrick how sorry...how much...how deeply I feel his loss. Lady Danneah was...dear to me as well."

The minister bowed and backed away. The hall was somber and silent in spite of the great crowd of people. Cordwin wanted to flee, wanted to be in his own room, away from the eyes of friends and strangers.

A quiet rush of wings brought him to attention. Through one of the high windows flew a grey-brown mourning dove. It circled three times above Cordwin, then fluttered to the stone floor before the dais. An iridescent mist gathered and swirled about the dove, growing to a glittering column. The crowd gasped as the bird transformed to a figure wearing a grey, hooded cloak. The figure bowed low.

Like arrows, Captain Daikin and five guards launched from the sides of the hall and surrounded the figure, their swords drawn. Amazed and wary, Cordwin grasped his sword hilt and tensed to defend himself.

"Don't be afraid of me, Lord Cordwin," a quiet, female voice assured him. "I mean no harm to you or your people." The figure pushed the hood back from her head and the cloak from her shoulders.

Cordwin gazed at her stunned, captivated. She was like the sun in a summer sky, chasing winter shadows from his heart. She wore a long-sleeved blue dress with rounded neck and gathered at the wrists and waist. The skirt was short enough to show her black slippers. She was pale and slender but not thin. Her short blond hair was ruffled and wind-blown. At her throat she wore a silver necklace with a pendant shaped like a dove.

He suddenly realized he was holding his breath. "Who are you?" he stammered, his eyes wide.

She stood staring at him, unmoving. Her eyes were bluer than her dress and wide open as if she were surprised. Her lips were slightly parted and trembled. "My lord," she said, not taking her eyes from him, her voice hushed.

"Who are you?" he asked again.

She stood still a moment longer, then genuflected. "My lord, I am Briella, great-granddaughter of Casslin."

"Casslin!" Daikin gasped, lowering his sword.

"The Wizard who served my father and grandfather?" Surprised, Cordwin touched the eagle necklace. It had stopped vibrating. "The one who gave me this amulet?"

For a moment, she bit her lips, and her shoulders drooped slightly before she replied. "He remembers the day he gave it to you. He's spoken of you so often, I feel we've met already. He sends good wishes upon your coronation. He sent me to you, to serve, advise, and protect you as I am able. And I swear I will protect you and your people with my life."

Cordwin glanced at Daikin, nodded. Daikin nodded back, and he and the guards went back to their places. Anxious and excited, he asked, "But where's Casslin? Doesn't he know how much I need him now?"

Briella's lips trembled. "He wanted to come. This time he couldn't. But I'll serve you as faithfully as he served your father and grandfather."

Cordwin's voice was barely audible, his grief burning in his throat. "But why did you wait so long? Why didn't you come when we needed you? When Vorlik was attacked? When Clevil and Ellisa lay dying and their son was stolen? Why wait 'til now?"

She gazed steadily into his eyes. Her smile was touched with deep sadness. "Grandfather sensed danger for Vorlik but was too late to stop the attack. He loved Clevil like his own son. Grandfather sent me to you as a token of his grief and regret, and asks that you accept my service." Gracefully, she bowed to him.

Cordwin almost ran down the dais steps until he stood before her. "Please, tell me who murdered Clevil and Ellisa," he said anxiously.

"That is beyond my powers, my lord," she said breathlessly.

"Then can you tell me where my nephew Bren is? Or if he's even alive?"

She shook her head. "I...I don't know, my lord. Baygor knows how much I wish I did."

Despair encircled Cordwin's heart like a glaze of ice. Tears crept to the corners of his eyes. "Then what good is your power?" he whispered. "What good are you if you can't name Clevil's murderer, can't tell me what I need to know so badly?"

Briella's gaze never left his face. "Do you hurt so much?" she whispered and touched her fingertips to his temple.

Light flared in his head. All his pain, anger, and grief poured from his heart like a flood until he could breathe freely and easily for the first time since Clevil's death. Dizzy and off balance, he staggered back, clutching at his chest, but he felt as if his heart had suddenly remembered how to beat, free of anguish for the first time since he'd found his brother dead.

Daikin rushed to his side. "Cord, are you all right?" he asked anxiously.

Cordwin held up his hand and nodded slowly. Daikin straightened, bowed, and took a step back, but only one.

Cordwin turned back to Briella. "Sweet Baramay," he said, gaping at her in amazement, "what did you do to me?"

She looked paler than before, her eyes filled with worry. She reached out her hand to touch his arm, but halted. "My lord, I never meant to harm you. I only wanted to ease your pain. I...please, forgive me, my lord." Her voice trailed off, and she sank to one knee. She kept gazing at him so intently, Cordwin felt as if she were reading his soul through his eyes.

"My lady," he whispered, "you have given me the first moment of peace I've had in many days. I'm deeply grateful for your...kindness." He held out his hand to her. Hesitantly, she placed her hand in his, curled her fingers around his hand, and stood up, gazing straight at him. Her hand felt so small in his, warm and soft, but not weak. For a few moment he felt her warmth seep into his heart. His eyes studied hers, only inches from his. Her nose was just slightly too wide; her lips were a bit too thin. But there was an openness and lack of guile in her face that he found captivating. He felt as if she belonged in his arms, as if she were part of him.

"My lord," she said, barely loud enough for him to hear, "please. Everyone is watching us."

Cordwin glanced around and realized he was standing in the Audience Hall, surrounded by scores of soldiers, nobles, and people of note, all gawking at him. He cleared his throat and released her hand reluctantly.

Briella's voice quivered as she spoke again. "My lord, Grandfather tried to learn what you want to know, about your brother and nephew. Grandfather tried so hard. He and the other Wizards couldn't find the answers, but they're certain Sorcery's hiding the truth. Grandfather wanted to tell you himself, but he's too ill to travel. He's...he's dying. He may have died already. I'll never see him again." Her voice cracked.

"Oh gods," Cordwin said under his breath, squeezing his eyes shut. Dying? Casslin dying? Would everyone he cared for be taken away? He remembered Casslin's emerald eyes and loving smile. The Wizard had taught Cordwin how to gentle a horse with only a quiet tone of voice. Casslin had shown him the magic of a flower, a bee, a falling leaf. Once the Wizard had shown Cordwin an ugly slingnet spider that made him shiver, then showed him the spider's dew-covered web, sparkling like diamonds in the sunlight. "Even something as fearsome as this spider can create a thing of extraordinary beauty," Casslin had said. "Look for beauty in all you see."

Cordwin had loved Casslin as much as his own father, perhaps even a bit more. Cordwin cried for days when Casslin left Vorlik. Even after he'd left, sometimes Cordwin thought he felt the Wizard's reassuring touch on his shoulder. He wished with all his heart that he could feel Casslin's comforting touch once again. He opened his eyes and saw Briella with her hand over her mouth to muffle her sobs. "I'm truly sorry," he said. "He was very kind to me."

Briella nodded, her blue eyes shining like liquid sapphires, and wiped the tears from her cheeks with her fingertips. She bowed her head and said, "Thank you, my lord." She straightened, reached inside her cloak, took a rosewood chest from her cloak, and presented the chest to Cordwin. "I've brought other gifts from my grandfather: silver bracers set with spells for your protection, and also an heirloom of your house, the silver and emerald ring that your father gave to my grandfather, a token of friendship and gratitude. He sent it back to you as a pledge of my service."

Cordwin stared at the chest, anguish creeping back into his soul, and shook his head slowly. "I don't want trinkets and ornaments," he said, his heart overwhelmed with too many sorrows. "I want my nephew back. I need to know who killed my brother. I thought Wizards could do anything."

Her eyes seem to stare beyond him, and her face grew paler. "Baygor knows I wish that were true," she said.

Cordwin felt as if he were in a whirlpool, unable to break free, unable to save himself, being sucked down to cold and empty darkness again. Hopelessness throbbed in his head. "If you can't help me, can't tell me what I need to know, then I don't need you." He turned away from her. "Go. Just leave." He paused. "I don't want to see you again." The moment he said it, he knew it wasn't true.

In a moment, Daikin was at his side. "Cord," Daikin whispered close to his ear, "what are you doing? She's a Wizard! We *need* her!"

"Don't!" Cordwin whispered back, glaring at his cousin. "Not in front of everyone!"

Daikin backed away and gave a stiff bow, but he didn't look Cordwin in the eye.

Cordwin looked back at Briella. She stood statue-still, gazing steadily at him, her eyes red-rimmed. Gracefully, she set the chest on the floor at Cordwin's feet, then backed respectfully from him. She watched him with sad eyes, which made him uncomfortable.

"My lord, I'll still serve you...even though you don't want to see me again. I'll do everything in my power to keep you and your people safe. I'll set a Wall of Warding around your borders so no army can attack Vorlik. I'll heal and teach and protect your people. I swear loyalty to you and your house. Long life to you," she paused a moment, then said, "and happiness and peace, Lord Cordwin of Vorlik. May Baramay and Baygor smile upon you."

She touched her fingertips to her forehead and bowed again. As she straightened up, she inhaled suddenly, pressed her hands to her temples, and sank to the floor, unconscious.

Murmuring swept through the audience as Cordwin sprang to her side, slid his arm beneath her, and cradled her against his chest. She felt light, as if she were made of a summer breeze. She looked young, no older than he was. He smoothed a stray strand of golden hair from her forehead and touched her cheek, soft as velvet. "Lady! Lady, are you ill? Briella!"

Finally, her eyes opened, focused on his face, then widened. She became paler than moonlight.

"What happened?" he asked.

"A vision." Her body trembled as much as her voice did.

"A vision?" He leaned closer. "What did you see?"

"A young man, who looked much like you, but not you. A man named Bren." She choked on the last word.

Cordwin's heart leaped. "Bren? Are you sure?"

"Yes." She swallowed hard. "Yes. It was him."

Cordwin's blood raced through his body. "He's alive," he whispered. He felt like laughing and crying at the same time. "He's alive!" He took Briella's hand and kissed it. "Thank you, Lady Briella. You've given me hope when I had none."

"I saw chaos, war, and death—so much death." Briella's skin felt warm to his touch, too warm, almost as if she had a fever. Her voice shook as she spoke. "When Bren returns, he'll destroy the peace of Vorlik, then save the land."

"But when?" Cordwin gazed excitedly at her. "When will he return?"

"When the child becomes a man," Briella whispered.

"But that's so many years from now!" Cordwin said, distressed.

"I saw him," Briella said. "A grown man. I saw a jeweled knife touched by evil. Its blade dripped blood. My blood. And at his feet . . ." she shuddered, "at his feet I lay bleeding. Beside me lay a sword with the word 'Truth' and his name etched on the blade: Bren." Her eyes grew wide with fear. "Bren is going to kill me. When he returns to Vorlik, he'll kill me." Her voice dwindled to silence.

"But you're a Wizard," he said, disbelief in his voice. "Bren couldn't kill you. No human could."

Briella's voice was so soft, Cordwin could barely hear it. "It will happen," she said. "Even Wizards die."

Cordwin brushed a tear from her cheek and felt her shaking. "Do your visions always come true?"

Her blue eyes were wide with terror, and she nodded. "Always," she whispered. "Wizards seldom have visions—once, twice, three times at most in a lifetime—but they always come true. Always."

"Maybe this time it won't." Cordwin tightened his embrace just enough to reassure her, as he would a frightened child. At that moment more than anything else he wanted to protect *her*, keep *her* safe. "Did you actually see him kill you?"

"No," she said thoughtfully. "I didn't see him kill me, but even so, it will happen. He'll come, and I'll die."

"But—" he halted, bewildered, "what will you do?"

"I don't know. I don't know! What can I do?" she said frantically. She hid her face in the folds of his velvet robe and shuddered against his chest.

Cordwin smoothed her wheat-colored hair and held her tenderly. "Lady, how can I help you? Tell me what I can do!"

She turned her head until she looked straight up at him. She shook her head slowly. "There's nothing you or anyone else can do," she said as she looked intently at him, "but I thank you for asking. Grandfather was right about you." She caressed his cheek.

Cordwin's heart beat as fast as a hummingbird's wings. *How can I feel so completely elated and at the same time so utterly peaceful, all from just a touch of her hand?* he wondered. He gazed at her face, so filled with fear, and he thought, *I would give my life to protect her.*

"Then what will you do?" he asked.

"What I promised to do," she said. "I swore to serve you and your people, and that's what I'll do, my lord: serve you...and await my fate."

Cordwin felt her shudder, her skin prickling with goose bumps. She whispered words he didn't understand, and she seemed to shrink away from him. He started to ask her what she'd said when suddenly, his arms were empty. A dove hovered before him a moment, then flew through the high window. He leaped to his feet.

"Wait! Come back!" he called, but the dove didn't reappear. He stared after her for a long while before he realized she wouldn't return. People began talking all at once, chattering like a flock of blackbirds. Cordwin just stared up at the windows.

9

Briella winged from the high window, still shaken by her vision. *I'm going to die,* she thought, her heart pounding. *I won't live three hundred or more years. Perhaps only a few decades. When Bren is grown to manhood and returns, I'm going to die. And he may be the one who kills me. Lady Baramay, why let me know this now? Why let me live with this fear?*

She wanted a place to hide, a place she felt safe. She wanted to go home, but she couldn't. She'd sworn to serve Cordwin, and she couldn't break that promise. She scanned the castle for a place to land, a place to rest, to calm her racing heart. She spotted a narrow windowsill on the third floor facing west. The shutters had been left open. Gliding to the sill, she hopped down and glanced around the small and sparsely furnished room. No one else was there. Changing back to her natural form, she leaned against the cool stone wall between the window and a narrow bed.

She wanted to cry, but tears didn't come. She felt as if all her tears had frozen around her heart. Even with her cloak wrapped around her, she felt cold, and she wondered if she'd ever be warm again. *Grandfather, did you know?* she thought. *When you sent me here, did you know I was going to my death?*

Her chest hurt, and she felt as if she couldn't get enough air no matter how fast she breathed. *Bren won't come for years, twenty or twenty-five or more,* she thought. *Twenty years at least. Twenty years to live. Only twenty years.*

She slid down the wall until she sat on the floor, knees pulled close to her chest and her arms wrapped around them. She felt as though she were moving though honey thick with winter's cold. Leaning her forehead on her knees, she closed her eyes. She wanted to escape to the quiet darkness of sleep, and she prayed that she'd wake up to find the vision was only a bad dream. But in her heart, she knew it was real, that she would die. Her stomach was churning so badly, she felt nauseated. If she'd had anything on her stomach, even simply water, she knew she would vomit. She opened her eyes, pulled her cloak closer, and tried to stop shivering.

Cordwin was more than she'd expected. The moment she'd looked into his eyes, she'd felt such a sweet ache in her heart that she could hardly speak. She'd never felt so completely entranced by anyone, and Cordwin wasn't even a Wizard. Just thinking about putting a name to the sensation that filled her mind, enfolded her heart, made her tremble. It was too close to love, and she could never love a human. Only one Wizard had ever loved a human, the Wizard Timmree, and Briella couldn't do what Timmree had done. But Briella's heart told her that Cordwin was her lifemate, and that frightened her almost as much as the vision of her death.

Cordwin's grief had almost overwhelmed her when she'd touched his temple. His heart was in so much turmoil, yet she'd felt his compassion, his gentleness in spite of his grief. Her grandfather's face appeared in her mind, and she opened her eyes. *I know how Cordwin feels,* she thought, *losing the people he loves.*

She brushed her fingertips over her cheek where Cordwin had touched her, and she remembered the warm, exciting fear she'd felt when he'd held her in his arms, the pleasant tightening around her heart, the sudden catch in her breath when she'd looked in his eyes, the tingling that raced over her skin. The sensations made her want to run from him, run far away, but somehow she knew that even the Wizard's Vale wasn't far enough to escape him.

Something else bothered her. When she'd first appeared in the hall, she'd felt suddenly cold and off balance, as if she were standing on a ledge and about to fall. She'd never felt anything like that before. She didn't know what had caused it, but it unnerved her.

Weary down to her bones, she crossed her arms on her bent knees and rested her head on her arms. She struggled to keep her eyes open, but the lids kept drooping. *I need to rest a moment,* she told herself, *only a moment, and then I'll go on.* She closed her eyes and fell asleep almost instantly.

Suddenly, she heard the door open. Jerking her head up, she rubbed her tired eyes. Sunlight crept through the window, touching the stone floor beneath the window sill and stretching toward the other side of the room. Opposite the window, Cordwin stood in the doorway, staring at her, his eyes wide and his mouth open. He still wore his crown and coronation clothes.

"Lady Briella?" He entered the room and quickly closed the door behind him. "What are you doing in my room?" he asked.

"*Your* room?" She couldn't move, startled. "This is *your* room?" She kept her eyes on Cordwin but groped for the windowsill with her left hand. "Forgive me, my lord. I wouldn't have trespassed if I had known." She stood and started to turn toward the window.

"Wait, please," Cordwin said as he strode toward her. "Don't leave."

She hesitated. His eyes held her captive until he had almost reached her. *No,* she thought frantically, *if he touches me again, if his fingers caress my cheek, if he holds my hand one more time, I won't be able to leave him. Ever.* She changed into a dove and darted through the open window, seeking the safety of the woods south of the castle. She settled on the branch of a great oak tree, flexed her wings, then nervously cleaned and smoothed her feathers to calm the confusion swirling in her mind.

I need a sanctuary, someplace quiet and safe, she thought, *and away from Cordwin. A place I can sleep and maybe eat something. I haven't eaten in days.* Her stomach felt painfully empty. She glanced around the woods for a moment. *Didn't Grandfather say there was town with an inn south of here? A meal, bath, and a night in a warm bed would be wonderful.*

She spread her tired wings and flew south. After passing over a large wood, solitary cottages, fields, and numerous vineyards, she sighted the village of Yarrow. Circling the cluster of stone and wooden buildings, she spied a small stone chapel, its roof painted blue and gold, and directly across the road was a two-story inn. A wooden sign painted with brightly colored wheels proclaimed it the Singing Wheels Inn – Hollester Fitch, proprietor. Alighting in a stand of dogwood and maple trees near the village, she changed to her own form and trudged the short distance.

Ivy nearly covered the road-front side of the inn. Warm sunlight and spring air poured in through the open door. Laughter and tempting aromas tumbled out. Peering into the rectangular room, she saw many tables and benches. Several villagers were seated for the noon meal, delivered by a plainly dressed matron with walnut eyes and a braided crown of brown hair. A red-haired man washed the counter while chatting with several dusty, beer-sipping travelers. He wore a white apron over a rolled-sleeved shirt and dark brown trousers.

As she entered, the man looked up, dropped his rag, and bustled to greet her.

"Welcome, lady," he said, bowing slightly. "I am Hollester Fitch, innkeeper. How may I serve you?"

"I'd like a room for the night and a bath if possible, perhaps some food, but especially the bath," Briella said hopefully.

He beamed, drying his hands on his apron. "Of course. The water will take a while to heat, but if you would care to eat first, your bath will be ready when you're finished."

Just wanting rest, Briella sighed but gave him a weak smile. "All right, but I'd like something simple to eat. Maybe some fruit and cheese. And something to drink."

"Of course. Will you be wanting a private room?"

"Yes."

"I have only one private room left, and it's four coppers a night, and one for meals."

Briella took her drawstring purse from a pocket in her cloak. Opening it carefully, she took out a ruby the size of an apple seed. "Would this cover the cost?"

The innkeeper's eyes blinked and flew open wide. "More than cover," he said breathlessly. He led Briella towards a table near the fireplace, far from the other diners. "Have you come from the castle?"

She hesitated. "Yes."

He gave a deep, wistful sigh. "We'd loved to have seen the coronation, but with so many visitors needing a place to stay and not everyone can stay at the castle so. . ." He spread his arms wide, gave a shrug, and walked back to the bar.

Briella slumped to the bench and leaned her back against the wall. The coolness of the stone soaked through her clothes and felt good against her too warm skin. She felt exhausted, as if even breathing was too much effort.

The matron soon brought a wooden tray with a large wedge of a firm white cheese, a small round of brown bread, a wrinkled apple and a bowl of small red berries Briella didn't recognize, as well as a mug of wine. "Is there anything else you wish?"

Briella looked at the food, then gave the matron a smile. "No, thank you."

The woman gave Briella a curious stare. "You're a stranger in Vorlik, aren't you?"

Briella nodded.

"I just picked these tyneberries this morning. And I'm sure you'll like the wine. Yarrow's famous for its vineyards, you know. I'm the innwife. If you need anything at all, please let me know."

"Thank you," Briella said, grateful for her concern. "I will."

Briella's stomach was empty and she felt lightheaded, but she was almost too tired to eat. She nibbled at the cheese and tyneberries and started to feel better. The brown bread was crusty but soft inside. The wine was good, light, as clear as water, and sweet. The innwife refilled the mug several times and brought a small honey cake when she filled the mug a second time. Briella almost turned down the sweet but changed her mind. The cake was lightly spiced with nutmeg and cinnamon and filled with raisins and dried cherries. By the time she'd finished licking the crumbs from her fingers, she was warm and relaxed and feeling much better. The innkeeper approached the table, smiling with satisfaction.

"Can I get you anything else?" he said, chuckling.

"No, thank you," Briella said, feeling content. "All I need now is a bath and a good night's sleep."

"Your room and bath are ready. If you'll follow me." The innkeeper led her between the puncheon tables and benches, up a narrow set of stairs, and to a small but spotless room with a fireplace. The red shutters on the west facing window were wide open, letting in the early afternoon sunlight and a gentle breeze. A quilt-covered bed, a lamp table, a straight-backed wooden chair, and a washstand with pitcher and basin were the only furniture. On the floor before the crackling fire was a deep, round wooden tub of steaming water. Folded towels and a cake of lavender soap lay on the chair beside the tub.

"My wife will be up soon to assist you if you wish," the innkeeper said.

"Yes, please," Briella said with a weary sigh.

He bowed and left.

Stripping off her cloak and dress, she laid them across the foot of her bed. She started to remove her dove pendant, but stopped, remembering her promise to Amaly. She kicked off her shoes, pulled off the rest of her clothes, and tested the water with her foot. Not uncomfortably hot. She inched her way down into the wooden tub.

The warmth soaked into her sore, stiff muscles, soothing even the bruised area on her arm where she'd fallen so hard when she'd passed out from the vision. Scrunching down as far as she could in the water, she closed her eyes. Her thoughts wandered to her grandfather, and she wondered if he were still alive. She thought of Cordwin and how his touch had made her heart race, of her own loneliness and the shadow of death looming before her. Shoulders sagged, and tears bubbled over her lashes.

"No," she said suddenly, pulling herself rigidly straight and wiping her eyes. "I won't cry. I won't! There's so much to do, and I don't know how much time I have to do everything."

She washed with the lavender-scented soap, then eased herself deeper into the comforting warmth. "Tomorrow is soon enough to begin. Tonight, tonight I'll rest and forget."

After soaking for a while, she wet her hair and scrubbed it vigorously, inhaling the soap's familiar fragrance. Lavender was Amaly's favorite scent, too. Her shoulders sagged; she bit her lower lip. The room was so quiet, so empty, so lonely. Her throat tightened, and she blinked back tears.

Suddenly, there was a knock at the door. Startled, she slipped deeper into the water. "Who is it?"

"The innwife. Could you use more hot water?"

"Yes. Please, come in."

The innwife pushed open the door then lifted a black, iron kettle she'd momentarily set down. Carefully carrying the iron kettle, its handle wrapped with a thick folded cloth, she shut the door with her foot and waddled cautiously toward the tub. The innwife smiled. "Ah, washing your hair. I'm just in time, I see. Bend your head, and I'll pour. Close your eyes so you don't get soap in them." She held the kettle over the tub.

"All right."

Briella bent her head down and shut her eyes. Suddenly, hot water scalded her head and shoulders, and she yelped.

"I'm sorry, I'm sorry!" the innwife exclaimed as she set the kettle on the hearth and examined Briella's burned skin. "My daughter said the water was just right, and I didn't think to check it myself! I'll fetch a salve to relieve the pain immediately."

Briella gritted her teeth and winced. "No, wait. In my cloak there's a salve that'll heal the burn quickly."

The innwife looked at her with a touch of skepticism. "I'd like to see that, since I'm a healer myself."

"In the left inside pocket is a dark blue jar."

The innwife searched inside the cloak until she found the jar, then brought it to Briella.

"Apply it sparingly to the burned areas, even the scalp," Briella told her.

The innwife pulled the waxed cork stopper from the jar. A wholesome fragrance of mint and wintergreen and something sweet yet subtle filled the air. The innwife gently smoothed a thin film of the salve on Briella's scalp, neck, and shoulders. Almost instantly, Briella felt a cooling numbness replace the painful heat.

After setting the jar beside the tub, the innwife touched Briella's shoulder. "I don't believe this," she said, awe in her voice. "The skin was fiery red only moments ago, and now it looks as if it had never been burned! I've never heard of a salve like this! Where did you find it?"

"Very far away," Briella said wistfully. She looked up at the innwife. "Would you like it?"

"Oh, yes!" the innwife said.

"It's yours," Briella said.

The innwife blinked. "Truly?"

Briella nodded.

"Baramay bless you!" The innwife put the stopper back in the jar. "Is it useful for other things than burns?"

Briella nodded. "Cuts, scraps, bruises, boils, any inflammation of the skin—healed in hours, instead of days. It prevents infection and scarring when applied within four days of the injury. Use it sparingly A little will heal most wounds."

"Wonderful! But it won't last forever. Where can I find more?"

"I may come back this way again and bring you some." Briella thought for a moment. She didn't want to take the chance that Cordwin might see her again. "Or a peddler woman named Old Mam might come to Yarrow someday. She'll have more salve and other medicines you might find useful."

"Thank you so much!" the innwife said. "What about your hair? Should you leave the salve on or can you wash it out now?"

Briella touched her scalp gingerly. "I can wash it now. It feels much better." She rubbed the lavender soap on her hair until she worked up a good lather and washed her hair again.

"I'll mix some cooler water to rinse this time." The innwife poured water from the kettle into the basin on the wash table, then added cold water from the pitcher and tested the water with her fingers. She frowned, added more cold water, and tested it again. "Just right. Whenever you're ready."

Briella gently massaged her scalp until it felt clean. "Ready."

The innwife slowly poured the basin of water over Briella's head while Briella ruffled her short hair until the soap was rinsed away. She squeezed out as much water from her hair as she could, then relaxed in the tub.

"Is there anything else I can do for you?" the innwife asked.

Briella smiled at her. "No, but thank you."

"Call if you do." The innwife smiled back, picked up the dark blue jar, and left.

Briella rinsed off and stood up, the rapidly cooling water splashing down her body. She wrapped her hair in a towel, wrapped another one around her body, then stepped from the tub and dried off before the warm fire. As she ruffled fingers gently through her hair, the fragrance of lavender spread throughout the room. The scent was comforting, but made her homesick. She'd never felt alone before. She missed Amaly even more than she'd imagined she would. And her grandfather—no, it hurt too much to think about him.

She slipped into a light sleeveless gown, climbed under the down-filled quilt and soft cotton sheet, and snuggled deep into the feather mattress. Although it was only midafternoon, she fell asleep.

She woke after the sun was well above the horizon, after a fitful night of dark dreams. The tub was no longer in the room. How it had been removed without waking her up, she didn't know. *I must have been sound asleep,* she thought.

Splashing cold water from the bedside basin didn't refresh her much. Her eyes still ached. She dressed quickly in the chilly room, repacked her few possessions, clasped on her cloak, picked up her pack, and left for the common room where the innkeeper greeted her.

"Good day, lady," he said with a bow. "I hope you had a restful night."

Briella gave him a weak smile. "The room was very comfortable."

"And what would you like for breakfast?"

"Just some porridge and milk," she said and sat down at the closest table, setting her pack on the stone floor beside her.

The innwife brought a large bowl of hot porridge, a pitcher of milk, a jar of honey, and a thick slice of fruited bread, toasted and buttered. Briella ate half of the porridge and a few bites of the bread. When she'd finished, she rose, picked up her pack, and sought the innkeeper to settle her account.

He smiled as she gave him the promised ruby. "I hope everything was to your liking?"

She nodded and returned his smile.

"Thank you, and come again, lady." He bowed graciously.

When Briella turned to leave, the innwife stopped her. "Here's enough food for a week and a small water skin," she said, handing Briella a sack. "Payment for the salve. I'll use it wisely, I promise."

"Thank you," Briella said as she slipped the sack's drawstring over her shoulder. "You are very kind. Watch for Old Mam the peddler woman. She might come through any day."

The innwife smiled. "Oh, I will."

Standing in the open doorway, Briella gazed out at the village. The midmorning sun felt warm on her face, but the air was cool and filled with the scent of freshly cut hay, charcoal and hot iron, and peppermint, and the clang of the blacksmith's hammer. Across the road from the inn, a young priest of Baygor walked between the chapel and a small house, his hair like spun copper, his arms filled with stalks of peppermint. Briella smiled and nodded to him.

He smiled back and said, "Baygor bless you."

"Thank you," Briella said and gave him a small curtsey, then walked across the wide dirt road that ran through the center of the village. "That's a lot of peppermint."

He grinned, making him look even younger. "Baygor's the patron of farmers and gardeners, and he's blessed me with a bumper crop."

"Do you have a few plants to spare?"

He laughed. "More than a few. You're welcomed to take as many as you like."

"I can't take any with me at the moment, but I'll be passing through again."

"I look forward to that. My name's Liska. Stop by anytime, and I'll make you some peppermint tea." He gave a slight bow, then crossed the street to the inn. Briella turned south and plodded through the bustling town. A brown-haired boy stopped hoeing a kitchen garden and waved to her. He looked to be a year or two younger than she was. A woman who must have been his mother cleared her throat and stared at him with a raised eyebrow and her fists resting on her waist. The boy grinned at Briella, shrugged, and went back to hoeing.

After she passed the last house at the edge of the village, she walked down the road until she was certain no one from the village could see her. Still, she looked over her shoulder to be certain, then changed into a dove and flew south.

Green fields of wheat were beginning to head. Herds of cattle and sheep grazed in wide pastures of clover and alfalfa and drank from the many creeks and small rivers that watered the land. Wild briars were heavy with small red tyneberries. Apple, plum, and pear trees were filled with small green fruit, promising baskets of ripe fruit in the fall. *This is a rich land,* Briella thought.

Farther south she flew over the great city of Tironza, where many men worked to rebuild fire-damaged buildings. Sadness filled her heart when she saw the remains of the Temple of Baygor. Grandfather had always said Tironza was the most beautiful city he'd ever seen. She hoped to see it when it was completely restored.

Beyond the city to the south were the Circle Mountains, gleaming in the noon sun. She flew westward through the mountain passes, searching for a place to build her house. Finally, she found a wide meadow hidden by ridges on all sides. Alighting, she changed to her natural form and surveyed the meadow. She sent her thoughts deep underground until she located a stream. "Yes, this is the perfect place for my home," she said to herself.

Speaking a word of power, she hollowed out a well from the rock to contain the water, then picking up a small pebble, held it in her outstretched hand and said, "From the earth where you were formed by Baramay the Creator, *tasrin amnia kreya barason.*"

Briella felt power leaving her. The pebble disappeared, and rocks and mortar appeared lining the well above and below the ground.

Opening her drawstring purse, she took out a small sapphire. She held it in her palm, raised her other hand above her head, and said, "From the earth where you were formed by Baramay the Life-giver, *tasrin amnia pyron barason.*"

The sapphire vanished from her hand as Briella felt her strength draining away. Blue crystal walls sprang from the ground, forming a broad kitchen and sitting room facing north, a bed chamber and a bathing room on the south side.

From another pocket she took a tiny silver box. Inside were five red seeds the size of large peas, nestled in black dust. She planted a seed with a few grains of the dust, and on the small mound she poured water from the water skin the innwife had given her. Stretching her hands to the sky, she called out, "By the power of Baygor the Preserver who gave all life the gift of offspring, *tasrin callum queesala barason.*"

A tiny, pale-green shoot pushed its way through the soil, stretching, reaching upward. Quickly, it grew into a hundred-foot callum tree with pale grey-green bark and silver-green leaves, which shaded the ground like hundreds of fans.

She entered the house and set down her pack and the innwife's sack on the sapphire floor. Opening her pack, she took out a wooden box, unhooked the catch, and opened the lid. Inside were bits and pieces of things. With a small piece of the substance needed, Briella created all the furnishings for her house. She selected several splinters of rosewood, and speaking the proper words, she created a table, chairs, and shelves for the kitchen. An oak shaving became a wooden sink. A bit of maple became plates, bowls, mugs, and spoons. A piece of baked clay became a brick-lined fireplace. A bead of iron became a kettle, a dipper, a knife, and pans. Another bead of iron became hearth hooks and a small cauldron.

A bit of oak became a bed frame, a wash table, and a chair. A bit of down and a piece of cotton thread became a feather bed mattress and pillows. Another length of cotton thread became sheets. Woolen yarn became a blanket. A small fleck of silver became a mirror. A bit of pottery became a pitcher and basin. A sliver of ash wood became a bathing tub. Finally, she created a wooden bench seat just outside the door and cloaked the house with the illusion of a thatched cottage.

Exhausted, she sat at the kitchen table and took out some fresh bread and dark honey from the innwife's sack. Late afternoon sun shown in the kitchen's northern window as she spread the honey on the bread and took a bite. The bread was soft and chewy and filled the growling emptiness in her stomach, but she was so tired, she almost fell asleep holding the last bite of bread.

Tomorrow, she thought as she stretched and groaned, *no, the day after tomorrow, I'll start the Wall of Warding around Vorlik. But tonight, I'll sleep.* She popped the bread in her mouth, pushed to her feet, shuffled to her bed, and stretched out on the mattress, not bothering to undress.

She rested most of the next day, although she created a wooden bucket, rope, and pulley for the well, and unpacked most of her possessions and stored them. She set out the items she'd need to cast the Wall of Warding, deciding to begin the Wall at the western border with Drambit. *That's the most dangerous site,* she thought.

Next, she inventoried the food left from the innwife's sack. The bread and cheese would last another four to five days if she were careful, the dried fruit maybe longer, but she'd need more, quite a bit more. She tapped her bottom lip with her forefinger thoughtfully. She'd have to buy some as she went. She knew she wouldn't have the strength to create more food after casting the Wall of Warding.

She refilled the sack, filled the water skin with fresh water from the well, and set them on the table next to the box of bits and pieces. In her pack she put her purse, a blanket, and her second dress. She went out to the callum tree and picked up all of the grey-green bark the tree had already shed and all the leaves that had fallen, then carried them inside. The bark she broke into pieces and stored in a small cloth bag. The leaves she crushed and mixed with peppermint oil, wintergreen oil, comfrey, woundweal, roborant, and aloe to form the healing salve. Finally, she used a bit of pottery to make small jars for the salve, filled them, then stowed them in her pack.

Enough for today, she thought as she sank down on a chair. *Now I have things to sell and trade for food. Time to rest and eat.*

She nibbled at some bread and cheese, a few dried apples, and drank some water. Feeling better, she wandered outside and sat on the bench.

The sun was dipping toward the tops of the western edge of the Circle Mountains. A chill breeze blew from the east, making her shiver. She rubbed her arms to warm up. *I'll plant an herb garden when I have the time,* she thought, *especially lavender. And some roses. Maybe a few fruit trees. It will be just like home.* She shivered again, and her eyes blurred with tears. "No, not like home," she whispered. "Never like home. But it will do."

She watched as the sun slipped behind the mountains, glowing orange and red and magenta, until the sky was dark and the stars glittered overhead.

10

Briella woke at sunrise. After a small breakfast, she put on her blue dress, stowed the last of her items in her pack, fastened on her cloak, and slipped her pack over her shoulder. Whispering a word of power, she changed into a dove and flew north from her house.

The city of Tironza was already stirring. She saw women hanging out clothes on lines stretched across alleys, and children running through streets, playing games. Smoke rose from chimneys, bringing the scent of fresh baked bread and hot iron. Horses clopped through streets, pulling wagons and carts loaded with goods from warehouses. Some headed south on the road through the Circle Mountains; some were going north toward Yarrow and Tarolin. Merchants hawked wares in Market Green, and craftsmen were already at work rebuilding the Temple of Baygor.

Veering west from Tironza, she followed a road that skirted a small river flowing at the base of the mountains. Farmsteads, encompassed by stone fences, dotted the land. She passed a few clusters of houses and a larger village, but mostly she saw solitary farmhouses, surrounded by fields of wheat, oats, and barley, and pastures with herds of sheep, goats, and cattle.

The sun had reached its zenith when she spotted a sizable town east of the mountains and just south of the crossroads of the road from Tironza and the east-west road that led into Drambit. Houses built of wood or limestone, many with small vegetable and herb gardens, lined the streets on the south end of town. A green and white chapel of Baramay faced west just south of the town square. Shops of all kinds lined the square. And in the center were stalls selling all sorts of food, trinkets, pottery, and hand-made baskets.

North of the square were warehouses where men loaded timber, blocks of stone, crates, boxes, and bags. Smoke belched from a blacksmith's shop to the clang of hammer on anvil. A cartwright replace a wheel on a wagon while two strapping boys steadied it.

It looks like a prosperous town, she thought, *and a good place to buy food.*

Alighting in a small copse of maple trees south of the town, she changed into the form of an old peddler woman leaning on a staff, a sack of goods slung over her shoulder.

She took one jar of salve from her sack, then hobbled along the wide rutted road leading into the town and called out, "Salves for sale! Healing salves for sale! Good for burns, cuts, scrapes! Soothes all kind of rashes! Salves for sale! Healing salves for sale! Soothes itches! Eases bunions! Salves for sale! Healing salves for sale!"

She passed the chapel of Baramay and wove through the crowd in the village square, past the Merchants Guild Hall on the east, past a jeweler's shop on the north edge of the square, hawking her wares. Several people stared at her curiously, but no one stopped to buy. Briella turned south on the western side of the square, but suddenly, she felt dizzy, cold, and off balance. She stumbled and fell to one knee, dropping the jar of salve and her staff.

A pair of strong but gentle hands grasped her arms. "Old mother, are you ill?"

Briella looked up into violet eyes in a young woman's face. "I, um, I felt dizzy."

The woman helped Briella stand. "Have you eaten today?"

"A little."

"Come with me." The woman picked up the jar and staff Briella had dropped, handed the staff back, took the sack from Briella's shoulder, and put an arm around Briella's waist to steady her. The woman led her to a two-story grey stone building bearing a sign painted with two trees and the words: Two Oaks Inn, Kam Winsell proprietor.

"Kam, I need a cup of water," the woman called as she eased Briella into a chair at a table near the door, then set Briella's sack on the floor and the jar on the table. "And a bowl of soup. And some bread." She turned to Briella. "You just rest for a moment."

Briella clutched the woman's arm. "I have little money to pay for the food."

The woman grinned at Briella. "Don't trouble yourself about it," the woman said. "Kam can afford a bit of food. I should know. I'm his wife." Tying a white kerchief over her light brown hair, she bustled off to the kitchen while Briella tried to catch her breath.

What happened? Briella wondered, holding her head as the dizziness subsided. She felt...exactly as she had when she first appeared at Cordwin's coronation: cold, dizzy, disoriented. What could have caused it?

The woman came back with a wooden tray heaped with bread, a large wooden bowl of soup and a wooden spoon, and a wooden cup of water. "Here, you eat your fill, and if you want more, just ask." She placed her hand on Briella's forehead. "Hm, no fever. You feel a bit cool in fact. You probably just need a good meal." The woman withdrew her hand, and Briella looked up at her.

"Are you a healer?" Briella asked.

"Yes, I studied the healing arts after I wed," the woman said. "Innwives are often called on to tend injured travelers as well as townspeople. My name's Maiya, and I'm married to the most generous innkeeper in Vorlik." She looked across the room at a young man with nut-brown hair and a round face, and she winked at him. "I have to keep an eye on the purse strings or he'd give everything away." She grinned at Briella. "Of course, once in a while is all right. You're a stranger to Leflin, aren't you?"

"Yes. I'm called Old Mam."

"Then you don't have a place to stay, do you?"

"Uh, no," Briella said, "not yet."

"Well, Old Mam, this is the best inn in town." She laughed and rested her slender hands on her narrow waist. "Of course, this is the only inn in town, but we're still the best. There're several rooms available at the moment. Too early in the year yet for our busy time. The trade caravans are just starting to come in. I could let you sleep in one of the small rooms for the night."

Briella shook her head. "I can pay for the room...or maybe you'd be interested in a trade." She picked up the jar from the table. "This is a healing salve unlike any you've ever seen. It's yours for a night in a bed."

Maiya took the jar from Briella, pulled out the waxed stopper, and sniffed the salve. "Hm," she said thoughtfully. "Mint, wintergreen, roborant." She sniffed the salve again. "Woundweal, aloe." She looked puzzled. "And something else, something unfamiliar."

Briella smiled. "My secret. Maybe someday I'll tell you. But you'll find this is a good salve for any kind of cut, scratch, or rash, any kind of skin problem. It'll heal burns in half the usual time, and if you apply it right after the injury, there's no scarring."

Maiya looked skeptical. "No scarring?"

"You'll see," Briella said with a wink. "Just try it."

"All right. You eat and rest, and I'll get one of the rooms ready for you." She hurried off to the kitchen.

The soup was loaded with chicken, carrots, barley, turnips, and onions, and seasoned with parsley, oregano, and rosemary. The bread was a hearty brown bread with chewy crust. Briella ate all the meat and vegetables from the soup, then dipped bread in the bowl to soak up the broth. *I was hungrier than I realized,* she thought. *Maybe that's why I was dizzy. Maybe I really did need to eat something.*

Maiya came back carrying a pitcher and refilled Briella's mug with water. "Can I get you anything else?"

Briella shook her head. "No, but thank you. I feel much better now."

"Would you like to lie down for a while?"

Briella hesitated. "Maybe. Yes. I could use a nap."

Maiya picked up Briella's sack and offered an arm to lean on. Picking up her staff and taking the proffered arm, Briella stood up and let the innwife lead her past the kitchen and down a short hall to a small room on the ground floor.

The room was just big enough for a narrow bed, a wash table, a chair, and a small hearth, but it was clean and warm. A narrow window, just to the right of the head of the bed, looked out on the town square. A candle sconce hung on the wall near the door.

Maiya set the sack on the floor, settled Briella in the chair, then pulled down the dark brown comforter on the bed. "Rest for now. You might want to close the shutters against the noise and light."

"Thank you," Briella said, feeling surprisingly fatigued.

Maiya smiled and left the room, closing the door behind her.

Briella took a deep breath. "I need to buy food, but I'm just too...drained. The stalls will still be open in a few hours. I'll sleep just an hour or two."

She stood slowly and shuffled to the window to close the shutters. Shadows were still very short, just past midday. People wandered from stall to stall in the town square while merchants enticed passersby to stop and consider the merchandise. On the far side of the square was the Merchants Guild hall. A caravan was assembled in front of it, several wagons with teams of matching white horses. Hulking men loaded crates, bags, and boxes in the open top wagons, then spread tarpaulins over them, tying them down securely.

The lead wagon was wooden, enclosed, with a small window on the side. Beside the wagons rode a blond young man on a pale horse that had strange blue-green eyes. The young man gave orders to the teamsters, who hurried their pace. Soon the drivers were on the wagon seats, reins in hand. The blond man held up his hand, and the wagons started to move toward the crossroads at the north end of town. Just before the caravan moved out of sight, the blond man frowned and glanced across the crowd, then looked straight at the inn, straight at Briella, with cold blue eyes that widened suddenly. His lips moved, and he drew a symbol in the air.

Suddenly, Briella felt cold and dizzy. She felt as if she were choking, she couldn't breathe, and her vision turned dark with yellow spots. She clutched the edge of the window to keep from collapsing, but her legs felt so weak, she could barely stand. Finally, she knew what had caused the weakness: a Sorcerer! Quickly gasping out a word of warding, she raised a shield around the room. The oppressive dizziness started to subside, her strength began to return slowly, and warmth flowed through her body again.

A Sorcerer in Vorlik! She'd never been near a Sorcerer, hadn't expected to face one here, and hadn't even known she would react to the presence of one. Now she was certain that Sorcerers had been behind the attack on Vorlik. *He* must have been at Cordwin's coronation! That's why she had felt dizzy!

The caravan and the Sorcerer moved out of her line of sight. The wagons were going west, and she didn't have the strength to follow the Sorcerer, not yet. He had been at Tarolin Castle two days ago. He was probably heading for the Drambini border. The Wall of Warding was more important than ever now. She staggered to the bed and sank down on it, feeling exhausted.

I have to start the spell as soon as I'm able. I can't wait for another day. She glanced at the window, her eyes narrowed. *I'll keep my disguise up, but the Sorcerer won't catch me unprepared again!*

She lay down, not bothering to take off her shoes and cloak or to slide under the comforter, and fell asleep.

A knock on the door wakened her. Making sure her disguise was still in place, Briella sat up slowly. "Come in," she said.

The door opened, and Maiya smiled as she entered. "I let you rest as long as possible, but it's late afternoon and I thought you might not want to sleep too long," the innwife said. "Are you feeling better?"

"Yes," Briella said, blinking her eyes until she could see clearly. "Yes, I am. Much better. In fact, so much better I think I'll travel until at least nightfall today."

Maiya's eyes widened, and she frowned. "Are you sure? There's no place to stay within half a day's walk, and the nights can be quite chilly in spring."

Briella stood up and nodded. "I'll be fine. And I'll be back this way again."

Maiya raised an eyebrow, then shrugged and sighed. "All right. But please take care of yourself."

"I will." Briella picked up her sack and staff, and followed Maiya back to the main room.

Maiya ducked into the kitchen and came out holding a small bundle tied up in a blue cloth. "Just a few meat pasties, one of the few apples left from last year's crop, and piece of pumpkin cake," she said as she handed the bundle to Briella.

Briella smiled at her. "Bless you for your kindness and concern."

"Baygor watch over you, Old Mam."

Briella nodded. "And you."

She walked out into the town square, hobbled toward the jeweler's shop, and peeked in the only window. A scarecrow of a man sat behind a counter polishing a sapphire, then he carefully set it in a gold ring. The man looked up as Briella walked through the open door. His greenish-brown eyes scanned her appearance. "Baramay's blessings, old mother. Can I help you?"

"Yes." Briella pulled out her purse and chose a tiny ruby. "Would you be interested in this?"

The man took the ruby from her and looked at it closely. His eyes widened, and his mouth dropped open a bit. "Yes, this is—" he halted, cleared his throat, then said, "this is moderately valuable stone. I'll give you . . ." he scrunched up his thin lips, then continued, "two silver towers for it."

"Two silver pieces! Hah! It's worth at least two gold pieces," Briella said.

"Two gold castles? I wouldn't give my own mother two castles for that! Six silver."

"One gold. That's fair."

"Fair for you. Not for me," the jeweler said. "I have to make a profit to stay in business. Ten silver. That's half a gold, and more than fair."

"Make it fifteen silver and it's yours."

"Done." The jeweler set the ruby down on the counter, pulled out a wooden box from under the counter, opened it, and counted out fifteen silver coins stamped with a tower and placed them in Briella's hand. "And if you come across any others like this, I, uh, might be interested."

Briella smiled and poured the coins into her purse. "I'll remember."

She left the jeweler and went to a farmer's stall. There was little available this early in the year, but she bought onions, beets, peas, radishes, a small waxed round of hard cheese, and some dried tyneberries. Adding them to what she had in her pack and what Maiya had given her, she thought she'd be able to eat for a week or more. Now to start the Wall.

She walked past the north edge of town until she came to a small cluster of trees. Slipping behind them, she changed into a dove and flew toward the mountains.

The western road was deserted, and the sun was nearly touching the mountain tops. The Sorcerer had long ago crossed into Drambit. At the base of the mountains she flew over a long wooden building cloaked in evening shadows. Two soldiers in blue and gold uniforms stood guard before the main door, while a dozen other guards lined the road leading into the mountains. Pairs of guards practiced with swords in the yard north of the building. And east of the barracks was a carefully stacked tower of wood and small brazier, guarded by two soldiers.

The road ascended into the mountains and was just wide enough for two wagons. A narrow stream bordered the road, flowing down to Vorlik's grassy plains. Maples, poplars, and oak trees covered the lower slopes of the mountains. Higher up, picket pines replaced the deciduous trees. At the top of the pass, only mosses and lichens covered the ground, and snow still clung under jutting rocks. The road descended to the west, twisting and turning, into the flat barren Drambini plains.

Briella alighted on the road at the top of the pass and changed to human form. *This is where I'll begin the Wall,* she thought.

She searched both sides of the road until she found two smooth faces of rock facing each other. Taking a small dagger from her pack, she jabbed her index finger. Blood began to ooze out. She drew a zigzag pattern on both rock faces with her blood, then stood in the center of the road. Holding her dagger above her head and squeezing three drops of blood onto the rock- and-dirt road, she said, "By the power of Baramay who made the land and mountains and all that is, *tasrin queesala vardigen barason!*"

The air in front of her shimmered, as if an iridescent curtain hung across the road from rock face to rock face and as high as the mountain tops, then vanished from sight. She changed to a dove and flitted to the top of the slope to the north. Choosing another rock face, she opened the barely clotted wound on her finger, drew the zigzag design on the rock, and spoke the words of the spell. A curtain shimmered again, connected to the first part.

She continued creating the Wall of Warding bit by bit moving northward until by sunset she was worn out. Too weary to create a fire, she ate one of the pasties Maiya had given her and drank a bit of water. She rubbed some salve on the cut on her finger, then huddled under her cloak and gave a quiet laugh. *And I thought making my house was tiring.*

In moments, she was asleep.

Each morning she began weaving another section of the Wall. Each night she collapsed, sleeping wherever she finished the day's work. When she ran low on food, she flew to the nearest village or farmstead and traded her salves, silver, or healing services for food. At the end of a month she'd covered the entire border of Vorlik. She smiled as she wove the last threads of force together at the Drambini border. No army could march through the passes now; no invaders could sneak through the mountains. The Wall would bar them from entering Vorlik.

She rubbed her neck and tight shoulders. Her headache almost kept her from feeling her weariness. She had barely enough strength to change into a dove and fly home. Numb fingers fumbled with the door handle. Legs trudged across the floor, as if they were weighed down with lead. Her knees buckled, and she fell across her bed.

For nearly a week she slept, mind drained, body exhausted. Even dreams didn't penetrate her sleep.

Sunlight, tinted blue by the crystal walls, seeped through her closed eyelids. Birdsongs and insect chirps disturbed her rest. She opened her eyes, blinked, and tried to swallow. Her mouth was too dry, and her tongue seemed glued to her palate. Hunger growled in her stomach. Slowly, she rolled to her side, then pushed up on shaky arms. Her legs quivered as she stood. Every step was uncertain.

Finally, she reached the kitchen table and sank onto a bench. A half full water skin and her sling pouch lay on the table where she'd dropped them on her return. She dragged out her last two rounds of twice-baked bread and a string of dried apples, and started eating. Between frantic bites, she gulped the stale, room-temperature water.

Suddenly, she stopped, still clutching a piece of bread. There was a metallic taste in her mouth. Her jaws tightened; her stomach churned. She staggered toward the front door, but didn't reach it. She fell to her hands and knees, then gagged and vomited. It had been too long since she'd had solid food. *I should've known better than to eat so fast,* she thought, a sour acid taste in her mouth.

She crawled to the door, pushed herself to her feet, and sagged against the frame. The late afternoon sun cast long shadows eastward. The air was cool and scented with spring flowers. Crickets started singing in the meadow. Briella inhaled slowly, exhaled slower, until her stomach felt steady again.

Vorlik is safe now, she thought. *At least as long as I live. I can only protect them until...Bren comes.* She choked at the thought of her death and tore the piece of bread in half. "It isn't fair!" Her words echoed back at her, and she gave a bitter laugh. "Ah, but who said life was fair?"

She pinched off bits of bread and scattered them for the snow sparrows then went to clean up her floor.

That night Briella changed to a dove and flew to Tarolin Castle. She wanted to tell Cordwin that the Wall of Warding was complete, that his land would be safe from invasion. Or maybe she just wanted to see him again. Maybe both. She couldn't be certain.

Just as the full moon reached its zenith, Briella sighted the silver-grey towers. She circled the castle, searching for Cordwin, seeking his presence within the stone walls. There—she found him in his room. She flew through his open window, touched the smooth floor soundlessly, and resumed her own shape.

Cordwin lay asleep on his side, facing toward the window, his head resting on one arm. Dark hair fell back from his face, revealing thin brows and long, dark lashes. His chest was bare except for the eagle amulet which glittered with magic. A blanket covered him from the waist down. He looked so young, so sad, so beautiful.

Briella knelt beside him, a strange warmth growing in her chest. Her heart beat faster, and her breathing quickened. Even a month away from him hadn't lessened his effect on her. She lightly touched his cheek. He stirred but didn't wake.

Bending close to his ear, Briella whispered, "My lord, the Wall of Warding is complete. Your people are safe. Sleep peacefully now. I'll watch over you. As long as I live, no one will harm you."

Cordwin woke suddenly, as if aware of another presence. Startled, Briella froze. She knew he saw her, and for a moment, she was glad he did. She wanted to feel his arms around her again, gaze into his eyes, and feel his hand holding hers. Was this what it felt like to recognize a life mate?

Stop this! she thought. *You can't walk that path. Leave. Fly away. Quickly!*

Instantly, she spoke a word of power, transformed into a dove, and flew through the window. Before she turned south, she glanced back at his window. He stood there, moonlight glowing on his bare skin, and called her name. She almost forgot how to fly.

She had to see him again, even though reason told her it was foolish and dangerous. She knew she would come to him again.

11

Sunlight struggled through the dust-clouded window as Paxell paced impatiently in his study. He forced himself to concentrate on his campaign against Vorlik. Other thoughts tiptoed at the edges of his mind, images of Dannee, sweet and painful. He squeezed his eyes shut, trying to drive her ghost from his heart. She was gone, gone forever.

Stopping before the window, he gazed down at the stone houses of Abasettown, huddled like beggars along the south road. He studied the road that led from the town to the eastern mountains, wishing he could travel that road and ride triumphantly into Vorlik. But he didn't feel very triumphant.

He turned from the window and gazed at the ancient leather-bound book lying on his desk, the book of Sorcerer's spells. He'd learned much from it, gained power beyond any he'd imagined. Yet he hadn't gained what he had hoped: control of Vorlik. He'd lost the only one he'd ever loved: his wife. Now he had an infant daughter and the heir of the house of Vorlik on his hands.

"Greetings, Lord Paxell," a low voice whispered.

Startled, Paxell whirled to face the door. "Grimmin! I didn't know you were back." His eyes narrowed, surveying the man who blended with shadow and stone. He walked around his desk. "What news do you have from Vorlik? Tell me quickly. I haven't had any news since they closed the borders."

Not replying at once, the shadowed man moved into the room with panther stealth, halted two feet from Paxell, and pushed back the hood of his grey-blue cloak. A golden-haired young man with innocent, blue eyes gazed back at Paxell, but the Drambini lord read consuming fire and indeterminate age in those eyes. The spy had served him well and been well paid for his service. Still, Paxell didn't think he'd trust Grimmin at his back.

"My lord," Grimmin said with a bow that was just enough to be civil, "Vorlik has a new ruler. Cordwin has taken his brother's place."

"But my army—what happened?"

"Cordwin led Vorlik's forces since Clevil had been ill. The mercenaries were completely overwhelmed. The survivors fled south, back to Beltrin."

Paxell's mouth fell open; his eyes widened under raised brows. "Even the Tanavari?"

"The reports say they declared they wouldn't surrender. They never do. They fought. They died. Every tattooed one of them."

Paxell clenched his fists. "Hound of Darkness! All those soldiers gone! And I still don't rule Vorlik!"

"If I may continue," the spy said with cold arrogance.

Infuriated, Paxell grabbed Grimmin's cloak at the neck. In the deadly cold voice Paxell used to intimidate others, he said, "You'll be more respectful when addressing me, or you'll be missing your head."

"And you," Grimmin said quietly," should be less quick to anger."

Paxell glanced down to see the point of a dagger poised a hair's breadth from his chest. A shiver ran down his back. He released Grimmin's cloak and retreated a step.

Grimmin sheathed his weapon, a hint of cold satisfaction glinting in his eyes. "As I was saying, when your army was destroyed, Cordwin discovered they were merely the diversion from the true objective: Tarolin Castle. Cordwin arrived to find the castle burning, the inhabitants murdered, Clevil and Ellisa dead, and their son missing.

"Cordwin was ill for days—"

Paxell interrupted him. "But he not dead," he said, seething.

"No," Grimmin said, his eyes fixed on Paxell, "he recovered, unfortunately. During his illness, Captain Daikin, Cordwin's cousin, closed all borders. I couldn't get out of Vorlik until today, but I'd learned something that I thought would interest you."

"What?" Paxell asked, his head cocked.

Grimmin stared out the window, frowning intensely. "I was at Cordwin's coronation. Briella, great-granddaughter of the Wizard Casslin," Grimmin almost spat out the name, "appeared and swore loyalty to Vorlik. She said she would place a spell, a Wall of Warding, around the entire border to prevent any army from entering. I crossed into Drambit just before she began the spell."

Grimmin paused, his eyes half closed. "I doubt you'll have another chance to take Vorlik." He looked askance at Paxell. "At least as long as *she* is alive, and I hear that Wizards have very long lives."

Anger and frustration flowed through Paxell like liquid fire. He clenched his teeth and pounded his fists on his desk. "Damn her to Barsallin's hell!"

Grimmin inhaled sharply and stared at Paxell. "One does not use that name...casually," he said, his silken voice now winter cold.

Paxell stiffened, and his skin went cold. He'd named the Hound of Darkness, god of evil, god of the Sorcerers, the god feared by most lands but worshipped only in Drambit. Few dared to say the name openly. "But how can I fight a Wizard?" He paced across the room. "Casslin stopped my grandfather from taking Vorlik a hundred years ago, and now Casslin's great-granddaughter is stopping *me*. Hound of Darkness take all Wizards!"

"Tasrin," Grimmin whispered, touching the fingertips of his left hand to his forehead, then to his chest.

"What?" Paxell asked. He'd never heard the word before.

Grimmin just looked at him, then a slow smile bowed his mouth and he shook his head. "It will take years to rebuild an army. The Wizard's Wall of Warding will prevent any attack—even if you had the troops." Grimmin paused. "Oh, one more thing. When Cordwin arrived at Tarolin Castle after it was attacked, he found the old nurse who cared for Clevil's son. She was still alive, and before she died, she told Cordwin the child had been taken by raiders from the north."

"Does he know—" Paxell started to ask, then halted.

"Know what?" Grimmin asked, his voice quieter than owl's wings. "That you have Clevil's son?"

Paxell's eyes flew open wide with surprise.

"You do have the heir to Vorlik, don't you?"

Paxell cleared his throat. "How could you know that?" he whispered.

"I know." Grimmin leaned over the desk and casually touched the cover of the ancient book on the desk, tracing the inscribed symbols with his index finger and whispering words Paxell didn't understand. Grimmin looked up and gave the lord a slow smile. "You needn't worry. No one else knows. The boy would be useful if he were twenty years older, but a baby is nothing but a nuisance." He walked toward Paxell until they were barely a hand's breadth apart. "If you'd like me to dispose of the boy," Grimmin said softly, "there'll be no trace for anyone to find, not even a Wizard."

Paxell backed away from the spy, shivering, walked to the opposite side of the desk. What *could* he do? He braced his hands on the desk on either side of the magic book and stared at the tome. There might be an answer in it, if only he could find it, could learn to control the power. A spell, a weapon, something he could use to break the power of the Wizard. If it took the rest of his life, he'd find a way to destroy the Wizard and conquer Vorlik.

"I'm not certain what I'll do," Paxell said thoughtfully, "but I'll keep Clevil's get. He may be useful, perhaps not now, but someday. He could be the key to conquering Vorlik." He turned toward the eastern window, staring at the mountains, and crafting a plan. "I'll raise him as I would my own son, train him, and mold him to my will. And I have a daughter. If there's no other way, I'll marry her to the boy. Once they're married, he'll die unexpectedly, leaving Miria to rule Vorlik—under my guidance, of course."

"Of course," the spy said wryly. "And if I may serve you further, you merely need to ask—for the usual fee."

Paxell smiled. Grimmin was dangerous, but Paxell admired the man's skills grudgingly. Going to a large trunk behind his desk, Paxell opened the heavy lid, withdrew a bulging leather pouch, and tossed it to Grimmin. "I'll need information about the

Wizard, how many troops Vorlik still has, and Cordwin's attempts to find the child. See if a ransom or a trade would be acceptable, but don't draw attention to yourself."

"I'm always discreet," Grimmin said with a cold smile. "I won't be going back to Vorlik for a long time, but I have friends who will gather information for me. I'll return to Drambit five months from now, when the harvest is nearly complete." He paused. "His name is Bren."

"What?"

"Clevil's son—his name is Bren. It might be wiser *not* to call him that. If you're going to keep him, then keep him hidden as much as possible. Someone in the castle might have a loose tongue. Call him by another name until you can be certain of his loyalty."

Paxell nodded, admiring Grimmin's craftiness.

"If you have no objections, I'll take my leave." Grimmin bowed slightly. "Look for me in the autumn."

Pulling his hood over his face, the shadowy figure blended into the grey-blackness of the stairwell and silently disappeared.

Paxell stared after him, wondering how Grimmin could look like an honest young merchant and be trusted in every land. A most intriguing and useful man, but dangerous. Paxell shuddered, then turned back to his desk.

Paxell caressed the black and silver tome. *The real power is here,* he thought, *waiting for me to discover it. This is how I'll conquer Vorlik. But why stop there? I can control the world if I learn the power of this book. Nothing will be beyond me! Nothing!* His vision blurred. He blinked back tears that threatened to spill down his lean face. *Nothing except returning Dannee to life.*

Bitterly, Paxell stared out the window at his bleak land. He spotted a small caravan of wagons rolling through Abasettown. A hooded figure, mounted on a pale horse, rode to join it as the wagons drove south.

Paxell turned back to his desk, opened the yellowed pages, and began to study the scarlet words of dark power.

Five months passed rather quickly as Drambit's bleak spring became a sweltering summer, then cooled to a temperate autumn. Paxell provided nurses for his daughter Miria and the boy called Pyccis. The nurses kept the infants, as well as Callas' son Malbar, from the lord's sight. Paxell couldn't look at Miria without remembering Dannee. The wounds in his soul bled fresh pain whenever he saw his daughter.

He concentrated on the black and silver book, searching daily for something to destroy the Wizard and a way to defeat Vorlik. Finally, he found one, but not exactly what he'd hoped to find. On a yellowed page near the back of the book, in spidery crimson letters, was written the following spell:

DAGGER OF SLAYING

Paxell drew his fingers lightly down the page. "This," he whispered, "this may be what I've been searching for." He continued reading.

"To make a Dagger of Slaying, first obtain a dagger of the finest quality steel, worth at least one hundred vaelas of gold. The blade must be etched with the name of the one to be slain and with the word of power: *rahala*, meaning death. Heat the blade until it glows red-gold then pour fifty drops of your own blood on the blade while saying,

"By the power of Barsallin, god of darkness, be the purpose of this blade to shed the blood of the one whose name be written upon it. Death to that one! *Tasrin roh Canzet utana*!

"Finally, the dagger must be immersed in a mixture of powdered ovrin horn, blood from a newborn fawn, and spittle from a sea snail.

"The Dagger of Slaying must not be wielded by the maker, but by one who has never slain a man and who believes that the intended victim is worthy of death. He must say the name of the victim while holding the dagger. Only then will the dagger seek its intended target."

Paxell tapped the page thoughtfully. *I'll have to commission the best craftsman in Tukkus to make the dagger. How much is a vaela? Where will I find powdered ovrin horn? What is an ovrin? And where will I find someone to wield the knife, someone I can trust, someone who hasn't killed before, someone who truly believes the Wizard must die?*

He paused, his mind racing like thunderclouds. "Bren!" he said breathlessly. *He would be the perfect choice, if he weren't so young. Of course, with a Wizard guarding Vorlik, I may have to wait until Bren's grown so he can kill her. A long time to wait. Still, if it's the only way to destroy the Wizard and the Wall of Warding,* he smiled to himself, *I can be patient.*

A silken voice interrupted Paxell's thoughts. "Greetings, Lord Paxell."

Instantly, Paxell slid his dagger from its belt sheath and simultaneously stood to face the intruder.

Grimmin stood in the doorway, hood thrown back from his young face. His hands rested lightly on his narrow hips. "I've returned, just as I said I would." He glanced at the open book on the desk. "I see you've been studying. Have you learned anything... interesting?"

Paxell sheathed his dagger and relaxed his stance slightly. "I've learned many things since you last were here. But have *you* learned what you were paid to learn?"

Grimmin nodded and sauntered toward the Drambini lord. "Vorlik's forces were only slightly diminished by your mercenaries. The five Guards are still strong enough to win a war against Drambit, especially considering how decimated your army is. Rumor says the Wizard lives in the south, though no one seems to know exactly where, not even Cordwin."

Paxell's hands tightened into fists at Grimmin's insolent tone. *Someday the man will pay for it,* Paxell thought, *someday very soon.*

"Cordwin's searched all the surrounding lands—except, of course, Drambit, he wouldn't ask you for water if he were dying of thirst—for news concerning his nephew. He even contacted your father-in-law Lord Merrik for information. Bren of Vorlik has vanished from the face of Baramayan." Grimmin smiled, but it was a humorless smile.

"I wouldn't suggest a ransom or trade," the spy continued. "Cordwin's in no mood for either. He'd probably make war on you at the mere hint you had his nephew, and right now you couldn't win a war against a group of Vorlikian children. Your choices are to keep the child hidden for future use or," Grimmin's eyes sparkled like sunlight on snow, "kill him now."

Paxell sighed. "I thought so."

"I'd do it for you," Grimmin said quietly, rubbing his fingers against his palms, his blue eyes glittering like sunlight on ice. "I'd kill him for you right now, without payment. The heir of Vorlik would vanish forever, and we'd both be avenged against the lords of Vorlik."

"Both?" Paxell asked, astonished. "I know why *I* hate Vorlikians. Drambit and Vorlik have been enemies since the beginning of time. Why do *you* hate the house of Vorlik?"

Grimmin was silent for a moment, his eyes narrowed. "It is a very old grievance."

Paxell turned and scowled thoughtfully out the window. There would be immense satisfaction in the death of the heir of his ancient enemy, but Cordwin and the Wizard would still have to be dealt with. "No," he said at last, "I suppose I'll keep him alive since he fits into my plans."

Grimmin was silent for a while, then said, "As you wish. Is there anything else you want from me?"

"Yes." Paxell turned back toward the spy. "How much is a vaela?"

"A vaela?" Grimmin raised an eyebrow, and a smile barely tugged at the corners of his mouth. "It's an ancient measurement equal to . . ." he paused and glanced at the ceiling, "two Peltik gold castles."

"Have you ever heard of ovrin?"

"They are similar to cattle but have very long horns, white to dun colored hide, blue-green eyes, and the temperament of a mad dog. They live in the south beyond lands inhabited by civilized men and never range nearer than the Rensle Steppes. Wild tribesmen hunt ovrin as part of their coming-of-age rites. I've seen horns and hides several times in the markets of the seacoast cities."

"What about a sea snail?"

"Certainly, in the port of Hixus. It's considered a delicacy by the rich merchants there. After tasting it myself, however, I can't understand why."

"I need an ovrin horn and a live sea snail."

Grimmin looked curious. "Why would you need such things?"

"You are not paid to question. I'll pay you well as always. I also need a dagger made of the finest steel found in Tukkus, at least two hundred castles worth."

"I can get these things for you, but it'll take some time." Grimmin gave him a sly glance. "The ovrin horn will be the most difficult. It may take more than a year, possibly two. The sea snail won't be difficult to find, but keeping it alive may not be easy. The dagger's no problem. I'll bring them to you when I have them all. Of course, payment must be in advance."

"Of course," Paxell said, an edge to his voice. He took a small pouch from his waist. Opening the leather thong, he counted out twenty flawless emeralds into Grimmin's outstretched hand.

Grimmin chose one and held it up to the sunlight streaming in the window. "The emeralds of Drambit – perfect in color and clarity." He turned and gazed at Paxell intently. "You must want the items very much to part with such wealth." He shrugged and dropped the emeralds one by one in his own pouch. "No matter, you'll have what you want. Long life to you, Lord Paxell." With a slight bow, he slipped from the room.

Now I must wait, Paxell thought. *I'll study and plan and be patient. And I'll shape Bren – no, Pyccis to be my instrument of destruction. I have to ensure that he'll trust me completely. But will I tell him? What can I say that will make him do whatever I ask?*

He paced the room several times, then leaned against the window frame and stared out at his kingdom. *I'll tell him...that . . .,* he smiled slowly, *that a witch killed his parents, and he must avenge them. I'll be his savior, his guardian, his father, and I'll instill such hatred for the Wizard, he'll beg me to let him kill her.*

He turned back to the desk and the open book of spells. Carefully, his fingertips caressed the yellowed parchment. "And Vorlik will be mine," he whispered.

12

Cordwin reined in Moon Shadow at the top of the rise. Daikin pulled his horse to a halt beside his cousin. Cordwin gazed out at Tironza a mile ahead in the center of the southern plains. The city shone in the late morning sunlight like a pearl set in the center of emerald fields.

"Beautiful," Daikin said softly. A breeze from the south blew the hood of his cloak back from his wavy copper hair.

Cordwin just nodded and pushed his hood back from his face. He found it hard to believe a large part of the city had been destroyed by fire almost five years ago. Two mounds on the northern edge of the city were the only visible reminder of the tragedy, but those mounds were covered with flowers. The citizens of Tironza remembered the dead, and so did Cordwin.

A small cottage stood now between the barrow ground and the road. Beside the cottage was a flaming brazier and a beacon tower of stacked wood, guarded by two soldiers in the yellow and gold uniform of the Southern Guard. Both the tower and cottage had been built as part of a warning system Cordwin had established running from the four border crossings to Tarolin Castle.

Cordwin gazed at the tower and nodded to himself. *Vorlik will never be attacked again without warning,* he thought.

Moon Shadow shuffled impatiently, and Cordwin sighed deeply.

"Barg's Breath, Cord," Daikin said with a laugh, "how can you look so melancholy when you're going to the Autumn Fair in Tironza? Cheer up, cousin. Time to drink and laugh and forget."

Cordwin chuckled and shook his head, the breeze ruffling his dark hair. "Daik, how can I be melancholy when I'm with you? And I know exactly why you came along with me." He held up a hand when Daikin started to reply. "Don't bother protesting that it's for my protection."

"But there have been several attempts on your life," Daikin said, his freckled face looking innocent.

"Not for two years."

"But you are the lord of Vorlik, and you can't go anywhere without a bodyguard. An entire squad would have come with us if we'd told anyone else we were leaving the castle, especially for the chance to go to the Autumn Fair." Daikin grinned, and his green eyes sparkled. "And the Fair is neutral ground. Even if you came face to face with the Drambini lord himself at the Fair, you'd both be bound to honor that. Where could you be safer than at the Fair?"

Cordwin nodded. "Anyone could have been my bodyguard. You just wanted to enjoy the dancing, drinking, and women — especially the women — at the Fair."

Daikin grinned wider. "The counselors will be furious, especially since we sneaked out of the castle to go peasanting."

Cordwin laughed out loud. "I am glad for your company, though. Come on. Let's enjoy the Fair." Clapping knees lightly against his horse's sides, Cordwin rode toward the city, his cousin keeping pace with him.

Tents and wagons covered the grassy area west of the city, the same place the healers had set up their tents five years before. Tironza had many inns, but there were never enough rooms during the Autumn Fair. Many people simply camped outside the city in the comfortable autumn air.

Cordwin and Daikin reached the city gates, but soldiers wearing the yellow and gold surcoats of the Southern Guard stopped them. "Sirs, you can't bring–" a sergeant started to say, then halted, his eyes growing wide as he stared at Cordwin's face. Bowing his head, the sergeant clapped his fist to his chest and said, "Your pardon, my lord, but there's no room to ride in the city. The streets are too crowded."

"But what can we do with our horses?" Daikin asked.

"You can leave them here," the sergeant said. "We will tend your horses ourselves."

Cordwin stroked Moon Shadow's neck, then said, "All right. Take good care of him." He dismounted and handed the reins to one of the guards. Daikin did the same.

"We will guard them as we would guard you, my lord," the sergeant said, fist to chest again. "May you enjoy the Fair."

Daikin winked at his cousin, nodded toward the city, then the two of them pulled their hoods to shadow their faces and entered the gates.

The week-long celebration was the greatest event in the northern lands, and the day was absolutely perfect. The sky was clear blue and dotted with cotton-boll clouds. A southern breeze was warm but carried a hint of the coming winter winds. Trees displayed leaves of apple-red, corn-gold, melon-orange, and cinnamon-brown. The air carried whiffs of smoke and spices, fruits and breads, flowers and flummeries.

Merchants and traders from as far away as Hixus on the southern sea flocked to Market Green to bargain for the best merchandise at the many stalls and wagons. People prayed at the beautifully restored Temple of Baygor the Preserver, giving thanks for the bountiful harvest. Food was plentiful, and the wines were the best in many years. Puppeteers delighted children. Laughter echoed through the streets and alleys, and people clapped while young couples danced a circle dance to the music of pipes, drums, lutes, and harps.

Cordwin breathed deep as he looked around Market Green, then sighed. "It's good to escape for a time."

"And the Autumn Fair is just what you need," Daikin said with a grin. "Here you aren't the lord of Vorlik. You're just another visitor. You can enjoy yourself without anyone annoying you." He scanned Cordwin from head to foot. "No one could tell that you're more than you appear. Just keep your hood up."

Cordwin nodded. He'd carefully dressed in a simple white shirt, brown vest, black pants and hooded cloak, and had worn only his silver eagle pendent and the silver-and-emerald ring Briella had given him. He hoped no one else at the Fair would recognize him.

"I need time to relax, to laugh." Cordwin closed his eyes and listened to the joyful sounds of chaotic voices and music. His heart felt lighter than it had in weeks, maybe in months, and he felt slightly wicked for leaving the castle for a bit of fun. But only slightly wicked. "I know the counselors will make me pay for this escapade with long lectures, but at the moment I don't care. It's time to celebrate life."

Daikin grinned and clapped Cordwin on the arm. "That's the spirit!" He glanced over Cordwin's shoulder.

Cordwin turned to see what had caught Daikin's attention. A blond-haired woman, whose eyes twinkled with sapphire mischief, smiled at them. Cordwin turned back to Daikin and said, "I see you've already made plans to celebrate."

Daikin grinned at Cordwin and clapped him on the back. "Well, I think I'll stay here for a while," Daikin said. "I'll meet you at Olney's Inn for supper. Enjoy yourself!" He strolled toward the woman.

Cordwin chuckled and wandered away. As he wove through the crowds, he began to feel almost content, relaxed, and peaceful. Just as he passed a pastry stall, two slender arms clasped around his neck, and a pair of soft lips kissed him so soundly and unexpectedly, he was breathless by the time the kiss ended.

"Welcome to the Autumn Fair," said an adolescent girl, her arms still locked around Cordwin's neck. There was an impish gleam in her violet eyes.

Cordwin grinned back at her. "You're one of the Fair Greeters."

"Yes," she replied, using one hand to adjust the wreath of ribbons and fall flowers on her wheat-colored hair, but keeping her other arm around Cordwin's neck.

"And I'm Fair Game."

"Of course. I gave you a Kiss of Greeting, so you owe me a dance. What's your name?"

Cordwin hesitated, uncertain what to say since he was incognito. "I'm...Cord of Yarrow."

She smiled and said, "Well, Cord of Yarrow, Tressie of Tironza claims her dance."

Tressie clutched his hand and almost dragged him to an area in the center of Market Green that was roped off by garlands of flowers. Half a dozen other couples had begun in a circle dance. Cordwin and the girl broke into the chain and joined in, skipping and whirling to the lively tune. By the time the musicians ended their piece, Cordwin and Tressie were flushed and laughing.

"I thank you, Cord," she said with an exaggerated curtsey. Her wreath of flowers fell to the ground, and she swooped down to pick it up. She set the wreath back on her hair and grinned. "May you enjoy your time at the Fair."

He returned her bow, breathless but happy. "I thank you, Tressie, fairest of the Fair Greeters."

She giggled and slipped away.

Thirsty from the dancing, Cordwin bought a small mug of fresh cider. It was sweet yet tangy and delightfully cool. He returned the mug, then ambled around the perimeter of Market Green. The buildings on the east and west sides of the town plaza had been refaced with new limestone and set with lintels and sills of polished granite. The Temple of Baygor was the most impressive of the restored buildings. Eight columns of polished blue marble held up the overhanging roof and the great dome covered in gold leaf. A stained glass window, showing golden Baygor creating the stars and the sun, had been set above the main entrance. *No one could tell it was ever destroyed,* he thought, smiling. *The craftsmen rebuilt it even more beautiful than before.*

As Cordwin reached the western side of the plaza, he saw a crowd had gathered beside the shop of Shiffin the Jeweler. Curiosity tugged at Cordwin.

"What draws such a crowd?" he asked a brown-haired youngster, who was trying to worm his way through the tight pack of onlookers.

Frowning at Cordwin, the boy tried to squeeze between two men. "It's the blind storyteller, and I can't get close enough to hear her!" He circled around until he found a space to wedge his way through.

Pressing closer, Cordwin wove his way almost to the front row of the standing adults and strained to see what attracted their attention.

Seated on a wooden crate and surrounded by a semicircle of eager children was a grey-cloaked figure. A hood shielded the face within from view. A sun-baked hand gripped a sturdy staff. The crowd grew quiet as a resonant voice spoke from the hood.

"What shall it be today, good listeners? A tale of battles and heroes? Of good and evil? Of Wizards and Sorcerers and mortal men? A tale of love?" The story teller halted, sitting as still as a stone. She turned her head from side to side as if listening or searching for something until she was facing Cordwin. She cleared her throat and began again. "Or perhaps a tale of all of these things? And if the tale pleases you, perhaps your generosity will show your approval. Hear now the tale of Timmree the Wizard and Cavolin, Lord of Vorlik.

"Long ages ago, before your grandfather's grandfather's grandfather was born, the Sorcerers were banished to the south, the Wizards hid themselves in the north, and Cavolin was lord of Vorlik. He was tall as a picket pine, fierce as a Formian bear, and agile as a mountain deer. His grey-blue eyes shone with kindness and wisdom, and his smile spoke of his honesty. His black hair swept back from his lean, golden face like waves on a stormy sea. He was the best swordsman in Vorlik and could gentle any horse with love. His people adored him, and his enemies feared him."

The storyteller lowered her voice until she could barely be heard above the music. "But the Sorcerers envied Vorlik, craving the land that had once been their own. But they feared the Wizards and the wrath of Baygor, feared that the god would strike them down as he had destroyed the first Sorcerer Canzet. So the Sorcerers decided to use Vorlik's greatest enemy, Drambit, to conquer the land."

Children booed, women shivered, and men cursed at the mention of Vorlik's ancient foe.

"The Sorcerers sent Armir and Lorasa, two of the most powerful of that evil race. They came secretly to Malikai, lord of Drambit, appearing to him in his own room while he was in bed. The lord of Drambit felt the Sorcerers' presence before he saw them. Malikai was frightened by the men with hypnotic eyes and honeyed voices.

"'Do not fear us, lord of Drambit,' Armir said softly with a smile. 'We've come to offer you your heart's desire.'

"Malikai pulled the covers up to his pointed chin and asked, 'And what's that?'

"Lorasa smiled and said, 'Why, we'll help you conquer Vorlik.'

"Malikai sat up instantly and asked, 'But how? Do you have a great army or spies to aid me?'

"'No,' Armir answered slowly, his smile widening to a grin. 'But we have magic.' He moved closer to the Drambini lord and whispered, 'We are Sorcerers, Malikai. We are kinsmen. Our blood flows in your veins. Would you like to see Vorlik crushed, its lord groveling at your feet? Would you like the wealth of that land to be yours?'

"Malikai swallowed hard as he thought of the farmlands, the herds and flocks, all the riches of Vorlik he coveted. 'Yes,' he said, 'I want to be lord of Vorlik. But why are you willing to help me? What will you gain?'

"'We wish to live in Vorlik when you've conquered it,' Lorasa said.

"'Just you two?' the Drambini lord asked with his natural skepticism.

"'Oh, no,' Armir replied with a smile, 'all the Sorcerers.'

"Now Malikai was no fool, so he asked, 'But how long will I be lord of Vorlik if all the Sorcerers are living there?'

"'You may rule Vorlik any way you wish,' Lorasa said with a dismissive wave of his hand. 'It matters not to us. We only want to destroy the house of Vorlik and reclaim the land that was once ours.'

"Malikai was uncertain about the bargain, but he wanted Vorlik so much, he didn't care how he obtained it. 'All right, I agree,' he said. 'Tell me your plan.'

"Beginning that night, Malikai and the Sorcerers began to plot Vorlik's destruction."

Again children booed and men cursed.

"At the same time in the Wizards' Vale lived Timmree, daughter of Pollemos. Her hair was golden as sunlight, and her smile was warm as a southern breeze. Her eyes sparkled like sun on the sea, and her lips were as pink as a wild rose.

"The night Malikai made his pact with the Sorcerers, Timmree had a dream, a vision of evil coming to Vorlik. Waking suddenly, she ran to her father's room. 'Father, something terrible is happening in Vorlik. We must help them. Please, let me go there.'

"'No!' Pollemos said, his eyes hard with resolve.

"Timmree was startled. 'But why?' she asked. 'How can you refuse to help?'

"'I'm not refusing to help,' he said, turning away from her. 'I just won't allow you to go. Someone else will do as well.'

"'But Father, I have to go! The dream told me I must!"

"When Pollemos turned back to his daughter, his face was filled with anguish. 'I can't let you go. If you leave the vale...' He put his arms around her and held her close.

"Timmree felt her father shaking, and she was frightened. 'What will happen?' she asked. 'What will happen if I leave the vale?'

"Very slowly, Pollemos pulled away from his daughter. He gave her a sad, hopeless smile and said, "I had a vision, too. I saw that if you leave the vale, you will never return. I will never see you again."

Timmree was torn by the terrible choice she had to make. Either she had to leave her father forever or she had to allow Vorlik's destruction. Now Timmree loved her father more than anyone else in the world, but she couldn't let the people of Vorlik suffer if she could prevent it. Her eyes filled with tears as she said, 'Father, I have to go. In your heart you wouldn't want me to make any other choice.'

"Pollemos hugged her tightly, and tears filled his own eyes. 'You're right,' he said. 'You must help.'

"Quickly, Timmree prepared for her journey.

"Just before she left, her father came to see her. He handed her a small box. 'Take this with you,' Pollemos said.

"Timmree open it. Inside was a silver and emerald ring.

"It was my father's. He'd want you to have it now." Pollemos hugged her tightly. "Please, take care of yourself. Remember I love you. I'll always love you." Releasing her, he quickly left the room.

"Timmree's eyes blurred with tears as she watched him go. 'I'll always love you, too, Father,' she whispered as she closed the box and slipped it into a pocket. Turning to her open window, she changed into an eagle and flew from her home. Riding the currents of the winds, she arrived at Tarolin Castle two days later.

"Cavolin was in his council chamber along with his captain and lieutenants when she flew through an open window and changed back to herself right before him. He leaped to his feet and drew his sword.

"My lord," she said as she knelt before him, "I am Timmree, daughter of the Wizard Pollemos. I've come to help you, for I've had a vision of evil. War's coming to Vorlik, war and death. Drambit will invade your land today."

"She looked up at the lord of Vorlik and did not move. She was like a bird transfixed by a snake, but she wasn't afraid. She felt as if a part of her heart had suddenly come to life. At that moment she knew why her father hadn't wanted her to go, why she would never return to the vale." The storyteller paused for a few moments. "She knew from the moment she saw Cavolin, she would love this lord of men and would stay with him, that he was her life mate.

"Cavolin stared at her just as astonished and mesmerized as she was. He no longer felt the sword in his hand nor heard the voices of his lieutenants. All he felt was the comforting warmth that filled his chest, the surging of life through his entire being. He walked to her, took her hand, and kissed it. And he knew he would love this Wizard all his life.

"At that moment, a messenger knocked and entered the room. 'My lord,' he said as he saluted, 'Drambit is marching an army into the western pass!'

"Cavolin glanced from the messenger to Timmree. 'Sound the battle horn!' he ordered. 'Assemble the troops and prepare to ride!' The officers saluted and left.

"Cavolin helped Timmree to her feet and gazed at her intently. 'My lady, thank you for your warning. I'll thank you properly when I return from battle.'

"Timmree's heart filled with fear. 'My lord,' she said, 'I must go with you!'

"'My lady, I can't let you face such danger,' he replied."'But I'll be able to help you,' she said.

"He pressed her hand to his chest and said, 'No, I...couldn't bear it if you were hurt.'

"She smiled at him and said, 'My lord, I've less chance of being hurt than do any of your soldiers. In fact, I might prevent injuries. Please, let me help. That's why I came to Vorlik.'

"At last, he agreed. He took her to the courtyard and ordered his mount and a horse for Timmree. Together, they rode at the head of the troops. Several hours later, they reached the western plains beyond the town of Leflin.

"Blood stained the green fields as Drambini clashed with Vorlikians. The dust of thousands of horses' hooves clouded the air, and the sound of striking steel echoed through the mountains and valleys. Horses cried as they fell; their riders screamed, pierced by sword and shaft. Watching the battle from the Hills of the Axe, Cavolin and Timmree feared Vorlik's forces were overmatched and outnumbered.

"As the Vorlikian troops retreated before the Drambini army, Timmree sensed evil, but not from the invaders. Her vision blurred, and she saw Armir and Lorasa sneaking through the mountains just south of the pass. Turning to Cavolin, she said, 'My lord, Sorcerers have come to Vorlik. I must face them.'

"Before Cavolin could protest, she changed into an eagle and winged to the spot she'd seen in her mind.

"The two Sorcerers had reached the eastern side of the mountains when Timmree found them. Landing in the snow and returning to her own shape, she called to them. 'Leave this land, servants of the Hound of Darkness! I won't let you enter Vorlik unchallenged!'

"Armir laughed. 'Do you think you can defeat both of us? We'll kill you and leave you for carrion.'

"'You can try,' Timmree said, 'but you won't succeed.'

"'We'll see,' Lorasa replied with a smug grin.

"Above the mountains lightning split the sky. The ground shook, and trees toppled like twigs. Globes of red, green, and yellow fire lit the sky and burst into fiery sparks that fell to earth. Timmree struggled to defend herself, and at the same time, strike at the two Sorcerers. Armir became an eagle and tore at Timmree's face. Summoning a raw north wind, she sent it toward the bird, battering it from the sky. Lorasa threw a globe of fire which shattered against Timmree's wall of ice. Armir attacked as a snow leopard, raking claws down her side. Timmree countered as a Formian bear, her powerful paw pounding against his head, knocking him unconscious.

"Timmree felt searing pain on her back, fire burning through the thick fur and leathery hide. As the Wizard-bear rolled in the snow to put out the flames, Lorasa cast small, red seed at Timmree, which burst into flames on her arm. Howling, the wizard struck the ground with her huge paws. The earth trembled, throwing Lorasa on his face in the snow.

"Armir stirred and changed into a crow. He fled the mountain, heading south to the Sorcerers' haven. Timmree returned to her normal form and flung a stiff breeze after him to speed him from Vorlik.

"At that moment, Timmree felt a dagger, as cold as ice, pierce her side. Lorasa had crept up behind her while she'd been concentrating on Armir. Timmree faced the Sorcerer, her hands held high, gathering green fire in her palms. Lorasa reciprocated, red fire swirling about his hands. Arcs of ruby and emerald strove against each other as Timmree and Lorasa strained to maintain their power. Weakening from her wound, the Wizard faltered for a moment, and the red fire almost touched her hands.

"Drawing deep from her soul, from her love of life, she called the last of her strength into a final effort. Green drove the red back to Lorasa's hands, then engulfed the Sorcerer. He twisted and writhed, vainly trying to escape the green globe. His flesh hardened and grew cold. When the green flames disappeared, a granite statue stood where he had been. Timmree was faint and weary, but she transformed into an eagle and flew toward the battle.

"Cavolin's forces drove the Drambini army back toward the border. When Malikai no longer had felt the Sorcerers' power, he'd decided he didn't want to fight alone. Sounding retreat, the Drambini forces fled west, pursued to the border by a portion of the Tarolin and Western Guards.

"Timmree alighted near Cavolin, transforming from eagle form. She knelt, even though she was hurt. 'My lord, I've defeated the Sorcerers who entered Vorlik.'

"At that moment, she collapsed. Cavolin jumped from his horse and lifted her in his arms. Fear gripped his heart as he mounted, holding her close to his chest, and galloped for Leflin. Reaching the physicians' tent, he shouted for help. The chief physician and two aides ran to take Timmree from Cavolin's arms.

"'Will she live?' he asked anxiously. 'Can you save her?'

"'I don't know,' said the physician as he examined the burns, slashes, and knife wound. 'She's lost a lot of blood, and I've never treated a Wizard before.'

"Cavolin gripped the physician's arm and pleaded, 'You have to save her. She must live!'

"The physician nodded and took her to a bed. He tended Timmree for days, and all that time Cavolin never left her side. When she opened her eyes again, the Vorlikian lord was sitting beside her, holding her hand.

"'My lady,' Cavolin said with a relieved sigh, 'I've been so worried...I thought...I was afraid...' He halted, wanting to say so much but not knowing how. 'Timmree, Vorlik owes you so much, and so do I. I have no way to repay your great kindness. I can only say that I love you and offer you my heart and my ring. Marry me and be the lady of Vorlik—and my wife.'

"Timmree hesitated. She knew if she accepted him, she'd never be able to leave Vorlik and she'd never see her father again, just as Pollemos had said. But as she gazed up at Cavolin, the choice was simple. 'Yes, I'll marry you,' she answered.

"Their wedding was a great celebration. Wine flowed like rivers. The dancing lasted seven days and nights, and everyone in Vorlik rejoiced.

"So the blood of Wizards and men was mingled in the lords of Vorlik only. Cavolin and Timmree lived a long and happy life and had many children. And there's still a hint of magic in their descendents.

"And somewhere, high in the Circle Mountains, is a stone statue, worn by wind, rain, and cold, that was once a Sorcerer."

The children cheered, and the adults clapped. Some threw coins at the storyteller's feet. Cordwin tossed a coin, too, the only gold one. The hooded figure set her staff down beside her and bent to the ground, groping for the money.

Cordwin pushed his way through the departing crowd. "Please, let me help you," he offered and knelt to help collect her earnings. "I haven't heard the story of Timmree and Cavolin since I was a boy. You tell it with such..." he searched for the right word, "passion. Yes, that's it. Such passion." Standing, he poured the recovered coins into the teller's hands, soft hands which trembled at Cordwin's touch.

The woman let the coins spill onto her lap. Taking one of Cordwin's hands, she touched the ring he wore. "It's her ring, Timmree's ring. Only one person would wear that ring." The teller remained quite still. "You're Lord Cordwin, aren't you?"

"Y-yes, I am," he replied, astonished that the blind woman had recognized him, and even more astonished she'd known he was wearing the ring. "How could you know?"

She held open Cordwin's hand and returned the coins to him. "Here, give these to the poor of Vorlik."

"No, you need..."

She shook her head and cupped her hands around his. "No, other people need the money more than I do." Her voice quivered even more than her hands did. She withdrew her hands and picked up her staff, leaning to her left against the jeweler's shop.

"If that's what you want," he said, "I'll gladly see the money's given to the orphans of Tironza." He poured the coins into a pocket on his trousers.

"Thank you, my lord." The teller's voice was a whisper but intense. Raising her head, she seemed to look straight at Cordwin.

A flash of light caused him to squint. The sun reflected off an amulet that had peeked from beneath the grey cloak, a silver amulet shaped like a dove. His heart beat faster, and he inhaled sharply.

"Briella," he said breathlessly.

13

Cordwin sank to one knee before Briella and took her right hand. It felt small in his hand, as soft and warm as the first time he'd held it

"I thought I'd never see you again." He tried to glimpse her face, hidden in the shadow of the hood. "But I hoped. I hoped."

"I...I didn't know you were coming to the Fair," she said, her voice barely audible. "I've tried to stay away from you as you asked--"

"No, please, don't," he said, cringing. "I'm so sorry I said that. Truly, I didn't mean it. Please, forgive me." He raised her hand to his lips and kissed it chastely. Even that light kiss made his heart dance.

"My lord," she said, her voice trembling almost as much as her hand, "my lord, there's nothing to forgive. You had suffered so much grief and loss. I should thank you for your courtesy and concern when I collapsed."

"If you would thank me, my lady," he said, "then please, let me escort you at the Fair."

"I...I, uh, have to leave," she said, "now. I need to go." She tried to pull her hand away from his, but he held hers firmly.

"Don't go," he pleaded. "Please don't go."

"There are things I must do...people who need help." Her voice sounded strained, as if she couldn't breathe. "I...I can't stay."

"Briella," he said earnestly. Even her name quickened his pulse. He held her hand against his chest and gazed at her fervently. "My lady, you and I will always have more things to do than there's time to do them. But this moment we're at the Autumn Fair, and it's a glorious day. Let us take a little time to walk among the people we both serve. For just one day let's be simply Briella and Cordwin, and enjoy the Fair as everyone else is."

She gazed at him for a while, then nodded slowly. "All right," she said, "just for today." She paused, then cleared her throat. "I have something for you."

"For me?" Cordwin said, surprised.

She set her staff down, reached inside her cloak, and pulled out a bundle as long as her forearm, wrapped in red velvet and tied with a golden cord. "I finished making this for you only a few days ago. I don't even know why I brought it with me. I didn't imagine that I'd see you today." She held it out to him.

Reluctantly, he let go of her hand, dropped to both knees and sat back on his heels, then took the bundle. He untied the cord and draped it over his arm, then slowly unrolled the red velvet on his lap. Inside was a recorder, carved from a reddish wood with a scent of oranges, polished but not lacquered. He brushed his fingertips slowly down the smooth wood from the narrowed mouthpiece to the slightly flared end, and the recorder seemed to warm at his touch. Placing his fingers on the evenly spaced holes, he put the mouthpiece to his lips and blew steadily. The sound was a clear as a summer morning yet as intense as a winter storm. Cordwin had never played an instrument with a tone so pure or so achingly beautiful, as if Baramay herself were singing through the recorder. The sound wrapped around him like a warm blanket on a cold night, comfortable and comforting.

Amazed, Cordwin put the recorder back on the velvet, touching the wood again, then rewrapped it carefully and retied the golden cord. He held the bundle to his chest and looked straight at Briella. "My lady," he whispered, so astonished he could barely speak, "I want...this is...how can I thank you for so precious a gift?"

Briella was silent for a few moments, then said, "Promise me something."

"Anything you ask," he said.

"Play for me."

Cordwin's eyes grew wide. "Play for you?" he stammered. "That's all? You want me to play for you?"

"Yes."

He stared down at the cobblestone pavement and swallowed hard, suddenly self-conscious. "I'm not very good."

"Yes, you are."

He looked up at her, surprised. "How do you know?"

"I've heard you. Many times."

"How did you...no one could..." Cordwin's face felt too warm. "I was all alone. No one else was awake."

"I was," she said. "Many nights I've sat on your windowsill and listened to you. Your music is so beautiful but often melancholy. Promise that you'll play a song for me, just me. Something lighthearted."

Cordwin nodded. "I promise," he said, slipping the recorder inside his shirt, close to his heart, "but promise me you'll dance with me, here, today."

She sat very still for a moment, then said, "A blind woman wouldn't dance."

"But you're not really blind."

"No, but those who see me believe my illusion."

"Then banish the illusion. Be as you are," he said, taking her hand again, "as you were the first time I saw you."

"I can't," she whispered. "Not here. Not where people would see me change."

"But why wear an illusion at all?"

"To protect me from my enemies."

"Enemies?" Cordwin gaped at her astonished. "Who would want to harm you?"

"Sorcerers," she whispered. "I have to be on guard against them always. I can't let them see through my illusion."

Cordwin glanced around the plaza. People surged around them, some of them looking askance at the two of them. "Then let's go somewhere you *can* change."

She didn't speak for a long time. "Let me lean on your arm and lead me to a place where no one will see us."

She picked up her staff and stood. Cordwin rose, moved to her right side, and placed her hand around his arm. He led her cautiously through the crowds to the main avenue running south. They turned down a narrow street in the southern part of the city, then entered a shadowed alley far from the crowds and curious eyes. Looking both ways to make certain no one could see them, he turned to her and said, "Now you can change."

She spoke a word Cordwin didn't understand, then she pushed the hood back and unclasped her cloak.

Cordwin stood staring at Briella, speechless. He hadn't seen her for five years, but she was more beautiful than he remembered. Her eyes were as blue as the clearest sapphires. Skin smooth and with the blush of health. She wore a simple form-fitting sky blue bodice over a white blouse with loose sleeves. Her full skirt was of the same shade of blue as the bodice. White moons and silver stars were embroidered around the hem – the symbols of Baramay and Baygor. Soft brown slippers showed beneath her hem. Her only jewelry was the silver dove pendant. Golden hair brushed her shoulders, bangs almost touching her light brows. Her lips were like deep pink rosebuds.

Cordwin's chest felt tight, and he could hardly breathe.

She took off her cloak, folded it into a tiny square the size of her hand and slipped the cloak into a pocket on her skirt. She leaned her staff against the wall of the building, spoke a few quiet words and passed her hand over the staff, and it vanished from sight. She turned back to Cordwin.

"Briella," he said, savoring her name, "let us go to the Fair." He held out his hand to her.

Deliberately, she placed her hand into his, glancing at him nervously. He entwined his fingers tenderly with hers. *How warm her hand feels,* he thought. *The lightest touch of her hand delights me in ways I never knew.*

Her eyes widened, and her hand quivered in his grasp, but only for moment. She gave him a tentative smile. "Lead on, my lord."

"Cordwin," he said softly, stepping close to her and gazing into her eyes. "My name is Cordwin."

She hesitated, then said, "Lead on, Cordwin."

They walked back to the center of the city.

Market Green was ringed with poles draped with ribbons and garlands of dried flowers and brightly colored leaves. Vendors called to passersby to try the pastries and pasties, tarts and cakes, or buy the finest cloth from Hixus or furs from the Formian lands. Merchants hawked jewelry and ribbons, knives and tools, and wooden toys for children. And in the center of the Green by the fountain were pipers, drummers, and players of lutes and viols, and couples danced a jig to the lively music.

Ducking beneath one of the garlands, Cordwin and Briella wandered past a puppet theater surrounded by a crowd of laughing children. So many people filled the Green, Cordwin had to lead Briella single file toward the Temple of Baygor.

A grey-haired priest stood beside the temple door, wearing a blue and gold surplice embroidered with silver stars, and he smiled at the crowds. Burn scars twisted down one side of his face. Cordwin halted, staring at the priest for a moment, then cleared his throat. "Baygor's blessings, priest." He bowed his head.

The scarred priest turned to Cordwin with an open smile. "Baygor's blessing, to you and your lady."

"I have a gift for the temple." Cordwin took out the money Briella had given him from his pocket. "I hope this will help the orphans." He poured the coins into the priest's lean hands.

The priest stared at the coins, then looked up at Cordwin with glistening eyes. "This will help a great deal." He held up the gold coin, the one Cordwin had given. "And this – this will buy an apprenticeship and a good life for two of our children." A tear trickled down the scarred face. "Baygor bless you."

Embarrassed, Cordwin glanced at Briella, then said, "Thank you, but this is from the blind story teller."

The priest gazed at both of them, then smiled. "Then Baygor bless her as well." He bowed deeply and went back inside the temple.

A light breeze brought the scent of hot bread, and Cordwin's stomach growled. He looked over at Briella. "Are you hungry?" he asked.

At that moment, her stomach growled, too. She smiled and nodded her head.

He laughed and led her toward a stall covered with a brightly colored awning.

A robust man stood behind a wooden table and called out, "Pasties, beef pasties, fresh from the ovens of Olney's Inn. Hot savory pasties, two for a copper. Eat them while you see the Fair. Pasties, hot fresh pasties. Come and buy, come and buy."

Cordwin opened his coin pouch and took out a copper coin stamped with a gate design. "Two pasties, sir." He handed the coin to the merchant.

"Klaymar's my name, merchant of Beltrin, and two pasties it is," the man said. Quickly, he wrapped two golden half-circles of stuffed bread in clean corn husks and handed them to Cordwin. "Still warm, so be careful," the man said with a wink.

Cordwin handed one to Briella, then took a bite of his own. The tender bread crust was sprinkled with crushed salt. Inside, small chunks of beef and potatoes were seasoned with sage, onion, and pepper. The filling was so hot, it burnt Cordwin's tongue. "Ach!" he said, panting out the heat.

"Told you it was hot," Klaymar said, his chestnut eyes gleaming merrily. "Some sweet cider would cool your tongue, and I just happen to have some right here. Only a copper a mug."

Cordwin frown at him a moment, then laughed. "You did warn me the pasties were hot. Let's have two mugs of cider then." He took two copper coins from his pouch and handed them to the merchant.

The man pocketed the coins, then filled two wooden mugs with cider from a large keg. "You'll have to drink it here, unless you'd like to buy the mugs as well," Klaymar said as he handed Cordwin the mugs.

Cordwin stared at the man a moment, then looked at Briella. She smiled and rolled her eyes. Cordwin handed her one of the mugs, then he looked back at the man and asked, "How much for the mugs?"

"Well, these are hand carved from the finest maple with a polished bone handle," Klaymar said. "I'd let them go for five coppers. Each."

Cordwin gaped at the man, then burst out laughing. He counted out ten copper coins and handed them to the merchant. "You'll go far, Klaymar."

"I hope so," the man said, grinning. "I have a wife, a daughter, two sons, and another child on the way."

Cordwin held up his mug and grinned. "Baygor grant you a healthy child, and Baramay grant you prosperity."

The man smiled. "And Baramay grant you happiness and good fortune." He paused and glanced at Briella. "But I see she already has."

Cordwin gazed at Briella. *Yes,* he thought, *she has.*

Briella blushed and began sipping her cider.

"Enjoy the Fair," Klaymar said. "Come back again if you get thirsty. I'll refill your mugs for free."

Cordwin nodded. "We'll take you up on that later." He and Briella left, eating pasties and drinking the cool, sweet cider.

They wandered through the rows of stalls, looking at ribbons, jewelry, pottery, and fine cloth. There were merchants selling knives, shoes, belts, and hats. Bakers sold buns filled with dried fruit and confections made of ground figs and raisins then rolled in ground almonds. An old man sold wooden toys, flutes, recorders, and lutes. Farmers sold honey combs, bushels of apples and pears and pumpkins, and heaps of winter radishes and turnips. A matron sold dried flowers, scented dream pillows, and fragrant creams, as well as culinary herbs. And music floated above all.

Cordwin leaned close to Briella. "Shall we have our dance now?"

She smiled and nodded.

Cordwin led her back to Klaymar's stall. "Refill these and hold them for us," Cordwin said, placing the mugs on the table. "We're going dancing."

Klaymar grinned and winked at Briella.

A new dance had just begun when Cordwin and Briella arrived at the roped off area. They joined in with the hop-skip step and a twirl and clap. Briella laughed when Cordwin bumped into a couple next to them. He grinned and said, "I'm out of practice."

At that moment she stepped on his foot. "So am I," she said, laughing.

When the jig ended, the musicians began a square dance. With a bow and a curtsey, the dance began. Cordwin felt freer than he had in months, dancing with Briella. When she moved on to the next partner with the next verse, he kept glancing at her while trying not to step on his new partner's feet. When the final verse brought Briella back to him, he was delighted.

They danced a reel and several more circle dances, then went back to Klaymar's stall for another cider. The merchant grinned and sighed as he gazed at Cordwin and Briella.

"Ah, to take a turn at the dance," Klaymar said. "It's been too long. But I have to tend to business. Have a dance for me."

Cordwin finished his mug of cider and wiped his mouth on his sleeve. "Oh, we will. We will. And we'll be back for more cider." He took Briella's empty mug and set both mugs on the counter. Taking her hand, they hurried back to the dance.

The sun was westering and shadows grew long while Cordwin danced with Briella until he was sweating and breathless. The dance ended with his arm around her waist and her arm around his waist. Her face was flushed. Her golden hair was windblown, and a lock of hair was stuck to her damp cheek. She laughed breathlessly.

"I haven't danced in a very long time," she said.

"Neither have I," Cordwin said. He gazed into her eyes and felt as if he were held captive by them. A warm sweet ache bloomed in his chest. "Briella, I would dance with you for the rest of my life." He brushed the strand of hair from her face, then touched her cheek.

Briella leaned her cheek against his palm and closed her eyes for a moment. "Oh, Cordwin," she whispered, "I would--" Suddenly, she stiffened and turned pale. "I can't," she whispered, shaking her head and pulling away from him. "I can't. I couldn't do what I have to do, not if I stayed with you. I'm not Timmree."

"I don't understand!" he said. "What do you mean?"

She melted into the crowd before Cordwin could stop her.

"Wait!" he called. "Please, don't go!" He tried to push through the throng, but there were so many people. He crashed into a couple, stumbled, called a quick apology, but kept running. He spotted her heading for the side street where they'd been before, and he followed as fast as he could. "Please wait!"

She ducked into the alley where she'd changed. Cordwin ran as fast as he could until he reached the entrance to the alley. Briella was slipping on her cloak and fastening it at the throat.

"Briella, don't go!" He ran toward her. "Please don't leave me!"

She gazed at him for a moment, then said, "I can't be what you want me to be. I couldn't protect you or your people if I did. I'm sorry. So very sorry." She grabbed her staff, whispered something, then changed into a dove and flew to the sky on a gentle breeze.

Cordwin leaned against a wall in the deepening late afternoon shadows, breathing hard, and stared up between the buildings to the sky where Briella had gone, a cold ache filling his heart.

14

Briella alighted outside Tironza, beside a tree far beyond the edge of the tent city, and changed back into her normal shape. Her heart beat so hard, her chest hurt. Her breath came short and fast, and her face felt too warm and damp.

She hadn't expected to see Cordwin. She still felt his touch as he'd poured coins into her hands, still heard his voice and saw his dark eyes gazing at her, still felt his arm around her and his hand touching her cheek. His nearness troubled her, yet she wanted to be close to him again. A feeling filled her heart, sweet and warm, and the feeling frightened her. *He* frightened her. He didn't understand what he was asking of her, what she would have to give up. And she'd have to break her promise. She couldn't do that, not even for him. No matter how much she wanted to.

Twice, assassins had come through the Wall of Warding, bent on killing Cordwin, but she hadn't felt them cross into Vorlik. Only a feeling that some danger was near Cordwin had warned her to protect him. The Wall of Warding would keep out armies, but one lone assassin could sneak through undetected. She hadn't realized that when she'd created the spell, and she had no remedy for that flaw.

If I made Timmree's choice, she thought, *if I gave up what I am, how could I keep him from harm? If anything happened to him because I was powerless to protect him, I would die.*

She leaned against the tree, her heart still racing. *What if I didn't make Timmree's choice but stayed at the castle to watch over him? Could I do that? Could I see him every day, be near him every night without wanting more? No. My heart couldn't bear that. And Wizards are always chaste until they wed. I have to stay away from him if I want to be true to my promise. Lady Baramay, give me the strength to keep my vow.*

Confused, she changed back into a dove and fled west from Tironza to the village of Selmdin.

The sun was sinking toward evening as she alighted and changed into Old Mam the peddler, bent and grayed. "Potions for sale," she called as she hobbled down the deeply rutted road through the center of the village. "Cures for fevers. Cures for colds. Healing salves and herbal tonics."

A few people came from their houses, staring curiously.

"Come and see. Come and see." She waved one hand and patted her bulging leather bag, slung over her shoulder, with her other hand.

"It's Old Mam," said a brown-haired woman named Pella.

Adults hurried to surround Briella, smiling. Children tugged at her robe for attention. She traded medicaments for food and supplies until the sun began to sink behind the Circle Mountains.

"Do you have a place to stay tonight?" Pella asked.

Briella smiled and said, "I sleep under the stars most nights."

"Stay the night with us. We have an extra bed, and the nights are getting chilly."

"Thank you, and Baygor bless you."

The evening was happy and chaotic. Pella, her husband, five children, her mother, and her husband's two younger brothers all crowded on benches around a table, but they gave Briella the only real chair in the house. A fire crackled in the hearth on the north side of the kitchen, holding back the cool air creeping through the open windows on the south.

Hands passed around platters of roasted chicken and fried ham, bowls of baked potatoes, boiled turnips, baked and mashed squash mixed with honey, fresh greens and cabbage drizzled with a sweet herbed vinegar, and a plate with slices of hot bread and fresh butter. There were bowls of mustard, pickles, relishes, and sauces to complement the foods. A pitcher of fresh cider sat at each end of the table. And on the sideboard were a deep dish apple pie and an applesauce cake loaded with raisins and walnuts.

"Where have you been lately?" Pella asked as she handed Briella the plate of bread.

"I spent a day at the Autumn Fair in Tironza then—"

"The Autumn Fair!" exclaimed a boy about twelve years old. "What did you see? What did you do?"

"Was there dancing and music and handsome young men?" asked a dark-haired girl with wide brown eyes.

Briella smiled. "Yes, there was dancing and music." She paused and remembered Cordwin's face. "And handsome young men."

The girl sighed and frowned. "Mother, when will I ever get to go to the Fair?"

Pella looked askance at her husband and gave him a knowing smile. "Maybe next year," she said.

"But I'll be an old maid by then!"

"Sixteen is not an old maid," Pella's husband said, winking at his wife.

The girl rested her elbow on the table, propped her chin on her hand, and glared at her plate. "I'll never get to be a Fair Greeter."

"Probably not," said her father.

Pella rolled her eyes and covered her mouth with her hand to hide a smile.

The family laughed and talked and ate until everyone was full and happy and drowsy. Evening gave way to a full moon night so bright, it was like daylight shining in through the windows.

"Time for bed," the husband said.

The children grumbled even though most of them were yawning.

"Off you go," Pella said, kissing each child in turn. The children trudged up the stairs, calling "Good night" to everyone.

Briella helped Pella and her mother put away the leftover food in the cool root cellar, then washed up the dishes. The two younger brothers went off to their room behind the kitchen. Pella's husband said, "Good night," and went to the bedroom east of the kitchen.

Pella led Briella to a door on the west side of the kitchen. "This is my sister Sheelagh's room. You can stay in her room for the night. She's off helping my other sister, Melvene. Do you remember her? She's very ill." Pella looked away, a worried frown on her face.

"What happened?"

Pella sighed. "She was on a ladder picking apples and slipped and fell and broke her leg. Mother is too old to travel that far, and I couldn't leave her to do all the work for this family. So Sheelagh went to help."

"Where does Melvene live?" Briella asked.

"On a farm southeast of Leflin." She paused and inhaled a short breath. "Is there anything you could do for her?"

"Maybe," Briella said, resting a hand on Pella's shoulder. "Tell me how to get there, and I'll see if I can help."

Pella told her how to find the farm.

Briella nodded. "I'll leave tomorrow morning."

Pella placed her hand over Briella's. "Thank you," she said earnestly. "Baygor bless you." She turned to the door and opened it.

The room was small but cozy. A single bed was pushed against the western wall. A three-legged stool sat beside the bed. Three wooden pegs stuck out from the wooden walls; Briella's pack hung from one of them. A wash stand with brown bowl and bucket stood against the north wall. A window opened to the south toward the center of the village.

"I hope you'll rest peacefully tonight," Pella said.

Briella smiled. "I'm sure I will."

"Good night."

Briella entered the room and closed the door. She took off her cloak and hung it on a peg next to her bag. She didn't bother changing clothes, just took off her shoes, and placed them beside the bed. The stone floor was cold as she crossed to the window to close the shutters.

Moonlight coated the landscape like a blanket of snow, white and clean. The air was scented with smoke and apples and spices. Winter would come soon. Briella could feel it. Snowflakes would cover the land like moonlight. The earth and trees would go to sleep until spring. People would huddle in warm houses, telling stories, knitting, carving wood, making cured hides into coats and shoes and hats. And *she* would be alone.

She leaned against side of the window and remembered Cordwin's dark mesmerizing eyes, his gentle voice, his laughter, the sensuous touch of his hand. A tear rolled down her cheek as she closed the shutters, darkness filling the room.

Music coaxed Briella from a dreamless sleep. The piper was outside but close by. For a moment her heart stopped beating, and she couldn't breathe. "Cordwin?" Had he followed her somehow? She rose silently and listened. No, it wasn't Cordwin playing, but the music was as sad and mournful as his.

She slipped on her shoes, took her cloak from the peg and clasped it on. Quietly opening the door to her room, she glanced around the large kitchen. The room was dark and empty, not even embers glowing on the hearth. She crept to the front door, opened it, and slipped out.

The moon overhead was as round as a plate and blue-white as fresh milk. Dry leaves fluttered in the chill autumn breeze. Music floated in the air like mist, tenuous, variable. Following the sound, she found Del, Pella's young brother-in-law, at the foot of a tree growing from the side of a gully behind the house.

"Del?" she said softly.

He jumped to his feet, dropping his pipe.

"What are you doing out here?" he asked nervously.

Briella inhaled sharply. In the moonlight Del reminded her of Cordwin, as he'd looked on the day they'd met. Same wavy hair, lean face, same dark eyes filled with grief and despair. Swallowing tightly, she said, "I heard your music."

Even in moonlight, she could see Del blush. "I-I'm sorry. I didn't mean to wake you."

She smiled. "It's all right. Would you play for me?"

He nodded, a shy smile brightening his face. She sat on the dry ground beside the tree. He picked up his flute, rubbed it clean on his shirt, and began to play.

The music was quiet as a zephyr, gentle as a mother's touch, but there was such pain, such terrible loneliness in the song. Tears glistened in Briella's eyes. She'd heard that despair many times before—in the music Cordwin played on his flute late at night, when all but the night watch were asleep. Cordwin tried to hide his loneliness from others, but his music betrayed it. Tears trickled down her cheeks as Del's music stirred memories of Cordwin sleeping, his bare chest rising and falling as she knelt beside him. She could almost feel his warmth, hear his breathing. If only she could touch him at that moment...

The music stopped. "Are you ill, Old Mam?" Del asked.

Briella looked at him, startled. "No...no, I'm all right. Your music was so beautiful, I couldn't help crying. But it's so sad, so lonely."

Del turned away, shadows hiding his face. "I..." he swallowed hard. "There's a girl—Jen—I love her, but she doesn't notice me. She doesn't care about me at all."

Briella smiled to herself. First love was always painful. "Have you told her you love her?"

Del's face jerked back towards her. Astonishment gleamed in his eyes. "No—of course not!"

She spread her hands palms up and shrugged. "Then how could she know?"

"But...I...She..."

"Do you think she can read your thoughts?"

He looked uncomfortable. "Uh, no, I suppose not."

She put a hand on his shoulder and squeezed lightly. "Then tell her. You might find she loves you, too."

"But what if she doesn't? Could you give me a potion to make her love me?"

Briella shook her head. "That wouldn't be love, only a trick."

Del hung his head.

"Why don't you play for her, perhaps make a song just for her? She'd like that."

"Do you truly think so?" he asked eagerly.

She smiled. "Yes, I do." She stood and stretched. "But now, it's time for sleeping. You can play for Jen tomorrow."

He stood, too, and they walked back to Pella's hut. They crept through the kitchen, trying not to wake anyone. Del whispered, "Good night," then tiptoed to his room. Briella returned to her room and climbed back into bed. As she fell asleep again, she thought she heard a sad flute playing. It wasn't Del's.

15

The next morning Briella left Selmdin and flew to Pella's sister's farmstead. An apple orchard spread south of a sturdy two-story wooden house. Sheep and goats grazed in a meadow north of the house. Behind the house a young woman with golden-brown hair, Pella's sister Sheelagh, pulled up a bucket full of water from a well. Briella landed in the orchard, changed into Old Mam, and trudged up the dirt track to the house.

"Hello," she called. "Anyone about?"

Sheelagh stepped around the back corner of the house and shield her eyes against the morning sun. "Old Mam? What are you doing here?"

"Pella told me Melvene had broken her leg and that you'd come to care for her. I thought I might be able to help."

"I don't know what else to do," said Sheelagh. Her eyes were red and dark-circled. "If you can help, I'd be grateful."

"I'll see what I can do, child," Briella said.

She followed Sheelagh inside the house to a bedroom off the kitchen. A woman lay in a bed, left leg splinted and propped on a folded quilt. Her reddish-brown hair was slicked back from her pale thin face, and her eyes looked sunken and bruised. Her forehead was terribly hot when Briella touched it, and the woman mumbled incoherently and tossed restlessly.

Briella ran her fingertips lightly over Melvene's leg, broken halfway between the knee and ankle. It was a clean break and well splinted, but the skin was fiery red and hot to the touch. An angry red streak crept up the leg.

"Blood poison from infection," Briella whispered. Turning to Sheelagh, she said, "I need a kettle of boiling water as quickly as possible. And clean cloths. And a cup and basin."

Sheelagh dashed from the room and outside. Briella opened her pack and took out roborant, woundweal, callum bark, and callum leaf salve, and her willow wand. She spread a thin layer of the salve on the leg. Instantly, the skin began to cool, but the red streak was still there.

Sheelagh came back with several clean cloths and a glazed basin and wooden cup.

"I need the cloths here, but take the basin and cup back to the kitchen. Fill the basin with cool water, then bring it back," Briella said. "Is the kettle on to boil?"

"Yes, but it might take a while," Sheelagh said.

"All right. As soon as the water boils, call me."

Sheelagh hurried from the room with the basin and cup. A few moments later she came back carrying the basin in her arms, walking carefully and trying not to slosh the water.

"Set it down and go check on the kettle," Briella said.

Sheelagh set the basin down on a stool and carried them to the bedside. "I'll call you when the water's hot." She glanced at Melvene, then hurried from the room.

Briella dipped a cloth into the cool water, rung out the extra water, then bathed Melvene's feverish face and dry cracked lips.

"Water's boiling!" Sheelagh called.

Briella took the herbs and wand into the kitchen, then stopped and listened for a while. "I don't hear any children's voices."

Sheelagh sighed. "She doesn't have any children. Four years married and she's never been pregnant. For someone who loves children as much as she does, it's heartbreaking."

Briella nodded thoughtfully. "I want you to bathe Melvene's face while I make a potion." Sheelagh nodded and went to her sister.

Briella tossed the herbs into the boiling water and stirred them with the willow wand until the infusion was green-gold. A sweet clean scent filled the room. She dried her wand on her cloak, ladled the potion into the wooden cup, and carried it to Melvene's room.

Sitting beside Melvene, Briella wafted the fragrant steam toward her. The woman lay still and quiet. Briella blew on the potion to cool it. When it was cool enough to drink, Briella slipped her arm behind Melvene and helped her sit up, then pressed the cup to the woman's lips.

"Drink," Briella said.

Melvene's eye flickered toward Briella.

"Drink as much as you can."

The woman took a sip, then rested her head against Briella's shoulder.

"Drink some more," Briella coaxed.

Melvene took another sip, but she seemed too weak to take more than one at a time. Slowly, sip by sip, she drank the entire cup, then fell asleep. Briella laid the woman back against the pillows.

"Let her rest now," Briella told Sheelagh. "When she wakes, she'll feel better. Give her more of the potion, as much as she'll drink." She handed Sheelagh a jar of the callum leaf salve. "Apply this once a day to her leg, just a tiny dab the size of a pea. And I'll measure out enough herbs to make another kettle of potion."

"But will she be all right?" Sheelagh asked anxiously.

Briella smiled. "She'll be climbing ladders within a couple of months, although I hope she'll be more careful."

Picking up her pack, Briella followed Sheelagh to the kitchen, leaving Melvene sleeping. Briella measured out the herbs and instructed Sheelagh how to make callum bark tea to speed the healing. "I'll check back in a week," Briella said. "Melvene may feel well enough to want to get up, but don't let her put weight on that leg for at least three weeks."

"I'll remember," Sheelagh said. "Baygor bless you, Old Mam."

Briella smiled and patted the girl's cheek.

She turned to go when Sheelagh said, "Wait! It's midday, and you haven't eaten anything. I have some soup and some fry bread. Jake and the farm hands will be back from the orchard any minute now."

"Thank you, but I have a long journey yet. Next week, when I come back."

"All right, but don't leave yet." The girl grabbed a sack and filled it with apples, some fry bread, and a piece of apple walnut cake. "For the road," Sheelagh said as she handed the sack to Briella. "Baygor keep you safe."

"And you, too."

Briella left the house and walked past the orchard, tired and pensive. She stopped and looked back toward the house, then sat down beneath one of the apple trees. *I can't be everywhere at once, even if I can change into a dove and fly as fast as I can. And I won't be here forever,* she thought with a shudder. *I need to train other healers to make salves and potions. But they don't have a callum tree for leaves and bark.*

Her eyes widened. *That's it! I have four more callum seeds. If I give them to healers in Vorlik, I can teach them how to make the potions and salves. Then they can teach others. And more people will be tended much sooner than now! And I'll start with Maiya in Leflin. Sweet Baramay, why didn't any of the Wizards think of this before?*

She stood up, stuffed the sack of food in her cloak, shuffled far enough from the house no one would see her, then changed to a dove and flew to Leflin. Landing near the town, she changed to Old Mam and hurried to the Two Oaks Inn.

It was early afternoon when Briella found Maiya washing tables at the inn.

"Old Mam!" Maiya said. "It's good to see you again. It's been months since you were last here. Would you like a cup of wine?"

"No, but a cup of water would be welcomed."

"Here, sit down and rest. I'll bring you some water, and we can talk."

Briella sat down at a table near the kitchen. Warm scents of sage and apples and smoked ham trickled into the main room, and she suddenly realized she was hungry.

As if reading her mind, Maiya came back with a platter of food and a mug of water. "Thought you might want something to go with the water." She grinned and sat down beside Briella.

Briella laughed. "I didn't know I was hungry until I smelled your cooking." She took a piece of bread, dipped it into a bowl of bean soup and ham, and took a bite. The soup was filled with carrots, onion, garlic, celery, barley, tomatoes, and white beans, and seasoned with cloves, bay leaves, and pepper. "Oh," she said, savoring the flavors, "you are the best cook in all Vorlik."

Maiya smiled proudly. "So where have you come from?"

"Oh, I mended a broken leg. And I went to the Autumn Fair."

Maiya sighed. "I haven't been to the Autumn Fair since...since before I married Kam. Can't just close up an inn and go off to the Fair. But someday, when the children are grown and can run things without us, I'm going to drag that husband of mine down to Tironza for the Fair. Oh!" She clutched her abdomen.

Briella touched Maiya's arm. "Are you all right, child?"

Grinning, Maiya nodded. "Yes, the newest Winsell just kicked me. Must be a boy."

Laughing, Briella said, "Congratulations. You didn't tell me you were with child last time I was here."

"I wasn't sure myself."

"So where are the other two?

"Taking a nap. Although Eran thinks he's too old to take naps. He's four now and very independent." She leaned close. "Actually, I need an hour without having to keep track of the kidlings so I insist they take a nap. So, what did you see at the Fair?"

Briella was silent for a moment, remembering Cordwin and the joy she'd felt in his company.

"Old Mam? Old Mam, are you going to sleep?"

"Oh, um, no, I was just remembering the Fair. Lots of things to see and do. Anything you could ever dream of for sale. Dancing, singing, puppet theaters, story tellers, jugglers, tumblers, and food of all kinds. Not as good as yours, but good. And..." she paused, "Lord Cordwin was at the Fair."

"Lord Cordwin!" Maiya placed her hand over her heart. "He came to Leflin three years ago on an inspection tour of the Western Guard. All the young women were swooning over him. Now I'm a happily married woman with two lovely children and another one on the way, but I have to admit that even my heart skipped a beat when I saw him."

"I know what you mean," Briella said softly.

Maiya looked surprised, then grinned. "I guess you're never too old to appreciate a handsome young man."

Briella quickly took another bite of bread and a spoon of soup, not looking at Maiya.

"So, are you staying the night?" Maiya asked.

"If you have room."

"We always have room for you."

"And I have something for you." Briella reached inside her cloak, took out a tiny silver box, and opened it. Inside were the four red callum seeds. Taking out one of them, she placed it in Maiya's hand. "This is a callum seed. Plant it this fall in a place with lots of room. By next fall it will be taller than you are, and in five years it will grow to the size of a large oak. Its bark is used for healing potions and its leaves are used in the healing salve I gave you. When it's grown, I'll show you how to make the potion and salve."

Maiya gazed at the seed, then looked at Briella, astonished. "Where did you find this?"

"A very long way from here," she said. "But I'm not as spry as I used to be. I can't make enough medicine on my own. I need to pass on my knowledge, and I have no children. So if you'd be willing, I'll teach you everything I know about healing."

Maiya's eyes glistened. "Baygor bless you," she said, taking Briella's hand in hers. "I'd be honored to learn from you."

The next day Briella flew to Yarrow to see Germaine, the innwife at the Singing Wheels Inn. She gave Germaine a callum seed. "I promised I'd tell you my secret one day. This is the secret ingredient. Plant this seed. When the tree is grown, I'll show you how to use the leaves and bark to make salves and potions. And I'll teach you everything I know about healing."

Germaine was delighted. "Thank Baygor you came to Vorlik! Our people will long remember your kindness."

Briella gazed out the front door of the inn. Mid-morning sunlight spilled in, bringing the spicy scent of peppermint and crushed grapes. "Being remembered is my immortality," she said softly.

She shared lunch with Germaine, who let her know all the latest gossip about who was betrothed and who'd had a baby and whose son was keeping company with whose daughter. Briella smiled and laughed at the comforting mundane matters of ordinary life, but in her heart she felt melancholy. *I'll never truly be part of their lives,* she thought.

She left after lunch and flew to Tribbia, the northernmost village where the northern road wound through the Circle Mountains to the lands of the Formian council. Lena, the local healer and Old Mam's friend, was amazed by Briella's gift of the callum seed and the offer to share her knowledge.

Briella stayed the night, then flew to Yertz on the eastern border, where she gave the last seed to Citee, innwife and healer.

I've done more today than I've done in the last five years, she thought. *People for generations will be healed long after...,* she shuddered, *long after I'm dead.*

16

Lord Paxell sat on the windowsill of his tower room, his back leaning against the window frame. With his black hair and neatly trimmed beard and black clothing, he looked like a shadow in the window. He gazed at the Circle Mountains, their snow-covered tops gleaming in the midday summer sun. Legend said Baramay raised the mountains around Vorlik after Baygor had destroyed Canzet, the first Sorcerer. Paxell glared at the barrier and clenched his fists. "Will I ever cross those mountains and see the land my fathers dreamed of ruling?" he said to himself.

"Who knows what the future will bring?"

Startled, Paxell leaped to his feet and turned toward the voice. Grimmin stood just inside the doorway, a wry smile on his young face. His grey clothes were covered with dust, as if he had just arrived.

"I brought you the dagger you commissioned, Lord Paxell," the blond merchant said, "fashioned by the best Tukkus smith, formed and engraved as you instructed. I haven't located an ovrin horn yet, but I've left word with people I know that if they come across one, to keep it for me. And I'll find a sea snail for you." He held the dagger, hilt first, out to the lord.

Paxell quickly crossed the floor and took the gleaming short dagger from the merchant. The hilt was gold and silver, shaped like a dove with a blue gem for each eye, and a large perfect emerald on the end. The weapon felt surprisingly light in Paxell's hand and well balanced. The word "*rahala*" was etched into one side of the blade, and "Briella" etched on the other side. He smiled as he rubbed the edge against his thumb to test the sharpness. "Beautiful," he said softly. "This may bring me what I want most in life."

"Especially since the assassins didn't succeed," Grimmin said.

Paxell jerked his head up and stared at Grimmin. "Assassins?"

Grimmin chuckled. "Neither one of the assassins succeeded in killing Cordwin." He held up a hand when Paxell started to speak. "Don't bother saying you had nothing to do with them. I *know*. You need to hire someone more skilled than the last ones were. I know several who might do."

"You, perhaps?"

"Me? Kill Cordwin?" Grimmin's hands twitched slightly, and a hungry look filled the merchant's blue eyes. "If there wasn't a Wizard in Vorlik..." his voice was hushed, almost wistful. He shook himself, then smiled at Paxell. "No, you couldn't pay me enough to try."

Paxell tightened his grip around the hilt. For a moment he wondered what it would feel like to drive the blade into the merchant's belly, but only for a moment.

Grimmin's blue eyes narrowed. "You'd have more luck with a Formian bear than you would with me."

"I *know,*" Paxell said through gritted teeth, and he turned toward his desk. Opening a small wooden box, he placed the dagger inside and closed the lid. He rested his hands on the box, then said over his shoulder, "Bring me the other items when you have them."

"Of course," Grimmin said, "but there is the small matter of payment in advance. I believe we agreed on emeralds."

Paxell turned slowly and said, "Yes. We did." He opened the black velvet pouch tied to his belt and removed twenty perfect emeralds. As he dropped them into the merchant's hand, he said, "Why do you need so many emeralds?"

Grimmin stared at Paxell a few moments, then smiled coolly. "I'll return when I have the other items you seek." He gave a slight bow, then turned and exited down the darkened stairwell.

Paxell stared after the merchant and shuddered, then glanced over his shoulder at the box on his desk. *One step closer,* he thought, *one day nearer to my heart's desire.*

He walked down the dimly lit spiral stairs, pausing at Captain Callas' office only long enough to nod at him. Continuing down the stairs to the ground floor, he walked through the Audience Hall and crossed the wide marble-floored foyer to the heavy oak doors open to the courtyard. Guards saluted as he passed into the sunny but surprisingly cool summer day. Soldiers practiced sword play and archery in the dusty courtyard. A wagon lumbered toward the north side of the castle, loaded with baskets of vegetables and bags of flour. Near the stables, men unloaded sacks of feed from another wagon.

A light breeze ruffled Paxell's dark hair. He breathed deeply, catching the scent of dust, the musty odor of horses, and a fragrance so faint, he couldn't identify it at first. Suddenly, his eyes widened, and his breath caught in his throat. Roses – the fragrance of roses, Dannee's roses, that's what he detected. She had planted roses in a walled garden on the south side of the castle, not long after they'd wed. He hadn't been there since her death. He'd forgotten the garden was there.

Haltingly, he walked to the south side of the courtyard to a limestone wall. In the center of the wall was a wooden door with a sliding latch. His hand trembled as he slid the bolt back and opened the door.

The fragrance of roses surrounded him, caressing him gently. An ache began in the center of chest, and his vision blurred. He saw Dannee dancing in the garden, her golden hair shining in the sunlight. She laughed as she tossed handfuls of pink and white rose petals into the air and whirled in circles as they drift down around her. She stopped, facing him. Her blue eyes grew wide, she gave a small gasp, then she ran toward him, her arms outstretched to him.

It had been six years since Dannee had died, but anguish tore through his heart, as deep and fresh as if she'd died only moments before. His knees felt too weak to hold him. He sank to the grass, his eyes filled with tears. He covered his face with one of his hands, trying to block out the sight of Dannee's ghost, and shook with sobs.

Small arms wrapped around his neck, and a soft cheek leaned against his. "Father," a high pitched voice said softly in his ear, "Father, don't cry."

The arms released him, and tiny fingers pried his hand from his eyes. He blinked his vision clear. Standing before him was a little girl, six years old, blond, pale, with deep blue eyes like Dannee's. She wore a blue dress with pink roses embroidered at the neck and hem. A few rose petals clung to her hair.

"Miria," he whispered, his chest so tight, it hurt to breathe.

"Did you hurt yourself, Father?" she asked.

He gazed at her for long moments, then cleared his throat and said, "No. No, I'm all right."

"Then why are you crying?"

"I..." Paxell stopped, not knowing what to say. "You...you looked so much like your mother, dancing in the sunlight. She loved to dance, too."

Miria's shoulders drooped, and she stared at the ground. "Thinking about Mother makes me sad, too. That's why I come here and dance. I don't feel sad when I'm dancing. Why don't you dance with me, and then you won't feel sad either."

She took his hands and tugged him to stand. Slowly, he stood up and looked beyond her. Two boys, both looking about Miria's age, stood near a trellis covered with white roses. One of the boys was raven-haired and grey-eyed; he looked like a smaller version of Captain Callas, probably his son. The other boy had dark brown hair and gold-flecked blue eyes, and a lean oval face. Paxell stared hard at the boy, who looked much like Cordwin.

"Come here, both of you," Paxell said.

The boys stiffened, looked at each other, then cautiously approached Paxell. In unison they bowed and said, "My lord."

"You're Captain Callas' son Malbar," Paxell said to the first boy.

"Y-yes, my lord," the boy said.

Paxell turned to the other boy. "And you're Pyccis," he said, his voice strained.

"Yes, my lord." The boy bowed but kept his eyes on Paxell.

Paxell stared at the boy. "Yes, I remember now. I haven't seen you in months. You've...changed." He kept staring at the boy until Miria tugged on his hands.

"Father, I've never seen you here before."

Paxell looked down at his daughter. "This was your mother's garden. She loved roses. She planted these with her own hands and tended them. I never come here anymore."

"Why did you come today?"

"I don't know," he said softly. "Something drew me here." He brushed a few petals from her hair, then gently cupped her chin in his hand. "You look so much like your mother, so much. You're all I have left of her."

"Tell me about her, Father," Miria said. "No one talks about her or tells me what she was like."

Paxell gazed at her. "That's because talking about her hurt too much. I couldn't bear to think about her."

Miria glanced up at Paxell, then turned her face away. "Is that why you don't come to see me? Because I look so much like her?"

Suddenly ashamed, Paxell knelt and put his arms around his daughter and held her close. "My little Miria," he said as he kissed her hair, "forgive me. I'm sorry I haven't been a good father to you, but I swear I'll change. We'll be together always, and we'll talk and remember your mother together."

Miria flung her arms around his neck. "Oh, Father, thank you."

Paxell hugged her back. *Part of Dannee is still with me,* he thought, tears filling his eyes.

"Now where did the rapscallions run off to this time?" a gravelly woman's voice muttered behind Paxell. "Malbar! Pyccis! Princess Miria! Where are you?"

Paxell glanced over his shoulder to see the children's old nurse coming waddling through the garden door. She faltered, staring open-mouthed at Paxell.

Instantly, she dropped to one knee and said, "Forgive me, my lord. I didn't know the children had intruded on your presence. I'll take them from here, and I swear they won't bother you again. Pyccis, Malbar, Princess Miria, come away now!"

Paxell stood, faced the nurse, and held up one hand to silence her. "These children are here by my leave, and they may enter my presence whenever they desire. Do you understand, woman?"

She blinked her bulging eyes, her mouth dropping open. "Uh, yes, my lord."

"And I want them to be taught to read, to cipher, and to play music as well as dancing and riding. And my daughter is to have her own maid."

"Yes, my lord."

"And her rooms are to be closer to mine."

"Yes, my lord. I'll see to it immediately."

"Then go." Paxell waved the nurse away.

Then nurse stood, curtseyed, and left as quickly as she could move.

Paxell looked down at Miria and smiled. He felt lighter and more alive than he had in many years.

Miria's blue eyes filled with tears as she gazed up at him. "I love you, Father."

He took her hand, leaned over, and kissed the top of her head. "I love you, too."

17

The callum seeds sprouted in spring and grew almost ten feet the first year. Briella taught the healers how to care for the callum trees. "You must not take the bark from the tree," she told them. "The tree will shed bark on its own. And use only leaves that have fallen to the ground. They have the greatest healing in them."

She often visited Liska, the young red-haired priest of Baygor from Yarrow. She'd taught him the healing ways at the same time she'd taught the innwife Germaine and even showed him how to make the healing salve from callum leaves. She always appeared to him as she truly was, since that was how he had first seen her, although she'd never told him her true name.

He was very pensive one warm autumn day. "Would you come to my house and have a cup of peppermint tea with me?" he asked. "There's something I'd like to speak to you about."

Briella smiled. "I'd like that."

Liska's house was next to the chapel. The cottage was made of white limestone and roofed with slate. The single room contained a bed, wooden pegs set into the wall for clothes, a small wooden table with two chairs, and a hearth built into the south wall. Bundles of drying peppermint, lavender, sage, and woundweal hung from the wooden rafters and filled the cottage with the fragrance of all the herbs. The house was small but cozy, and comfortable enough for one person.

Briella sat down in one of the chairs and waited. Liska was silent as he took two cups from a shelf and set them on the table, then plucked deep green peppermint leaves from some plants he had harvested a short time earlier. He placed the leaves in the two cups, then fetched a steaming kettle from hearth.

"Who are you?" he asked, pouring boiling water over the leaves in her cup. Instantly, the clean sweet fragrance of mint filled the house. "After six years I still know so little about you. You know more about herbs and plants and healing than even the senior priests and healers I know, and you don't look a day older than the first time I saw you. I don't even know your name." He halted, watching her intensely. "Are you the Wizard Briella?"

She sipped her tea before answering. "Does it matter who I am?"

He studied her for a moment, then smiled. "No. You are who you are. I've been thinking, though, that what I've learned should be shared with all the priests of Baygor. If you *were* the Wizard, you couldn't be everywhere you're needed. But if every priest of Baygor could make this salve or have access to it and the callum bark and leaves, the people of Vorlik would always be near someone who could heal them."

Briella blinked, her eyes wide and her mouth slightly open. "You're right! That's why I gave Germaine the callum seed – to make healing more available. But if the all priests of Baygor could provide the salve and healing potions to the villages of Vorlik."

"Or wandering priests took their healing skills to all the farms and cottages."

"All the people would be near a healer whenever they needed one," Briella said.

"But there's only one callum tree," the priest said.

"No, there are four others."

"Four?" Liska looked at her startled. "But are they enough? Germaine's tree hasn't produced seeds yet."

"No, but one will next year. Callum trees produce seeds when they're seven years old, then every seven years after that. Not many seeds, but a few. Each one must be planted and tended carefully. I've taught Germaine and the other caretakers," Briella smiled at Liska, "and you how to care for the trees. You each must teach the ones who receive the new seeds."

"I will," he said. "I'd like to start with the Temple of Baygor in Tironza. A city so large has greater need for healers. And it's almost time for the Autumn Fair. You could come with me and teach the priests at the temple."

The Autumn Fair, Briella thought as she sipped the peppermint tea. She was tempted to go. *But what if I see Cordwin again?* she thought, fear and elation swirling in her heart. *What if he sees me? I could go as Old Mam. He's never seen me as the peddler. He wouldn't know me, but I could still see him, still hear his voice.* She started to take a drink of tea but halted, chewing her lower lip. *No, if I saw him again, if he looked into my eyes or touched my hand, my heart wouldn't have the strength to stay away from him.*

She sighed. "No," she told Liska. "I can't go to the Fair. I'm needed elsewhere. Besides, you can teach the priests as well as I could. But I promise I'll give you some seeds to plant next fall."

"Thank you." He blew on his cup of tea to cool it, took a sip, and set the cup down but held it between his palms. He gazed at the cup for a few moments, then said quietly, "I swear by Baygor, I'll keep your secret, Briella."

She touched his arm, and he looked up at her. "I know," she said.

Autumn was tiptoeing into winter as painted leaves fell to the ground, a blanket for the earth's winter sleep. Soon ice would edge ponds, and snowflakes would flutter down to cover the world in white. Families would huddle together before warm fires and tell stories of brave deeds and great battles. *But I'll still be alone,* Briella thought.

A late afternoon sun crept toward the Circle Mountains as Briella left the eastern village of Ambrell. She had delivered two babies, set a farmer's broken leg, and treated an old man's gout. As soon as she was beyond the villagers' sight, Briella dropped her old peddler's disguise and changed into dove form. Her wings ached as they beat against the brisk mountain air. She wasn't sure she could reach home, she was so weary, but soon she saw her thatched roof.

Large fan-shaped leaves and grey-green bark littered the ground around the callum tree. The herb garden needed harvesting before the first frost blackened the leaves. The deep red climbing rose on the trellis beside the door looked worn by the long summer, the last blossoms drooping in the fading light. Briella sighed. *So much to do before winter comes,* she thought.

It felt good to walk through her door, safe and comforting. She called fire to the hearth, and soon a crackling blaze warmed the kitchen. She ate some cheese and bread a farmwife had given her for healing her son, and sipped a cup of spring wine from Yarrow, given to her by Germaine the innwife.

The setting sun glowed through the crystalline walls, warming her, comforting her. Her head drooped until she rested it on her arms, crossed on the table, and she slept.

"Cordwin, look out! The dagger, it's poisoned!" Briella's cry woke her abruptly. "Cordwin?" She glanced around the room. She was in her own kitchen, but Cordwin had seemed so real, so close. Her hand was stretched out in front of her, reaching for...what? She rubbed her eyes and sat up. Her neck was stiff from the awkward position. A dream, it was only a dream, but it still seemed too real. A vision? Perhaps, but present or future?

"Lady Baramay, let him be all right," she prayed, still shaking, heart hammering in her chest.

Her stomach felt like a lump of ice as she changed into a dove and launched herself on the night wind. Her tiny heart was nearly bursting, and her wings were pushed to their limits. In spite of her fatigue, she couldn't stop until she sighted the grey walls of Tarolin, until she knew Cordwin was safe.

A black spider climbed the stone wall towards Cordwin's window. No, not a spider! A man, like a black shadow within shadows, creeping up the shadowed stone of the castle. An assassin! It had to be.

Briella landed on the castle wall, changed into an eagle, then dove at him. Talons tore deep into his shoulder. Wings slapped at his eyes. Her beak cut through his leather gloves to flesh. A dagger flashed arrow-quick toward her, but she banked away in time. She rose steeply, then plunged toward him again. This time, her talons sank into his throat and ripped. Blood sprayed the wall before the man fell. He couldn't scream. He didn't make any sound until he hit the ground, then he made a liquid thud, like a smashed melon.

Gliding through the window, Briella transformed in the waxing moonlight. Cold sweat ran down her face; her gasps for breath were almost as rapid as the blood pulsing through her. She sagged against the window frame, muscles aching, and gazed at Cordwin.

He was asleep, covered only with a blanket from waist to mid-thigh. His smooth bare chest rose and fell with each breath. Even in sleep his face was pensive, troubled, lonely. Dark hair lay across his forehead, and his lips parted slightly.

Thank Baygor, he's all right, she thought, warm relief trembling in her chest almost as much as fear had. She fought back sobs gathering in her throat. Silently, she crept across the floor and knelt beside his bed. She took Cordwin's hand and pressed it to her lips.

Cordwin stirred and murmured her name.

Suddenly, she wasn't certain she wanted him to see her. She shrank back into the shadows, her back against cold stone.

Cordwin sat up and glanced about the darkened room. "Who's there?"

She remained silent, longing to answer yet afraid.

He grabbed a dagger from the table at his bedside. "Someone's there, I know it."

She still said nothing.

His voice as soft as moonlight, he asked, "Briella, is it you?"

Her heart pounded, and her skin tingled at the sound of his voice. Her mouth was so dry, she could hardly speak. "Yes."

Cordwin rose from his bed, wearing only loose-fitting knee-length underwear made of thin light cloth. "Where are you?"

Hesitantly, she stepped from the shadows into the moonlight streaming through the window. "Here."

Discarding the dagger, he crossed the room until they stood face to face. "Briella." He caressed her hand at her side. "At last."

The look in his eyes made her shiver with delightful dread.

Cordwin glanced down at himself. "Oh, I'm not presentable. Please forgive me." He hurried over to the chair by the hearth, grabbed a pair of trousers, and quickly pulled them on and tied them at his waist. He hurried back to her.

"When you left me at the Autumn Fair, I was so afraid I'd never see you again, but I still hoped," he said softly. "I hoped we'd have another dance or drink a cup of cider together. See," he said and pointed to the mantel over the hearth. The two wooden mugs sat side by side. "I kept our mugs, hoping we'd use them again." He stepped closer. "And finally, you came to me tonight."

Briella tried to keep her voice from shaking but didn't succeed. "I—I had a dream."

"So did I. I was dreaming about you. Did you feel it?"

"No, I dreamed you were in danger that someone was going to attack you a poisoned dagger. After the other attempts on your life, I had to come. If anything happened to you—

I had to be certain you were safe." She looked out the window at the crumpled body on the ground below. "I'm glad I did."

Cordwin followed her gaze and stepped closer to the window. He looked down into the courtyard, then gasped. "Merciful Baygor!"

"He was climbing the wall. He was going to kill you."

"You saved my life again." He turned toward her, his eyes wide, and took her hand.

"If I hadn't come..." Her voice failed.

He stepped closer, and his voice became a husky whisper. "Do you care so much? Do I mean that much to you?"

Cordwin's touch became softer yet more intense, and she felt frightened. She tried to pull her hand away, but he wouldn't let go. Confusion and fear tingled down her neck. She knew she should flee, escape, hide from his searching eyes, but she couldn't move. "Please, my lord, let me go."

"You know my name," he said, moving closer until he held her hand against his bare chest. "Say it, please."

"Cordwin," she whispered. "Cordwin, please, please let me go."

"How can I let you go?" He drew her against his chest, his arms encircling her tenderly. "I love you."

She felt a moment of panic, but it was swept away by his gentleness. Briella leaned against him, listened to his heartbeat, felt the warmth of his arms, and breathed in the cedar wood scent of his skin. She felt safe and peaceful, as if some part of her had been missing and she'd found it at last.

"Briella." Cordwin caressed her hair and kissed her forehead. "I've wanted to hold you in my arms since the moment I first saw you. I love you with all my heart. I'd die to protect you." His lips brushed her ear, and he whispered, "My ring, my house, my heart and love are yours for as long as I live. Be my wife, my friend, my counselor, the mother of my children. Tell me, please, tell me you love me as much as I love you."

She longed to accept him, wanted to feel his arms around her always, wanted to sit beside him, lie beside him, wake beside him for the rest of her life. *All I have to do is say yes,* she thought. *Just tell him what's in my heart, how deeply I care for him.* She wrapped her arms around him, delighting in the touch of his smooth skin, and held him close.

"Cordwin," she whispered, her lips brushing his bare chest, "I love you."

Moaning happily, Cordwin pressed her closer. "I'll make you happy. I swear by Baramay, I will."

He pulled back just a little, then leaned down and kissed her, gently at first, then more intense, passionate. And she kissed him back fervently.

Shouting outside in the courtyard drew her attention from Cordwin, and she glanced out the window. Guards had gathered around the body of the assassin, torches lighting the dark courtyard. Suddenly, a cold chill clutched her heart. *I saved him tonight,* she thought, *only because I'm a Wizard. If I become human, give up all the power I have, the next time I couldn't protect him. He'd be dead, and I couldn't do anything to stop it. And I couldn't live with the knowledge that I let him die.* Tears filled her eyes, and desolation filled her heart.

She looked up at his face and caressed his cheek. "Cordwin, I love you," she said as she gazed into his dark eyes, "with all my heart, but I can't be your wife, even though it's my dearest wish."

"But you love me," Cordwin said, looking bewildered and frightened. "You said you love me. Why can't you be my wife?"

"If I married you," she halted, her throat so tight with despair, she could hardly speak, "if I became your wife, I couldn't protect you and your people the way I do now."

"I don't understand!" Cordwin said. "Why can't you marry me?"

She gazed at him for timeless moments, then said, "On the night before Timmree wed Cavolin, Baramay visited her."

"But what does that have to do with us?" Cordwin asked.

"Baramay came to Timmree and told her she had to choose which race she would be: Wizard or human."

"But why?"

"Baramay created Wizards differently than humans. That difference allows us to use magic, but it also prevents us from having children with humans. Timmree wanted to be Cavolin's wife and bear his children." Briella touched Cordwin's face. "She chose to be human so she could marry a human. And when she did, when she spoke her vows, Baramay took away Timmree's magic, even her longer life span, and made her human."

"She gave up everything?"

Briella nodded.

"We don't have to have children," Cordwin said, holding her to his chest. "We don't even have to marry. I couldn't ask you to give up who you are. Just stay with me. Please don't leave me."

"And would you make me your mistress," she asked in a hushed tone, "your concubine, a woman with no honor?"

"No," Cordwin whispered, "no, I want you for my true and lawful wife. But if that's not possible...please, stay with me. Please."

Briella nestled against him, her tears dampening his skin. "I can't do what Timmree did, no matter how much I want to. If anything happened to you or your people because I gave up my power and I couldn't protect you, I couldn't live with that." She shuddered. "And...my time's limited."

"We *do* have time," he insisted. "We do! Bren won't come for years, maybe never."

Briella shook her head, a cold lump like lead in her throat. "He'll come, and he'll kill me."

Even in the moon shadows, Briella saw Cordwin pale. "No," he whispered as he kissed her hair. "I can't lose you, not now."

"When Bren returns, I'll die. Tomorrow or years from now, I'll die when he returns. Could you live with the thought that your nephew killed your wife?"

"Yes!" he said. "But he won't kill you! I won't let him!"

"You couldn't protect me from him anymore than I could protect you and your people if I became human." He started to protest, but she shook her head and rested her hand on his cheek. He turned his face and kissed her palm.

"As much as I love you," she said, her voice shaking, "and as much as I want to, I can't stay with you. There isn't time. I swore to protect Vorlik, and I've never broken a promise."

"No," he said, shaking his head, "no, I won't let you go."

"Cordwin, you are still young."

"So are you!" Cordwin said, despair in his voice.

"Find someone else to love, someone who'll share your life and fight at your side, a woman to give you children. I can't. I don't dare. I'm sorry." Tenderly, she kissed him. "I love you, Cordwin, and I always will."

She whispered a word of command, turned into a dove, and fled the castle.

"NO!!!" she heard him cry as he raced to the window. "Come back! Don't leave me!"

She saw him sag against the window frame and heard him whisper, "I'm so lonely, so very lonely."

At that moment she was glad she was a dove. Birds don't cry tears.

18

Pyccis and Malbar raced out the front entrance to the sunlit courtyard of Drambit's Abasette Castle. The boys were about the same height and age, being "almost eleven years" as they said proudly when asked. Both were lean, bronzed, and full of energy as all boys of that age are. Dressed in brown trousers and matching thong-laced vests over white shirts, the two companions ran around to the north side of the castle and hid in the shadow of the castle wall near the kitchen.

Pulling a strand of his walnut-colored hair from his mouth, Pyccis peeked around a stack of wooden crates, his gold-flecked blue eyes checking for pursuit. "I think we've fooled old Varlin," he whispered, smiling triumphantly.

Malbar swept his raven hair from his square face. Laughing, he jumped high, his fist aimed at the clear, autumn sky. "Yeah!!" Quickly clapping his hand over his mouth, he cast a worried glance around the courtyard, pale grey eyes squinting at the sun's brightness. Looking back at his friend, Malbar hissed, "No more lessons for us! What'll we do today?"

Pyccis thought a moment, wrinkling his forehead and scrunching his lips as he slowly ground his teeth.

"Why don't we sneak out the back gate to our secret place?" Malbar suggested. "We haven't been there in two weeks."

Pyccis nodded. "All right. Did you bring any food? I filched some cheese and bread."

"I sneaked some pieces of jerky and two apples." Malbar opened his pockets to reveal a cloth-wrapped bundle and two red, knobby apples. "Come on. Let's go."

Moving with the stealth only boys intent on avoiding adults employ, the two slipped behind the kitchen, through the smithy, and around the walled-in cistern to the castle wall's north side. A stream had been diverted under the castle through a stone conduit and blocked with iron grating. The boys had long ago found a narrow gap in the bars under water. With the aid of files borrowed from the forge, they'd enlarged it enough for them to wiggle through. Their secret exit hadn't yet been discovered by Varlin, their teacher, or by Captain Callas, Malbar's father. Still, they were always careful never to be followed on their escapes.

Stuffing their stolen goods into a waterproof bag Pyccis had remembered to bring along, they slipped into the water, dove under the surface, and swam through the gap. They resurfaced far enough upstream to be hidden by trees and rushes, then the boys swam to the muddy shore. Crouching behind a cluster of tyneberry briars, they peered at the castle to make certain they hadn't been spotted by the battlement guards or the inhabitants of the cluster of rock-and-timber huts at the base of the castle.

Malbar wrung water from his clothes. "Fooled them again!"

Pyccis grinned. "Let's go!"

The boys followed a path north through hills covered with scrub trees and briar thickets, unseen from the castle. The land was less desolate than in past years. Grass grew thick enough that even the wild sheep ate their fill. Squirrels and rabbits skittered across decades of fallen leaves, hiding in the wooded dells and copses. Everbearing tyneberry briars still bent low from the weight of their fruit. The air was clear with a nip that added a glow to the boys' cheeks.

With the Circle Mountains to their right, the boys threaded their way through brush and bracken. They crunched brittle leaves underfoot, spreading a spicy, earthy fragrance in the comfortably warm air. They skipped stones across a pond below a small cataract, then climbed up the rock face to cross the stream above the waterfall. Several hours after they'd left the castle, they reached a little dell, tree-hidden and lined with thick layers of fallen leaves. Crawling through a narrow gap in the encircling hedge, the boys tumbled to the floor of their secret retreat and laughed exuberantly at their successful escape.

"We did it!" Pyccis lay flat on his back and gasped for breath.

Malbar stretched out beside his friend, hands locked behind his head. "Varlin will be furious!"

Panting with excitement and grinning with immense self-satisfaction, Pyccis stared at the cloudless blue sky overhead. He reveled in the scent of damp earth beneath him. The air in the shaded dell was cooler than on the sunny path and felt good on his flushed face. He was glad just being alive.

Malbar broke the long silence. "You know we'll both receive an hour lecture and at least twenty pages of Drambini history to learn for punishment."

"I know." Sitting up, Pyccis said, "I don't care! It's worth all the punishment just be free from their constant watching for a while. Even if Lord Paxell himself punishes us, I'll still slip away to our secret place."

"Not as secret as you think," a tiny voice came through the hedge, startling the boys to their feet.

"Who are you?" Malbar asked, picking up a stick.

Pyccis clenched his fists in front of him, prepared to defend his territory. "Show yourself, if you dare!"

The hedge rustled as a dirty and bedraggled figure crawled through the hedge and stood up. The intruder smoothed leaf-studded golden hair from a grubby face, brushed dirt from a dark blue shirt and trousers, and stood facing the two.

Pyccis looked at Malbar, seeing his own astonishment reflected in his companion's face. Turning back to the interloper, he and Malbar said simultaneously, "Princess Miria!"

Miria frowned as she tried futilely to brush the dirt from her clothing.

"How did you find us?" Pyccis asked, amazed and annoyed.

Miria gazed at them with summer sky eyes and beamed proudly. "I've been watching you for months. I saw you sneaking food from the kitchen and knew you were planning another adventure. I just waited until I was certain you were out of sight before I went through the portcullis and found your tracks so I could follow you. Your footprints were easy to follow in the dry dirt, and I kept close enough I could hear your voices easily. I'm surprised someone else hasn't found you before now."

The boys frowned as they stared at their feet.

"I thought we'd been so careful," Pyccis said.

Miria laughed at them. "Don't worry. I won't tell anyone about this if ..."

"If what?" Malbar asked, his eyes narrowed.

Miria grinned smugly at the two boys. "If I can join."

"Join what?" Pyccis asked.

Resting her hands on her waist, Miria grinned wider. "Join *you* on your adventures from the castle."

"Oh. Well, um, we've got to talk about this privately." Pyccis motioned to Malbar. "Maybe you'd like to wash your face, Miria?"

"Yes, I would," she said.

Pyccis dug under a pile of leaves near gnarled tree roots, took out a waterskin and a stained but relatively clean cloth, and handed them to Miria. Putting his arm around Malbar's shoulder, he led his friend to the opposite side of the dell.

Malbar folded his arms and frowned. "If we let her come with us every time, we'll get caught, I know it."

"But if we don't, she'll tell her father about our secret." Pyccis scrunched up his mouth and raised one eyebrow. "And she did follow us without giving us away, without us even knowing we were being trailed. Besides," he glanced back at the princess, who smiled sweetly at him as she scrubbed her face, "I'd like to have her join us. She could bring more food with her. After all, no one questions her word in the castle. She could ask for a whole ham, and no one would refuse."

"She'd have trouble carrying it," Malbar said with a sour look. "Oh...I guess it'd be all right."

Turning back to a rather smug Miria, Pyccis said, "I guess you can join us, but you have to swear to keep our place a secret."

Miria rolled her eyes. "Of course."

"Then swear. Swear by the Hound of Darkness that you'll never tell anyone about our secret place."

She stood up straight, touched her forehead and chest with her first two fingers of her left hand, and said, "I swear by the Hound of Darkness never to tell anyone about our secret place."

"Now spit," Pyccis said.

She wrinkled her nose, but then she spit on the ground.

"Ok," Pyccis said, "now you're part of our secret circle."

Miria glowed. "I'm so glad. We'll have so much fun together. You," pointing to Pyccis, "can be my prince, and you," pointing at Malbar, "can be captain of my army, and together we'll conquer the world."

Pyccis bowed grandly and grinned. "Ah, my princess, I'd conquer a thousand lands for you."

Glancing sharply at his friend, Malbar also bowed. "And I, princess, I'd fight the greatest armies and slay them by myself for your sake, dying for your honor if I must."

Miria struck a grand pose. "Ah, with devotion like yours, I'll be queen of the world."

Yes, thought Pyccis as he looked at his companion with a little jealousy, *but who'll be your king?*

All day long they played in their leaf-choked dell, eating their small hoard of food, laughing and talking. Having never been beyond the borders of their land, they felt like their secret place was a paradise, a place to be free from the constant surveillance of guards and teachers.

Afternoon became evening. The red-gold sun sank toward the western plains. The wind became brisk and cool. Miria shivered.

"I guess we should go back," Pyccis said with a sigh.

Malbar's shoulders drooped, and he nodded.

Reluctantly, Pyccis crawled through the hedge and led the other two as they all plodded back toward the castle. Sneaking cautiously, half-crouched, Pyccis retraced the path to the stream and helped Miria down the rock face. When they reached the sheltering grove just north of the portcullis, Pyccis said, "I'll go first, then you," pointing at Miria, "then you last," to Malbar. "That way I'll make sure it's clear, and Miria will be safe."

Pyccis dove in the chilly water and swam for the castle wall. As he squirmed through the hole in the grating, he was grabbed by the back of his vest and jerked upward so suddenly, he inhaled water. For several minutes he choked as he crouched on hands and knees. Soon, he heard Miria and Malbar choking as well. Pyccis looked up and stared through watery eyes at Lord Paxell and Captain Callas, both of whom were frowning grimly at them.

"So you've come back from your little adventure, eh?" Paxell asked, his eyes burning with anger as dark as his clothes. "And where have you been all this time?"

"We didn't go very far, my lord." The chilly air and his wet clothing weren't the only reasons Pyccis shook. "We were in no danger."

"No danger!" Paxell's face was livid. "No danger! Beyond the protection of these walls, without guards, no one knowing where you were? And Miria with you? You don't know what danger you might have met!" Paxell halted, his fists clenched as he stared at Pyccis. "If anything had happened to her or you, I couldn't bear it!"

"Father--" Miria began.

"Oh, Miria," Paxell said, kneeling and wrapping his arms around her, "Do you know how frightened I was, how frantic I became when I couldn't find you?" He looked over her shoulder to the shivering, dripping boys. "There are those who'd think nothing of killing you—thieves and Vorlikian spies! You won't leave this castle again without guards, and then only by the front gate! This particular entrance will be sealed off! I can't take the chance that you might be in danger again!"

"Father, please." Miria looked more like a stringy-haired peasant girl instead of a princess. "We meant no harm. We just wanted to play."

Paxell stared at her for a moment, then his tight jaw relaxed slightly. He smoothed a tangle of blond hair from her dirt-smudged face and touched her cheek gently. "I know, Miria, but your days of playing are over. You're my daughter, my dearest and only child. One day you'll be Drambit's ruler. You must learn the discipline and responsibility that come with power. All of you will begin preparing for your roles in life. Miria, you'll learn the ancient writings, history, military and political strategy, and the uses of power." He turned to the boys. "You two will stay safely within the castle walls and will learn strategy and history, tactics of combat, and how to fight with and without weapons." Paxell gazed at both boys intently. "And we'll see who's better."

Pyccis turned toward Malbar, studying him carefully, and for the second time Pyccis saw the other boy, not as a friend, but as a competitor.

19

"You have to consider Vorlik's future, my lord," said Counselor Kenna. The look in his hazel eyes was as adamant as his tone. His short trimmed beard was as white as his hair. "It's been more than fifteen years since you became Vorlik's lord, and you still haven't married."

Cordwin cringed as did the two scribes, the other counselor, and three lieutenants seated around the long narrow table in the council room. The room was a little too warm as the afternoon sunlight poured in through the high windows. *I wish Daikin were here,* Cordwin thought, rubbing the knotted muscles of his neck, *or better yet, I wish I were with him, inspecting the newest recruits for the Tarolin Guard. Anything's better than listening to Kenna again.*

"The people of Vorlik are frightened," Kenna said. "They need to know the land is secure, for them and their children."

Cordwin sighed. "Please, counselor, not today." He didn't want to discuss the subject. Like a child's repetition of the only word he knew, Kenna made the same point at each council meeting. Cordwin was too tired to listen one more time, but he could tell from the counselor's reproving stare that Kenna wasn't going to drop the matter. Cordwin turned to Lieutenant Rayvil. "How are Vorlik's defenses?"

"The signal towers are in place at all four border crossings and maintained constantly," the grizzled guardsman said. "Each Guard has as many soldiers as the barracks can contain. And the troops are constantly training for an attack." He paused. "But it is wearing on the soldiers to be always on alert."

"That's true," Cordwin said, pondering Rayvil's words, "but how can we relax our guard?"

Rayvil rubbed his scarred chin and frowned pensively. "Well, we could give the soldiers leave from the barracks for a few days each week to visit their families. Give a quarter of the soldiers three days off one week, another quarter would have three days off the next week, and so on until everyone has some time off each month. We'd still have enough troops to protect the land, and the soldiers would come back renewed of spirit."

"An excellent idea," Cordwin said and turned to Scribe Vel. "Send the order to each of the four border Guards, and we'll implement the order here immediately."

"There are other ways to protect Vorlik," Kenna said.

Cordwin winced. Hoping to evade another argument, Cordwin turned to Scribe Vel and asked, "Are there other matters we need to consider?"

The lean, pale scribe shuffled through several sheets of paper. "Lord Roth of Hargrim has sent messengers to bargain for our surplus grain."

"How much?"

"Two hundred wagon loads."

Cordwin gasped. "Two hundred wagon loads? Was Hargrim's harvest so poor this year?"

Vel nodded and handed Cordwin a letter in tight script. "Heavy rains caused late planting, then there was no rain for almost two months. Several hailstorms just before harvest time destroyed more than half the remaining crops. Many of Hargrim's people may starve this winter."

Cordwin well remembered the only time he'd visited Hargrim. He'd been barely fourteen and had been astonished by the barren land ruled by Lord Roth, his mother's great uncle. The country was aptly named: a hard, grim land of marginal fields and scrub pastures, tormented by too much wind, too little rain. "Buy up as much grain as possible," Cordwin told the scribe. "Send a letter to Lord Roth telling him we'll gladly sell him our surplus and ask one half of the usual price. I'll make up the difference from my own treasury."

Eyes bulging, Vel kept opening and closing his mouth, but no sound came out. Finally, he said, "But that's...that's outrageous! You can't afford it!"

"Our harvest this year was almost more than the granaries can hold. I can't let Hargrim's people go hungry when I can do something to prevent it," Cordwin said. "Could you?"

Vel frowned and shook his head.

Looking like a cork popping from a bottle, Kenna bolted to his feet. "Since we're speaking about Hargrim, Lord Roth has inquired about a possible match between you and his niece. She's well educated and intelligent, a pretty girl not quite twenty who could produce an heir within a year."

Cordwin gritted his teeth. *Doesn't he ever get tired of harping the same tune?* he thought.

"There have also been inquiries from Lord Elgin of Tukkus regarding his daughter, Lord Orl of Beltrin regarding his granddaughter, and the mayor of Tironza regarding his sister," Vel said. "All of them are young, eligible, and capable of producing numerous children."

Kenna turned toward Vel and held out his hand.

Cordwin turned toward Vel, who shrugged, then extracted several letters from the pile of paper in front of him and held them out to Cordwin. Taking the letters, Cordwin glanced through them. All sounded polite and hopeful. Cordwin sighed and handed the letters back to Vel. "Give them my thanks for the honor they do me, but make it clear that I'm not interested, Vel."

Kenna's face looked like heated metal. "My lord, whether you want to discuss this or not, we must talk about your marriage."

"Must we?" Cordwin murmured to himself. He knew Kenna would keep pushing his point until he'd had his say.

"You are thirty-four and still have no heir. The house of Vorlik needs to continue. Your people depend on it. You must marry and give Vorlik its future lord."

"Bren is Vorlik's future lord."

Kenna threw up his hands in disgust. "That's what you say every time I bring up this subject."

"Then don't bring it up again!" Cordwin said, although he knew there was no hope of that.

"No one even knows if Bren's alive!" Kenna said.

Cordwin turned slowly and stared at Kenna. "Bren *is* alive. The Wizard Briella told me he is. Do you doubt *her* word?"

Kenna shifted in his chair as if it were full of splinters. "Well...no," he said grudgingly. "But we still don't know when he'll return. It might be years from now. And, Baygor forbid it, you might die before that. Who'd rule Vorlik then?"

Cordwin massaged his temples and closed his eyes. "Kenna, we've discussed this before. As my closest kin, Daikin would be regent until Bren returned."

"But--"

"No!" Cordwin pushed to his feet. In a quiet voice like cold steel, he added, "The matter is closed."

Kenna folded his arms and pursed his lips. His face became stony, but the glint in his hazel eyes told Cordwin that the argument would continue—later.

Cordwin leaned against the cool, stone wall of his room. Resting his forehead on his wrist, he gazed out his window toward the western mountains. Sunset had colored them and the autumn clouds magenta and steel blue. A chill breeze ruffled his dark hair with invisible fingers and gently brushed his face. *If only it were Briella's hand touching me, her fingers caressing my face,* he thought.

He had searched for her everywhere, following rumors of the blind story teller or other disguises she might use, but he never found her. Only tales of her healing and kindness.

Loneliness filled his heart with an ache that never stopped. Sometimes he could still feel the echo of her heartbeat against his chest, the touch of her hand on his cheek, the warmth of her lips on his. The scent of lavender had surrounded her like a mist, and every time he caught the scent, tears threatened to spill from his eyes. The memory of holding her so near was incredibly pleasant and deeply painful.

A knock brought Cordwin to attention.

"My lord?" Daikin's voice called from the other side of the door.

Cordwin sighed listlessly. "Come."

Entering and closing the door behind him, Daikin smiled openly, his green eyes glinting. "A long day?"

Cordwin nodded. "You?"

"Inspecting the new recruits is not one of my favorite duties. You forgot to mention that one when you made me captain of the Guard. Sorry I missed the council meeting."

"Oh, yes, I know how sorry you are." Cordwin pressed his palms against his eyes. "Barg's breath, I hate arguing with my counselors."

"Kenna again?"

"Who else?"

"When he thinks he's right, he's as single-minded as a Beltrin merchant."

"And as persistent."

Daikin grinned. "How would a mug of ale go down now? I'm heading for Leez's Tavern in Tarolin Town. He has a barrel of the finest ale I've ever sampled. Why not come with me? We haven't been out on one of our adventures for quite a while, and you're long overdue for some enjoyment. I know two delightful women who'd love to be our companions for the evening."

"You're trying to tempt me, aren't you?"

Daikin's red fox grin lacked only chicken feathers. "Of course. Just forget Kenna, forget everything else, and come with me."

Cordwin gave him a half-hearted smile. "Thanks, truly, but I don't want to be around a crowd tonight."

"Then let's go for a gallop. It'll get you away from the castle—and Kenna—and give you a little peace."

"Well..." Considering how late it was, Cordwin almost said no, but changed his mind. "Why not? I need to get away for a while."

"Wonderful! I'll grab a couple of wineskins—"

"Make that water skins," Cordwin interrupted.

Daikin looked hurt. "All right. Water skins. And I'll meet you by the stables. It's about time you listened to me."

Cordwin just smiled.

By the time Cordwin had changed into some comfortable riding clothes and walked to the torch lit courtyard, Daikin was waiting for him, horses saddled.

"Ready for some fun?" Daikin asked as he mounted.

Cordwin climbed up on Moon Shadow and started to answer when he spotted Kenna coming down the steps, waving his hand and calling, "My lord, a word with you."

"Barg's breath, not now," Cordwin muttered to himself. Darting a pained look at Daikin, he clapped his knees against his horse's sides and held on as Moon Shadow leaped through the gateway. Daikin caught up with him and kept pace, even when Cordwin swerved west.

Wind dried his eyes and plastered his hair against his head. His face felt cold, but sweat ran to his temples. His blood felt like molten steel surging through his body; his heart pounded faster than horse's hooves. He felt as light as milkweed fluff and carefree.

How long they rode, he didn't know. He heard Daikin laughing. Cordwin laughed, too, laughed for the dark red sun as it sank out of sight, for the sweet air scented with wood smoke and spice, for apples hanging heavy on trees. He laughed at Daikin, red hair blowing wildly as he urged his horse on, faster, faster. And he laughed just for being alive.

At last, Cordwin reined his horse to a stop, dismounted, and sat on the damp grass with his back to a tree, still laughing between quick breaths. Daikin plopped down on the ground beside his cousin, leaned back, and propped himself up on elbows.

Twilight shadowed fields and woods. A harvest moon rose orange and full over the eastern mountains. The quiet was broken only by crickets and night birds.

"That felt wonderful!" Cordwin said between gasps.

Daikin chuckled. "Well, we should do it more often. You spend too much time in your room. You need to get out and see your people more often." He prodded Cordwin's shoulder. "You need to enjoy life a little! Find yourself a pretty girl."

Cordwin groaned. "You sound like Kenna now."

"Gods forbid!" Daikin said wincing. "But he has a point."

"He always has a point—which he makes over and over and over." A long sigh escaped Cordwin's lips. "Why can't he just let it be? I'm all right the way I am."

Daikin turned to Cordwin, leaned on his shoulder, and gave him a "your-good-friend's-about-to-have-a-serious-talk-with-you" look. "Cord, I'm worried about you, and I'm not the only one. Everyone in the castle has noticed how you walk around hardly aware of your surroundings. Sometimes when people talk to you, you don't seem to see them. It's as if you're looking through them, like a window." He paused, as if uncertain whether to continue. "You love her, don't you?"

Flinching, Cordwin tried to hide his surprise. "Who?"

"Briella."

Cordwin started to speak, then glanced away. "Am I that transparent?"

"Look, you can fool others with the excuse you're saving the throne for Bren, but I know you better than anyone else. Whenever her name is mentioned, your eyes glitter and you absolutely glow."

Cordwin tried to interrupt, but Daikin held up his hand for silence. "Let's suppose Bren does return and takes the throne. What will you have? Captaincy of Vorlik?"

"You're Vorlik's captain."

"Don't interrupt! The devotion of all the people? That's small comfort on a cold night. Cord, why don't you just marry her?"

"I asked." Cordwin smiled dolefully. "She refused."

"She what?" Daikin's eyebrows shot up, and his mouth dropped open. "But—why? It wouldn't be the first time a Wizard married a lord of Vorlik. Our ancestress Timmree was a Wizard."

"I know. So does Briella, but she still refused." Corwin leaned his head back against the tree, then turned his head toward Daikin. "I won't ask anyone else. I can't." He paused. "I love her."

Daikin lowered his eyes and nodded.

Cordwin stared up at the few stars bright enough to shine in the moonlit sky. "I saw her at the Autumn Fair in Tironza, years ago when you and I went together."

"You did?" Daikin said. "You never told me that."

"I don't tell you everything," Cordwin said softly. "I held her in my arms, and we danced and danced until almost sunset. And she came to me the night the last assassin tried to climb the wall to my room. She's the one who saved my life, and I asked her to marry me that night. I held her in my arms and kissed her. She almost said yes, I know she wanted to, but she said she couldn't protect our people or me if she married me. Then she flew away. I haven't seen her since that night."

Cordwin gave his cousin a sad smile. "You don't know how much I envy the sick who feel her healing touch. I want to hear her tell stories to children or sing the ancient ballads. I wish she were singing and talking to me. Just to me." He glanced at Daikin. "I suppose I sound selfish."

Daikin grinned. "No, you sound like a man in love."

"I need her," he whispered, "as much as I need food and water and air."

"I wish I could give you some comfort." Daikin clasped his cousin's arm. "I don't know any medicine for an aching heart—except time. And who knows, time may change her mind," he said in a lighter tone. "Why don't you change your mind about joining me at Leez's place? It's still early in the evening. We can have some of that ale, sing a few songs, and still have a good night's sleep."

Cordwin stared at the darkening sky for a moment before he answered. "All right. If Kenna's going to complain anyway, I might as well make it worthwhile."

They mounted up and rode back, slower this time, to the little town just east of the castle.

Leez's Tavern was packed with locals and merchants and drivers from several caravans. Leez greeted them at the door with a bear hug. Apropos, since he looked like a Formian bear.

"Welcome, my lord! Welcome, captain!" the tavern keep said, his voice rich as aged wine. "You've stayed away from my tavern too long. Come, sit. I'll bring you some ale that you'll swear was made by Baygor himself."

Cordwin smiled as he watched Leez plow through the rows of tables. It did feel good to be there. Maybe Daikin was right; he should get out more among his people. Maybe it would take his mind off other things.

Leez hadn't exaggerated about the ale. It was dark, not too bitter, with a hint of sweetness, perfect. Cordwin took several long, slow swallows before he spoke. "How much do you pay Baygor to make this?"

Leez grinned with pleasure. "I have one more barrel of the same brew. If you'd like, I can send it to the castle."

Cordwin took another sip and let the beer rest on his tongue a moment before he swallowed it. He wiped his mouth on his sleeve. "No, all your customers should have a chance to sample ale this good. But I thank you for the offer."

Bowing, Leez left.

Someone strummed a lute. Another began to sing. Soon, everyone joined in, clapping hands, stomping feet, clanging mugs on the tables. Cordwin joined in with as much enthusiasm as Daikin. One of the locals, a stout pig-faced man, leaped onto a table and began dancing. The wood creaked but held.

Many mugs and several hours later, the two cousins stumbled back to their horses. It took several tries before they managed to climb up into the saddles. Shoulders slouched, they kept the horses to a slow walk.

"Barg's breath, I'm tired," Daikin groaned.

"Not as tired as I am," Cordwin groaned back. "But happy. Very happy."

"See?" Daikin said with laugh. "You should always listen to me. I know what's best for you."

"You did tonight."

The full harvest moon shone overhead, making the night almost as bright as dawn. Night-blooming starflowers spread their heavy sweet fragrance on the light cool breeze. Crickets scratched and night birds sang. Somewhere in the distance a dove called to its mate, but there was no answer.

They'd reached the barrow ground between the town and the castle when Cordwin shivered, not from cold, but from dread. A wind, colder than death, rustled through his hair and trailed down his neck. His eyes and head cleared instantly, and fear trickled like sweat down his back. He looked down at his eagle amulet. It glowed bright red in the dark. He didn't know what it meant, but he knew it couldn't be good.

"Baygor protect us," he whispered, reaching for his sword and glancing at his cousin.

Daikin's eyes were round as coins and glittered emerald bright, but his face was paler than normal.

Suddenly, Cordwin felt as if he couldn't breathe, as if invisible fingers tightened around his throat. His heart pounded in his chest. His head throbbed. He felt as if he were sinking in water. The next thing he knew he hit the ground hard and lay on his back. His vision was edged with black and yellow, and he saw Daikin slumped against his horse's neck. Cordwin tried to move, but couldn't.

"Cord," Daikin croaked. He slowly drew his sword, but fell to the ground. He crawled to Cordwin's side, raised up on his knees, and gazed into the darkness. "Whatever you are, you won't touch Lord Cordwin!" Daikin gasped, holding his sword with both hands.

A dark form rose from the barrow ground and strolled toward them, moonlight revealing his face. Hair as dark as raven feathers fell in waves around a lean face. Dark eyes glittered as the man smiled.

"Lord Cordwin of Vorlik," the raven-haired man said in a deep resonant voice. Dressed all in black, the man was like a shadow within a shadow. "I've been waiting to meet you for so long. Such a pity our first meeting will also be our last." He held out his left hand, spoke some strange words, and slowly began to draw his fingers toward his thumb.

Cordwin's throat tightened. His head pounded as hard and fast as his heart. *A Sorcerer!* he thought as his vision began to dim. *A Sorcerer in Vorlik! Lady Baramay, protect my people!*

At that moment, a dove fluttered to the ground in front of him. A mist swirled around the dove, and suddenly Briella stood between him and the Sorcerer. The hood of her cloak slipped off her head. A light breeze brushed the cloak back from her arms. In the bright moonlight, Briella seemed to glow. With palms facing the Sorcerer, she moved her hands in two contiguous circles in front of her and spoke words Cordwin didn't understand. The invisible fingers squeezing Cordwin's throat disappeared. He gasped and choked and sucked in a deep breath.

"Get him back to the castle!" Briella called. "Now!!"

Daikin put his arm under Cordwin and helped him sit up.

"No," Cordwin whispered, his throat too raw to speak louder, "help her."

"He can't!" Briella said. "Get back to Tarolin! I can't fight if I have to worry about you both! Go! Quickly! And don't come back!"

Daikin helped Cordwin stand, and they staggered to their horses. Daikin heaved Cordwin onto his saddle, then mounted his own horse.

Cordwin slumped against Moon Shadow's neck, too weak to sit erect. His chest ached, and his lungs burned with each breath. "Home," he whispered.

The horse broke into a gallop. Cordwin wrapped his arms around Moon Shadow's neck and held on. Unable to focus his eyes, he closed them and prayed, "Lady Baramay, keep Briella safe."

He heard Daikin's horn blowing as they neared the castle gate and the creak of the portcullis being raised. Voices shouted his name. Moon Shadow halted, his coat slick with sweat and his sides heaving. Hands clutched Cordwin's arms, and he opened his eyes. He was in the courtyard of Tarolin Castle. Guards ran from the barracks and from the castle itself, surrounding the two horses.

"Help him down gently," Daikin said as he dismounted next to Cordwin. Daikin stumbled and fell to one knee. Two guards helped him stand.

Several guards caught Cordwin as he slid off Moon Shadow. His legs felt too weak to hold him. He sagged in the guards' arms.

Suddenly, blue fire crackled through the air beyond the castle walls. Red fire arced toward the blue and exploded into a red shower of sparks. Thunder shook the trees and echoed through the courtyard.

"We have to help her," Cordwin croaked.

"What do you want me to do?" Daikin asked. "I can't fight a Sorcerer, and neither can you!"

"Daikin, I have to see!" Cordwin said, reaching toward his cousin. "I have to know she's all right!"

"I'll climb up to the balustrade and watch and tell you what I see," Daikin said. "Will that be enough?"

Cordwin nodded weakly

"Take him to his room," Daikin said. Cordwin started to protest, but Daikin held up his hand. "I'll report as soon as I know what's happened."

Cordwin didn't resist when the guards put his arms over their shoulders and mostly carried him into the castle. The guards took him up the stairs to his room, placed him on his bed, then lit a candle and left him to rest. His throat was bruised and raw, causing coughing spasms that left him breathless. A short time later, the door opened, and Tothim came in, carrying his bag of medicines. Tothim felt Cordwin's forehead, then checked his pulse on his wrist. Taking the candle from the bedside table, Tothim held it near Cordwin's face and peered closely at him. The candle seemed painfully bright.

"Your eyes are as red as blood," Tothim said, "and there are bruises and some swelling on your throat. You shouldn't talk for a few days. I'll have some roborant tea sent up to you, and you need to rest. No work for at least three days."

Cordwin gave a grim, hoarse laugh. "At least I won't have to see Counselor Kenna for a while."

Tothim smiled. "Rest now. I'll send up the tea. And no talking." He turned and left.

No sooner had he left than a dove flew through his window and changed into Briella. Her blue dress was torn near the hem and was peppered with tiny burns. He tried to sit up but was too weak.

"Lie still," she said, kneeling beside his bed.

She laid her hand on his forehead, then touched his throat. She took a small jar from a pocket in her cloak and opened the waxed lid. A fragrance like spring flowers and sweet herbs filled the room. She spread a small amount of salve on his throat. Immediately, it felt better, although it still hurt to swallow, and his chest still burned.

"Are you all right?" she asked.

"Are you?" he whispered. He touched her golden hair and caressed her cheek. She looked as young as when he had first seen her, except for her eyes. They seemed much older or perhaps just weary. "Are you all right?"

"Yes," she said quietly, her shoulders drooping.

"The Sorcerer?"

"Dead." She shuddered. "A stone statue now stands in the barrow ground."

"How did you know he was here? That I needed you?"

She took his hand and held it to her cheek. "I'm often near you, even if you don't see me. I was in Tarolin Town tonight and saw you go to Leez's tavern." She paused. "Something told me I needed to be there. That's when my amulet began to glow blue, and I felt dizzy. I knew there was a Sorcerer nearby."

"My eagle pendant glowed red when I neared the barrow ground," Cordwin said. "It happened once before, at my coronation just before you appeared."

"A warning," she said as she gazed at the pendant. "Watch for it. If you ever see it turn red again, flee. Don't look around. Don't take time even to think about where the Sorcerer might be. Just run for the nearest safe place. Promise me you'll do it. Please!"

He nodded slowly.

She kissed his palm. Tears glittered in her eyes. "Now you know why I can't marry you. If I were human, I couldn't have protected you tonight. And if anything happened to you . . ." She kissed his palm again.

"If you won't marry me, then stay with me and protect me here," he said. "Just don't leave me."

She gazed at him silently for a few moments, then shook her head. "Could you be this close to me every day without wanting more? Could you?" She paused and rested her cheek against his hand. "I couldn't. I'm not that strong."

Someone knocked on the door. "My lord?" a gravelly female voice said.

Briella stood instantly and started to bolt for the window, like a deer startled in the woods.

Cordwin grasped her hand and held tight. "She's bringing tea," he said. "Tothim sent it up."

"My lord?" the woman called again.

Briella reached in a pocket on her dress, took out a small pouch, and handed the pouch to him. "Add one piece of this bark to the tea. It will heal your throat much quicker." She pulled her hand from his grasp.

"No! Don't leave!" he cried in a hoarse voice. He held out his arms toward her. "Please!"

"I can't stay," she said, tears flowing down her face. "I can't."

"My lord, are you all right?" the voice on the other side of his door called. "My lord!"

"Far-thell, my love," Briella said.

The door burst open, and four guards and a portly matron poured into the room. Briella glanced at them, then looked back at Cordwin for a moment. Speaking strange words again, she changed into a dove and flew out his window.

20

Fatigue throbbed like a headache as Briella leaned against the callum tree near her house and shivered from the cool breeze and warm memories. The landscape was blurred and distorted, like looking through flawed glass, until she wiped her eyes.

Her memories were of the night when Cordwin had held her and asked her to marry him, almost fourteen years ago. The feel of his arms around her, the scent of his skin, set her blood thrumming throughout her body. His desperate cry of loneliness as she left him still echoed painfully in her heart.

She rubbed her arms to chase away her chill. Her thoughts shifted to the night the Sorcerer tried to kill Cordwin. *I almost lost him that night. I wish I could've stayed with him, married him, and shared whatever time we had,* she thought, *but if I had, I couldn't have protected him. He would have died because of my selfishness.*

The Wall of Warding had kept Vorlik free from invasion. Forty-five callum trees now grew across the land, and more seeds had been harvested for planting next year. The priests of Baygor had created an order of itinerant healers to make the healing potions and salves from the callum trees and to minister to all parts of Vorlik. Briella had kept her promise; she'd served Vorlik. But she'd spent twenty years alone.

Leaning back, she gazed at the Sparks of Baygor sparkling in the new moon sky. "Oh, Cordwin," she whispered like a night wind's sigh, "I wish fate had allowed us to be together, to be happy, if only for a while."

She'd seen Cordwin many times since then. He always looked at every face with desperate hope in his eyes, searching for her. Once when she'd been in Leflin at the Midsummer Fete, he'd come with Daikin to the celebration. Cordwin seemed to recognize her in spite of her disguise as Old Mam, but she'd melted into the crowd before he could reach her.

Still shivering, Briella hurried inside her house and tried not to think of him. She had only a short time left to finish her last and most powerful creation: a special sword for the house of Vorlik. After a five-year search, she'd bought a flawless Drambini emerald, the size of a robin's egg and shaped by Shiffin the Jeweler of Tironza, for the hilt. It had taken her two more years to find the smith from Tukkus who was skilled enough to forge the blade according to her directions. In the last three years between her normal rounds of Vorlik, she'd infused the sword with power, though the spells had drained her.

The final spell, to seal the magic in the sword, would require seven days of concentration to complete. The effort would leave her weak and vulnerable. In her days as an apprentice, someone—usually Amaly—had always kept watch while she'd recovered. Now, she had no friend to protect her. The thought made her loneliness even harder to bear.

"Amaly, I wish you were here. I miss you so much. I need your help, now more than ever." She sighed, took a deep breath, and began her greatest spell.

From sunrise to sunset for seven days she concentrated on the spell, barely taking time to eat or drink. At night she collapsed in dreamless sleep. By the time the spell was completed, she was gaunt and so drained, she fell to the floor, too weak to move. For five days she drifted in and out of dreams of her grandfather and Cordwin. On the fifth day she crawled to the table where there was some dry bread, dried fruit, and stale water, placed there before she began the spell. She sat on one of the chairs, choked down a little food, and swallowed some water, then folded her arms on the table to pillow her head and slept again.

Her cheeks were damp and chapped when she awoke, several hours before dawn. She'd had a dream, a dream of Cordwin. The dream was so real, she could feel the softness of his lips on hers, the comfort of his arms.

"I want to see him again. I *need* to see him again, one last time," she whispered to herself before she drifted off to sleep again.

In the morning she woke, stood, and stretched to relieve the aches in her arms, neck, and back. Gazing at the sword on the table, she drew her fingertips lightly over letters etched on the blade. It gleamed as if it contained sunlight or fire. Sleek and clean of line, the sword was a weapon of beauty and strength.

Glancing around her silent, empty house, she thought of Cordwin. She was still too weak to fly to Tarolin Castle, so she ate the last bit of bread she had, slept, and waited until the next night.

Stars twinkled overhead, so close she felt she could touch them. The air had the bite of winter as she stood before the callum tree, spoke the words of power, and changed into a dove. She sped northward though the mid-autumn night with a moon, nearly full, shining silver on her grey wings. Tironza was dark and quiet, only a few points of light gleaming in the night. Farther north, no lights shone from the inn at Yarrow or from Liska's house across the road. The closer she was to Tarolin Castle, the faster her heartbeat, almost as fast as her wings. A few torches lit the courtyard as she flew past the castle wall. She fluttered through Cordwin's window and transformed in the moonlight.

Cordwin slept restlessly, blue-white moonlight casting soft shadows on his lean face. His dark wavy hair was tousled. He was covered to his chin with a blanket, one arm crooked beneath his head.

She sat on the window sill and leaned her cheek against the cool stone, content merely to look at him. *He's so beautiful,* Briella thought, tears threatening to spill down her face.

Kneeling beside him, she touched his arm. "Cordwin," she said softly, "Cordwin, wake up. I need to speak to you."

Waking with a start, Cordwin's eyes were half-closed with sleep, then shot wide open when he looked straight at her. "Briella!"

He circled her with his arms, kissed her face, and pulled her down to his bare chest. "You've come back to me! I thought I'd never find you!" He pressed his cheek against hers and whispered, "Don't leave me again, please! I love you more than my life. Marry me. Marry me and be my wife."

Pushing herself up, Briella started to speak, but Cordwin put his fingertips over her lips and shook his head. "I don't care if we have only a little while. Whatever time we have, it'll be enough."

If only that were true, she thought. *I want to believe it so desperately, but I can't.* She had to remind herself that she'd come for a specific reason. "Come with me. I want to show you something I've made for Bren."

Cordwin held her tighter. "No, please, just stay with me."

"You must see this. Please." She touched his cheek. "Cordwin, please." She felt him tense, then relax.

"But...All right."

Briella pushed herself up and stood up. Cordwin rolled off the other side of his bed, grabbed a furred robe lying on the chair beside the glowing hearth, and slipped the robe on.

"Where are we going?" he asked.

"To my house."

He looked puzzled. "How?"

"I'll use a translation spell to carry us both, but it's difficult and draining. I have to know exactly where I'm going so I can only travel this way to places I've been before. That's why I usually travel as a mourning dove. But I need you to come with me."

"What should I do?" he asked.

"Put your arms around me, and trust me."

"I do trust you, with my life," he said as he encircled her with his arms.

She started to spread her cloak around them when he said, "Wait! There's something I have to show you!"

He rushed to his trunk, opened it, and took out two items: one was wrapped in red velvet and tied with a golden cord; the other, wrapped in black woolen fabric and tied with a leather thong. He slipped both of them inside his robe, then hurried back to Briella.

Wrapping her cloak about them, she spoke a word of command, and they became like breath on cold mornings. Swirling rainbows of light surrounded them. Cordwin gripped her tighter, his breath coming in short gasps. They rose together on the wind and sped towards her house. As they landed before her door, she transformed them back.

"Great Baygor!" Cordwin said. "To travel like that – it's amazing!"

"But very tiring." Briella smiled and took him inside. She called flame to the candle stands in the kitchen to light their way.

Cordwin's eyes were as wide as an owl's as he turned slowly, gazing at the room. "Beautiful," he whispered. "It's as if the house were carved from a hill of sapphire."

Briella took his hand and led him to the table, but she sank down on a chair, weary from the journey. She pointed to the sword, gleaming blue in the moonlight that seeped through the walls. She caressed the blade with pride and said, "This is a Sword of Truth. It's stronger than the finest steel, and the one who wields it will always discern truth from lie. Only the heirs of the house of Vorlik can use this sword. Bren will need it when he returns." She choked back a sob, remembering the vision of her death. "And he'll return soon. Too soon. And too late for us."

"No, it's not too late for us." Cordwin sat down beside her and held her to his chest as she shuddered with dread. He kissed her forehead and caressed her hair. "I told you I had something to show you, something that gives me such hope, I'm almost afraid to voice it." He reached inside his robe and removed the black woolen bundle. "Open it," he said and handed it to her.

Briella took the bundle, untied the leather thong, and unwrapped the cloth. Inside was a thin-bladed dagger with a silver hilt. She looked up at Cordwin, puzzled. "How can this bring you hope?" she asked.

"This is the dagger the assassin was carrying the night you saved me." He paused, trailing his index finger down her cheek. "The night you saved my life."

"I don't understand."

"You came to me because in a dream you saw me dying from a wound from a poisoned dagger."

She nodded.

"How do you know it was poisoned?" Cordwin asked.

"I saw it in the dream," she said.

"But how do you know *this* dagger, the assassin's dagger, was poisoned?" he asked.

"Because I saw you attacked with a poisoned dagger."

Cordwin smiled at her. "But I wasn't attacked, was I?"

"Of course not," she said, perplexed. "I was there to stop the assassin."

"Could you tell if this dagger were poisoned?"

"Yes."

"Then test it. See if it's poisoned."

Confused and uncertain what he was trying to prove, Briella held her left hand over the dagger and raised her right hand over her head. "By the power of Baygor whose light reveals the truth in all things, *tasrin kagali bhatticharya harason!*"

A golden light surrounded the dagger, shimmering orange and red at the edges. Briella's eyes grew wide as she gazed at the dagger. "It's not poisoned," she whispered, astonished. "But I saw it. I saw it."

"So your vision was false."

"That's...not...possible," she said, shaking her head. "What you saw didn't happen, did it?" Cordwin asked.

Briella felt as if she couldn't breathe. "No," she stammered.

Cordwin put his arms around her again. "If you were wrong about this vision, is it possible," he said quietly, "is it just possible that your first vision was false, too?"

Too overwhelmed, Briella couldn't answer. She felt dizzy and off balance, as if the ground under her feet had suddenly shifted. *Lady Baramay, help me understand this,* she thought. *Please, tell me I haven't lived lonely and alone for nothing!* Desolation struck her like a blow to her chest. "No, oh, please no," she gasped, tears streaming down her face. "All these years. All these years."

Cordwin pressed her close, kissing her forehead, her hair. "Sweet lady, don't cry. Don't cry. We have the rest of our lives together."

She gazed up into his eyes, desperately wanting to stay with him. *Vorlik is as protected as it can be,* she thought. *What more could I do as a Wizard to protect the land and its people?* "I've been so lonely," she said.

"So have I," he said. "But we never have to be alone anymore. Marry me. Marry me tonight."

"No, not tonight."

"But why?" he asked desperately.

She smiled at him. "Because if I marry you tonight, I won't be able to take you back to the castle."

"But you'll marry me when we return to the castle?"

"Yes," she said softly, "I'll marry you then."

Cordwin kissed her forehead, her right cheek and her left, then tilted her chin and kissed her lips passionately. "I love you with all my heart, for all my life," he said and embraced her tenderly. "When we return to the castle, our lives will become hectic. But right now we're alone together in this quiet, peaceful place. I'm holding you in my arms with Baygor and Baramay watching over us. This can be our wedding night."

Slowly, Briella raised her eyes to meet his. "Yes," she said, "our wedding night. I love you more than life itself."

Standing, she held out her hand. Cordwin took it, and she led him to her bed chamber.

As the sky became dove grey edged with dawn pink, Briella lay awake, nestled against Cordwin's chest. Her head pillowed on his shoulder, she felt completely content and deliriously happy for the first time in her life.

He moaned and stirred from sleep. A smile as warm as summer winds lit his face as he opened his eyes and gazed at her. "How did I live before you came?" he whispered.

She raised up on one elbow and caressed his cheek. "I knew the first time I saw you, the first time I looked into your eyes, that you were my life mate. A human lord? My life mate?" She smiled slightly. "I was so startled, I almost couldn't speak. And after I had the vision of my death, I fought against the feeling that began to flower in my heart." She bent down and kissed him. "But every time I saw you, every time I was near you..." She gazed at him, trembling.

Cordwin drew her closer and kissed her tenderly, then gathered her in his arms.

Briella's tears fell onto his smooth, bronzed chest. *It would be hard to die now,* she thought, *now I finally let myself love him. But will I die? Was the vision only an illusion, the dream only a dream? How can I know for certain?*

"Don't cry, my love," he said, his voice as soft as baby's breath.

Briella looked up at him and caressed his cheek. "They're only tears of joy." She glanced at the gathering light coming through the window. "It's almost dawn. I should take you back to your castle before you're missed. Daikin will tear the castle apart looking for you if he discovers you're gone."

Cordwin pulled her closer and grinned. "And won't he be surprised when we tell him we're married? He has to stand up with me for the formal ceremony. We'll have the biggest wedding feast since Cavolin and Timmree! And we'll dance until dawn and drink barrels of wine and declare holiday for a week! And I'll invite lords from all the surrounding lands to share our happiness!"

He glanced at the ceiling. "Let's see. Orl, Roth, Elgin, Merrik, chiefs of the Formian council — we might be able to have the wedding feast in a week, if we send out the messengers today."

Briella smiled at him. "We have to return to Tarolin Castle first, and then we'll marry."

"Not yet," he said, smiling. He rose and walked to where his robe lay on the floor. There he retrieved the red velvet bundle and came back to sit on the edge of the bed. "I promised I'd play for you, only you," he said as he unwrapped the recorder. "Do you remember?"

"Yes." She touched his shoulder and drew her fingertips down his muscular arm. "I remember. At the Autumn Fair, the day I gave you the recorder."

He put the mouthpiece to his lips and began to play a melody so sweet, tears welled up in her eyes and spilled down her cheeks. She closed her eyes and listened to each note, clear as morning, deep as a cavern, filling her heart with joy and serenity. The last note echoed a few moments like the trill of a songbird, then faded away.

Gradually, she opened her eyes and gazed at him. "I love you," she whispered and beckoned him to her arms.

Cordwin enfolded her and kissed her neck, and they lay down again, giving each other pleasure for pleasure, love for love.

The sun had crept well above the eastern mountains as Briella and Cordwin rose and dressed. She started to tie the Sword of Truth around her waist.

"Leave it here," Cordwin said.

Briella shook her head. "Bren will come sometime," she said, "and he'll need this. If I leave it here, it will be hard to retrieve once I've lost my powers."

Cordwin nodded slowly.

She wrapped her cloak around them and glided on the winds of morning toward Tarolin. When they reached his room, she transformed them. They stood silently holding each other. The journey left Briella weary, but she felt safe and content in his embrace.

"I never thought I'd be this happy," Cordwin said as he tilted her chin up. He smiled at her, then kissed the tip of her nose. "I'll have to tell Scribe Vel to send out the invitations to the formal wedding today. Is a week enough time to prepare?"

"Why do we need a formal wedding?" she asked and gave him a quick hug. "If we speak our vows, we'll be married."

"True, by all the laws of the land." He lifted her in his arms and whirled her around until she was dizzy and laughing. "But you're marrying the lord of Vorlik," Cordwin said as he set her back on her feet. "And tradition requires a public ceremony for royal weddings. Kenna will be thrilled I'm finally going to be married. But," he smiled at her, "let's say our vows now."

Briella smiled up at him and nodded.

Cordwin kissed her and caressed her cheek. Removing his silver and emerald ring, Timmree's ring, he slipped it on her finger. "Before Baramay the Creator and Baygor the Preserver, I give you this ring as a symbol of my faithfulness to you and my love for you. Please accept me as your husband for as long as I breathe."

She looked at the ring on her finger, Timmree's ring, then looked up at Cordwin. "Before Baramay the Creator and Baygor the Preserver, I accept this ring and vow my faithfulness to you and my love for you. You are my husband, and I–"

Suddenly, Briella stiffened as light lanced through her head, light so sharp and intense, she couldn't move or speak for a few moments. At first she thought Baramay was taking her powers away, but then an image formed in her mind, a face she'd seen once before in a vision when she first came to Vorlik. Her breath seemed trapped in her chest. She felt cold, so very cold. The Sword of Truth at her side suddenly felt unbearably heavy, she felt so weak. She grasped Cordwin's arms to keep from falling.

Cordwin's smile turned to a puzzled frown. "What's wrong? You haven't finished your vows."

"No," Briella whispered, her fingers digging into his arms, "I see...I see..."

"What? What do you see?" Cordwin asked softly as he tightened his embrace.

"Oh, no. Not now," she murmured, her heart pounding so hard, her chest hurt. Bren had come through the Wall of Warding; she felt his presence as clearly as she felt Cordwin's arms around her. "Please, not now," she prayed.

"What's wrong?" Cordwin asked as he held her close and stroked her hair gently. "Tell me!"

Pulling back far enough to gaze at him, she stood on tiptoes and covered his face with desperate kisses. Her eyes filled with tears, and her heart was torn between anger and fear. She pressed against him, trying to stop her shivering, but it didn't help. When her throat relaxed enough for her to speak again, her voice quavered. "The visions weren't false. The vision I saw of you just hasn't happened yet. Someone will come with a poison dagger to kill you. Be careful, my love. Be so very careful because I won't be there to protect you."

"What are you saying?" Cordwin asked, panic in his voice.

"Bren's come. There's no time left for us." She whispered a word, turned into a dove, and flew from his room.

Frantically racing to the window, Cordwin shouted as if his lungs were trying to explode from his throat. "NO!!! Not now! I can't lose you!" His fingers gripped the window sill like tree roots. "Briella, come back! Please, come back to me!"

Only his mournful echo replied as he beat his fists against the window frame.

"She can't die! Not now!" he cried. "I have to stop him!"

His chamber door burst open as Daikin charged into the room with sword drawn. Finding Cordwin alone, Daikin gave him a bewildered look. "Why're you shouting? I thought another assassin had somehow avoided the extra guards and attacked you—or worse!"

Cordwin hit the stones of the window frame again, hoping the physical pain would numb the pain in his heart. "It is worse! She'll die if I don't stop him!"

Daikin stared at him as if he were insane. "Stop who? Who's going to die?"

"Briella!"

Daikin grabbed Cordwin's arms and gave him a shake. "What are you talking about? Briella's a Wizard. She'll live for hundreds of years."

Fear as cold and hard as a rock gripped his heart. Cordwin clutched his cousin's shoulders. "No, she told me, when we first met at the coronation! She had a vision of Bren as a young man, coming back to Vorlik, coming to kill her! He's here, now, in Vorlik! I have to find him, stop him! I can't let him kill her!" He stared at Daikin, anguish pulling at the corners of his eyes. "She finally accepted me, said she'd marry me. I gave her my ring, and I spoke my vows, and she'd almost finished saying hers. Then she had a vision of Bren in Vorlik now. I can't lose her! Help me! Help me stop him!"

Silent for a moment, Daikin nodded. "All right. We can try. But...Briella's vision...if she's seen this..." He halted, chewing on his lip, then gave Cordwin a crooked smile. "Of course, I'll help."

"Send word to the commanders of the four border Guards to watch for Bren and for any sign of unusual activity on the borders. Keep the Tarolin Guard alert as well while I'm gone."

Daikin frowned. "What do you mean—gone? Where?"

"I'm going to find her. I'll protect her from Bren myself if he slips by the border garrisons. You're in command of Vorlik's forces until I return."

"But you can't leave now."

Cordwin ignored Daikin's remark. "Maybe I should send for a dozen Formian trackers. With their help I could cover Vorlik in a few days. We can start in the southern mountains. That's where her house is."

Daikin grabbed Cordwin's arms and gave him a slight shake. "That's foolish! You belong here, not dashing all over Vorlik like a whirlwind!"

Jerking from Daikin's grip, Cordwin shook his head stubbornly. "No."

"Look, Briella obviously didn't want you with her—"

"You don't know—"

"Yes, I do!" Daikin's eyes were like burning ice, like frozen fire. "She left you. She had a good reason. Wizards always have good reasons for what they do. Just think for a moment. She's seen a vision of her death by Bren's hand, your nephew's hand. She knows it'll happen—no matter how much you or I or the rest of Vorlik hope she's wrong. She cares so much for all of us, but especially for you. So she wants to protect you, to spare you any grief. And if a Wizard can't protect herself, what makes you think a love-sick human like you can?" He tried to smile but failed.

"I can try!" Anger almost covered the fear in Cordwin's voice. "I have to try! I can't just wait!"

"That's exactly what you have to do. You can't search Vorlik the way the five Guards can. Let them do what they've been trained to do. And let me do my job—or relieve me of command, if you don't trust my judgment."

Stunned by the offer, Cordwin gaped at his cousin. "You're serious."

Daikin's light brows raised slightly. His lips barely moved as he answered. "I wouldn't have said it if I weren't."

Cordwin wanted to resist, wanted to deny Daikin's words, but he knew Daikin was right. Cordwin's shoulders slumped as his gaze faltered. "I'll stay. You know your duties better than I do."

"Sensible of you," Daikin answered.

Cordwin jerked toward his cousin, angry. Daikin's crooked smile and the mischievous glint in his green eyes stopped Cordwin. Daikin was teasing. As always.

Cordwin gave a deep sigh and relaxed, suddenly realizing how tense and tight his whole body had been. "Making you captain was the best thing I ever did. What would I do without your good sense?"

"Make more mistakes."

Cordwin hugged his cousin, needing Daikin's strength and comfort. "Baramay blessed me the day you were born," he said.

Daikin hugged him back and said, "Come on. Let's save Briella." He released Cordwin, strode to the door, opened it, and called guards from the corridor. "Send word to the four border Guards. Tell them to watch for any young men of twenty to twenty-five years – strangers to Vorlik – and bring them under guard directly to Lord Cordwin. Also, be alert for any unusual activity on the borders."

Cordwin interrupted him. "If any of them has a jeweled knife, take it and give it to no one except me. Don't harm them, but don't allow them to escape. This is imperative! What about the Formian trackers?"

Daikin ground his teeth for a moment, then nodded. "Send a messenger to the Council of Formian Tribes requesting a dozen trackers for the usual fee. I want the Five Guards on full alert beginning now."

Bowing low, the puzzled guards left immediately.

Daikin bowed, too, and started to leave but hesitated, his back toward Cordwin. "I'll do my best. You know that."

"Yes," Cordwin replied softly. "I know."

"For your sake, I don't want her to die." Daikin bowed and strode quickly from the room.

Cordwin stared at the closed door, wishing he could say how much Daikin's help meant to him. Slowly turning back to the window, Cordwin braced himself on the ledge and stared past the courtyard.

The sun cast long morning shadows, but none were as dark as the fear that shadowed his heart.

"I'll save you, Briella, somehow," he said. "I won't let you die."

21

Briella flew south, fear and despair almost freezing her heart. "Lady Baramay, why?" she prayed. "Why let me find happiness only to have it ripped away so suddenly?"

She passed dark, quiet Rindolar Woods, passed fields and vineyards and herds of sheep grazing in still green meadows. By the time she reached Yarrow, she was exhausted. She flitted to the herb garden behind Liska's house and landed, changing to normal form only moments after touching the ground. She hoped no one saw her, but she was too tired to care.

Using the stone wall for support, she felt her way around to the front door and knocked. She heard the clatter of a chair being scooted back and footsteps on the wooden floor. The door opened, and Liska stood there with his mouth dropped open and his eyes blinking in surprise.

"Briella," he whispered.

"Please," she said weakly, "may I come in?"

"Of course," he said and stepped aside to let her enter. As soon as she was inside, he closed the door. "Please sit with me. I just heated some water for peppermint tea. Would you like some?"

She staggered to one of his two chairs and sank down onto it, unable to stand any longer. The Sword of Truth clattered against the chair leg. "Yes," she said softly, "please. Anything to warm up. I'm so cold." She rubbed her arms, but that didn't help.

Liska took a plain brown ceramic cup from a shelf on the wall and set it on the table in front of her. He pulled a stem of peppermint from a newly tied bundle hanging from the ceiling and put the stem in the cup. Using a thickly folded cloth, he took an iron kettle from one of the hearth hooks and poured steaming water into the cup, then put the kettle back on the hook. The cool soothing scent of peppermint filled his one-room house. "Did you want honey?" he asked.

"Yes." She untied the sword from her waist and placed it on the floor beside her.

He brought a small covered crock to the table and set it before Briella along with a wooden spoon. He gazed down at the sword on the floor. "Why are you carrying a sword?"

"It's a gift for the lord of Vorlik," Briella said softly. She took the spoon and drizzled a small amount of honey in the steaming liquid. She stared at the tea, watching as the water turned to greenish gold as the tea steeped. She held her hands over the steam that twisted and swirled up from the cup, and she shivered. Liska added more wood to the fire and stirred it to a roaring blaze. Briella barely felt it.

Liska took a folded quilt from the end of his bed, shook it out, and wrapped it around her shoulders.

"Thank you," she said, pulling the quilt snuggly around her shoulders. She felt as if she'd never be warm again.

He pulled his other chair to her side and sat down. "What is it that has you so troubled?"

She turned her face toward him slowly, shivering with cold fear. "I need you to do something for me."

"Anything," he said fervently.

"Do you know the mountains south of Tironza?"

He looked puzzled. "A little. I used to hike there when I was a novice at the Temple of Baygor."

"I need you to go there next autumn." She blew on the hot tea to cool it down. "In the mountains just west of the pass into Peltik, there's a high meadow hidden from below. There's a callum tree growing there. Next year it will produce seeds. I need you to gather the seeds and distribute them as you will." She blew on the tea again and tried to sip it, scalding her tongue.

"But why me? Why can't you gather the seeds yourself?"

"I...won't be able to," she said, shivering again. "You must promise me you'll gather the seeds then and again in seven years and every seventh year after that."

Liska was silent for a while. When he spoke again, his voice was slow and deliberate. "You sound as if you won't be here any more."

Tears filled her eyes, and her throat tightened. "I won't," she whispered.

"Will you come back?"

She shook her head.

He cleared his throat. "Where are you going?" he asked, his voice strained and quiet.

Briella tried to answer, but no sound would come. She took another sip of the hot tea.

He touched her arm, and she looked up at him. His red brows were pulled together in a worried frown.

"Where are you going?" he asked again.

"To Barg's kingdom," she said, her voice cracking.

He shook his head. "But you're a Wizard. You can't die, not now. Wizards live for hundreds of years if the legends are true, and you're still very young."

"But we can still be killed."

He inhaled sharply. "Merciful Baygor! What's happened?"

Clutching the quilt around her, she told him of her vision of Bren and her own death. "He's here now, in Vorlik. I felt him pass the Wall of Warding. My death is imminent. That's why I need you to gather the seeds from my callum tree."

"Is...is there nothing you can do?"

She leaned her elbow on the table and rested her forehead in her hand. "I don't know."

"Is there anything *I* can do?" he asked.

"Yes," she said. "Do you have any parchment?"

"No," he said, "I'm sorry. All I have is the book of records in the chapel."

"Even a small scrap of parchment will do."

"How small?"

"The size of a walnut would be enough."

"I might have that." Liska stood and went to a small trunk at the foot of his bed. He opened the trunk, dug under several folded robes, and pulled out a square of folded paper smaller than the palm of his hand. He carried it to Briella. "Would this do?"

She unfolded the parchment. Inside was a lock of chestnut- colored hair tied with a green ribbon. She looked at Liska questioningly.

"It's my mother's hair," he said, touching it reverently. "Can you use the parchment?"

Briella rested her hand on his arm and nodded. "But I only need a small piece."

"Take what you need then."

She tore off a small corner of the parchment, then refolded the rest around the treasured lock and handed it back to Liska. Raising her right hand and holding the scrap of parchment in her left, she said, "By the power of Baramay who created all that is, *tasrin revara selvaraj barason!*"

The scrap of parchment began to grow until it was large enough for a letter.

Liska stared at the parchment, his mouth open. "Great Baygor," he whispered. He gazed up at her, his eyes wide. "You truly are a Wizard."

"Do you have ink and a quill?" she asked, her strength sapped.

"Yes." He strode to his door, opened it, and hurried outside. A few moments later, he returned with a small ink pot and a pointed quill. "I hope these will do."

"Thank you." She set the ink pot on the table and pulled out the waxed stopper. "This letter must be taken to Lord Cordwin and placed in his hand as soon as possible. Tell him it is from me. He will understand."

"I will deliver it myself," Liska said.

She dipped the quill in the ink and started to write, but halted and looked up at the priest. "You have been a dear friend to me, and I'm grateful."

"Grateful to me?" he said, kneeling. "Briella, I'm grateful to you. All Vorlik is grateful to you."

"When I finish the letter, may I stay here and rest until I have the strength to leave?"

"Gladly. I'll be in the chapel for a short time and I'll have to talk to the innkeeper about borrowing a horse, but then I'll take the letter to Lord Cordwin. Rest as long as you need. No one will bother you here." He took her hand between both of his. "Baygor protect you, Briella, and give you...peace." He stood, strode to the door, opened it quickly, and left, closing the door behind him.

Briella drank the rest of the cooled tea, then began the letter to Cordwin. *He has to know that the Wall of Warding will only last as long as I'm alive. When I die, that's the most dangerous time, the time when his enemies will attack Vorlik. Cordwin, you must be ready to defend your land.*

When she finished the letter, she grasped the sword, stood, and stumbled to Liska's narrow bed. She collapsed onto it, hugging the quilt and sword to her, and fell asleep.

22

Bren was restless. He played with his quill pen, frowning in annoyance, his gold-brown eyes staring into the air. A slight breeze blew his walnut hair across his face, further irritating him. He smoothed his hair from his face, pulled at the collar of his robe, and wished he could get out of the study. He wanted to put on his fighting gear and ride to the practice field. At least then, he'd be out of the castle, out in the fresh air, and away from old Varlin's watchful eye. But Paxell had sent word that he wanted to meet with Bren in the study, and Varlin didn't let Bren waste his time while waiting.

Glancing at Malbar seated across the table, Bren saw the same look of annoyance on his friend's face as he struggled with a page of ancient Drambini history. Malbar looked up, grimaced at Bren, and cocked his head toward the old tutor. Bren nodded with a sigh and returned to the irksome task of translating the old text.

I'm a man now, he thought impatiently, *not a child. I don't need someone to watch my every move. It's time I had my vengeance against those who killed my family and stole my lands. I'll take back what's mine. I'll marry Miria and begin my own line. I'll be avenged...and soon.*

The door to the study opened, and Lord Paxell strolled in. His hair was streaked white at the temples and his forehead was creased, but he still looked like a powerful black wolf in his black and silver clothing.

Simultaneously, Malbar and Bren rose, then knelt and said, "My lord."

"I want a word with Varlin, then I'll speak with you, Pyccis." Looking at Malbar, he added, "Alone."

Malbar bowed, and with a glance at Bren and a shrug, he left.

For several minutes Paxell mumbled to the old tutor, who nodded several times. Bowing, Varlin looked askance at Bren then left the room.

Paxell ambled to a window and gazed out. "I understand you've had enough of studies today."

"Yes, my lord. I..." He hesitated and lowered his eyes. There was so much he wanted to say, but did he dare?

Paxell turned toward Bren. "There's no reason you shouldn't say what you're thinking. There've never been secrets between us. At least none since I told you of your true origins."

Bren swallowed tightly and straightened as he pulled the little bits of his courage together. Even though he loved and respected Paxell, Bren was awed by him, too, the feeling almost muted his voice. "I'm a man now. I want revenge for my parents' deaths." As he gazed at his foster father, Bren's courage wavered, and his mouth felt as if he'd tried to swallow cotton.

Paxell nodded. "I agree."

"You...do?"

"Yes, it's time for to set things right, to reclaim the heritage taken from you." Paxell put his arm around Bren's shoulder, gave him a gentle squeeze, then lowered his voice. "But there are things we need to discuss before that."

Bren looked puzzled. "What things?"

"Come. Sit down." Paxell motioned to a bench by the window. When they were settled, he continued. "You know about the night your parents died."

Bren remembered well the story he'd heard since childhood, and his heart felt like forged steel: glowing hot and hard. He nodded, his eyes narrowed with anger.

Paxell's hand on Bren's shoulder felt comforting, reassuring. "All the kings of Drambit before me hated Vorlik. But for my dear wife's sake, I made peace with Clevil, and we became friends, good friends. I thought we would be friends for life," he choked for a moment. "For three years there was peace and harmony between your father and me, and the rivalry between Drambit and Vorlik had ended."

Paxell's gaze hardened, but he seemed to be talking to himself. "At least that's what I believed. Until that witch Briella came and bewitched your uncle. They plotted to take the throne and murder all of you, but I foiled their plan. I tried to save all three of you, I tried very hard, but your parents were killed before I could rescue them. At least I was able to save you. I've kept you hidden and safe all these years."

"You've been like my own father," Bren said. He wished he were a boy again so he could hug Paxell and feel the warm contentment of the strong, protecting arms.

A smile softened Paxell's face, and his voice became gentle. "And you've been the son I never had."

I couldn't love you more if I were your own son, Bren thought.

"Your uncle might not have been responsible for his actions, being bewitched himself. But the witch Briella is guilty without doubt."

Bren cursed the sound of her name. "Hound of Darkness take her! I'll kill her with my own hands, then I'll deal with my uncle. I'll have as much mercy for him as he had for my mother and father. We'll crush his forces and free my people."

Paxell nodded. "It's taken me twenty years to rebuild my army to fighting strength. It was nearly destroyed in rescuing you. I barely had a handful of soldiers left to defend our borders. Luckily, Cordwin's troops were depleted as well or he might have attacked us. But now I have the troops to defeat Cordwin and place you on your rightful throne."

He smiled at Bren, then became solemn. "There's a problem. The witch has built a Wall of Warding about Vorlik. No army can enter. However, I discovered that one person could enter undetected. At different times over the years I've sent men, specially trained, to kill your uncle, but they never came back. The witch must have stopped them, murdered them, most likely."

For a moment, anger flickered across Paxell's face. He cleared his throat before he continued. "You must go alone and kill the witch to break the warding spell. When the Wall is gone, my army will help you regain your throne. But remember—we can only take Vorlik when she's dead."

Bren pressed his clenched fist to his chest. "I swear I'll kill her myself. I'll leave at once."

"Take this." Paxell handed Bren a beautifully crafted dagger, the name "Briella" etched on one side of the blade and the strange word "rahala" on the other. The hilt was gold and silver, shaped like a dove with a blue gem for each eye, and a large perfect emerald on the end. "This is a magic dagger. It took me years to acquire this. Its sole purpose is to kill the witch, and she can only be killed by this dagger. Never let it out of your possession."

He glanced around the room, as if he expected to see prying eyes, then leaned close to Bren. "You must be very cautious. They'll be watching for you, I'm certain. Disguise yourself as an old man and use your childhood name: Pyccis. Hide the dagger somehow, perhaps inside a staff. No one must suspect you or you will be killed."

"Thank you, my lord." Bren knelt, his eyes shining with love. "I won't fail you."

"One more thing," Paxell said, one dark brow raised slightly. "I know how you feel about Miria."

Surprise stole Bren's voice.

"Only a lord will marry her." His tone made it quite clear he was serious, then a smile brightened his face. "And I'm certain you'll be that lord. Good luck."

"I'll never be able to repay your kindness." Impulsively, he embraced Paxell, then pulled back, embarrassed. "But I'll always remember what you've done for me."

An almost imperceptible frown flitted across Paxell's face but quickly became a warm smile. "May you wash your hands in your enemy's blood."

Bren was startled by the luck-wish, used exclusively among Drambini soldiers. He felt pleased and proud Paxell had said it to him. Holding the dagger across his chest in salute, he stood soldier-straight and said, "May I be worthy of your trust."

Paxell nodded, rose, and strode from the room.

As soon as Paxell was out of sight, Malbar rushed back into the study, his eyes filled with expectation. "Well, what did he say?"

Bren smiled and leaned close to Malbar. "It's time for me to return to Vorlik and claim my throne. I'm leaving today."

"Wonderful! I hope you succeed, but...I'll miss you."

"When I return, I'll be lord of Vorlik." Bren strutted about the room. Facing Malbar, he grinned. "Has a magnificent sound, doesn't it?"

"You may be lord of Vorlik to others, but you'll always be Pyccis to me." Malbar smiled warmly and clasped Bren's forearm. "Good luck and come back soon."

Bren charged up the spiral stairs, then stood breathless in the entrance to Paxell's tower study. Miria was there as he knew she would be. He stared at her, his throat tightening more from the passion she stirred in him than from the rush up the stairs.

She stood beside the narrow window. Her skin was like apple blossoms, and her hair was spun sunlight. She was dressed in a rose-pink satin gown, and the curves of her body made his chest feel as if his heart were trying to smash through his breastbone.

She turned toward Bren and gave him a smile that made his hands shake and his face feel hot. "What's caused you to come running up the stairs?" she asked.

Bren slowed his breathing before he attempted to answer her. He wanted to sound coherent and calm, dignified. "I'm leaving today for Vorlik to take my throne from my uncle."

"Oh, that's what's so important." Miria's eyes twinkled mischievously as Bren finally stopped panting.

"I'll be lord of Vorlik when I return." He strode toward her until they were only inches apart. "I'll be worthy to marry you then, and we'll rule Vorlik together."

"Yes," Miria said, still smiling, "we will."

Bren slid his arms around her and kissed her willing mouth. He held her close, caressing her soft, thick hair. "I love you, Miria. I always have. I always will." Releasing her and turning, Bren strode quickly to the door and down the dark stairway.

23

Bren was rather pleased with his disguise. He'd streaked his hair grey and made his face appear ashen and lined. Standing bent as if from years of labor, he wore tattered clothes and well-worn sandals. He examined his appearance in his mirror and decided that no one would guess he wasn't an old man.

A sharp rap on his door was immediately followed by, "Lord Paxell to see Pyccis."

Bren wheeled toward the door, seeing if he could fool the Drambini lord.

Entering the room, Paxell stopped short as he looked at Bren, surprise cutting furrows on his forehead. Slowly, a smile widened Paxell's narrow mouth. "I see you've taken my suggestion. A very good disguise. It fooled me for a moment."

Bren bowed awkwardly, practicing his old man image. "Thank you, my lord."

"Now, you must leave today." His voice dropped low, and he leaned close to Bren. "Remember, be cautious; trust no one. Kill the witch first, then deal with your uncle. Good luck and may the Hound of Darkness not cross your path." He paused, then suddenly embraced Bren almost fiercely. "I wish you were my son," he murmured, "then all this wouldn't be necessary."

Something in Paxell's tone disturbed Bren. Perhaps the Drambini lord was more worried about him than Bren had realized, afraid he might be hurt or worse. Returning Paxell's fierce embrace, Bren said, "I wish you were my father."

The time that seemed to stretch for safe, comfortable hours was over too soon. Paxell pulled away first. Backing away, he stared at Bren with something like fear. Paxell turned quickly and strode from the room, leaving Bren empty and wishing he could've kept the closeness he'd felt for that short time.

Bren filled his sack with food, clothes, and enough money to see him through his trip. He'd bored a space in the large knob of the staff he'd carry, hidden the dagger, and stuffed the hole with clay. Slinging the sack and a water skin over his shoulder, he left.

The midday sun was slightly too warm on Bren's head as he walked out into the courtyard. Wagons, bringing food to the kitchen, creaked toward the north side of the castle, and a large number of soldiers practiced with swords, more than Bren had seen at one time. The ring of the blacksmith's hammer shaping swords and horseshoes echoed throughout the walled enclosure. Bren shuffled toward the front gate, bowed slightly to the gate wards, and wandered out into the streets of Abasettown.

The town spread out on both sides of the east-west road that ran toward Vorlik. Few people from Drambit traveled that road. Only merchants and wanderers crossed from Vorlik to Drambit and back. The town square was filled with foreign merchants seeking trade goods, local farmers bringing bushels of grain and root vegetables for winter storage, herdsman with flocks of sheep and goats, weavers bringing their prized woolen fabrics, and jewelers displaying their craftsmanship. Bren hadn't been to the town since he was a young boy, and then only with Lord Paxell and a dozen armed men. It was exhilarating and a bit frightening to be out with no guards.

The land between Abasettown and the Vorlikian border was hilly. Most trees were stunted. Only brambles and wild game were plentiful. It was poor land for farming but adequate for grazing; Drambit produced some of the finest wool and woolen cloth in the northern lands.

Bren had no trouble finding his way along the eastern road. His only problem was remembering he was supposed to be an old man. He wanted to run toward the border instead of slowly ambling the two days' journey. He had to concentrate on a slow, halting pace with a hunched back. It took him longer than he thought it would, since he had to move at a plodding pace. He had to camp a third night before crossing the border.

The Circle Mountains, grey ridges tipped white, rose sharply on either side of the road as it continued through a wide but rocky valley into Vorlik. He reached the guardian keep, carved from the mountains, before dawn on the third day. Twice as many guards were visible than Bren had been told to expect. The guards questioned all travelers before allowing them to cross the border.

It's just as Lord Paxell said, he thought. *They may be searching for me, but I'll fool them all. Nothing will keep me from my throne.*

"State your name and reason for entering Vorlik," demanded one of the guards.

"Pyccis," he said in a high, crackly voice. "I'm traveling to Norrin to see my only brother. He's very ill."

The guards passed him through quickly and turned to the next traveler. Bren smothered a smile as he hobbled past the stern-faced soldiers. They hadn't checked his staff. The dagger was safe. Now to find his parents' murderers: the witch, then his uncle. But how did one locate a witch? Surely, someone in the next town would know where to find her.

Leaning heavily on his staff, he walked with a slow, halting gait up the steeply climbing pass. It was wide enough for two large wagons or four horsemen to ride abreast. Picket pines stood like silent guardians along lower elevations, giving way to moss-covered slopes up higher. The air grew cold and thin. Snow edged the road. Walking became difficult even for Bren. He was young and strong, but unaccustomed to the height. Soon he halted, panting for air as he leaned on his staff.

A red-and-blue wagon, drawn by a team of sturdy Peltik ponies, reined to a halt beside Bren. Holding the reins was a rotund man with chestnut eyes. His voice echoed like a drum as he called to Bren. "Old father, I can see you aren't used to these heights. Would you like a ride?"

"Oh, yes," Bren sighed gratefully and dragged himself up beside the man. "Where are you going?"

"Why, to Vorlik, of course." The man laughed as he slapped the reins, his ruddy face crinkling with a smile. "I'm going to Leflin first, then on to Tarolin Castle, to Yertz on the eastern border, south to Tironza, then on to Peltik. My name's Klaymar, merchant of Beltrin. Who're you and where are you heading?"

"Uh, I'm Pyccis," Bren stammered. "I'm looking for a Wizard I've heard lives in Vorlik. Have you heard of her?"

The driver smoothed back his hair and stroked his beard, both honey-gold and showing the first few strands of white. "Briella? She certainly does indeed live in Vorlik. Why?"

"I need to find my son, who was kidnapped as a baby."

Klaymar looked at him sympathetically. "I've five sons and a daughter myself. I'd be heartbroken if any of them were taken from me."

Bren nodded.

"Well, the Wizard might be able to help you. I don't know much about her. Maybe the innkeeper at Leflin could tell you more. Ask for Kam Winsell at the Two Oaks Inn. He has clean, comfortable rooms and sets a good table, both at a reasonable price. He's full of curious information, and so's his wife, Maiya the Healer. You can ride with me all the way to Leflin if you like."

"Thank you," Bren said, rubbing his sore feet.

As they reached the summit of the pass midmorning, suddenly Bren felt cold and tingling all over for barely a heartbeat. He felt as if eyes were staring at him from every direction at once, seeing through his disguise, and he shuddered. The sensation faded just as suddenly as it had come.

Klaymar reined the horses. "Barg's breath, you're pale as a full moon! Are you ill?"

"I—no—I don't think so," Bren gasped, holding his head. "What was that? It's as if someone's been inside my head, reading my mind."

Klaymar chuckled, readjusting the grey-black wolf pelt that was thrown around his shoulders. "Oh, that's just the Wall."

"The Wall?"

"A Wall of Warding. They say the Wizard Briella placed it all around the borders of Vorlik to protect the land from attack. Affects people differently every time. Me, I just felt a tingling on my skin. Don't even feel it anymore. It's nothing to worry about."

Bren looked about uneasily, feeling unseen eyes still staring at him. Someone had discovered him, he knew it. He'd have to be doubly cautious.

The journey down the pass was steep and winding, narrower than before. Bren could see below where the road wound through the mountains to green, rolling foothills. White and brown dots indicated a large flock of sheep and goats grazing far below. A few miles past the foothills, the road cut through two large hills. East and south Bren could see the rich farmland and forests. North were green meadows cut by numerous streams. His land, his home—it was green and alive, so different from Drambit. No wonder his uncle and the witch had wanted to keep it for themselves.

Klaymar guided his team down the winding path until they reached flatlands. For the first time he noticed a long one-story wooden building north of the road. A score of soldiers, wearing blue and gold uniforms, stood watching as people and wagons passed; other soldiers practiced with swords. Twenty mounted men rode west toward the border.

Bren noted the large number of soldiers and the high level of watchfulness. *My enemies are taking no chances,* he thought. He smiled with satisfaction. *But I've come to claim my throne despite all their precautions.*

As the sun passed from morning to midday, Klaymar drove toward the cluster of houses which formed the town of Leflin. The Two Oaks Inn at the center of the town was his first stop.

"Here you are." Klaymar helped Bren down.

"Aren't you staying at the inn?"

Klaymar smiled. "No, I'll be at the Merchant Guild House across the way, but maybe we'll meet again. I hope you find the Wizard and your son." He slapped the reins and turned his wagon toward the eastern side of the town square.

Bren entered the main room of the Two Oaks Inn. A middle-aged man with leathery skin, periwinkle eyes, and a tuft of grey hair was filling a wooden mug from a barrel. Handing it to a customer, the man noticed Bren and asked, "How may I help you, old father?"

"Do you have a room for the night?" he asked in an appropriately crackly voice.

The man bowed with a grace that seemed unnatural for his gangly shape. "Certainly. I'm Kam Winsell, and this is my inn, the best inn in the district." He chuckled. "Of course, it's the only inn in the district, but that's beside the point. We've clean rooms and the best food and drink in all of Vorlik, and that's no boast. Two coppers a night. Evenings we've entertainment in the common room if you care to join us. If not, you'll find your room comfortable and warm. Do you have business here?"

"I've heard there's a wi--" Bren cut off the word "witch", "a Wizard in Vorlik. I'm trying to find my son, stolen from me as a baby. I've searched for him without hope until I heard of the Wizard of Vorlik. Where can I find her?"

The innkeeper looked surprised. "No one finds Briella Mourning Dove. She finds them. If she wants to see you, she'll come to you."

Puzzled and annoyed, Bren asked, "But...how will I know her?"

The innkeeper shook his head. "You might not, unless she chooses to reveal herself...or until she's gone. We're never certain about her. We think she might be a peddler of salves and potions, or the midwife who appears just when she's needed. Some say she's the old man who cares for sick animals. Who can say?"

Bren wondered at the respect in the man's voice and decided Briella must have the entire population bewitched. Swallowing his anger, he said, "I'll take the room for two days. Perhaps she'll condescend to come to me." He smiled tightly.

The innkeeper frowned slightly but said nothing. Kam showed Bren to his room, then left.

Keeping his disguise intact, Bren carefully removed the old robe and washed. After he'd changed clothes, he joined the local inhabitants in the common room and ordered lunch. The thick stew and fresh bread filled the hollow feeling in his stomach. His hunger satisfied, Bren turned to listen to the conversations around him. Some talked about the year's abundant harvest. Others spoke of the coming marriage of the son and daughter of two men present, who had toasted each other several mugs too many. Some spoke of the coming winter. Old men told of winters grown more severe with time. Most seemed curious about the stranger in their midst and questioned him about his reason for visiting their village.

Bren did his best to look old, tired, and desperate. "When I was much younger," he said, "I had a good wife and a son, just a baby, but my greatest treasure. One day while I was out tending my sheep, someone broke into my house, killed my wife," he faked a sob, "and took my son. I found tracks of three horses leading from the house. I followed the tracks until I lost them in the dry northern lands west of Formia. I searched for my son for months until I gave up and returned to my farm. Every once in a while I hear a rumor that my son might be alive somewhere, but every time I follow the rumor, it leads to nothing. I'd given up all hope of finding him before I die. Then about a year ago I heard rumors of a Wizard somewhere in Vorlik and thought there might still be a chance to find my son. So I'm trying to find the Wizard. Can any of you help me? Please!"

The crowd murmured their sympathy.

"I wish we could help you," said a man who looked about as old as Bren pretended to be. "But we don't know where she lives. No one does. She knows you're here. She knows everything that happens in Vorlik."

Bren shivered at that.

"Be patient. You've waited so many years. A few days more won't matter."

"Is there nothing else I can do?" Bren tried to keep the anger from his voice.

"Have another mug with us." The old man cracked a grin and motioned Kam for another round. "She'll find you if she wants to. Be patient and wait. She might come to you in many guises, so watch carefully."

After politely downing a mug, Bren returned to his room, unsatisfied. "I have to find the witch quickly." He touched the end of the staff knowing his weapon was safe. "And I'll take my revenge soon," he whispered intently. "Very soon."

24

In the tower room Paxell studied a map of Vorlik that lay on the desk, his eyes gleaming like the clear black schorl in his ring. With his index finger he traced the borders of the land he'd dreamed of ruling. *Almost in my hands, almost mine at last,* he thought. *The fields, the mines, the vineyards of Yarrow. I've waited two decades—no, all my life.* He cupped his hands. He could almost feel the wealth of Vorlik. *My father and his father dreamed of ruling Vorlik, plotted, schemed, fought to rule Vorlik. But they failed. I won't. Not with the magic I've learned from the Sorcerer's book.* He rolled his hands into fists. *This time, I'll lead the army myself. I'll run my campaign from the battlefield, and Vorlik will be mine.*

He smiled at Miria, standing beside him. For a moment he was breathless as he realized how much like Dannee his daughter looked. Then he met Miria's eyes, blue like Dannee's but with a cold hardness like his own. Her pale skin looked like white marble against her dress of Drambini black. The starkness was broken only by a silver snake amulet hanging at her breast. She smiled a cunning smile, then studied the map with the same intensity her father had.

Paxell pointed at the road east to Vorlik. "Bren left five days ago, so he should have reached the border the day before yesterday at the latest." A pang of regret tugged at his thoughts. *If only I didn't care for him,* Paxell thought. *This would be so much simpler if I could remember he's an enemy. Sometimes, sometimes he seems like my own son. Bren, I wish...I wish you were my son. If you were, I'd have given you anything you wanted, even if that meant giving up my dream of ruling Vorlik. Why couldn't you have been Dannee's child?*

He shot a guilty glance at Miria. He loved her, more than he wanted to admit, but she wasn't a son. Sighing briefly, he turned his attention back to the map. "I don't know how long it'll take him to find and kill the Wizard, but when the Wall of Warding is dispelled, I'll bring my troops through the pass."

He paused again, his fingertips caressing the map with more passion than during the occasional times when he'd taken a woman to his bed. "I've planned, prepared, and waited for this since before you were born." He turned his head toward his daughter. "Soon, Miria, I'll have what I've always wanted: the riches of Vorlik."

Her eyes narrowed, and her smile was like sunlight, but it was cold winter sunlight. "How will you know when the Wall's destroyed?"

He tapped the map. "A squad of my guards is hiding here in the mountains. Once each hour beginning tonight they'll try to cross the border. When the Wall's down, they'll signal men waiting in the foothills. The watchman will relay the signal from there to the camps here and here," pointing to areas north and south of the pass along the foothills of the mountains, "where I've massed my troops. Then," he savored a long, slow breath, "then I'll lead the army through the pass. We'll destroy the border guards at the guardian keep before they can warn the Western Guard. Cordwin will be completely surprised. I hope I'll have the satisfaction of killing him myself."

Miria gave him a look which made him uncomfortable, the kind of look he often used to intimidate others. "Why do you hate Cordwin so much?" she asked quietly.

"He's a Vorlikian. Isn't that enough?"

"No," she said with a discerning gaze, "it's more than that."

Paxell's hand clenched convulsively, and his eyes stared at the map. "He stopped me from conquering Vorlik twenty years earlier. It could've been mine all these years. If he had died then, you'd be living in Tarolin Castle right now. But in a week or two, you'll be there anyway. We'll take Vorlik by surprise."

"That doesn't seem reason enough to hate him so much."

"Maybe not, but it's all I'm going to tell you." Paxell's nails cut into his palm as he clenched his fists. He'd never told anyone how jealous he'd been of Cordwin, how he'd hated the Vorlikian because Dannee had cared for him. No, let Miria think it was because of the ancient rivalry between the two countries.

"A wonderful plan, if it succeeds," a silken voice said behind them.

Turning sharply, Paxell saw the familiar figure of Grimmin leaning against the doorway. His face was still youthful, unchanged by time. His hand rested casually on the hilt of a dagger tucked into his belt.

As arrogant as ever, Paxell thought, *and as dangerous. But one day I'll be powerful enough to humble even him.* He gazed at Grimmin and shivered. *Maybe.*

"Good day, Lord Paxell." Grimmin dutifully inclined his head although Paxell heard insolence in his tone. "And to you, Lady Miria. You're looking quite well. Yes, indeed, quite well."

Miria edged closer to her father, and he felt her shudder.

"What brings you here?" Paxell asked sharply. "I haven't sent for you."

Grimmin smiled wolfishly. "That's true. I missed your daughter's sweet voice and velvet skin, and I know she missed me, too. Tonight, she can show me how much."

"No one speaks to me like that!" Miria said, drawing her belt knife from its sheath.

His face became solemn, his voice intense. "Maybe someone should."

"You bastard son of a whore!"

Grimmin gazed at her in mock-shock. "Oh, such language from a lady! Miria, you wound me deeply."

"I'll show you just how deeply I can wound you!" Miria started to lunge at him, but he didn't even flinch.

Paxell grabbed her wrist, tightening his grip until she dropped the knife. "Leave it," he said, dangerously quiet.

Her usually fair skin glowing red, Miria rubbed her wrist. "Father, do something!"

Paxell glanced at Grimmin, then scowled at his daughter, and his voice was a dagger of ice. "Miria, be silent."

Fear widened her sapphire eyes. She gasped and shrank back from him.

Grimmin smiled slightly and turned to Paxell. "I thought you might need some information I have."

Paxell stared impatiently at him. "Well?"

"And the price?"

"I'll pay what it's worth! Haven't I always?"

"Indeed, you have," Grimmin said as he kept his eyes on Miria.

Paxell glared at the merchant. "Tell me what's so important."

"My caravan has just come from Vorlik. Cordwin's doubled the border guard. I don't know if he suspects anything, but everyone entering Vorlik is questioned and searched. All five Guards are on alert, and Cordwin's even hired some Formian trackers. Something to do with the Wizard," he spit on the floor, "but my agents didn't get any details on it. Cordwin's edgy, so you should be especially cautious now. Any unusual troop movement might alert Cordwin, and you'd lose the initiative."

"I'm no fool," Paxell said disdainfully. "I've been slowly moving my troops into place for the last month. Still, it's good to know their guard is up. I'm joining my troops today. In less than a week I'll be lord of Vorlik."

Grimmin's gaze shifted from Miria to Paxell, and his voice became as soft as snowflakes. "I wish I could be there to see Cordwin's defeat, but I have urgent business in the south I must tend to. Now, for my payment."

Feeling inside his pouch, Paxell withdrew a thumbnail-sized emerald and tossed it to the man. "There, that's more than enough."

Holding the gem up to the light, Grimmin examined the gem, then gave Paxell a satisfied smile. "Indeed, it is. Good luck to you, O future lord of Vorlik." Grimmin turned to go, stopping long enough to gaze at Miria again, then he seemed to vanish into the dark of the winding stair.

Paxell noticed that Miria shivered though there was no draft in the tower.

"Father, I trust him as much as I'd trust a thief to guard my treasure. He's more dangerous and has darker secrets than anyone I've ever known. He's like...death's shadow." She clutched her arms across her chest as if chilled. "He frightens me."

"As long as he does what he's paid for, that's all I care about," Paxell grumbled. He tried to appear unconcerned, but as he turned back to the map, he glanced toward the door, and for a moment he was afraid, too.

The sun colored the Circle Mountains blood red and slate grey as Paxell reined up his horse in front of his tent. Captain Callas stood waiting for him. An evening breeze, portending frost, ruffled the captain's dark hair.

Paxell glanced at the clusters of grey-green tents pitched beneath whitethorn trees. Blanket-wrapped soldiers huddled around dying embers, eating dried meat and hard bread. Paxell had ordered a cold camp, no fires to keep them warm. He wasn't taking any chance of being spotted by the border guards. Satisfied, he dismounted.

"My lord," Callas said, bowing, then followed Paxell into the tent and secured the flap.

A single candle cast pale light on a table in the tent's center, and on the map spread there. Paxell sat down, facing Callas expectantly.

"Everything is ready, my lord," Callas said, pointing out troop positions. "Our scouts reported that Bren crossed the border four days ago. The charms you made to prevent detection have been issued to First and Second Squads, and they are stationed on either side of the pass, here and here. They'll be the first into the pass and take the guardian keep. Third and Fourth Squads are stationed south of the road. Fifth and Sixth Squads, along with the mercenary troops, are camped with us north of the road and will follow as soon as the guardian keep is in our hands. The Seventh Squad is here in the mountains on this side of the Wall, checking to see when it's down." Callas gave Paxell half a smile. "Only a few more days, my lord, and you will be Lord of Drambit and Vorlik, as well."

"Yes," said Paxell. He didn't smile, but he felt satisfied. Vorlik was nearly his...and Cordwin was as good as dead.

25

All the next day and evening Bren asked the villagers about Briella with no success. Everyone knew about her, but no one really knew her well. The only information he got was from the innwife, Maiya the Healer.

"I've heard she lives in the south," Maiya told him, her violet eyes gazing at him curiously, "somewhere in the mountains, but exactly where I doubt anyone knows. And I doubt she's there often. She travels the land constantly, aiding those in need."

"My thanks," Bren said. "At least I have a place to start my search." Smiling to himself, he went back to his room, prepared to leave the next morning.

The innkeeper greeted Bren in the grey light before dawn and gave him a hearty breakfast, then walked with Bren to the front door. "Here," Kam said as he handed Bren his waterskin, so full it didn't slosh, and a bulging sack. "I've also packed dried food for your journey."

"Thank you," Bren said. "Thank you for everything."

"Far-thell."

Bren nodded, then turned and left the inn.

"I hope you find your heart's desire," Kam called after him.

"Oh, I will," Bren muttered to himself as he took the southern road out of Leflin. "One way or another, I will."

The sun rose scarlet over the eastern mountains. The air was warm but with a slight chill, a portent of winter winds. The spicy scent of fallen leaves and the hearty smell of wheat chaff floated on the morning breeze. From somewhere south Bren heard cattle insisting that their owner turn them out to pasture after milking. The sky was sapphire with wispy clouds like giant, pink feathers. Thousands of migratory birds winged south, casting shadows on the golden fields. To the west a smoky haze hung over hills and hollows, foretelling smoked meats for winter mornings. Everywhere he looked, he saw abundance, so different from the unproductive fields of Drambit.

A good morning to be alive, Bren thought. Filling his lungs with the crisp air, he stretched his arms to the sky.

The road to the south was deeply rutted and dusty. Several caravans passed, heading north for Leflin. At each one he asked, "Do you know where I can find the Wizard Briella?", then told his sad tale.

"She does indeed live in the south," the traders assured him, but no one knew exactly where.

"She'll find you if she chooses," one driver told him. "If you're in need, she'll find you."

She has the entire population bewitched, Bren thought angrily as he watched the caravan disappear northward, *but not for long. I'll break the spell and free them all!*

He walked the next two days without seeing another village, passing the most fertile farmlands he'd ever seen.

This will be a good land to rule, he thought, pleased. Fruit trees bent to the ground with apples and pears; fat grazing cattle; abundant quail and pheasant in the wooded areas; fields golden with grain. *Almost unbelievable,* he thought, *and soon it'll be mine.*

Near sunset he found a grove of hard maple and dogwood trees beside the track. Gold and crimson leaves carpeted the ground thickly and sent up a spicy wood scent as he trod on them. He scraped the leaves into a thick mat to make a suitable bed for the night. Bren cleared a circle from the leaves down to bare earth for a fire, then went in search of kindling. He came back, arms loaded with twigs and branches and one sizable log, and started a blazing fire. He skewered a chunk of smoked beef the innkeeper had packed for him and turned it over the fire until it crackled. The aroma made his stomach grumble.

Shadows deepened as the sun slid behind the mountains to the west. The air became chilly. Bren added a large branch to the fire, glad he'd gathered plenty of wood. He sliced a thick strip of the meat, and with a chunk of slightly stale bread, savored the smoky taste and stringy texture.

Darkness came quickly. Crickets chirped to one another; a single dove called to a mate that didn't answer. Stars shone dimly in the light of a waning moon. Leaves rustled as the breeze increased, causing Bren to pull a blanket about his shoulders.

From the darkness, silently, a cloaked and hooded figure stepped toward the fire. Startled, Bren grabbed his staff and jumped up, holding it like a club.

"May I share your fire tonight?" asked a soft, muffled voice, a female voice, as a delicate hand pointed.

The voice excited him, tingling his skin like sparks from wool. Power was in that voice, power like the wind: soft as a gentle breeze but with the potential for a destructive gale.

Could this be her? he thought, excitement and caution running through his heart. *Slowly now, Bren, carefully. Be cautious, but act as if you suspect nothing. Don't betray yourself until you're sure it's her.*

"It's cold," Bren replied evenly. "My fire's warm enough for us both."

The figure moved soundlessly until she stood facing him across the fire.

"It's going to be a chilly autumn." It was the only thing he could think of to say.

"And a cold, cold winter," she said so softly, he barely heard her.

Bren swallowed tightly, trying to keep his voice from shaking with anticipation and fear. "Where're you going?"

"I'm returning to my home in the south." The figure held slender hands toward the fire's heat, a silver ring set with an emerald on the left hand.

"Do you know the Wizard Briella?"

"Everyone knows about her, but only one can say truly he knows Briella." There was a trace of sadness in the voice.

He leaned toward her, the fire making his face feel tight, like it was covered with dried mud. "I'm trying to find her."

"Why?"

Bren rested his forehead in his hand and let his shoulders droop. "My son—he was stolen from me as a child. I need her help to find him. Please, can you help me find her? I'll do anything, pay anything to find my son! Please, do you know where she is?"

For a moment the woman was silent. When she did answer, her voice was flat and distant. "You have no son."

Bren was taken aback but quickly recovered himself. "Oh, gods, is he dead, then?"

"You never had a son." Her hands wove back and forth before the fire.

He tried to sound angry. "What do you mean? Of course, I had a son! How can you say such a thing? Why would I come all this way if I didn't?"

"I always speak the truth. As a result, I always know a lie when I hear one. You have no son. You've never had a son. You're not married, and you're not over twenty-five years old. What do you want from Briella?"

Bren licked his lips and cleared his throat. Shifting uneasily, he stared at the sizzling meat. "Do you want to share my fire tonight or sleep in the cold?"

For an instant Bren was afraid she'd leave until, in a voice like wind through grass, she said, "I'll share your fire."

Moving to his left, she sat down next to him, her back to the trees, and pulled her cloak closer about her.

"Are you hungry?" Bren asked curtly.

Her shoulders sagged, and her head bowed slightly. "Yes." She sounded terribly weary.

Cutting a piece of meat, he handed it and some bread to her, then sat down himself.

"Thank you," she said. "I haven't eaten all day."

Bren watched her surreptitiously. What did she really look like, hidden in the depths of the hooded cloak? "You must be thirsty." He offered her his water skin. "Here. It's all I have."

"Thank you."

As she raised the skin to her lips, the fire lit her eyes momentarily. They were as clear blue as the finest sapphires with the fire of blue opals, startling, so open, nothing hidden behind their blue veil.

This can't be her, he thought, strangely drawn to her. *She's too...too...guileless, too unwary to be the witch. But maybe that's only an illusion. I must be certain. I have to know!*

Finished, she handed the skin back to him, and their hands touched briefly.

The touch was soft as a kitten, light as a snowflake, but as piercing as talons. Bren felt as though his soul, his every thought, was visible to her eyes, and he trembled. "You can see me, know me with a single touch. Who are you?"

"I am Briella." Her voice was hushed, almost sad. "You are Bren, son of Lord Clevil and Lady Ellisa, nephew of Lord Cordwin, heir to the throne of Vorlik. And you are...my death. You've come as I saw twenty years ago."

Bren froze. Her power surrounded him, embraced him, crawled over him like hundreds of ants. *Hound of Darkness, she could kill me with a glance!* he thought.

"Why do you want to kill me?" she asked.

"Why?" he shouted. "You killed my mother and father!"

"I've never killed anyone...except one man who tried to kill me and another who would've killed someone dear to me." She steepled her fingers and whispered words he couldn't understand.

The fire in his eyes burned brighter than the campfire. "You're lying! Now I'll have my revenge and take back my land!"

He tried to lunge at her but found he couldn't move. He struggled to stand, but his body had become like stone. He stared at her, his eyes wide with fear. *She's trapped me,* he thought, panic growing in him, *and she'll kill me! With a word, a mere glance, she'll kill me!*

"Oh, Bren," she said softly, as if she'd read his thoughts. She held out her hands to him. "You've nothing to fear from me. I have no weapon, and I've no intention of harming you. I don't lie—ever."

He strained against the spell, willing his arms and legs to move, but he couldn't. Sweat beaded on his forehead and trickled down his face from the effort.

"Be still, Bren." Her voice, though barely a whisper, pounded against him like a smith's hammer. "I'll release you soon, but you won't hurt me...at least, not until I allow it. When we reach my house, I'll release you from this compulsion. Until then, you'll travel with me." Again steepling her hands, she murmured strange words again.

As though ropes had been removed, Bren felt the binding loosen. He tried to lunge at Briella again, but he couldn't. The binding was still there, waiting for him to test it. "You witch! You're a liar and a murderer! I'll end your spells and free my land and people! You've ruled Vorlik too long!"

Her lips barely moved as she replied. "I've said you're my death, but not until we reach my house."

"You knew I'd come to kill you?" His eyes narrowed suspiciously. "Why haven't you tried to stop me? Why don't you kill me now and free yourself? If I were you, that's what I'd do."

"Thank Baygor, I'm not you," she said sharply, her eyes reflecting flames. After a silence, she continued, her voice quiet and sad. "My fate is to die by your hand. I accept that—but at the place of my choosing."

Bren felt uncertain, confused. *This doesn't make sense. Why doesn't she just kill me? It has to be a trick to unsettle me,* he thought. He looked askance at Briella, his jaw aching from clenching his teeth. *I'll have to wait for my chance. Then I'll strike and free my land from her power.*

Pulling a heap of leaves together, Briella lay down near the fire. Her cloak wrapped tightly around her, she closed her eyes.

Bren tried to creep toward her, but invisible hands held him back. His resistance broke, and he sagged back to the dirt.

"Sleep, Bren," she whispered. For a moment her eyes opened.

Bren felt as if he were burning and freezing at the same time. Just as suddenly, the cold heat ended, replaced by comfortable warmth.

Briella closed her eyes. "You are safe. No one will harm you—not even me."

He gaped at her, puzzled. She was so small, not what he was prepared to face. He knew she was a murdering witch, but...why didn't he fear her? It had to be the spell, it had to be.

Banking the fire for the night, Bren lay down and closed his eyes. He hated her down to the deepest part of his soul, and yet he trusted her to keep her word. The contradiction made his head ache. Bewildered, he sank into sleep as if he were lying on a thick feather mattress.

26

Bren woke to find an old man, wrinkled and stooped, tending the fire. Leaping to his feet, Bren scanned the grove for Briella. *She's disappeared! She escaped!* he thought. Turning to the old man, he asked, "Did you see her? A woman cloaked from head to foot? Where did she go?"

Turning a small pheasant on a spit, the old man looked up. "I'm still here."

Bren stared at the same clear blue eyes he'd seen the night before. "Why do you look like that?"

The old man shrugged. "I'm needed to tend a horse at the next farmstead. They know me in this guise."

Bren's mouth and throat suddenly felt dry. He reached for his water skin and was surprised to find it heavy and completely full again. He gaped at the old man but said nothing, and took a long slow drink of water.

Besides the pheasant, the old man had toasted bread and spread it with melted cheese. Bren didn't ask where the pheasant had come from. When the old man offered half the fowl and toast, Bren took them and ate in silence, though he glanced uncomfortably at the weathered man.

This is foolish, pure madness, Bren thought as he slowly gnawed the dry, delicious flesh from the bone. *How can she—he—sit there, knowing I mean to kill her? It makes no sense! What evil is she plotting behind that face? Be on your guard, Lord Paxell told me. He was so right!*

Briella held her hands out to the fire and spoke a strange word. The fire disappeared; even the glowing embers turned to grey ash and gave off no heat that Bren could feel. She shouldered her pack and motioned Bren to do the same. Patched clothing had replaced the cloak she'd worn the night before. A white fringe of hair fell about a dried-apple face. Gnarled hands clutched the pack.

What does she look like behind her illusions? Bren wondered. *What does she truly look like?*

Briella nodded down the road. "The farm's not far, but I'll have a full day's work. I want to arrive early, so hurry up."

Without hesitation, Bren rose. Hefting his own pack, he followed the old man's lead, hurrying to keep pace with him. After they'd walked for nearly an hour, he sighted a large whitewashed farmhouse where several bare-footed children scampered about the grassy, tree-shaded yard. Soon, he and Briella stood before the door which opened to reveal a stout farmer. The fragrance of spices and baking bread tumbled out the door.

"Good morning, Hallifan," Briella said, inclining her head.

"I knew you'd come in time." He gave her a faint smile, then gazed at Bren with curiosity.

Briella nodded. "Take me to the horse. She needs me now. It'll be a long day."

Hallifan led them to a stall in the warm, well-kept barn filled with the scent of fresh hay and straw dust. On a bed of clean straw, a red-gold mare lay, ready to foal, but she seemed to be having trouble. Briella placed her hands on the horse's swollen belly and waited until the mare tossed her head and gave a pathetic whinny. Briella frowned and felt various places on the mare belly.

"What's wrong?" Bren asked.

She looked worried. "I'm not certain yet." Turning to Hallifan, she said, "I need boiling water, a bottle of wine or mead, and some clean cloths."

The farmer sent a young farm hand to fetch the things.

Rolling up her sleeves, Briella signaled Bren to kneel beside the mare. "Put your hands here," she placed them on the mare's belly, "and tell me when you feel the contractions."

"But why?" Bren asked, puzzled.

Briella glanced toward the children looking over the wooden rails bounding the stall. She lowered her voice so only Bren could hear her. "I think the colt is in the wrong position. If I can't turn him, he'll cut the mare's insides with his hooves, and they'll both die."

Bren blanched. He'd seen a horse die like that once, when he was nearly nine. He'd never forgotten how the mare had thrashed about in pain as her baby had slowly ripped her apart inside. Looking askance at the children, he turned to Briella. "Do you think the children should be here?" he whispered.

Briella raised a bushy eyebrow and shook her head as she gazed at him. "No, they shouldn't," she whispered back. Turning to Hallifan, she said, "Please send the children outside for a while. I'll call them when the baby is born."

Hallifan opened his mouth to say something to her, then stopped. He lifted his youngest daughter off the rail, set her on the ground, and motioned to the others. "You all have chores to do. Go on."

"But we want to see the baby horse," the little girl protested.

"You will—when it's born," Hallifan said. "Now go along. We'll call you when it's time."

The children shuffled out, grumbling all the while.

The young farm hand returned with a bottle of wine and several cloths, then said, "The water will be ready soon."

Briella opened the bottle, poured some wine over her arms and hands, then handed the bottle to the farm hand. She inserted her hand into the mare's birth canal and slowly pushed until her entire arm was inside. The horse twitched its legs and tossed its head, but Briella spoke to her in a calm, quiet tone until the mare lay still.

Bren watched Briella intently as she examined the horse. Her eyes narrowed, and she chewed her lower lip while she probed inside the mare.

"So?" Bren asked, feeling a strong contraction.

Briella withdrew her arm and wiped it on a cloth. "The colt is definitely turned wrong. I'll have to have help. Hallifan, I want you to keep the mare's head down. Don't let her thrash about. It'll only make what I have to do harder. I'm going to turn the colt, then we'll have to pull it out quickly, before it can hurt its mother any worse. You," she looked straight at Bren, "when I tell you to, brace yourself solidly behind me, wrap your arms around my waist, and pull hard. Don't stop until I say so. Do you both understand?"

Bren and the farmer said, "Yes."

A sun-baked woman with cow eyes waddled in, carrying a small cauldron of steaming water and a long-handled dipper.

"Set it down there," Briella said, pointing near the stall gate. "And I need a bowl."

The woman put the cauldron down, then left. She came back shortly with a wooden bowl.

Briella took out dried herbs from her pack and crumbled them into the bowl and ladled steaming water over the herbs. A clean, comforting fragrance filled the air, and everyone breathed easier, including the mare.

"What is that?" Bren asked, vaguely recognizing some of the scents.

"Comfrey, wintergreen, woundweal, roborant, and callum bark," Briella said as she stirred the infusion. "It'll soothe the skin and numb the pain." She dipped a cloth in the solution, held it above the bowl until cool enough to handle, then squeezed out the excess liquid. Returning to the mare, Briella pressed the cloth against the outside of the birth canal.

"All right," she said with a sigh, "it's time. Hallifan, keep her head still, and you," she tossed the cloth to Bren, "get behind me and find a way to brace yourself."

As the men took their places, Briella slowly wedged both her arms inside the mare. Bren slid his arms around the bony waist and waited as he felt her twist and tug at the new life waiting to be born. "Now, pull!"

Bren strained but didn't have any leverage.

"Again."

Bren pulled until his jaws hurt from clenching his teeth so hard, but still he couldn't pull the colt free.

Briella sagged a little against Bren. "Hallifan, do you have any rope?"

"Of course," the farmer replied. "How much do you need?"

"Enough to tie around me and wrap around that wooden support behind me. We'll use it as a pulley."

"Better grease the support first then," Hallifan said as he sent his hired hand to fetch a rope and a bucket of axle grease.

Soon the young man returned with the items. Bren tied the rope around Briella, smeared grease on the support, then looped the rope around the wooden support three times.

"Ready?" Briella asked, sounding tired.

"Ready," Bren said as he wrapped the rope around his hands several times for a firm grip.

"Pull!"

Bren's arms bulged as he hauled on the rope, backing up slowly. The mare struggled, but Hallifan did his best to keep her still. Briella dug in her heels and took a step back, then another. Finally, almost like a cork suddenly popping from a bottle, the colt was born, all wet and covered with a bloody white membrane. The mare bent around and began licking her baby clean.

The colt was weak but a fighter, a little chestnut colt with a white star on his forehead. He lay in the straw for a while. The mare nudged the colt's tiny ribcage, trying to get him to stand. After several tries, the colt stood on wobbly thin legs. The mare nudged her baby toward her teats, but the newborn didn't seem to know what to do.

"Come on, little one," Briella coaxed. "Try to suckle. Come on, now. Taste this." She squeezed a little milk from the mare's teats and rubbed it on the colt's lips.

The colt licked the milk but just stood still.

Briella pressed out more milk and tried again. "Come on. You'll like this. Try again."

The colt licked the milk from its mouth, then took a step toward his mother.

"That's right, little one," Briella said. "There. That's it."

The colt took the nipple and began to nurse.

The sun was halfway from zenith to the western mountains as Briella wiped her hands and sweaty face. "He'll live," she sighed as she slumped against a wooden rail. "You can let the children in now."

Hallifan strode to the barn door. "You can see the baby horse," he called.

The children scampered in and climbed up on the wooden stall. They giggled and pointed at the colt's faltering steps. Hallifan gazed at the wobbly, little colt proudly.

"Oh, he'll be a fine horse when he grows up." He turned to Briella. "Thank you. It's nearly supper time. And you know how good a cook my wife is. You'll stay with us, won't you? Both of you? We've an extra room you can sleep in."

"We'd be honored to accept." With a crinkled smile, Briella bowed slightly. She took a cloth, dipped it into the cauldron, and scrubbed her arms clean, then motioned Bren to follow her to the house.

The stonewalled kitchen was crowded with laughing people and delicious aromas. The farmwife was busily tending a kettle of soup while keeping an eye on several rounds of bread in the side oven. She smiled a welcome to Briella and nodded to Bren. Five children played tag around the long trestle table until their father warned them sternly to stop.

When all were gathered at the table, Hallifan turned to Bren and said, "This is my wife, Gwin. My children: Kort, Alcinda, Jole, Joslyn, Sarris. And those," he pointed at two young men just out of their gangly youth, "are Willum and Pak, my hired help. And you are?"

"A fellow traveler..." Briella paused, "Uh..."

"Pyccis," Bren answered.

"You are welcome to our home, Pyccis." Hallifan spread his hands and turned his face upwards. "Baramay's blessings on all who gather here." He sat, and the meal began.

The table was heaped with hot bread, sweet butter, baked tubers, a round of yellow cheese, red-blushed apples and deep blue grapes, and a rich meat-and-barley soup. Noisy laughter and good cheer made the food even more enjoyable. Bren was delighted with the spicy apple pie Gwin took from the oven, steaming and browned and served with thick cream.

Everyone seems so happy, Bren thought as he studied the faces around the table. *I wish I could have grown up in a family like this, lots of brothers and sisters, a mother and father*. Even as the thought crossed his mind, he gazed at Briella. *But she cheated me of a family, she and my uncle.* Anger seethed in him, and he clenched his fists, enraged.

After supper, Hallifan offered Briella and Bren chairs by the fire, then leaned against the mantle and smoked a pipe filled with musty-sweet leaves. His two youngest children chased the smoke rings, colored magenta-gold by the firelight, that he sent drifting in the warm shadows. Gwin sat on a chair near her husband and picked up a shirt she'd been repairing. Kort and Jole washed and dried the dishes while Alcinda sang of the land blessed by Baramay.

"That's the second time I've heard that name," Bren said.

Hallifan smiled after he'd blown a particularly large ring. "What name?"

"Baramay. Who is it?"

The entire room became uncomfortably quiet. Even the children stopped their play.

"Is he being silly?" asked little Sarris, her green-apple eyes wide.

Gwin's voice was strained as she said, "That's not polite, Sarris. Apologize to him."

The little redhead looked at Bren, then back at her mother. "But everyone knows who Baramay is."

Hallifan tapped his pipe in his hand, avoiding Bren's eyes. "Sarris, tell him you're sorry."

She looked back at Bren, and in a voice smaller than her size, said, "I'm sorry you don't know about Baramay."

Gwin looked stricken until Bren laughed, then she laughed, too. Soon everyone but Sarris joined them, the tension gone. Sarris just stared at them all as if they were crazy.

When Bren finally controlled his laughter, he smiled at the little girl. "I'm sorry I don't know about Baramay, too. I grew up very far away from here, and no one in my homeland knows about Baramay."

Sarris' mouth fell open in disbelief. "No one? Nobody at all?"

Bren shook his head and smiled. "Nobody at all. Do you think you could tell me?"

Sarris looked skeptical.

"Please?" Bren asked.

She scrunched up her mouth a moment, then nodded. "Baramay made all the trees and flowers and animals and the whole world, and the moon is a shiny white rock she had on her head, and the birds try to sing just like she does, and she made all the people and takes care of us."

Bren stopped the smile he felt inside from showing on his face. "Thank you, Sarris. Now I won't be so silly."

Sarris held her chin up and glanced triumphantly at her mother. Gwin looked as if she was torn between laughing out loud and hiding her face from embarrassment. Everyone else laughed.

Hallifan told Willum and Pak "good night" as the two left for their room in the barn. With a kiss and hug he sent his children to bed. Sarris looked back at Bren as she reached the stairs and sent him a wink before she skipped up to bed. Gwin put the shirt back in the basket beside her chair, and with a "good night" to both visitors, went to a room behind the stairs.

Hallifan led Briella and Bren to a small room with straw-mattress cots and a tiny window. "It's not large," he said, "but it's clean and warm. I hope you will be comfortable." He nodded to Briella, then to Bren. "Good night. Sleep restfully."

After the farmer left, Briella collapsed on the bed, exhausted, and fell asleep immediately. Bren stood beside her, confused, excited, lonely, and angry all at once. How different his childhood had been from little Sarris'. He watched Briella awhile, doubt creeping into his mind.

This is the witch Lord Paxell told me to kill? he wondered. *Is it just possible I'm wrong? Or am I completely bewitched?*

Finding no answers, he lay down on his cot, facing her, and closed his eyes in fitful sleep.

27

The aromas of bacon and biscuits, of eggs and fried apples, opened Bren's eyes. The pink light of dawn stole through the small window, and he noticed that Briella looked as exhausted as she had when she went to sleep, even though she was still disguised as an old man. Her eyes were red, sunken, and dark-circled. She was slow to rise from her bed and slower to move. She stared at him for a moment, then said, "Your disguise need repairing." She sank down on the bed again.

Bren touched his face, then glanced around the room. On one wall was a tiny mirror, smaller than his hand. He scrunched as close as he could and looked at his face. The makeup was smudged and streaked. Bren sighed. *What do I do now?* he thought.

"Come," Briella said, motio.ning him to sit beside her. Hesitantly, he sat on the bed, facing her. She touched his face and spoke strange words. A moment later, her shoulders sagged and her head drooped. "There," she whispered, "that will hold for a while."

Bren rose to gaze into the mirror. His disguise was in place, looking more natural than before. "Thank you," he said. "But why should my disguise matter to you?"

"Because it matters to you," she said. She stood and clutched at the wall for support.

In spite of himself, Bren offered her his arm. "Breakfast smells wonderful," he said.

With a listless nod, she took his arm.

She feels so...light, he thought as he guided her down the stairs, *as if she's made of air.*

They joined the family at the table, heaped with platters of eggs and fried bacon, a basket of hot biscuits and a crock of sweet butter, bowls of milk gravy and fried apples, and a pitcher of fresh milk. Gwin smiled as Bren ate hungrily. "Fill your plate again," she said. "No one leaves my table hungry."

Briella ate only one biscuit and drank a cup of peppermint tea. She started to leave the table, but Gwin stopped her.

"No one leaves my table hungry," the farmwife said. "Have another biscuit. I have tyneberry jam to spread on it."

Briella hesitated, then smiled. "How can I say no to that?"

Gwin grinned, hurried to a pantry off the kitchen, and came back with a small crock. Briella took another biscuit, split it, and spread the purplish-red jam on the steaming halves. She took a bite and closed her eyes while she ate. A slow smile bowed her mouth, and she opened her eyes. "Did Baramay give you the recipe for this?"

Gwin laughed.

Briella finished the biscuit and jam, then excused herself to check on the colt. Reluctant to leave such delicious food, Bren stuffed a final biscuit in his mouth, then followed her.

The little colt was still shaky on its long, thin legs but was much stronger and healthier. The mare nudged him toward his breakfast. Now that he understood, the colt suckled greedily. Briella stroked the soft, brown coat.

Bren surveyed the colt with a keen eye. "He's beautiful."

"A new life always is." She sighed, turned, and left the barn.

Bren walked just behind Briella. Suddenly, she stumbled. Without thinking, he caught her, put one arm around her waist, and draped her arm around his neck. She tensed and started to pull away, then relaxed and let him help her. When they reached the farmhouse door, she shrugged off his arm.

"Thank you," she said quietly. "I'm all right now." Holding her body rigid, she walked inside by herself.

Bren didn't understand why he'd helped her, why she'd resisted, why she'd finally accepted his help, then refused any more. He didn't understand anything. Bewildered by her and his own feelings, Bren followed her up to their room and packed his sack while she did the same.

Hallifan thanked Briella for her help, then Gwin handed her a large, woven basket. "Here's some food for your travels. It's small thanks for what you've done. Whenever you pass this way, please, stay with us. You're always welcome here."

Briella accepted the basket, lightly squeezing Gwin's hand. "Baramay watch over you."

Sarris peeked out from behind her mother's dress and giggled as she gazed up at Bren. "Maybe next time you come by, I'll tell you another story."

Bren chuckled and crouched down to her level. "I'll look forward to that."

"Far-thell." The little girl waved her chubby hand. "Baramay watch over you."

Bren and Briella left the house and started southeast again. Doubts troubled Bren's mind. *How could someone so gentle with animals, so loved by children, be as evil as I've always been told? This is the murderer I've hated? The one who killed my parents so callously for power? She couldn't be...But why should I doubt Paxell?* he thought. *He's been like my own father.* His jaw tightened. A dull pain pulsed through his temples, his forehead, at the base of his skull. *Stop thinking about it!* He rubbed his neck and tried to push the questions from his mind.

The land became hilly with brown oaks, yellow maples, and crimson dogwood. The road wove through passes piled deep with fallen leaves. A sun the pale yellow of winter egg yolks filtered through partially bare branches as an easy breeze creaked limbs. At midday they found a spring bubbling from beside the track and decided to rest. Sitting in a shaft of warm sunlight, they nibbled bread and cheese, then crunched tangy apples, all courtesy of the farmwife. Neither spoke but Bren watched Briella surreptitiously.

Finally, Briella creaked to her feet. Her shoulders were hunched, and her voice sounded weak. "Fill the skins, then we'll leave."

Bren held the water skins in the icy spring until they'd bubbled full and his hands were purple with cold. Hefting his gear, he matched her easy pace.

An hour later the road left the hills, opening to farmlands again. No sooner had Bren sighted a village in the distance than Briella murmured strange words and changed in midstep to an old woman.

Bren stumbled, nearly dropping his pack from surprise. Standing in the middle of the road, he gaped at her. "What are you?"

"Midwife," she replied.

"You know what I meant."

"Yes, I do." She said nothing more.

Ten huts comprised the village of Wherryn. The deeply rutted road ran southeast straight through the center. At the edge of the village, a frantic man in rumpled, patched clothes paced the dusty road. He glanced up the road, then halted, staring at them. His face lit up with relief. He ran to meet them and grasped her hand.

"I knew you'd come!" he said. "It's my wife Cilla! She's in pain, and I'm afraid for her! Please, help her, save her!"

Briella smiled and touched his hand. "I'll try."

Motioning to Bren, she followed the man to a small hut, freshly chinked with mud for the coming winter. When his eyes adjusted to the dimness inside, Bren saw a pale, blond woman, hardly more than a girl. Far along in the first stages of labor, she lay on a straw mattress, her belly far too large for her body.

"Bring a light," Briella ordered the husband.

When he returned with a sputtering tallow candle, even Bren could tell that the woman was exhausted, sweat-drenched.

Whimpering pitifully, fear shining in her eyes, the woman clutched Briella's hand. "Help me. It hurts. It hurts."

"You'll be fine. Everything's all right." She patted Cilla's hand, then turned to the husband. "Fill a kettle with water and boil it."

The man grabbed two wooden buckets and fled the house.

Briella motioned Bren to the other side of the hut and whispered, "Her heart's too fast. She's weak, feverish, and showing signs of swelling—very dangerous. This isn't going to be an easy delivery. I don't have much time to prepare...and I'm already worn out. You'll have to help me."

Bren shrugged, uneasy, and muttered to himself, "I don't know what I can do. I'm not a midwife."

The husband sloshed back inside, dumped water into a kettle, and added more wood to the shrinking fire.

"I need a small amount of wine. And bring me a bowl of water when it boils," she called to the man as she searched through her pack. "Let's see, foxglove, valerian, mint, wintergreen, roborant, and callum bark."

As soon as the kettle boiled, the nervous man hurried to bring a bowl of steaming water to Briella, half-spilling it.

"Carefully!" she snapped, giving him a dark look. The man stepped back, surprise and fear in his face. Briella closed her eyes and massaged just above the bridge of her nose. "I'm sorry. I know you're just worried. Leave her to me and wait outside. You stay," she said as she pointed at Bren.

Bren's eyes widened. "Me? But—but..."

"But he's a stranger!" the husband protested.

A glance from Briella silenced him. Slowly, he retreated to the door and stomped outside, slamming the door after himself.

Briella handed Bren the bowl. "Bring me more water."

Careful not to spill any, he carried the nearly full bowl to the bedside.

Briella cast the herbs into the water, stirring the infusion with a willow wand. A sweet, refreshing fragrance filled the air, lightening Bren's anxiety. Briella cradled Cilla's shoulders in her arm. "Sip this, slowly now. You'll feel better, and the pain will ease."

Gradually swallowing half the tea, the woman seemed less pale. She dozed a few minutes.

After a while Briella listened to Cilla's chest, felt her wrist, then smiled. "Her breathing's less shallow. Her pulse is slower, and she's stronger. Good signs. Keep the kettle full and boiling." She sponged Cilla's face, neck, and arms with the tea while Bren added water to the kettle and wood to the fire.

At last, Briella breathed a sigh. "The fever's broken, and the swelling's subsiding."

The woman pulled up into a ball as a hard contraction hit her.

"Relax, relax, now short breaths, that's it," Briella said. She motioned Bren over. "Pull that stool over here and set the bowl on it. Now lift her shoulders and straddle the bed behind her so she can lean against you."

Bren froze. "What?"

."There's nothing for her to pull against, so you'll have to help her."

Blushing sunset red, he gasped, "I can't do that!"

"Then I'll do it, and you can deliver the baby!" she snapped at him.

His hands shook as Bren helped Cilla sit up, then he straddled the bed behind her.

Briella nodded. "That's right. Now, bathe her forehead with the tea again. Wet her lips if she asks you to. Have you ever helped at a delivery before?"

Bren swallowed nervously. "No."

".Well, I'll need your help. This may be a difficult birth. Her life and her child's may depend on you doing exactly what I tell you instantly. Do you understand?"

Bren nodded, subdued.

"Good. Now the real work begins. When I tell her to bear down, you prop her up and support her back during the pains. In between times, massage her back or her belly, whichever she chooses."

"Her belly?" he stuttered. "You want me to touch her...like that?"

"Of course. Here." Briella placed his hands on the swollen abdomen and made slow circles. "And talk to her, help her relax between pains."

Bren's face felt hot. He'd never touched a woman in such an intimate way. *I can't do this!* he thought, panicking. Suddenly, he felt the child move inside, new life, fragile, tiny, struggling to be born. He was so surprised, he forgot to be afraid. "Relax and breathe. Everything's fine."

Bren watched as Briella washed her hands with wine, dried them on a clean cloth, then knelt at the end of the bed. Bren massaged the woman's back during contractions to ease the strain, but Cilla was too tense.

"It hurts!" she sobbed. "It hurts! Make it stop, please!"

Bren stared wide-eyed at Briella. "What should I do? What should I do?" he asked frantically.

"Calm down," Briella said. "It's her first pregnancy. She's just scared. Keep talking to her. She'll be fine if you keep your head."

Bren did his best to reassure Cilla, wiping her sweat-beaded face and cradling her as she leaned against him.

When the last intense pains doubled Cilla's body, Briella said, "Bear down, now. That's it. Once more, harder. Harder! Again. Wait. Wait. All right. Bear down one more time. There! Oh, look, look! You have a son! A beautiful, perfect little boy!"

Cilla slumped against Bren, half-laughing, half-crying. "My baby! My baby! Let me see him."

Briella cut the umbilical cord, wiped the tiny boy with damp cloth, and wrapped him in a soft blanket.

Suddenly, Cilla bent over and screamed.

Bren panicked. "Something's wrong! What should I do?"

.Quickly placing the infant in a wooden cradle, Briella hurried to examine Cilla.

Bren's stomach churned like a waterfall pool. "What's happening? What's wrong?"

Briella looked at him and shook her head. "Nothing. There's another baby...twins!"

Soon Briella held a tiny girl in her hands. Briella wiped the baby's face and wrapped her in a soft blanket. Briella held the little girl for a while, caressed the round, r.ed cheek, and whispered so low he barely heard her, "Cordwin, if only we'd had time --"

She glanced up as Bren stared at her. Her face became like a closed door, hiding whatever she felt behind her eyes. She placed the baby girl in the cradle beside her brother. "It's time to leave. We still have a day's journey left until we reach my house. Then," she choked, "we'll settle matters between us."

"Yes," he said, no longer certain he knew how he would deal with her.

Calling the new father, Briella presented his son and daughter and handed him a dark-blue cloth pouch. "Give your wife an infusion of these herbs three times a day for three days then once a day for three days. She'll be well then." She clutched his arm. Lines in her forehead grew deeper as her voice became intense. "Please, take care of them and love them."

"I will, always." The man's eyes were round as saucers, as if he, too, heard the disturbing tone in her voice that Bren heard. As she turned to go, he grasped her hand. "Please, wait." He went to a leather-bound chest, opened it, and removed a wool blanket along with a skin of new wine which he presented to Briella. "Thank you. I hope you have as much happiness as you've given me today."

Briella bowed mutely, but Bren noticed how pale she'd become. He followed her from the village as the neighbors crowded around to congratulate the father as shadows grew long and the air began to cool.

28

Briella sighed, her head drooping, as she whispered, "I've one more stop before we rest, but I don't have time to walk. I have to reach a cottage by sunset, and it's nearly already that. We'll wait until we've left the village, then I'll change us."

"Change?" Bren asked.

Instead of answering, Briella trudged past the curious people who watched silently but respectfully. Bren followed, more confused than before.

When they were beyond the village boundary, Briella faced Bren. "Hold me tightly. Close your eyes if it helps."

"But...I, uh..." As cautiously as if she were a bundle of thistles, Bren put his arms about her but didn't close his eyes. Colors and light swirled about him. Wind stung his face, and he felt dizzy. Breathing was painful; moving, impossible. When he thought he couldn't endure another moment, he realized they were standing still.

He was holding a woman with wheat-colored hair that brushed her shoulders, eyes like summer skies, and skin as soft as a snow rabbit. Was this what she truly looked like? He felt her warmth, her gentleness, her compassion, and he was drawn to her in ways he'd never been drawn to Miria. He was astonished and confused by Briella.

He winced as her name echoed through his mind. Briella — she was the one who killed his parents! Anger filled his heart, and he pushed her away. "Stop it, stop it! Get away from me! You can't trick me, you can't, no matter how you make yourself appear. I can't be bewitched so easily. I'll have my revenge. It's my right. You said I'd have my chance at the right time, and I will kill you!"

Briella watched him with sad eyes. "Oh, Bren," she whispered with such gentleness, Bren cringed with shame.

Turning her back to him, she murmured something and became an old peddler woman, bulging sack bowing her back. "Hurry," she called over her shoulder. "We have to reach the cottage by sunset." Back bent, she trudged on at such a fast pace, Bren had to run to keep up with her.

The sun was touching the tops of the Circle Mountains when they reached a rickety, thatched cottage with a stone-walled well beside it. No light shown through the ragged curtains at the only window. There was a disorderly woodpile beside the door, but no smoke curled from the stone chimney rising from the back side of the hut. Slowly, Briella pushed open the wooden door.

In the small, dark room, a young girl of perhaps eight years knelt, shivering beside a narrow cot and wringing out a rag over a chipped bowl. Her hair was as pale as her skin. Her patched shift hadn't been washed for weeks. Tears had left trails on her grimy cheeks. When her dull blue eyes saw Briella, the girl smiled feebly. "Please, help him."

On the cot lay a man, perhaps thirty-five years old, unconscious, terribly thin, and breathing like a rusty hinge. His beard was many days old, his lips were cracked, and he stank from sour sweat. Moaning in delirium, his eyelids fluttered, then he lay still.

Briella went to the cot and touched his forehead. "He needs liquids. That fever will kill him if I can't break it tonight."

"I tried to take care of him," the girl said as tears cut new paths through the dirt on her face. "I tried, but he got sicker."

Briella cradled the small face in her hands, thumbs smoothing away the streams of tears, and said, "You did a good thing by wiping his face with water. It was the best thing you could do for him."

The girl blinked back tears and tried to smile.

Sinking to a small stool beside the bed, Briella glanced at Bren. "Please, build a fire. Fetch some water and boil a kettle. And give the child some food from the basket."

Bren went outside to the haphazard pile of wood and loaded his arms. Bringing the wood inside, he started a small fire which soon warmed the hut. He went to the well, drew a bucket of water, and poured it into an iron kettle hanging over the fire. It took several trips back to the well before the kettle was full. While the water heated, he brought out some cheese, bread, and apples, and offered them to the child.

"Are you hungry?" he asked.

The girl nodded.

"Here."

The girl just looked at the food for a moment, then shyly reached for it. She tore at the bread as if she had not eaten for some time, stuffing it in her mouth until her cheeks bulged like a chipmunk's. Looking about, Bren could see no food at all. The girl had evidently tried to keep the room clean and swept. However, the roof needed repair. The walls needed to be plastered with mud to keep out the wind. She was just too young to do the work of an adult.

He felt uncomfortable, guilty. He'd always had more food than he could eat, always had clothing and warmth. The poor of Drambit had never been more than faceless creatures who'd provided whatever Bren had wanted. They'd never been people who were hungry and sick. This girl was frightened and cold and too young to deal with hunger and death. He decided to leave all but a few meager supplies, including the money he'd brought with him, in a cupboard. He smiled at the girl, and she smiled shyly back at him.

"I need a bowl of warm water," Briella called over her shoulder.

Bren found a wooden bowl on a shelf, and using a wooden ladle, nearly filled the bowl and brought it to Briella.

"Set it on there," she pointed to a small table beside the bed.

Bren set it down and watched as Briella examined the girl's father. She removed the man's sweat-soaked clothing, then bathed him completely with warm water from the kettle. The man shivered, moaned, and grasped for a cover.

"Bring me the blanket the new father gave me," she said.

Bren grabbed the blanket and spread it over the sick man.

Briella felt the man's pulse, rested her hand on his chest, then motioned to Bren.

"His pulse is very fast," she whispered, "and his breathing's raspy. Maybe pneumonia, maybe worse. I hope I've enough strength left to heal him."

"But why don't you just cure him with your magic?" Bren asked.

Briella gave him a crooked smile. "If he were dying right now, at this moment, I would. But there are hazards to such cures. First, he's so weak, any sudden shock to his body—even healing—might damage his mind. Second, I don't know if I have enough strength to do it. As weak as I am from traveling, I'd probably be unconscious for several days. Herbs and a little healing will work as well, just take a little longer."

"Maybe you should take some of your herbs, too," Bren said, then started, surprised that he cared whether she was well or not.

Age lines smoothed from Briella's face, and her eyes glistened. Her voice was gentle as her smile. "Maybe. Maybe I will." She turned away.

As Briella walked toward the hearth, the girl tugged at Briella's robe. The child's face was full of hope and fear. "Will he get well?"

Bren watched as Briella gave the girl a reassuring smile and stroked the tousled, flaxen hair. "I'll take care of your father. You go finish your meal, then to bed with you. All right?"

The child nodded slowly and went back to the table to finish her food.

Briella retrieved her pack and ruffled through it. "Mint, wintergreen, and callum bark," she said as she took small bottles from her pack. She opened each bottle, shook a small amount from each into her palm, and tossed the herbs into the kettle. When it boiled, she ladled some of the infusion in the wooden bowl and returned with it to the bed. A fragrance like springtime filled the cottage. Bren breathed in the sweet scent and felt refreshed and peaceful.

Briella sat beside the man's head and wafted the steam toward him. Soon his breathing was easier, less raspy. He stirred and opened his eyes slightly.

Returning to the hearth, Briella took more bottles from her bag. "Valerian, monarda, foxglove, roborant, and liverwort," she murmured as she measured a small amount of each herb. She dropped them into the kettle, stirred the liquid with her willow wand, and let the infusion steep for several minutes. A musty floral scent pervaded the room, like flowers in an old forest.

"I need a cup," she called to Bren.

He found several wooden cups on the shelf where he'd found the bowl and brought the cup to Briella.

She filled the cup with the green-gold tea and returned to the bedside. She blew on the cup to cool it. Supporting the man's head, she forced him to drink the steaming liquid, then refilled the cup.

"You need to drink a little more," she told him when he balked. "That's right. More. A little more. Good. Another sip. All right. That's enough for now."

She lowered his head back to the pillow. Filling a bowl with the tea, she dipped a cloth in the bowl and bathed his face and chest even while he slept.

Bren gazed at Briella, almost dizzy from the double image of her in his mind: Paxell's description of a murdering witch and Bren's own observation of a selfless healer. Two different pictures, much too different to be one person, but there was only one Briella. *Who is she truly?* he wondered.

A quiet sniff distracted him from the chaotic confusion in his mind. The little girl sat beside him, her knees drawn up tightly to her chest, her tiny hands clenched around them.

Trying to put the little girl at ease, Bren smiled at her. "What's your name?"

"Lufian," she said in a tiny voice.

"Lufian. That's a beautiful name."

"It was Mama's name, too."

"Well, Lufian, it's late and you should be in bed sleeping."

She shook her head. "No, I want to stay with Papa."

"But your papa's sleeping. That's because he knows he needs to rest. So do you. You want to help your papa, don't you?"

She nodded.

"Then you have to take care of yourself. You must be strong and well if you want to help him get better."

Lufian frowned slightly, her little forehead and thin brows scrunched in thought, then nodded slowly. She climbed into a small cot and covered with a hole-filled blanket. Glancing once at her father, she closed her eyes and fell asleep almost immediately.

Bren covered Lufian with his own cloak, sat on the wooden floor beside her bed, and smoothed her silky hair from her face. He grew drowsy and lay his head on the edge of the girl's bed. Watching Briella encourage the man to take more tea, Bren fell asleep.

A loud crash woke him up. The fire had burned low but still gave enough light to show Briella sprawled beside an empty bucket, water splashed across the wooden floor. Lufian whimpered in her sleep. Bren stroked her hair gently twice, then turned to help Briella stand. Her legs buckled. Bren scooped her up and set her in a chair which had a worn but usable pillow for her head.

Bren seized the handle, surprised at his anxious concern for her. "Why didn't you ask me to draw the water for you?"

She closed her eyes and rubbed her forehead. "I have to make more tea and didn't want to bother you. You've helped so much already." She started to stand.

"No, sit down." Gently, he forced her back into the chair. "You rest for a while. I'll watch him and make the tea. Just tell me what to add."

She didn't protest. After showing him which herbs to use, Briella slumped in the chair and slept immediately.

Bren took the empty bucket out to the well, shivering in the chilly air. A light frost had settled on the ground, making the grass crunch beneath his feet. He lowered the drawing bucket into the well, then pulled the rope until the drawing bucket was within reach. Pouring the icy water into the empty bucket, he carried it back into the hut, dumped it into the kettle, and added the herbs as Briella had told him. Trudging back outside, he filled his arms with more wood, brought it inside, and added several branches and one large log to the fire.

Bren sat on the chair beside the man's bed, waiting for the tea to brew, and gazed at Briella resting in the chair. He noted her ashen face and thin body. Still, he remembered the desirable woman he'd held in his arms a brief moment. *Am I bewitched?* he wondered. *Can I trust what I've seen or is this just an illusion to convince me not to kill her? How can I tell what is the truth? I just don't know what to believe.*

Even while he tended the sick man, he watched Briella until she opened her eyes about an hour before dawn.

Briella groaned and slowly pushed to her feet. "It's nearly time to leave." Checking the man's forehead, she smiled. "No sign of fever. His heartbeat's regular. His breathing's normal. He's still weak, but I think he'll recover completely."

Leaving a full kettle of tea over the fire, she retrieved her pack and went to the door. She looked back at the two sleeping forms once more, then silently motioned for Bren to follow her.

Reluctantly, Bren removed his cloak from Lufian. "I wish I could leave this for her."

Briella touched his arm and smiled approvingly. "Wait."

She set her pack on the floor. Walking to the man's bed, she pulled a thread from the blanket which covered him. She held the thread up in one hand, stretched her other hand over her head, and said, "By the power of Baramay who made all that is, *tasrin adessal rasheesah barason*!"

To Bren's astonishment, another blanket, identical to the first, appeared in her hand where the thread had been. "Hound of Darkness! How did you do that?" he gasped.

"Barsallin had nothing to do with it," she said, her tone flat, her eyes cold.

Bren nearly choked. She'd spoken the name that no one in his country dared say!

Briella spread the blanket over Lufian, turned, picked up her sack, and left. Bren stood staring at Lufian, more confused than ever. He tossed several logs on the fire, left nearly all his traveling food and the small pouch of money he'd brought with him in the cupboard, then hurried after Briella.

Stars overhead vanished in the grey light of dawn. The autumn morning was foggy and cool, frost clinging in low places. Briella pulled her cloak around her tighter and trudged down the road silently. She stumbled once, but Bren caught her.

"Let me help you," he said, mystified by his concern.

She leaned against him for a minute, her body light, almost ethereal. Her eyes closed, and for a moment her disguise blurred, revealing the soft, vital woman Bren had held before. Just as quickly, the old peddler reappeared. She pushed herself away from him slowly. "I'm sorry. I'm just...tired," she said and shuffled down the road.

Bren trudged behind her, deep in thought.

In half an hour they reached a tidy, darkened cottage. Briella knocked at the door. A light shone through the shutters, and the sound of quiet footsteps came towards the entrance which opened cautiously.

A red-haired woman in her early thirties stood in the doorway, her eyes wide with delight at seeing Briella. "Old Mam! Please, come in. Do you have time for breakfast? I just put some biscuits in the oven."

Briella shook her head. "I haven't time to stay. You know the hut just north of here?"

The woman nodded, a hint of a smile playing at the corners of her narrow mouth.

"The man's very ill."

"Oh, no!" The woman's skin became paler than its natural shade. "Will he live? What about Lufian? Is she all right? How can I help?"

"I've tended him all night. He'll recover with food and attention. I left a kettle of medicine on the fire. He must drink one cup every two hours until it's finished. Also, his daughter needs a woman to look after her. Could you take care of them until he's well?"

"Oh, I'd be glad to," the woman said enthusiastically, then blushed.

Briella gave the woman a supply of the herbs and explained their use. After Briella had said "Far-thell", she turned away and started down the road again. Bren walked close beside her as the cottage disappeared behind them in the morning fog.

29

"We can't waste any more time," Briella murmured, her eyes red. "I think I can convey us once more. Hold on to me tightly again, and we'll be at my home in a heartbeat...I hope."

Bren hesitated. He wanted to hold her again, wanted her so much his desire frightened him. Paxell's words of caution came back to him. Still, he felt safe, and that disturbed him more than ever.

How can I trust her not to harm me? he thought, baffled. *She knows I intend to kill her. Why hasn't she killed me? If I were her, I'd have killed me already*. He gazed at her silently. *She's not anything like I thought she'd be. But how do I know this feeling isn't a spell she's put on me? What can I trust?*

Cautiously, Bren placed his arms about her and closed his eyes. She felt like sunshine in his arms, warm, light, exhilarating. After a moment of dizziness, he opened his eyes and looked around.

They stood in a kitchen with walls made of blue crystal. The early morning sun shone through the outer walls, casting a faint blue glow on everything. Briella was still in his arms. Her disguise was gone. Her dress was as blue as her eyes, and her hair was the color of ripe wheat. She felt as desirable as she'd been the first time he'd held her in his arms. She reminded him of Miria, but Briella's eyes didn't have the hard, proud glint he'd seen in Miria's eyes. He felt awkward and clumsy, like a boy whose body had grown too fast. Slowly, he released her, and she backed away from him.

She whispered a strange word and passed her hand before his face. Bren's disguise disappeared, although his worn clothes remained. Briella turned toward her table, picked up a folded stack of clothing and black boots, and held them out to Bren. "These are worthy of the lord of Vorlik."

He rested his staff against a chair and took the clothing and boots from her. The long-sleeved shirt was of the finest white linen. White cotton stockings and linen undergarments lay on top of a wine-colored vest. Black trousers and black leather belt were next. The boots were as soft as goose down.

Briella turned her back to him and braced her hands on her table. "Dress quickly, Bren, and then we will finish what is between us."

He stared at the clothing, astonished. *Why is she doing this?* he wondered. *I don't understand her. I just don't understand.*

He peeled off his old clothes and worn sandals. The clothes were as soft and comfortable as they looked, and were finer than anything else he'd ever worn.

Briella turned back to him and spoke words he didn't understand. Suddenly, his staff disappeared. In his hand was the Dagger of Slaying. He stared at it. Did she want him to kill her? Immobile and speechless, he looked at her, waiting for her to speak.

She steepled her hands and whispered something. "You're released from my spell."

Bren felt as if an invisible rope around him had snapped. He shook himself and blinked his eyes. He was free.

She gazed at him calmly, though her lips trembled a little. "I won't stop you from avenging yourself. I gave my word, and I don't break promises. Wizards never do. But tell me what you accuse me of. At least, let me defend myself."

Bren cleared his throat, pointed the dagger at her, but when he tried to speak, no sound came. He cleared his throat again and finally found his voice, though it was weak and unsure.

"You bewitched my uncle," he began, repeating what he'd heard all his life, what he'd believed in, what had driven him from childhood, "bewitched him and plotted with him to murder my father, Lord Clevil, and my mother, Lady Ellisa. You've sealed this land against any interference with your power. Despite the way you've tried to fool me these last few days, I...I know what you are. All the good you may have done won't make up for what you did to my parents, and I'll have my revenge."

"Who told you all these things?" Briella asked softly.

"Lord Paxell, the man who saved me from death."

"Who else?"

"No one, but—" Bren started when Briella interrupted him.

"No—no, I see now," she whispered. Worry lined her forehead; her wide eyes stared beyond him. "It was Paxell. I should've guessed." Her gaze swung back to Bren. "Oh, Bren, don't you know? He was your father's enemy before you were born. Drambit and Vorlik have been enemies since the days of the first men and the wars between the Wizards and the Sorcerers. Generations of hatred were instilled in Paxell from the time he was a child."

Briella's eyes seemed to stare beyond Bren, beyond the room, seeing something he couldn't see. "It was his army that invaded southern Vorlik to draw off the East, West, and Tarolin Guards so he could attack the castle and kill your parents. Why he spared you, I don't know. Leverage in dealing with Cordwin, ransom perhaps, I don't know.

"As for bewitching your uncle, I didn't come to Vorlik until two weeks after your parents were buried. I was sent by my great-grandfather, the Wizard Casslin, to protect

Vorlik. The Wall of Warding I raised has prevented the repeated invasion of this peaceful land. Oh, yes, Lord Paxell would like nothing better than to have the Wall dismantled. He's rebuilt his army enough to attack Vorlik once the way's been cleared by my death."

Bren's face was purple in the blue light. "That's not true! It can't be true! He said he saved me from death, protected me. He's been a father to me!"

"Only because it fit his purpose."

"No, he loves me. I'm going to marry his daughter. He's helping me regain Vorlik."

"He'll take Vorlik for himself." She stared evenly at him.

"You're lying!" he shouted.

Briella straightened. "I told you once I don't lie. It's your choice, to believe me or not."

"I won't believe you," he said. "I can't."

Briella stared at the dagger in Bren's hand. "When I appeared at Cordwin's coronation, I had a vision of your return and the dagger you hold."

Bren kneaded the hilt impatiently.

"I saw my death at your hands." Her voice trembled. "I knew twenty years ago you'd come. If I were afraid of death, I'd have hidden or tried to kill you. Instead, I've served your people. And--" she looked deeply into his eyes, "I have a gift for you." She motioned to the table where the enchanted weapon lay.

The double-edged sword drew Bren like a lodestone. An emerald the size of a robin's egg glittered in the pommel. The word 'TRUTH' and his name were etched on the blade. It glowed as if it contained the fire that forged it. Shifting the dagger to his left hand, he reached out to take the sword, but stopped short.

Briella's eyes glistened as she gazed at her creation. "It's a Sword of Truth."

Bren looked questioningly at her.

"The sword will always let you know truth when you hear it. It can only be used by you and your heirs." She paused, caressing the slender blade as long as her arm, then knelt and offered it to him. "Take it, Lord Bren of Vorlik."

Warily, Bren grasped the hilt and raised the sword. It felt made for his hand, heavy but not unwieldy, a well-balanced, finely crafted weapon. "How do I know it will tell me the truth?" he asked. "If you are a liar, the sword may tell me only what you want me to hear."

"Then test it," she said. "I can only say what is true." She paused. "You must speak a lie, say something you know to be false."

Bren thought for a moment. "I came to Vorlik to thank you for taking care of my people."

Instantly, he saw a vision of his journey from Drambit to Leflin, felt the anger and determination to kill Briella. The intensity of his rage nearly took his breath away. The feeling was so intense, he had to lean on the table to steady himself.

"Now speak a truth," she said.

Bren swallowed tightly, almost afraid to speak. What could he say? "Paxell saved me from being murdered by you and my uncle. You bewitched everyone in this land and tried to keep it for your own. Paxell protected me and kept me safe, and now he's helping me to reclaim my throne."

Abruptly, almost painfully, he saw the truth in what Briella had told him: the murder of his parents, his own abduction, and her coming to Vorlik. He saw the people Briella had helped, the lives she'd saved. And he saw Paxell waiting at the Drambini border for the collapse of the Wall, ready to invade with his army. He dropped the sword. The very touch of truth seared his heart. Pain pumped from his soul like blood from a severed artery. "Lies! All my life has been lies!" His vision wavered like ripples on water.

Briella stepped toward him, her eyes filled with gentle pity. "Bren, don't blame yourself. You're only guilty of loving the man who raised you."

Her words made the hurt sharper, deeper. "But why? Why did he lie to me? He loved me, I know it. I felt it. How could he do this to me? How could he? Briella—"

The instant he said her name, the dagger jerked in his hand. Before Bren realized what was happening, the enchanted blade drove deep into her chest as if the dagger were guided by its own will. She staggered and screamed, a scream that cut down to Bren's soul, then he screamed, too.

"No!!!" Unable to move, he watched her plummet to the floor like a kite cut loose from its string.

Bren stared at the blood that splattered his hand and soaked her dress. He flung the dagger to the floor. Dropping beside her, he cradled her in his arms and moaned. "Oh, no. No. I didn't mean it. I didn't mean it. I'm sorry, so very sorry."

Sweat beading on her face, Briella struggled to speak. "The Wall of Warding – it dies with me. You must warn Cordwin about Paxell's invasion. Take the sword. It'll help you in ways you don't know. It gives you the power to travel from place to place instantly." Her skin became cool and pale as moonlight. She shuddered and lay limply in his arms, her eyes closed, but she clutched his arm and struggled to speak again. "Don't let me die in vain. Fight for your people, Bren. And tell Cordwin...tell Cordwin I loved him...more than life."

As her last breath escaped her lips, blue fire outlined her body, swirling like mist, shimmering like moonlight. Bren fell back and crawled away from her body. A whirlwind enveloped her, blue lightning arcing, thunder crashing through the room. And above the thunder was a cry of despair, of terrible loss. Slowly, the whirlwind shrank, the light dimmed until only the dove pendant glowed blue, then even that fire vanished. The room was quiet, deathly still.

Stark blue light filled the room as he crept to her side and took her in his arms. She was pale and soft as snowflakes, as cold and still as a windless winter night. She felt almost weightless as Bren carried her to the table and placed her on it tenderly. He smoothed her hair from her face, still so vibrant he could hardly believe she was dead. He sank to a chair and wept.

Straightening, he retrieved the sword from the floor. Power flowed through him. Strength and courage filled his whole being. "Now, I'll avenge my parents and you, Briella, and I'll stop Paxell. I'll fight for the people you loved and served so well. I swear I'll protect Vorlik. And I'll always remember you."

Raising the sword, he said, "Take me to Cordwin in Tarolin Castle."

30

Cordwin paced frantically in the Audience Hall, barely aware of the guards standing at the double doors leading to the main foyer. There's been no word from the trackers or any of the Guards, he thought, fear sitting on his chest like a lump of lead. *If they can't find her, what will I do? What more can I do to find her and keep her safe?* He halted for a moment, his throat almost too tight to swallow. *What if...what if Bren finds her before I do? No!! I won't even consider that! I have to find her! I can't live without her! Briella, please, please, come back to me!*

Sunlight crept through the high windows. The early morning air was warm, but he shivered. A shadow clouded his mind. Why, he didn't know. Something dark and dangerous was in the air, almost tangible, and it frightened him. He climbed the dais steps and sank onto his throne, his heart troubled.

He placed his hand next to his heart and felt the letter Briella had sent him, delivered nine days ago by the priest of Baygor from Yarrow. He'd read and reread the letter, but he pulled it from his shirt and read it again.

My dearest love, my husband who almost was, I will die soon. I know this, as surely as I know that my heart is in your keeping. Bren's arrival has shattered any hope we had of a life together.

You need to know that the Wall of Warding will last only as long as I live. When I die, that is when Vorlik will be in danger. That is when you must be strong and protect your people, because I won't be able to protect them anymore. Be wary. Be vigilant. Be brave.

Cordwin, know that you gave me more joy and happiness in our short time together than I ever thought possible. In my heart we are husband and wife, now and for always. I will speak your name with my last breath, and I'll wait for you in Barg's kingdom, where we will never be parted again. Baygor protect you, my sweet love. Briella.

Cordwin folded the letter and slipped it next to his heart, tears trickling from his eyes.

A sound like wind sighing through trees filled the Audience Hall. Suddenly, a young man appeared before him, holding the jeweled sword Briella had shown Cordwin only a few days earlier. The two door guards raced to place themselves between Cordwin and the stranger, their swords drawn. The stranger held the sword hilt, point touching the stone floor, but remained completely still.

Slowly, Cordwin stood and descended the dais. He felt off balance, as if he were walking the crumbling edge of a cliff at night. With halting steps he approached the young man. "Stand down," Cordwin said to the guards without looking at them. They took a step back and sheathed their swords, but stood close by.

His pulse pounding in his ears, Cordwin stepped toward the stranger until Cordwin was barely an arm's length away, their eyes on the same level. The stranger's face was shaped like Clevil's, same blue eyes, but his hair was walnut brown like Ellisa's had been. Cordwin stared at the sword, dread making his mouth so dry, he could hardly speak. "B-Briella's sword...how did you..."

"She gave it to me."

"Are you...are you..." Cordwin stammered.

The young man's gaze faltered, and he trembled. Softly, he said, "I'm Bren."

Cordwin gaped at Bren, unable to speak, until he looked at Bren's right sleeve. Cold sweat crept down Cordwin's neck. His hands felt clammy. He almost touched the dark stains on the right sleeve of Bren's shirt, then drew back. "Oh, gods," he whispered, panic thrumming through him. "There's blood on your hand, on your clothes."

Bren hung his head. "It's her blood. The dagger...it..." He fell silent for a moment, straightened, then said, "My dagger killed her."

Cordwin's eyes flooded with tears, and he shrieked, "No!!!" Agony nearly doubled him over, as if he'd been stabbed through the heart. He grabbed Bren's shirt with both hands and violently shook him. "You killed her! You killed my wife!"

Bren stiffened. His eyes widened, and he dropped the sword. "Your *wife?* Briella was your *wife?*"

"Yes, she was my wife! And you killed her! You have no idea what you've done!" Roaring like a Formian bear, Cordwin struck Bren with his fists until Bren's face was a mass of cuts and blood, but Bren didn't fight back. He fell to the floor, but didn't resist at all.

Bren wiped blood and sweat from his eyes, then retrieved his sword and scrambled to his knees. Holding the blade in his left hand, he offered the hilt to Cordwin and said, "Kill me. Avenge her death. It's your right, and I don't want to live anymore, not after this, not after what I've done."

Enraged and devastated, Cordwin jerked the sword from his nephew's grasp, swung the blade above his head, and tried to strike. Something held him back, as if invisible hands restrained his arms. He tried again, but all he could do was stare at his nephew. Blood dripped on the slate floor from gashes in Bren's left hand, gashes from the sword. Bren still knelt, his arms flung wide, head tilted up toward Cordwin, eyes wide with resignation and remorse. Eyes filled with tears. Blue eyes like his father's.

The sword felt unbearably heavy in Cordwin's hands. He let the sword tumble from his grip, and the blade clanged against the slate, echoing in the Audience Hall. Tears blurred his vision, edged in black and with colors fading to shades of grey. His legs felt shaky, and he staggered back a step. "Why?" he cried, glaring at the ceiling, his voice echoing in the empty hall. "Lady Baramay, why did you let her die? Why didn't you prevent it? What kind of god are you that would kill Briella, my wife, my love?"

Bren picked up the sword and held it out to Cordwin again. "The gods had nothing to do with her death," Bren said, his voice bitter and trembling. "Two men killed her: one man who was utterly deceitful; and one who was too gullible to know he was being used. Uncle, I'm sorry. I'm so sorry. Let me die. Take my life to pay for hers."

Cordwin couldn't speak. He collapsed to his knees and wept unrestrainedly. Bren put his arms around him, and Cordwin laid his head against Bren's shoulder. Cordwin willed his heart to stop beating, but it wouldn't obey. *Let me die,* he prayed silently, his body taut with anguish. *Let me join Briella in death. Let me stop breathing. Why should I keep living when Briella is dead?* He wept until he was nearly numb with grief.

Bren held him while he wept, and when Cordwin's tears had subsided to a few sobbing gasps, Bren whispered, "Briella told me that the Wall of Warding would begin to dissipate with her death. She asked me to warn you that the Drambini army waits at the border for the Wall to collapse." Bren paused. "And she asked that she not die in vain."

Cordwin was too choked to speak. At that moment, the doors to the Audience Hall crashed open. Cordwin lifted his head slowly and saw ten sword-wielding soldiers, including Daikin, charging into the hall. They surrounded Cordwin and Bren, swords ready to strike.

"Release Lord Cordwin or die!" Daikin shouted, glaring at Bren.

Cordwin held up his right hand. "Hold, captain, I'm...as well as I can be at the moment."

Daikin didn't relax and kept glaring suspiciously at Bren.

"Sound the alarm!" Bren said. "The Drambini are preparing to invade. Ready the castle guard and alert the towns between here and the western border. Hurry!"

"And who are *you* to give orders to *me?*" Daikin asked as Bren stood and faced him.

Cordwin rose slowly to his feet and said, "Bren, son of Clevil."

Daikin inhaled sharply, and his face turned pale. He turned to Cordwin. "Has everything...Is she...Are we too late?"

Cordwin could only nod. He could barely feel anything. He felt as if he were drowning, and he didn't want to struggle anymore. He wanted to sink into the dark, quiet place that pulled at his soul, promising an end of pain and sorrow. But a voice, Briella's voice, whispered, "Don't let me die in vain. Protect our people." He clutched at his chest, for a moment, then straightened. *I swear, my love,* he vowed, *I'll protect our people with all that I am, to my last breath. I swear it.*

"Baygor help us now," Daikin said. He turned back to Bren, glared at him a few moments, then knelt slowly. "My lord."

The guards followed Daikin's example and knelt before Bren. "My lord," they said.

Bren shifted uneasily but nodded to them.

"And Drambit?" Daikin asked.

"Lord Paxell is likely on his way, if he's discovered the Wall is down," Bren said. "We need to ready the troops now."

Daikin looked at Cordwin, who nodded again. "As you command, Lord Bren," Daikin said.

"Have Scribe Vel send out messages to all the Guards," Cordwin said. "But warn the Western Guard first. Light the signal fire. And send out scouts now."

The guards rose and hurried from the hall. Daikin gripped Cordwin's arm firmly and started to say something, but shook his head, turned and left. Moments later, a horn blast rang throughout the castle.

Alone in the hall except for the two door guards, Cordwin stared at Bren silently. Cordwin cleared his throat and blinked his eyes free of tears. "Where is she?"

"She lies in her house." Bren held out his right hand. "If I could trade my life for hers, I would. I swear I would."

Cordwin gazed up at the high windows where he'd first seen the grey dove flutter into the Audience Hall and change into a woman...and change his life forever. "She knew from the day she appeared to me, she would die by your hand. But she wouldn't leave. Her promise kept her here, even though she knew her fate. She saved my life more than once. And I loved her more than my own life. I would have died for her." He turned his bleary eyes toward Bren. "When we've defeated Paxell, would you take me to her? I need to see her once more, touch her face, and hold her in my arms one last time."

Bren stared at him. "Why would you want to hold a corpse?"

"Wizards aren't like humans," Cordwin said, remembering the story of Timmree. "Their bodies don't decay as men's do. It's said a Wizard's body remains untouched by corruption for weeks." He halted, his throat so tight, he could barely breathe. "I need to see her again. I need to."

Bren nodded. "When Vorlik is safe and if I still live, I swear I'll take you to her."

"Thank you," Cordwin said woodenly, anger and sorrow too evenly matched in his heart. "Let's go. We have a battle to win for her...and your mother and father," he said. "Paxell will pay for their lives...and more."

Bren picked up the sword, slid it through his belt, and Cordwin strode side by side with Bren from the hall to the foyer. "Send Physician Tothim to my room," Cordwin told one of the door wards. "I have a patient for him. And summon the priest."

Cordwin plodded up the stairs, forcing his feet to move one step at a time, and led Bren to the third floor. Cordwin pushed open the door to his room and shuffled inside. Pellin was there, laying out Cordwin's armor. A squire now and a capable fighter, the thirty-one year-old man was wearing a chainmail shirt and red tabard over all, a sword and scabbard belted on. A simple helmet nearly covered his auburn hair.

"It's war then," Pellin said, his deep voice as filled with worry as his eyes were.

"Yes," Cordwin said.

Pellin stood straight, his chin held high. "I'm ready. This time I'm going with you. I'm not afraid."

Cordwin nodded. "I know."

White-haired Physician Tothim arrived not long after, carrying a bag over his shoulder. He walked slowly now, his joints creaking, wheezing from the climb up the stairs. "Where's my patient?"

"Here," Cordwin said, pointing to Bren.

Bren held out his left hand.

Squinting his eyes, Tothim examined the wounds. "The wound has stopped bleeding, but the gash is raw." He took a jar of salve from his bag, opened the waxed lid, and spread the salve on the wounds. A springtime scent filled the room.

Cordwin froze. He'd smelled that scent before, when he'd been injured by the Sorcerer. "That salve," he stammered, "where did you get it?"

"The priests of Baygor make it from a curious tree," Tothim said. "It has amazing healing properties."

"Briella's tree," Cordwin whispered.

Tothim bandaged Bren's wounds gently and gave him soft, pig-skin gloves to protect his hand. "He'll be all right, but he shouldn't use his hand for a week."

"I can't wait that long," Bren said and tucked the gloves beneath his belt. "I have to fight today."

Tothim threw up his hands and looked beseechingly at the ceiling. "Why do I bother trying to heal patients when they won't follow my advice?"

Cordwin smiled. It was comforting to know that Tothim never changed, even if the rest of the world was turned upside down.

Tothim bowed to Cordwin. "My lord, if you will excuse me, I have to gather the healers and load the wagons." Turning away, he opened the door and left.

Pellin helped Cordwin put on his armor. Cordwin pulled on his red and gold surcoat over his armor and belted on his sword. He glared at Bren for a moment, then turned to Pellin and said, "Bring a candle and follow me." He motioned to Bren. "Come with me. I have something that is rightfully yours."

Walking to the door, Cordwin opened it and walked out to the corridor. He paused, slowly turned his head to the right, and gazed up the hallway. His stomach knotted, and it was difficult to breathe. He swallowed hard, then strode toward rooms he hadn't entered in twenty years.

He halted in the corridor at the spot where Clevil had died. For just a moment, like a flash of lightning, he saw his brother's body lying there, then just as quickly the memory was gone. Carefully stepping around the spot, he walked on down the corridor. He stopped before a door and rested a trembling hand on the dark wood. An iron key hung on a hook driven into the stone wall beside the door. Slowly, he reached for the key. *I swore I'd never enter this room again,* he thought.

He took the key from the hook, inserted it into the lock, and turned it. Closing his eyes, he pushed the door open, gathered his courage, and opened his eyes.

The room was dark; Cordwin couldn't see anything. The odor of dust and stale air filled his lungs. Reluctantly, he took a step into the room, then another. Pellin brought the candle in and lit several candles still in the room.

Dust covered everything. Cobwebs and spider webs hung from the ceiling. At the end of the bed was a dust-covered chest. Cordwin went to it, brushed away the dust, and opened the chest. Inside was a blanket-wrapped bundle. He ran his hand lovingly over the blanket. Cordwin took the bundle out of the chest and set it on the bed.

He pulled back the blanket. Inside were a steel breastplate with chain mail sleeves, bracers, a winged helmet, and a surcoat of the Tarolin Guard. He brushed his fingertips over the armor, remembering the last time he saw Clevil trying to put on the armor. Sometimes that day seemed so long ago. Other times it felt like yesterday.

"These belonged to my brother, your father," Cordwin said, looking at Bren. "Now they're yours. You'll need them today."

"Father's?" Bren picked up the bracers and gazed at them. "My father's? These were his?"

"Yes," Cordwin said, "his and his father's and his father's father's. They wore this armor to protect the people of Vorlik. Now it's your turn." He rested his hand on Bren's shoulder. "Wear this armor with honor and make your father proud of you."

"I'll try," Bren said. "I swear I'll try."

Pellin helped Bren put on with the breastplate and fastened the clasps on the sides. Bren put on the bracers, then the red and gold surcoat of the Tarolin Guard over all. Last of all, Pellin set the winged helmet on Bren's head.

Cordwin stared at his nephew, dressed in Clev's armor and the uniform of the Tarolin Guard. Bren looked so much like Clev that for a few moments Cordwin couldn't breathe, couldn't move. Shaking off his lethargy, Cordwin took a sword and scabbard from the chest, pulled the sword from its sheath, and handed the scabbard to Bren. "You'll need a sheath for your sword," Cordwin said.

Bren handed the scabbard to Pellin, who threaded Bren's belt through the scabbard, then buckled it on, looped the leather around and through, pulling the knot securely. Lastly, Bren pulled on the pigskin gloves Tothim had given him.

"Now," Cordwin said, clasping Bren's forearm, "let's fight for our people...and for her."

Bren nodded. "For her."

With Bren and Pellin following close behind, Cordwin hurried down the stairs, crossed the wide foyer, and passed through the castle doors. The priest of Baygor waited outside, dressed in his formal blue and gold robes. Cordwin bowed to the priest, then proceeded down the steps to the courtyard. Most of the Tarolin Guard were mounted and waiting. Daikin sat on his chestnut horse at the head of the Guard.

A stable boy held the reins of Moon Shadow and a second horse, a dappled grey, at the foot of the castle steps. Another boy held the reins to Pellin's jet black mare. Pellin took the reins and climbed up into his saddle. Cordwin handed Bren the reins of the grey horse, then took Moon Shadow's reins and mounted. Shadow was twenty-three years old, but was still strong and steady and Cordwin's favorite horse.

Cordwin gazed up to the highest turret of the castle. The signal fire was blazing there, warning all the signal posts of danger.

The priest held his arms outstretched at his sides. "Great and merciful Baygor, preserver of life, grant you protection to these your servants and keep them safe in this dark time. Give them courage and strength to defend your people. Hand to heart." He placed his right hand over his chest. "And heart to heaven." He raised his left hand to the sky.

"Hand to heart and heart to heaven," the soldiers said prayerfully.

Drawing his sword, Cordwin shouted, "For Vorlik and Lord Bren! Baygor protect us!"

"Baygor protect us!" the Tarolin Guard shouted.

The soldiers parted to let Cordwin, Daikin, and Bren ride to the gates first, with Pellin riding behind Cordwin. As soon as they reached the road, they turned and galloped west, the Tarolin Guard following them. Dust rose like columns of smoke in the morning sky.

Lady Baramay, let us be in time, Cordwin prayed as he raced westward. *Let us reach the border before Paxell crosses into Vorlik. And let us have the strength to defend the people Briella died for.*

31

The western border was several hours' ride from Tarolin Castle. Cordwin rode past the great Temple of Baygor, past the western reaches of Rindolar Woods, past farmsteads and orchards, past blazing signal fires. All along the route, wagon loads of women, children, and the elderly were heading east to the castle. Men on foot or riding horses used for plowing joined the army heading west. Some shouldered bows; some had axes or swords thrust through belts.

Cordwin almost ordered them back to guard their families, but reconsidered. *It's their land, their homes,* he thought. *They have as much right to defend it as we have.*

Half an hour before they reached the village of Leflin, Corporal Alswick and several other scouts returned with reports.

"My lord," Alswick said, saluting, "they've crossed the border: three hundred horse, four hundred footmen, and one hundred archers. The first companies could be in Leflin in less than two hours, and they outnumber us, at least until the rest of our troops arrive. The Western Guard has tried to delay them but has been driven steadily eastward. They can't hold out for long without reinforcements. At their present rate of movement, we'll meet the enemy barely a mile beyond Leflin."

Cordwin summoned Daikin, Bren, and the lieutenants to the front of the troops where they formed a close circle. "We have to protect Leflin at all costs. Lieutenant Linaria, you take fifty men and set up a defensive line there. Also, help Tothim and the healers set up tents to care for the wounded. Organize the men of the town to build defenses around the town and also evacuate as many women and children as possible to Tarolin."

"Yes, my lord," Linaria said and clapped her fist across her chest in salute. Suddenly, she looked uncertain. She glanced at Bren, then back at Cordwin. "I mean, yes...sir?"

"Bren is Clevil's son and heir," Cordwin said quietly. "He is lord of Vorlik now."

"No," Bren said. Staring straight at Cordwin, Bren shook his head. "You are lord of Vorlik until I ascend the throne. Lead this country as you always have."

Cordwin scrutinized his nephew and nodded. *Clevil would be proud of you,* he thought. Turning toward the rest of the group, he said, "We'll split the rest of our soldiers into three groups. Captain Daikin and Lieutenant Rayvil will take a hundred men south of Leflin to join with the Southern Guard; they should be well on their way here. Lieutenant Tude and I will take a hundred to meet the Northern Guard and attack Drambit's left flank. Lieutenant Loren will ride to Leflin with Linaria then take the rest of the troops straight west." Cordwin paused and studied his nephew. "Bren, if you agree ..."

Bren clapped his fist across his chest exactly the way Linaria had. "Whatever you need of me," he said quietly, "I am yours, Uncle."

"You'll ride with Lieutenant Loren west to Leflin, then you'll lead the remaining hundred and fifty straight west toward the border." Cordwin heard gasps from the troops. "You'll likely be the first to face Drambini troops." Cordwin stared at him intently. "Can you do that? Can you fight against people you've known all your life?"

Bren looked away for a moment. He touched the hilt of the sword hanging from his belt and nodded. "Yes," he said, meeting Cordwin's gaze.

Loren stared at Bren for a long moment, then turned back to Cordwin. "I won't follow his orders, my lord. He killed the Wizard Briella. How do we know he's not a Drambini spy? How do we know he's not waiting for a chance to lead us into a trap?"

There was dead silence.

"He's right," Bren said, surprising Cordwin. Even Loren blinked at him in amazement. "I shouldn't be in charge. I have to prove I can be trusted, and I'll do whatever's necessary to do that. Give Lieutenant Loren charge of the troops. I'll be under his command, the same as any other soldier."

Cordwin looked at Loren, who nodded his head slowly, but his eyes were narrowed and fixed on Bren.

"All right. Loren will lead the remaining forces straight west, and Bren will be under his command. Discussion?" Cordwin glanced around the circle at his lieutenants. They all gazed back at him silently. "Then Baygor protect us all."

The lieutenants saluted Cordwin solemnly. "Baygor protect us." Quickly, they divided the troops.

Cordwin turned to Pellin. "I want you to go with Lieutenant Linaria and defend Leflin."

"But my lord, can't I fight by your side?" the squire asked. "Please."

Hesitating, Cordwin nodded slowly. "All right. But take care. Good squires are hard to come by." He smiled slightly.

Pellin smiled back and turned his horse to join the ranks of soldiers.

Cordwin shifted toward Bren, grasped his nephew's forearm, and stifled a gasp. "You look so much like your father," he said. "Your hair, your mother's hair was the same color. But I don't know *you*. Not yet." He paused, almost afraid to let Bren go. "Be careful. I don't want to lose you again, not now. I spent too many years trying finding you."

"We'll win today, uncle," Bren said. "We'll win for her. I swear it. I swear it on my life."

They sat unmoving, neither one speaking. Finally, Bren wheeled his horse and quickly rode westward, falling in with Linaria's troops.

As he disappeared into the west, Cordwin sat silently. For a moment his mind wandered to Briella. *If only she and I had had time,* he thought, *time to love, time for children, time to grow old together. Now there's no time left, no time at all.*

Daikin broke his reverie. "Cord, take care. May a friend guard your back."

For some reason the old luck-wish made Cordwin shudder. Looking sharply at his cousin, Cordwin clutched Daikin's outstretched hand and softly gave the reply. "May you not die alone." Daikin turned to go, but Cordwin pulled him back, dread filling his heart. "Daik, be very, very careful today."

Daikin cocked his head and grinned slyly, his hair gleaming like copper in the midmorning sunlight. "I always am. Save a few Drambini for me. I don't want you to have all the fun." He clapped his legs against his horse's sides and galloped southwest. He and his troops disappeared in a grey-brown cloud of dust.

Shivering as if someone had put ice down his back, Cordwin stared after Daikin a moment, then led his men northwest to join the Northern Guard.

32

Bren and the Vorlikian troops reached Leflin half an hour later. People in the town square were rushing around frantically, loading children and goods into wagons, but they all stopped when the soldiers rode into the square.

"What's happening?" cried a young woman clutching a small child.

"Yes! What's happening?" shouted several others until a chorus of frightened cries echoed through the square.

Suddenly, a gangly middle-aged man with periwinkle eyes and a tuft of grey hair leaped up on a wagon. "Silence, all of you!" he shouted. The crowd grew quiet instantly.

Bren's eyes widened. He recognized the man as Kam Winsell, the owner of the Two Oaks Inn.

Kam turned toward Linaria. "We've seen the smoke to the west," he said, his arms folded across his chest. "And we've seen several soldiers wearing the uniform of the Tarolin Guard racing back and forth through town. I think we have a right to know what's happening."

"Yes, you do," Linaria said. "Drambit has invaded the western pass."

Guilt tightened Bren's throat and made him cringe.

Cries of dismay ran through the crowd.

"We have to flee!" cried a woman with several children gathered around her.

"No, we have to fight!" shouted a brawny man with soot-smudged skin.

"You're both right," Linaria said. "We'll here will help you prepare to defend your town, but we need to get as many women and children away from here as quickly as possible."

"Wait!" Kam said, frowning. "How could Drambit invade us? Doesn't the Wall of Warding keep that from happening?"

"It does," a woman's voice came from the door of the inn. Maiya the innwife and healer, Kam's wife, stood there pale and shaking. "It does, as long as the Wizard Briella is alive." Her violet eyes glistened. "And that's it, isn't it? Briella is dead."

"The Wizard? Dead? What will we do?" one feeble old man asked.

Cries of despair mingled with shouts of anger.

"What we can," Kam said, holding up his hands to calm the crowd. He turned back to Linaria. "Tell us what to do."

Linaria and fifty soldiers began organizing the villagers' defense, while Lieutenant Loren and Bren rode westward with the remaining troops as fast as the horses could travel.

As they'd reached the edge of Leflin, a scout arrived. "The Western Guard has been destroyed. The first ranks of the enemy are only three miles away."

Loren frowned and clenched his jaw. "Much closer than I'd hoped. We'll have to delay the Drambini long enough for our other troops to arrive. All right, what options do we have?"

A sergeant spoke up. "Pull back to the village and join Linaria."

"No!" Bren said, although Loren glared at him. "We want to keep the Drambini away from Leflin."

"Then we could set up an ambush at the Hills of the Axe," Loren said.

"The Hills of the Axe?" Bren repeated.

"Hills on either side of the road ahead. Legends say a giant was walking through the land and didn't want to walk around the hill so he cut it in half with his axe. We could set up an effective ambush there."

"Ah." Bren remembered the hills when he ridden past them with Klaymar the Beltrin merchant. "That sounds like a good plan."

Loren smiled coldly. "Of course, to spring the trap, we need the right bait."

Bren raised an eyebrow. "Such as?"

"A small group of men who can strike fast, ride back, and keep attacking until the Drambini race into our trap."

"And who you would recommend to lead this group?"

Loren stared at Bren, no expression in his eyes. "I thought perhaps you."

Bren started, surprised. "You trust me so easily?"

"No," Loren said bluntly, "but I'd rather have you in front of me where I can see you. And if you're going to betray us, you would probably do it now."

Bren gave a bitter laugh and nodded. "Fair enough. I'll be the bait."

Two hills rose on either side of the road a mile further west: the Hills of the Axe. *They certainly look as if some giant had split a single hill in two,* Bren thought.

"This is where we should make our stand," Loren said. "I want skilled bowmen hiding on the eastern side of both hills." He turned to Bren. "What do you need?"

"You know these men. Choose forty guardsmen, the fastest and most skilled with swords. I'll lead them to the Drambini forces. We'll be your bait."

Loren had just finished choosing the riders when lookouts spied Drambini horsemen approaching, and another troop half a mile behind.

"Get the archers ready," Bren said. "We'll be coming back in a bit of a hurry."

Loren gave him a tight smile.

Bren led the forty guards out to meet the Drambini army. *This has to work*, he thought.

When Bren could see the Drambini soldiers, he drew his sword and shouted, "Hail, friends."

Some of the Drambini halted and stared at Bren, surprise on their faces. One of them raised his sword in salute and shouted, "Lieutenant Pyccis!"

Bren froze at the sound of his childhood name. *How can I do this?* he wondered, his heart torn between old friends and new loyalties. He knew these men he was facing, had sparred with them, had admired their skills, had wanted to be like them. How could he fight against them?

Vorlikian soldiers took advantage of the hesitation of the Drambini troops and plunged forward, slashing through their ranks. Bren suddenly had no choice but to fight for his life. His sword glowed like crimson fire. Black-clad soldiers fell to the dusty road, death freezing terror and disbelief on their faces.

The second wave of enemies joined the battle. Bren signaled retreat, horrified by what he'd done. The Tarolin Guards wheeled their horses and galloped east toward the hills, moving just fast enough to entice the Drambini to follow.

When Bren's troops were safely east of the hills, he wheeled to face the Drambini. He didn't care if he died now. He'd betrayed soldiers he'd known all his life, and he'd murdered an innocent woman. He wanted to die, wanted the anguish tearing his soul apart to stop. He held his arms straight out to his sides and shouted, "I am Pyccis of Drambit! Kill me if you dare!" And he prayed that a sword would find his heart and end his grief.

"Traitor!" the Drambini leader bellowed back and led a charge recklessly between the hills.

Vorlikian bowmen sent a barrage of pointed death, killing many. Confusion in the Drambini ranks caused jostling; colliding horses delayed their regrouping and retreat. A second and third volley of arrows took down many more, reducing the Drambini troops to half the original number.

The second group of Drambini horsemen joined the fight. Crossbows bolts sank deep into Vorlikian chests, killing many Vorlikian bowmen. But not one bolt touched Bren. He slashed at Drambini soldiers, his sword blazing in the sun as he led the charge, hoping that one of them would end his pain. But no one could withstand the force of his sword.

Loren ordered his men to attack again. When their arrows were spent, Vorlikian bowmen dropped bows, drew swords, and jumped down on the Drambini. Many of the invaders were knocked to the ground and trampled or run through. Suffering too many casualties, Drambini forces withdrew while the Vorlikian troop cheered. Bren just stared at the dead, almost too numb to move.

"We've stopped...the vanguard...temporarily," Loren said from horseback as a hundred men regrouped on the road. "If we face the main body...of Paxell's army without help, we'll be...overwhelmed, destroyed."

"That's why we must attack again," Bren said, looking straight at Loren. "We have to attack again before they rejoin Paxell. We have to draw them back, delay them until Lord Cordwin and Captain Daikin arrive."

Loren studied him carefully. "You're right. We have to attack."

"Baygor protect us!" the men replied in a grim tone.

Bren scanned their faces. They knew they'd likely die in the attack. *If I'm lucky, so will I,* he thought.

"We might stand a chance if we could lure them to Cailan's Crag," said a veteran soldier, who had more sandy hair on his chin than on his head.

"Cailan's Crag?" Bren said.

The soldier nodded. "A rocky hill almost due north of here. I was born and raised in this area. I could find my way around here on a moonless night without a torch. Cailan's Crag is the most defensible place around. We'd draw the enemies away from Leflin and probably hold out until Lord Cordwin and Captain Daikin arrive." He paused, then added, "Hopefully."

Other soldiers nodded and agreed.

Loren clapped the man on the shoulder. "We'll attack the Drambini again. When I give the signal, you lead us to Cailan's Crag, soldier. Bowmen, gather as many arrows as you can, then ride straight to Cailan's Crag and wait. When you see us coming, hold your fire until the enemy is well within range. Now go."

The bowmen began searching the battleground for usable arrows.

"The rest of you," Loren turned to the swordsmen, "follow me. Bren, you'll be in the lead where the Drambini can see you."

Bren nodded slowly. He couldn't speak.

"We stop them here or they won't be stopped at all," Loren said. "And we will stop them! We have to!"

The swordsmen cheered. Bren led them on the trail of the retreating Drambini. Soon, his horse was laboring from the hard riding, but he didn't slow down. After a short while he sighted the Drambini again.

"Sound your horns to draw their attention," Bren ordered.

One after another Vorlikian soldiers took the horns strapped to their saddle and blew long blasts that echoed through the land. The Drambini wheeled their horses, stared at the small force of Vorlikians, and laughed.

"This time, traitor," the Drambini leader shouted, "you'll die!"

Hound of Darkness, let it be so, Bren thought. *Let me die now.*

"No, Bren," Briella's voice whispered in his head, "don't let me die in vain! Fight for your people! Fight for yourself!"

Shaking himself, Bren stared at the Drambini soldiers and held his sword ready. *I will,* he thought. *I'll fight to defend my people and my land. I'll fight for your sake, Briella.*

The Drambini charged. Metal clashed with head-jarring clang against metal. Howls of frenzy mixed with howls of pain. Bodies once clean and whole became bloody from sword-carved rents. Drambini fought well, but the men of Vorlik attacked as fiercely as Formian bears. The Tarolin guards were outnumbered, but they stood their ground. Drambini soldiers closed in on three sides.

"Sound retreat!" Bren shouted before they were totally surrounded. The guardsmen wheeled and galloped northeast toward Cailan's Crag, following the sandy bearded guardsman's lead.

Bren heard the Drambini leader shout, "Hound of Darkness take them all! No mercy!"

"No mercy!" the other Drambini shouted.

The plan's working, Bren thought grimly. *They'll follow us now.*

Bren drove Vorlikians as fast as their mounts would travel, plunging through rolling hills then trampling golden wheat ready for harvest. His horse's breathing was ragged, raspy, as if its lungs were filling with fluid. Dust clouds, kicked up from the dry ground, made the animal's breathing worse. *What if my horse collapses before I reach Cailan's Crag?* Bren thought, worried. He tried to block it from his mind. Too much depended on arriving at the Cailan's Crag.

Soon, he sighted a pile of fractured and tumbled rock rising from the center of a meadow. Boulders and slabs were tossed about the base like the collapsed ruin of some giant child's tower of building blocks. Bren reached the crag moments before the pursuing army and leaped from his horse.

"Take cover!" Loren called and dashed behind some rocks.

"We have them!" the Drambini leader shouted.

Drambini cheered as they reached the crag.

"Now!" Loren shouted. The bowmen loosed their arrows. Horses and Drambini soldiers fell together as they died. The Drambini crashed into other Drambini. Horses stumbled and fell. Men shouted curses. A few invaders ran toward the rocks, swords flashing in the sunlight. They fell, wooden shafts sunk deep into flesh. Volley after volley of arrows fell. Horses bolted. Men screamed as they were struck. The surviving Drambini fled southwest, leaving their wounded comrades.

Shouts of triumph rose from the men on the crag as the Drambini retreated.

Loren stood atop the rocky hill and raised his hands to still the men. "We've won the battle," he said, "but the war isn't over. Let's hope we've given the other divisions the time they needed to reach their positions."

Bren stared at the dead Drambini piled deep around the crag and at the blood on his sword and hands. He nearly vomited. He could hardly breathe. "Now we must attack the main body of Drambini forces and face Paxell," he said, dazed.

"Are you insane?" a sergeant said. "We've lost over half our men!"

"We have to attack!" Bren said. "If we don't, we could lose everything! Everything!"

Loren raised one eyebrow as he studied Bren. "You're not planning to live out the day, are you?"

Bren gave him a grim, determined smile. "We can't let the Drambini drive any deeper into Vorlik, no matter what the cost."

"Mount up," Loren said as he climbed into his saddle. "And Baygor have mercy on us all."

33

Cordwin crashed against the Drambini ranks, bloody mist spraying the air as his sword cut through enemy after enemy. The Tarolin and Northern Guards formed a wedge on either side of him, splitting the invading forces. Drambini forces closed in behind and attacked from both directions. Fighting was so tight, the horses had no room to move. Cordwin and fifty Tarolin guards were cut off from the main wedge. Cordwin lost sight of Pellin and prayed the squire was still alive.

"We've had it!" shouted Corporal Dinnit as she fought on Cordwin's left. Sweat slicked her short blond hair to her head. "There's not even room to swing my sword without hitting one of my comrades!"

"Widen that small gap to your left and push through!" Cordwin shouted back. "Stampede a few horses!" He turned to his right. "Tabbit, Jelt, take down that man with the axe! There'll be a hole big enough for your men to break through to the rear."

Tabbit and Jelt attacked the axe man, solid and unyielding as a stone tower. Jelt screamed as the axe sliced muscle and cleaved bone just above his elbow. Before his scream ended, the axe fell to the ground, a hand still grasping the handle. The stone-tower man clutched at the spurting stump of his wrist and howled. Tabbit silenced the howl as her bloody blade connected with vertebrae.

"Ride!" Cordwin ordered Tabbit. "Take Jelt with you! The rest of you, follow him before the gap closes again!"

Cordwin clashed with two Drambini, who tried to block the group from escaping. His sword plowed a furrow across the chest of one, then lodged in the collar bone of the second. More Drambini closed on him. Twenty Tarolin guards stayed to protect him, giving the other thirty the time they needed to squeeze through the small break in the Drambini ranks.

A sudden gust swirled dust away so that Cordwin glimpsed the ragged banner of the Southern Guard moving toward his position as slowly as honey in winter. Daikin was coming. But would he be in time? "We need a defensible position!" he called. "We need a wall at our backs."

The fighting drove him and his troops westward until they reached a slight rise with three oaks, an island in a bloody sea of enemies. There was no place else to go.

Cordwin jumped from his saddle. "Dinnit, six men, south side! Lon, six, north! Archers in the trees! Guard your backs!"

The Vorlikians dismounted, put the trees at their backs, and faced the Drambini footmen sweeping toward them.

Cordwin's sword was like the prow of a mighty ship, cutting through wave after wave of enemies. Wind-blown dust mixed with wheat chaff to blur Cordwin's vision for just a second, half a heartbeat, but enough for a Drambini sword to graze his forehead. Blood streamed down and forked above his left eye, running along the side of his nose and matting in the hair at his temple. He felt dizzy, uncertain he was standing, unable to tell up from down.

"Duck!" yelled a familiar voice.

Instantly, Cordwin folded at the knees just in time to feel air rush past his head. When his vision cleared, he saw Daikin wrenching his sword from a Drambini's back.

"Looks like I got here just in time," Daikin said with a raspy voice. "You were almost a head shorter."

Cordwin didn't have time to answer. Drambini soldiers crowded toward them again. Daikin and the twelve men he'd brought with him took up places around the trees, but even with the additional swords, Cordwin had little hope. Drambini were a swarm of wasps, flitting in to sting, flying out of reach, stinging again. Even though the invaders lay in heaps, more surged around the trees. A Vorlikian fell, then another, and another. Their quivers empty, the archers dropped their bows, drew swords, and jumped down to join the fight.

Dinnit and her last soldier pulled back to Cordwin's group. Three of Lon's men guarded the retreat of a fourth who dragged Lon, unconscious and bleeding from his thigh and head, behind the protective line of Daikin's troops. Fewer Drambini replaced their fallen comrades, but they still outnumbered the remaining fourteen Vorlikians huddled on the east side of the trees.

We're going to die, Cordwin thought. *All these men, they're going to die because I failed. They deserve better.*

Frustration pumped furious energy into his tired muscles. Yelling as he charged, Cordwin leaped over twisted bodies and dented shields, his sword like a scythe reaping a red harvest of death. The Drambini soldiers shrank from him, but he followed, vaguely aware of Daikin at his back. Cordwin felt a slight stinging in his side and knew he was bleeding, but ignored it. He felt numb, cold, and hot all at once. The sight of Drambini blood fueled the fire of his anger until all he saw was blood and his sword.

Something slammed into Cordwin's back, knocking him off balance. As he stumbled against a Drambini, Cordwin drove his sword through the man's chest, then fell on top of him. Trying to suck air into his lungs, Cordwin looked around and saw what had hit him.

Daikin lay on the ground, holding his shield above him, while a Drambini hammered at the dented metal like a smith. Cordwin stood but felt weak and tired, as if he were wading through knee-deep mud. The world looked flat and artificial, a battle fresco, unreal. He shook his head clear. He had to help his cousin, he had to. He took an unsteady step toward the Drambini.

"Daikin, I'm coming!" Cordwin called, his voice raspy.

The Drambini soldier kicked Daikin's shield aside and swung his sword down. Cordwin watched, helpless, as Drambini drove his blade just below the center of Daikin's chest. Daikin screamed, and so did Cordwin.

Rage boiled in Cordwin's heart, refining down to pure hate. He attacked, aware of nothing but the surprised Drambini. Blow upon blow, Cordwin cut the Drambini into bits of leather and red ribbons of flesh. Dinnit and another guardsman grappled Cordwin to the ground.

"My lord, he's dead! He's dead!" Dinnit shouted as Cordwin stared at her, wild-eyed and still struggling.

Cordwin froze. "Daikin's dead?" he stammered.

Dinnit looked at Cordwin's cousin, then back at Cordwin. "Not yet, but...maybe soon."

"No. Please, no, not him!" Cordwin cried as he dropped his sword and sagged in his comrades' grip. "Lady Baramay, please don't take him from me, too!"

Dinnit and her comrade released Cordwin who crawled toward his cousin.

Daikin was paler than moonlight except for the purple-red blood running from his mouth and pooling in the gut wound. His green eyes were dull, like leaves blasted by summer heat, but recognition flickered in his face as Cordwin leaned over him. Daikin grimaced as his breath bubbled in his throat. "I'm afraid I'm dying."

Cordwin clutched Daikin's hand, which was as cold as half-melted snow. "Don't leave me. I've lost Briella today. I can't lose you, too."

"I'm...sorry. I'm too tired...and too hurt."

"I'll get you to a healer." Cordwin put his arms around Daikin's shoulders and tried to lift him.

The wounded man screamed, "No!" Panting hard as Cordwin lowered him back to the ground, Daikin looked up with pain-squinted eyes. "Too late for a healer. Time for a priest."

Cordwin shook his head, refusing to accept Daikin's death as inevitable. "You can't die."

Daikin's smile was sad, but for a moment his eyes sparkled with the mischievous humor Cordwin knew so well. "I guess that's one order I'll have to disobey." His smile dissolved as pain cut dark lines in his pale face. "I guarded your back."

..Cordwin blanched and felt sick. The luck-wish had come true. He stared in horror at his cousin. "You did. You guarded my back. And I won't let you die alone."

Cordwin held his cousin's hand and watched as Daikin's green eyes closed. Cordwin sat beside Daikin, too numb with grief to move, a statue of despair, while Dinnit and the other guard protected him on either side.

The guard cried out as blood spurted from his upper arm. A sword through his chest silenced the cry. Blood gurgling from her mouth, Dinnit fell on top of Cordwin. Horns sounded retreat in the distance.

I wonder who won? Cordwin thought as he lost consciousness.

34

Lieutenant Loren and the Vorlikian troops recovered enough horses for the eighty-nine surviving guardsmen to mount. Bren led the soldiers as they followed the trampled path the Drambini had made through a golden field of wheat. Somewhere in the battle Bren .had lost his helmet. His dark brown hair flowed back, wind stinging his cheeks as he galloped after the enemies.

He'd almost reached the east-west road when he saw dust clouds and heard the clang of weapons just ahead. Captain Daikin and his guardsmen battled hundreds of Drambini footmen and bowmen. Bren charged into the mingled troops. His sword caught the sunlight, concentrating it, magnifying it until it blinded the enemies. Bren felt invincible, as if he could take on the Drambini army all by himself. In the distance horns rang out. The Northern Guard and Cordwin had arrived, but something else caught Bren's attention. Not far away he spotted Drambit's standard, a black banner with a silver snake.

That's where Lord Paxell will be, Bren thought, steeling his heart. *I have to face him. And only one of us will live out this day.*

Bren slashed his way toward the Drambini lord, fighting against men he had known all his life. He'd practiced swords with these men, learned how to care for horses from them, and had called them friends. Each blow he struck, each wound he inflicted, felt like a blow to his heart. But he couldn't stop. He had to reach Paxell, had to confront him with all the questions tearing his soul apart.

Finally, he fought to within a few feet of the Drambini lord's position. Covered with sweat and blood, he reined his horse to a halt before Paxell, who sat on his black horse.

"Bren?" Paxell gaped at Bren and the Sword of Truth. "What are you doing in a Vorlikian uniform?"

"What I have to." Bren's voice was strained, his mouth barely moving.

"But why?" Paxell's forehead creased, and his eyes filled with hurt. He held out his gloved hand to Bren. "Why're you fighting me? Are you bewitched now, too?"

"I. was," he said, shaking his head, "but no more. I know the truth. I know everything." He stared at Paxell. "Why?" he cried. His throat tightened until he could barely speak. "Why did you lie to me?"

The lord of Drambit shrank back, as if Bren's words were a blow to his chest.

"You killed my parents! You would have killed me, too, but for some quirk of fate!"

"Bren," Paxell said, his voice quivering, "Bren...I--"

Bren cut off his answer. "I loved you! I couldn't have loved you more if you'd been my own father! I would have died for you! How could you do this to me? Why? Just tell me why!"

Paxell's eyes were murky, black pools. He inhaled slightly before he answered in a voice Bren barely heard. "I wanted Vorlik more than I loved you."

The Sword tingled in Bren's hand; Paxell had told the truth, and the truth hurt down to the depth of Bren's soul. He fought back tears and pointed his sword in challenge. Slowly, Paxell reciprocated the ritual.

"Today you die," Bren promised.

Metal rang against metal. Bren attacked with such force, Paxell's eyes widened in disbelief. They fought in the midst of chaos, circling and striking, thrusting and parrying. Bren leaned too far over his horse and tumbled to the ground. Paxell charged and raised his sword for a crushing blow, but his horse stumbled on a discarded shield and threw the Drambini lord to the ground. Paxell stood quickly and faced Bren.

The Sword of Truth caught the sun's rays, distilling them into a white light that caused Paxell to stagger. Swinging the sword with all of his anger and hurt, Bren drove Paxell backward through the press of fighting men. Step by step, Paxell retreated until Bren had him pinned against a large boulder. Bren rained blows on him like hailstones in a summer storm. Paxell used both hands to wield his sword, as if it were growing too heavy to hold. He slashed upward, pushed aside Bren's weapon, but at the same time exposed his own chest. Bren swung the Sword around, plunged it deep into Paxell's chest, then jerked the shining blade free.

A puzzled look crossed Paxell's face as he clutched at his chest. Blood ran between his fingers. He laughed softly, but the sound was bitter. His dark eyes looked up at Bren, dark eyes squinting with pain. Blood bubbled from Paxell's lips, and he gasped for air.

Paxell reached toward Bren and whispered, "I love you, Bren. I did love you." Coughing convulsed his body. "If only you'd been my own son..." Paxell crumpled to the ground and lay still.

Bren stood over the body, his sword hand bathed in blood, his anger cooling. All about him the battle surged, yet he was only aware of the lifeless body at his feet. Paxell had taught him to hold a bow, praised him for winning his first sword contest, taken him on his first boar hunt and let Bren make the kill. All the cherished memories of his childhood were bound to Paxell, memories now just as dead.

Bren's vision blurred. His eyes were hot, but when he rubbed them, his hand came away wet. He still loved Paxell. In spite of betrayal, in spite of everything, he still loved him. In the middle of the clashing armies and the blare of horns sounding retreat, Bren sank beside Paxell and cried.

35

In the scarlet grass lay remnants of men. Broken spears and discarded swords littered the ground. Screams of the injured and the dying replaced the shouts of triumph that had filled the air moments before. Horses wandered riderless among the dead.

With Paxell's death, the leaderless forces of Drambit had fled through the western pass. Of the eight hundred invaders, over six hundred were dead; another hundred, wounded. Vorlik had lost nearly three hundred.

Bren picked his way through the battlefield, nearly numb from all the dead bodies surrounding him. He had never seen death like this before, never seen people hacked and bleeding like meat on a butcher's table. He felt shaky and nauseated. He could only shake his head and stare in horror.

Tabbit followed him through the carnage. "We need to bury the dead of Vorlik," she said, "and we'll burn the enemy dead."

Bren nodded slowly, then said, "All but Lord Paxell."

"What?" Tabbit said, her mouth dropping open. "You can't mean that!"

"Yes, I do," Bren said, gazing west toward the mountains and the only home he'd ever known. "He was the lord of Drambit. I won't have him burned."

"But he caused all these deaths!" she cried with wide-eyed outrage. "He should be left for crows!"

Bren turned slowly toward the guard and glared at her. "That may be, but his body will be treated with the respect due a lord. Place his body in a wagon and send it with a guard of captured Drambini back to h.is daughter."

Gritting her teeth, Tabbit saluted and growled at three men to help her. Bren watched silently as they lifted Paxell's body and carried it to a wagon. *He lied to me and betrayed me,* Bren thought, his chest aching. *So why do I still love him?*

His eyes widened, and for a moment he couldn't breathe. *Hound of Darkness, what will Miria think when she learns I killed her father? Now that I'm lord of Vorlik, will she ever forgive me?*

Glancing around, Bren saw a soldier organizing transport of the wounded and hurried toward him. "Soldier," Bren said as he approached him.

The man stopped, eyed Bren for a few moments, then asked, "Who are you?"

"My name is Bren."

The soldier's eyes widened. "Lord Clevil's son?"

Bren nodded. "Yes. Who are you?"

Curiosity mingled with suspicion in the man's face. "Lieutenant Kyris of the Southern Guard."

"Have you found any trace of my uncle yet?" Bren asked anxiously. "Please tell me you've found him!"

Kyris stiffened and said with an emphatic tone, "Lord Cordwin hasn't been found yet."

Bren cringed. He understood what Kyris meant. Cordwin was still lord of Vorlik until Cordwin, and only Cordwin, said otherwise. "We have to find him...Lord Cordwin."

The corners of Kyris' mouth quivered, possibly a muscle spasm or an aborted smile. "We're looking for him even now. You can join if you want."

Bren nodded, then turned away.

He searched through scores of bodies on the battle ground, hoping for some sign of his uncle. Finally, he found Cordwin dragging himself from under a soldier's body. Blood seeped slowly from Cordwin's side. Above his left eye dried blood forked down the side of his nose and into the dark hair of his left temple. His eyes seemed unfocused.

"Let me help you!" Bren cried as he knelt.

Cordwin winced with pain but gazed up at Bren. "You're alive," he whispered, clutching his side. "Thank Baygor."

"You'll be all right," Bren said. "Just lean on me. I'll get you to the healers." Bren placed his uncle's arm around his own neck for support and started to stand.

His breathing ragged, Cordwin clutched at Daikin's body. "He saved me. I can't leave him alone."

Bren scanned the area and spotted a guard nearby. "Soldier, come quickly."

The woman scowled until she noticed Cordwin. Scurrying over the scattered corpses, the soldier reached the two quickly.

"My lord, please, let me help you," she said, her face filled with worry as she reach down to take Cordwin's other arm.

"No," Bren said. "I can take care of my uncle...Lord Cordwin. But he won't leave Captain Daikin."

The soldier inhaled sharply. "Hound of Darkness take all Drambini!" Tears welled up in her eyes as she knelt and touched Daikin's chest.

Bren gazed at her, mouth dry and throat tight. "Will you see that Captain Daikin is buried with the honor he deserves?"

"Buried!" she exclaimed. "He's still alive! His heart's still beating!"

"Alive? Alive?" Cordwin said. Tears filled his eyes. "Merciful Baygor, he's alive!"

The guard called to several other soldiers who hurried to her side. "We have to get him to the healers! And Lord Cordwin, too!"

"I'll take my uncle," Bren said. "Get Lieutenant Daiken to the healers. Quickly!"

With gentleness and deep respect, six soldiers lifted Daikin and carried him toward the wains for the injured. Another soldier stayed behind to help Bren with Cordwin.

"Come, uncle, let me help you to the healers." Bren helped Cordwin to his feet, and Bren and the soldier carried the injured man. Joining the long line of wounded walking east, together they reached the village as Cordwin collapsed, unconscious. Bren spotted Lieutenant Linaria and shouted, "Help me! Lord Cordwin's badly hurt!"

Linaria and several others rushed toward them. They lifted Cordwin and carried him to the Two Oaks Inn, Bren following closely.

Please, let him be all right, Bren thought. *I couldn't bear to watch him die. There's been too much death today.*

Maiya the Healer glanced up from a patient she was tending in the common room. She paled as she gazed at Cordwin. "I have one bed left. Bring him," she said and led them to a room on the ground floor.

The soldiers place Cordwin on the narrow bed. Maiya checked his wounds. "Thank Baygor, nothing's broken. Take off his armor and shirt, gently, while I get some medicine and bandages." She ran from the room.

Bren and Linaria removed Cordwin's armor and bloody clothes while another soldier took off Cordwin's boots. Maiya returned with a slingsack and a bowl of steaming water.

"Will he be all right?" Bren asked anxiously.

"Hopefully," Maiya said as she added herbs to the water. A sweet clean fragrance filled the room. She looked up from the potion and studied Bren. "I never saw you before today. Who are you?"

"I'm Bren."

Maiya stared at him, her violet eyes wide. "Bren? The son of Lord Clevil and Lady Ellisa?"

"Yes." Bren gazed at Cordwin, then looked Maiya. "You have to heal him."

She smiled. "I promise I'll use all my skills to make him well." She cleansed his wounds with the infusion, then applied a salve, the same fragrant salve Tothim had used on Bren's hands, and bound Cordwin's wounds with soft cloth.

Cordwin lay in bed, feverish, constantly calling for Briella, while Maiya bathed his face with the tea and forced as much of the liquid as she could down Cordwin's throat. Bren never left his uncle's bedside, not even to eat or sleep.

Finally, Maiya confronted Bren. "If you don't eat and get some rest, I'll have Lieutenant Linaria's men hold you down, and I'll force food down your throat myself. Then I'll have the soldiers tie you in bed until you've rested. And don't think I won't!"

"You wouldn't," he said, his eyes wide.

"Wouldn't I?"

The narrow squint of her violet eyes and the tight set of her mouth told Bren she meant exactly what she said.

His shoulders sagged. "All right," he said, too tired to argue with her.

"And I want a look at your hand. Tothim told me about the cuts. I'll bet you haven't had them tended since he did."

Bren shook his head slowly. He suddenly noticed how much his hand throbbed. Maiya removed the glove carefully. Surprisingly, the gashes had nearly sealed.

Maiya cleansed, salved, and rebandaged his hand, while Bren clenched his teeth against the pain. She left for a few minutes and returned with a bowl of stew and bread.

"You eat this now," she said, "or I'll carry out my threat."

Bren ate a little stew, but he had no appetite. Maiya made him eat enough to keep up his strength, but he refused to go rest.

"I can't leave him," Bren said. "Let me stay here. Bring me a blanket, and I'll sleep in the chair or on the floor. I just need to stay with him."

"All right," Maiya said, "just as long as you get some rest yourself."

"I will."

Maiya left and came back shortly with a blanket. Bren wrapped it around him and sat on the floor beside the bed. He rested his head on the bedside, dozing occasionally, and waited, hoping Cordwin would be well, hoping that Miria would forgive him, and that he could forgive himself.

On the third morning Maiya felt Cordwin's forehead, then she smiled at Bren. "Cool and dry. The worst is over." She spread a sweet-scented salve on his wounds.

A few moments later, Cordwin blinked and opened his eyes slowly. "Bren?"

"I'm here." Bren knelt beside the bed and took Cordwin's hand.

Cordwin's voice was hoarse. "Is Vorlik safe?"

"We won the war," Bren said, "and Paxell is dead. Beyond that, I don't know."

"How long have I been here?"

"Three days," Maiya said as she rebandaged his wounds. "But you're going to be just fine."

Cordwin relaxed and closed his eyes. He seemed to drift off to sleep a few moments, then suddenly he came wide awake. "Briella! Daikin! Pellin!"

"Pellin?" Bren asked, not recognizing the name.

"My squire," Cordwin said, his voice shaky. "I lost sight of him. I don't know if he's alive."

"Your squire was injured, but will recover," Maiya said, smiling. "He's in another room and doing very well. And so is your cousin. So well in fact, I've threatened to toss him out of his bed if he doesn't behave himself."

"Thank Baygor," he said with a grateful sigh. "I couldn't bear to lose anyone else."

Bren hung his head, feeling ashamed and helpless. He held Cordwin's hand tightly. "I'm sorry, uncle, sorry for everything."

Cordwin closed his eyes again and slept until late afternoon. Bren never left his side.

Cordwin woke as the sun cast long shadows in his room. Bren wasn't in the room, but Maiya was. She carried a tray with a wooden bowl and a cup.

"Don't try to sit up," she said as she set the tray on a bedside table. "I'll prop you up enough you can eat."

Ignoring her warning, Cordwin tried to sit up and winced as pain shot through his side. He groaned and sank back to the mattress.

"That'll teach you to mind what I say." Maiya shook a finger at him. "You can't get up for at least another day. I brought you a cup of callum bark tea and a bowl of meat broth. Now you drink this tea, all of it, mind you, then the broth. I'll bring you something solid this evening. You need lots of food to regain your strength."

"Treating me like a child," he grumbled under his breath as he glared at her.

She gave him a knowing smirk. "If you behave like a child, I'll treat you like one."

A growl bubbled in his throat. Reluctantly, Cordwin tasted the tea, then looked at Maiya. "This tea, I've tasted it before," he said, his chest tight. "Years ago when I was injured. Briella – she gave it to me. What is it?"

"Callum bark tea." Maiya sat down beside Cordwin and looked at him closely. "A peddler named Old Mam gave me a seed thirteen, no, fourteen years ago. I use the leaves to make that salve I put on your wounds. The bark makes the healing tea." Maiya paused. "It was her, wasn't it? Old Mam was Briella. I was certain of it even though she never said anything. She gave us all so much." Maiya's eyes glistened as she stood and left the room.

Briella, my love, Cordwin thought as tears filled his eyes and spilled into the cup of tea, *even beyond death you're reaching out to protect me.*

At the end of the week, Cordwin was well enough to get out of bed, although his side hurt with every move.

"Let me help," Bren said.

Cordwin shook his head. Gingerly, he dressed himself, but he couldn't pull on his boots.

"Please, let me," Bren said.

His shoulders drooping, Cordwin nodded. When he was fully dressed, he faced his nephew. "It's time."

"Today?" Bren asked.

"Yes," Cordwin replied, his heart both numb and hurting. "Please, take me to her. I have to see her one last time before I accept it, know it's real."

"But she's been dead a week."

"I know. But wizards aren't like us. Our histories say that Timmree remained unchanged for weeks after her death."

"Timmree? Who was she?"

Cordwin told the tale, remembering how he'd heard Briella tell the story at the Autumn Fair and tears filled his eyes again. "Cavolin didn't want to bury her because she looked so alive."

"But you said Timmree wasn't a Wizard when she died," Bren said pensively, "that she'd given up her powers to marry Cavolin."

"I know."

"You think it'll be the same with Briella?"

"I hope so."

"All right." Bren took Cordwin's wrist, unsheathed the Sword of Truth, and held it over his head. "Take us to Briella's house."

Light prismed about them like spiral rainbows. They stood in a mountain meadow, the last flowers of the year scattered across the grass. The air was refreshing and chilled, but there was no house, no well, only a bare square of ground where the house had once stood. The callum tree, the climbing rose, and the herb garden were all that re"What happened?" Cordwin said desperately. "Where is she?"

Bren glanced about, puzzlement on his face. "This is the place, I know it is. I remember seeing the tree and the rose through the crystal walls."

Cordwin shook his head and clutched at his chest. "Oh, no. Don't you understand? Her house was like the Wall of Warding. When she died, the spell began to break down. It's gone, all of it."

"But what happened to her? Surely, wizards don't just disappear when they die."

"I don't know," Cordwin said, sobbing. "All I know is that I can't even see her one last time. Nothing's left. Nothing!"

Trembling, he sank to his knees, his grief too crushing a weight to bear, and he wanted to die.

Bren knelt and held him as Cordwin leaned against the younger man's chest. Suddenly, Bren whispered, "Look, there, on the ground."

Something sparkled on the bare earth before Cordwin, three shining objects. Bren picked up one: the jeweled dagger still stained with Briella's blood, almost black in the morning light.

Cordwin's hands shook as he picked up the other two: Briella's dove-shaped pendant and the ring Cordwin had given her. He clutched them to his lips, cold metal, colder stone. They were all he had left of her. He squeezed his eyes shut, his pain too sharp, too deep for tears.

A breath of wind stroked his hair, caressed his face, like unseen fingers. The touch was warm as summer, comforting, familiar. Lips brushed his temple, his hands. The fragrance of lavender, Briella's favorite scent, surrounded him like a gentle mist. His eyes flew open, but he saw no one. His heart thumped faster, blood surging through him like storm-driven waves. His breath was short, ragged gasps. Hope that was almost fear parted his lips and formed a word. "Briella?"

"I'm here, my love," her voice whispered, an invisible hand touching his cheek.

"Where?" he asked frantically. "Where are you?"

"Here." He felt a light touch on his forehead. "And here." He felt another touch on his chest. "And here." The dove pendent tingled in his hand. He opened his hand and saw a blue glow surrounding the silver pendant. It felt warm, almost alive.

"Wear this next to your heart," she whispered, "and I'll always be with you."

Quickly, he clasped on the dove pendent. It felt warm against his chest, as warm as the touch of her hand. He closed his eyes, felt her near. She was with him, in his heart, his soul. He opened his eyes and saw her standing before him, wearing her blue dress, her eyes like summer skies. She seemed to glow like sunlight through frosted glass.

"Uncle," Bren gasped, "do you see her? Is she real?"

"I see her," Cordwin whispered, tears of joy streaming down his face. "Briella, my love, my life." He leaped to his feet and held out his arms to her. She rushed toward him and brushed her f.ingertips down his cheek. To Cordwin, it felt like sunshine and summer breezes.

"My dearest love," Briella said. She rested in his arms, her head leaning against him.

Cordwin held her to his chest, his heart racing, breathing in the scent of lavender in her hair. "How can this be?" he whispered. "How can you be alive when Bren killed you?"

"I don't know," she whispered back. "I don't know if I'm alive or dead or somewhere in between. I don't know why or how this has happened. I only know that I'm here with you now, and I will always be with you. Always."

Suddenly, he felt as if he were surrounded with fire, warm but not burning, caressing him, soothing his spirit. He opened his eyes, but he couldn't see her anymore. But he felt her, felt her in his heart, his thoughts, and his soul. He smiled; he wouldn't be lonely anymore. She was with him, would be with him always.

From somewhere in the mountain glen came the call of a mourning dove.

About the Author

Deborah Millitello wrote her first SF story, her first poem, and her first play when she was in fourth grade, and she's been writing ever since. She loves gardening, growing herbs, berries, and orchard fruits, making jams and marmalades, baking, knitting, crocheting, good music, hot tea, and of course, reading. She lives with her husband Carl, who has put up with her writing obsession for over forty-six years. She lives in a small town in Southern Illinois and is retired.

Her first book, *Thief's Luck,* was published in 2006. Her second book, *The Water Girl,* was published in 2015. A collection of her short stories, *Do Virgins Taste Better? and Other Strange Tales* was published in 2016.

.

Word Posse Fun Fact

Marion Zimmer Bradley was one of the most mentoring writers in the field of SF & F. There are scores of writers who sold their first stories to her, including me. She offered guidance and criticism that helped me and many others become better writers. I was fortunate enough to meet her once at her home in the Bay area. I am so grateful for what I learned from her.

The cover art is by Deborah's 18-year-old granddaughter, Danielle Shimchick, who is studying art at SIU Edwardsville.

A sneak preview of

The Wizard and the Warrior

Book 2 of the Baramayan Chronicles

I

Winter mornings in Hixus were usually overcast and mild, although sometimes chilly. Snow this far south was a rarity and a cause for delight among the city's children. But it was so close to spring, there little chance of snow. Overnight, fog rising from the warmer ocean waters had crept into the streets and alleys of the seaside city. By now at midmorning, all but a few misty tendrils were gone, but the air was still damp and cool.

Smoke hung low over the houses. Soot blackened the rooftops and upper stories of most buildings south of the cobblestone plaza down to the dockside warehouses. Even the gold leaf-covered dome of the Temple of Baygor on the west side of the plaza and the green copper roof of the Temple of Baramay on the east side were dulled by a thin layer of soot. The faint cry of sea birds mingled with the rhythmic lapping of waves on the shore, and the aroma of baking bread, salt air, and the ever-present odor of fish permeated the city.

Softly strumming "Tellowee's Lament" on his lute, the Wizard Maren scanned the overcast sky. Pulled by a feeling of disquiet, like waking from a dark dream he couldn't quite remember, he wandered south to Hixus' central market in the plaza. A slight breeze trickled to the north from the sea, and he shivered although he wore dark crimson wool trousers and hat, and a wool jacket of the same shade of crimson over his linen shirt.

He'd just come from the prosperous north side of Hixus from the home of one of the most prominent families in the city. The master of the house had invited Maren to play and sing at a celebration of his daughter's betrothal in six days. Maren had gladly accepted and had left with a small bag of silver coins.

The market was filled with merchants, peddlers, craftsmen, and sellers, hawking wares to the few customers venturing out in the dreary weather. The aroma of rich roasted meat mingled with the scent of bread baked with honey, candied fruit, and spices. Maren's stomach rumbled, since he hadn't eaten all day, but his uneasiness dulled his appetite.

"Come and see the latest fabrics," called the cloth merchant from his open air stall. "Butter-soft wool and white linen, flowing silk and the finest cotton. Cloth in every color of the rainbow." He scanned Maren from head to toe. "Fine goods," he said, "but a minstrel should have clothes that draw attention. Now I have just the thing for you." He caressed a bolt of dark blue and gold brocade. "Imagine a jacket and hat made from this, and dark blue trousers with gold piping to match. And I know a seamstress who would make you that suit of clothes, fit for a lord."

Maren strummed a chord, smiled, and gave a quick bow. "Maybe for the Spring Fete."

The cloth merchant grinned. "I'll be here." He turned toward a well-dressed woman with a young girl in tow.

"Apples, last of the season," a balding grocer said, holding out a red-blushed fruit to Maren, "wrinkled but sound and sweet. Three for a copper gate."

"Three apples for one copper coin? That's a bit steep. Six for a copper."

The grocer sighed. "But I only have one bushel left, and there won't be any more until next fall. Four for a copper."

"Five. Five apples for a copper."

The grocer held up his hands and gazed at the sky. "How can I stay in business like this?" He looked back at Maren. "All right. Five apples for a copper."

Maren smiled at the grocer and gave him a copper coin stamped with the image of a castle gate. The grocer handed him five apples, one at a time, and Maren stowed four of them in his jacket. The last apple he tossed in the air, caught it, then took a large bite. The grocer hadn't lied. The apple was sweet and sound, and reminded him of autumn mornings and harvest moons, of pies and cider and cozy fires. He ate the entire apple except for the seeds, which he dropped in his belt pouch. *Seeds for tomorrow's apple trees*, he thought. *And cider.*

A group of children crowded around him as he walked down the cobblestone streets, and they begged him for a story. "Maybe a bit later," he said and strummed a verse of "Chellit's Cat" for them. "Now run home before it starts to rain."

"It's not going to rain," a gangly tow-headed boy said.

"Run home anyway." He glanced at the sky. "Run home now."

The children grumbled but scattered quickly.

The wide boulevard called Northway ran from the cliffs at the northern edge of Hixus through the center of the city to the seaside. The houses bordering Northway south of the market square were two- and three-story stone tenements crowded with large poor families, but the road and neighborhood were kept neat and clean. Children played stick ball in the street, and women hung clothes from balconies.

Several taverns and inns, catering to the locals and sailors just in port, were wedged between the houses. The Mermaid Inn, where Maren stayed, was ten blocks south of the central market. Jeral the owner, swarthy and black-haired, opened his front door and swept the doorstep. He'd spent twenty years at sea before he'd married and settled down to run the inn. As large and strong as a Formian bear, he never hired roughnecks to get rid of troublemakers. He could handle up to ten men by himself and often did for entertainment. If he won, he took half the pot. If he lost, he took half, too. The Mermaid's patrons enjoyed watching more than betting.

The taverner looked up as Maren walked by and held up his massive hand in greeting. "Come back later an' have a drink with me," Jeral said.

"That I will," Maren said with a nod. He dug the apples out of his jacket and handed them to Jeral. "Can you put these in my room?"

"That I will," Jeral said with nod.

When Maren reached the docks, he noticed only half a dozen men sitting in front of the wooden warehouses, weathered by sun and sea that crowded the water front. No ships were tied up on the docks. One of the dockhands called to him. "How about a song while we eat our lunch, minstrel?"

Maren glanced at the sea, uneasy, then nodded and began playing and singing "Chellit's Cat." The men tapped their feet in time to the music while they ate smoked fish and bread. At the end of the chorus one of the dockhands tossed him a copper coin. Maren pocketed the coin, bowed, then turned toward the sea, still strumming the tune.

Growing more apprehensive, he walked to the end of the longest pier, its pilings crusted with barnacles and moss, and stared out across the sea dulled by the clouds overhead. White and grey seabirds cried out as they circled and dove for fish in the sea. The lapping of white-capped waves on the shore was like the beating of the world's heart. He loved that sound.

When Maren had left the Wizard's Vale, he'd spent only a half a year in Vorlik, ancient home of Wizards, before he'd wandered south to the great forests of Peltik. He'd lingered there for almost three years before he traveled east to Tukkus, home of blacksmiths, coppersmiths, and the world's finest sword smiths. He'd even learned to form simple tools in one of the many forges in the country. Restless after nearly three years, he traveled back to Peltik then south to Beltrin, home of merchants, farmers, and mercenaries. He stayed there only a few months before he moved on to the Freelands, the wide, wild lands of farms and small villages stretching south all the way to the edge of the Southern Plateau. He'd spent more than five years traveling from village to farmstead. Then he'd come to Hixus on the northern shore of the sea. And he fell in love with the city and had stayed there for nearly ten years.

He glanced over his shoulder toward the city of Hixus. White stone and wooden buildings spread across the wide sloping shoreline all the way to the steep northern cliffs and winding road up to the Southern Plateau. Humans hurried through life in the city, working, playing, singing, celebrating with such intensity. Maren wasn't sure if it was because their lives were so short or because it was the nature of humans to take joy in everything.

The years had passed swiftly for Maren. He was forty-two years old, but for a Wizard he was still very young, since Wizards often lived for four hundred years. It seemed impossible that he'd left his home twenty-two year ago. He had gone back just once, but little had changed there. Except the woman he'd hoped to marry had left for the human lands. But there were still many years for love and marriage and children.

He glanced back at the city again and sighed. Time to move on before people noticed he hadn't aged, before they suspected that he was more than just a minstrel. He turned back toward the sea. *But I'll miss this,* he thought as he gazed at the water. *The sound of the waves that I hear even in my dreams, the salty scent of the air, how vast the sea is – I never imagined anything this majestic when I was growing up in the Wizard's Vale. Maybe I'll travel west along the coast so I can still be near the sea.*

He leaned against a weathered piling and squinted toward the horizon. His dark brown hair fluttered in the building breeze filled with the scent of rain and lightning. The air felt close, almost smothering. He gazed toward the western edge of the city where a rocky prominence jutted out into the bay. He shivered and wished he'd worn his heavy cloak that he'd left back at the Mermaid Inn.

A storm's coming, he thought, his stomach knotted with worry, *but something more. Something...dangerous.*

"Hey, what's that?" called one of the dockhands.

"Where?" a second dockhand said.

"There, right there!" the first one said.

Maren turned toward the wharf and saw the man pointing south. Turning back to the sea, he scanned the horizon. There, southwest of the city, black smoke rose to the threatening sky. Shading his eyes, suddenly he spotted a ship on the horizon, coming closer, closer. The ship was burning!

The wind picked up, nearly blowing Maren's hat off his head. The white caps of the waves grew larger and wider. Maren took off his hat, stuffed it inside his jacket, leaned against the piling for support, and frowned at the sky. Dark clouds thickened in the south and raced toward the seaport. Winter storms were extremely rare on the southern sea, and winter was almost over. But this storm made his skin crawl and his chest tighten.

Finally, the ship was close enough that Maren could see a merchant flag flying from the mast and pennants strung on the rigging: red for "Warning," black and red for "Enemies," and blue and white for "Help." The wind was driving the ship fast, but fire was spreading faster. Maren doubted the ship would make it to port before it sank.

Slinging his lute on his back, he wheeled and ran back to the warehouses and the dockhands standing there. "You," Maren said, pointing at one of the men, "go tell the mayor to send out the city guard! We don't know what kind of enemies or how many we might be facing! Warn everyone you see that they might have to flee to the plateau now! The rest of you, we have to rescue the men from the ship!"

The messenger darted up the street toward the center of town.

Maren turned back to the sea. The ship was closer. Flames rose from all parts of the ship. Some of the sails had caught fire. The ship neared the harbor then turned east and dropped anchor in the bay. Men jumped from the burning decks and swam for the shore.

Maren scanned the shoreline. Just beyond the eastern dock were half a dozen small fishing boats. Beside them, two weathered men had hung nets to dry and were mending them.

"We need those boats," Maren told a dark-haired dock man. "Get them in the water and rescue as many as you can."

The dark-haired man and three of his companions ran to the fishermen. Maren watched as the dark-haired man waved his arms then pointed to the sea. The fishermen turned toward the bay, dropped their net shuttles, and raced to their boats. The four dockhands pushed the other boats into the water, then each climbed into a boat, and began to row for the ship.

As the first sailors reached the shore, Maren and the last dockhand waded out into the cold water to help sailors to the docks. Most were all right, but a few were burned or bleeding.

"Who's coming?" Maren asked one sailor, whose left arm was burned severely.

"Pirates," the sailor gasped, "a whole fleet of pirate ships."

"How far behind?"

"Not far," the man said. "Maybe an hour behind us. An hour at most."

"That's not much time!" Maren opened his belt pouch, took out a small blue jar, and opened it. A wholesome fragrance filled the air as he dipped his fingers in a white salve and spread it on the sailor's burns.

The man winced, then relaxed and closed his eyes for a moment. When he opened them again, he gave Maren a weak smile. "Baramay bless you."

Maren helped him to his feet. "Now help your shipmates! Get them to the Temple of Baygor! The priests will tend their injuries!"

"This way!" the sailor called to his shipmates, and cradling his arm, led them up the street toward the town's center.

The fishing boats landed with dozens of rescued sailors. Maren ran from man to man applying the salve as needed, directing those uninjured to help those who were hurt to the temple. In the distance Maren heard trumpets sounded from the north. The city guard was being called to arms.

The merchant ship was completely engulfed in flames, black smoke billowing toward the dark clouds. A grey-haired man jumped from the ship just before the main mast crashed to the deck, then he swam ashore. Maren met the man in cold waist-deep water, put the man's arm around his shoulder, and helped him to land.

The man coughed and gagged, his lean face blackened with soot, burns on his hands, arms, and face.

"Are you the captain?" Maren asked as he lowered the man to the ground then knelt beside him.

The man nodded slowly. His eyes were glazed with pain, and his breathing was ragged.

Maren took out the salve again and spread it on the man's burns. "What happened?"

The captain tried to talk but started coughing again. Maren took a tiny cloth bag from his pouch, then opened the small wineskin tied to his belt. He sprinkled grey-green powdered callum bark into the wine, whirled it to mix, and held it to the captain's mouth. *Not as effective as callum bark tea,* Maren thought, *but it will help.*

The captain took a swallow, coughed, and took several more swallows. He cleared his throat.

"Pirates attacked us as we were coming out of Stejanik's Bay on the southern continent," the captain said. "All the merchant ships were sailing together. We thought we'd be safe in a large group. We were wrong." The captain coughed again. "We thought we could outrun the pirates since the wind was blowing from the south. But fires seemed to spring out of nowhere, setting the sails alight, running along the ropes and rigging, first on one ship then another. All the other ships burned. The pirates killed the sailors who jumped overboard. I could hear the pirates laughing as they slaughtered the sailors. Laughing!"

The captain coughed again. "Mine was the lead ship and we barely got away, but the pirates followed us. They're not far behind us. Strange fires started popping up all over the deck. We'd put out one flame and another would pop up. Thank Baygor we made it this far. I anchored the ship in the harbor. I thought since it's burning anyway, we could use it as a barrier. I know it won't last for long, but it might slow the pirates down. What they'll do when they reach Hixus..." the man halted and shuddered.

"How many?" Maren asked.

"A dozen ships at least."

Maren helped the captain to his feet. "Can you walk now?"

The captain nodded.

"Report to the mayor. Tell him what you saw and tell him the people need to leave everything behind. There's no time to pack. We have to get the citizens out of the city and have the city guards in place before the pirates get here."

"What are you going to do?" the captain asked.

"What I can! Now go!"

The captain nodded and hurried toward the city center.

Maren turned back to the sea and scanned the shoreline from east to west. The breeze was coming in strong gusts, blowing Maren's hair straight back. *What can I do?* he wondered. *And how can I do it without being seen?*

His eyes stared at the rocky prominence at the westernmost edge of the city. He ran along the boardwalk down to the sandy shore, past the houses and cottages and tumbled down shacks lining the western edge of the water front. The tide was rolling in faster than normal, lapping farther inland with each wave. Clouds thickened overhead and a few raindrops began to fall. Maren scrambled over the tidal pools, boulders, and fallen rocks, worn smooth by salt spray and crashing waves, until he had reached the narrow row of rocks sticking out into the bay. Edging around the prominence just enough he was beyond the sight of anyone from the city, Maren searched the horizon.

After a few moments he saw a small break on the sea that grew larger – the mast of a ship, then another, and another, two-masted ships with sleek hulls and full sails, driven by the whistling south wind. Standing with one hand raised to the sky and his other hand outstretched, palm up, to the sea, he said, "By the power of Baramay, who made the earth and sea and wind, *tasrin akelleya taychay barason!*"

The air began to swirl into a sphere in his palm, growing larger and larger. He hurled the sphere toward the masts. A wind rose from the shore, blowing counter to the southern wind, now almost a gale. The ships seemed to stagnate in the tumultuous waves. Rain became heavier, then poured down.

Suddenly, he heard dire voices in the wind speaking dark words of darker power. Sorcerers! There were Sorcerers on those ships! In all his years he'd never been close to a Sorcerer, never had to face one of them. And there were at least two of them with the pirate ships. Could he defeat them? Was he strong enough? "Lady Baramay, help me, please!"

He concentrated on the wind spell, trying to push the ships back, but he felt the will of the Sorcerers pushing against him. He braced himself against the cliff face and shouted, "*Tasrin akelleya makeesa barason!*"

The wind howled toward the ships, swirling like a water spout. As it reached the lead ship, a column of green flame crashed against the water spout, which shattered like a ceramic bowl. Maren was hurled back against the cliff, knocking his breath from him and bruising his right side. Stone ripped through the right sleeve of his jacket and shirt, and cut his upper right arm. He sagged onto one of the boulders and gasped for breath. A wave crashed against the rocks and drenched him. His arm stung and burned. Twisting it enough he could examine it, he saw blood oozing from a ragged gash a hand's width long.

Kneeling at the edge of the sea, he scooped up some water in his hand. With his index finger, he swirled the water in his palm and said, "By the power of Baramay who made the sea and waves and all within, *tasrin rasheek kah barason!*"

The water in his hand began to swirl on its own and turned dark blue. He poured the water into the ocean, then collapsed to the rocks, and watched as the streak of dark blue flowed toward the ships. The blue water grew wider and wider, until it touched the lead ship, circling the ship faster and faster. A whirlpool formed under the ship, turning the ship round and round until it was dragged down into the ocean. The whirlpool grew larger, drawing in ship after ship, pulling them into the dark blue water. Ships crashed into each other, listed on their sides, then capsized. Maren heard men screaming and Sorcerers shrieking above the howling gale as the ships sank out of sight.

Only two ships escaped the whirlpool, but they held course for Hixus. Maren lay on the rocks, nearly exhausted, trying to catch his breath. He tried to push himself upright, but his arms shook so much he couldn't hold himself. He lay still, his cheek against the cold, wet stone. A cold wave crashed against the rocks, drenching him. He gagged and choked on the water that filled his mouth. His throat and chest burned, and the cut on his arm felt as if a heated iron had been thrust into the wound.

"Lady Baramay," he prayed as he sprawled on the rocks, "please give me strength."

Rain began pelting down, stinging like hail, and the winds whipped the sea like a hurricane. The tide rushed in, almost reaching the top of the rocks where Maren lay.

I have to get out of here, he thought, *or the waves will drag me into the sea.*

He crawled across the slick rocks to the cliff face, leaned against it, and gasped for air. Every breath hurt his ribs. Fumbling with the wineskin, he untied it, opened the stopper, and drank the rest of the wine and callum bark mixture. Warmth flowed down his throat, filled his stomach, and radiated through his body. The pain in his ribs eased, and he felt a bit stronger.

Clutching at the rock face, he pulled himself upright, paused, then turned to face the storm. A huge wave was building on the sea, rising well over Maren's head. Lifting a hand to the sky and holding the other palm out to the sea, he said, "By the power of Baramay who made the wind to blow and the tide to flow, *tasrin rasheek hamania barason!*"

The wave kept rolling toward shore like a wall. Maren clenched his jaw and concentrated on the water. Slowly, the wave ebbed and receded until the water barely touched Maren's feet. Holding his hands together palms up, he called another sphere of wind and sent it south. Gradually, the winds calmed to a gentle breeze, and the rain diminished to a drizzle, then stopped though the sky was still overcast.

Maren crept to the edge of the prominence and peered around it toward Hixus. The last two pirate ships had reached the harbor, but one had been driven toward the burning ship anchored there. The masts snapped, and the hull cracked as the pirate ship rammed into the burning merchant ship. Men dove from the wreckage into the water and swam for shore. The last pirate ship had furled its sails and was nearing the piers where the city guard had assembled, sword drawn, arrows nocked.

I can't let the pirates land, he thought. *They'll loot and burn the city, and kill everyone they don't torture and violate. I have to stop them, even if the people of Hixus see me.*

Summoning all of his remaining strength, Maren stood erect on the prominence where he could see the city's shoreline and took his lute from his back. He whispered a word of command and began to play and sing a lullaby.

Pirates crowded the portside of the ship, shouting and cursing, their swords and daggers drawn as the ship approached the pier. Maren sang the lullaby with all his might. The pirates jumped from the ship to the pier and began running toward the guards. Slowly, the invaders stopped shouting and lowered their swords. Their heads began to nod. The guards attacked fiercely, but the pirates barely defended themselves.

Maren strained to keep singing, but his voice was growing weaker. The few pirates still on the ship tried to climb over the side onto the pier, but they yawned and draped over the side, sound asleep. Most of the pirates from the wrecked ship were halfway to the shore when they gradually stopped swimming. One by one they closed their eyes and sank beneath the waves. Suddenly, Maren's voice cracked; he couldn't sing another note. The pirates fighting the city guards seemed to shake off their drowsiness and plunged into the fight with renew intent. But the city guards fought until every pirate was dead.

Maren staggered, barely able to stand. *The city's safe,* he thought as his legs gave way, and he sank down to the stony shelf, exhausted.

77506060R00141

Made in the USA
Columbia, SC
01 October 2017